Martha's Gift

THE GIFFORD TRILOGY

CB SMAILES

ISBN 978-1-0686266-0-9

For Linda

Chapter 1.

February 1460

As the embers of the fire burned low, the hearth in the centre of the earth floor became a void of despair that seemed to swallow heat rather than offer warmth or comfort. Today I would not weep as I remembered them. That way lay vulnerability, and I would not allow myself to be hurt again, not on this special day. Today was the second of February, Candlemas Day, and had my mother and sister been here, we would have been to mass to celebrate the feast of the Purification of the Blessed Virgin. My mother was drifting from me into insubstantial wisps of memories of times past; her gentleness remained in my grasp, but even when I concentrated closely, I could scarcely hear the sound of her voice in my head. Hard to believe that it was four years ago. My sister Mary, although we always called her Molly, clutching her bonnet and with her skirts flying as she chased after me; she was slipping away from me too. This evening we would have lit the candle that had been blessed at church and mother would have told us stories of her childhood or strange beasts that lived long ago, or the faerie folk that dwelt in the forest. That was before the sweating sickness took them in the outbreak of 1456. Summer, June 1456, when we buried two shrouded bodies, and I buried all happiness and hope with them. I spat angrily into the fire and the globule of saliva roiled and hissed.

Life had been generous in the lessons it had distributed to me; the bruises on my face and ribs were fading now, but more would follow. If I were to die here tonight, would anybody miss me? I thought not, and my sixteen years would be swept away like the stone chippings off the workshop floor. Tom Gifford, the ragged son of a drunken stonemason would be just one more mound of freshly turned earth in the cemetery of St. Mary Magdalene. Mother and my sister Mary were both named after her; mother's name was Magdalene, although she was always called Maggie. The Bible says that Jesus cast out seven demons from her before she became a disciple. How well he would serve if he cast out the demon that now haunted my father.

Those who took the trouble to look at me shook their heads in resignation and moved on. My pallid complexion had long since lost its summer tan, my cheekbones were prominent, and my eyes seemed sunken in the dark shadows of their sockets. I knew I was close to starving and would probably have perished months ago, had it not been for the kindness of my godmother, and the charity of the monks at St. Wilfrid's, where I had taken my place in the queue at the beggars gate for a piece of bread and a bowl of gruel. There was help to be had at the manor house, too, and I stood outside the kitchen and waited for leftovers from the household to be distributed. The cooks had a soft spot for me so that on occasion they would save me scraps of meat. "Here now Tom Gifford, don't you go dying on our doorstep!" At Christmas the poor had been given alms at a meal provided for the paupers of the parish in the great hall. The warmth and cheer of that evening seemed so long ago now.

***

In spite of my endless hunger, I was strongly built and already had the upper body physique of an archer. I had practised with a bow for as long as I could remember until the muscles of my upper torso were hardened by the hours spent at the butts. All men from the age of fourteen to sixty had to practise for two hours on Sundays or face a fine, and a casual glance at my shoulders and arms announced me unmistakably as an archer; the regular drawing of an eighty pound war bow was shaping my upper body with the physical deformity that was the legacy of regular practise. I had wavy, light brown hair and a patchy, embryonic beard that I kept close trimmed so not to catch on the bowstring. In happier times, perhaps even I could have ambitions; the hiring fairs and regular work with money that I could use for myself.

A twig caught into a momentary blaze, and I looked down at my hands. They were becoming callused and rough just like his, and I gave an involuntary sigh. I was not destined for the life he had chosen. I knew something else was waiting for me, something that would lift me from this existence, but as I dared to consider what the future might hold, the impossibility of my dreams was crushed by realism. What other course could there possibly be? I had no rich patron and I knew that

I had no calling for the Church. In these bleak days where survival was a day by day achievement, my prospects were limited to earning a few coins as a bird scarer for Ranulf Griswold, bailiff of the manor of Upper Broomfield. I drew comfort from the thought that it was February. If I could see out the next few weeks, spring would arrive, and life might slowly become easier. Then I could perhaps slip away; seek employment at one of the big houses far from here, where I was not haunted by the bittersweet memory of mother and Molly. One day, I would have fine clothes and be respected; I would have coins to give to the poor at Easter ... but then there was father to consider. I knew he had no love for me; he needed me but he did not want me, and yet how could I leave him? He was already a broken man, soaked in drink and self-pity. How could I just abandon him? It would be a greater cruelty than ever he had shown me, and I knew that in spite of my yearning for a better life, when it came to the point of leaving, I would be unable to do it.

***

Thin wisps of smoke drifted lazily upwards to find their way out into the darkness through a hole in the blackened thatch. I was alone, apart from my dog Jip, a stray terrier that I had taken in last autumn. As I waited for my father to return, part of me was comforted by the prospect of having someone to talk to, but in equal measure I was fearful of the consequences of his homecoming. Another beating? Another tavern doxy hoping for easy pickings? With any luck she would take one glance and turn on her heel in disgust, laughing over her shoulder at the squalor of the place.

My father, John Gifford was in his mid-forties. Short, thickset with powerful hands and arms, he was a boulder of a man, hewn from the living rock. His jaw was overshot, and protruded aggressively, lending even a casual conversation the appearance of a confrontation. His grey, curly hair gave him a grizzled appearance, his skin roughened by coarse work and exposure to the elements. He seemed to trickle stone dust when he moved, as though he was composed of the grey powder.

He had been a stonemason all his life, and by all accounts he was a good workman. He must have been, or he would have been sent packing long ago. The tales of his drunkenness were common gossip in our small parish and over the four years since my mother died, he had offended many people. Most significantly, he had come to the attention of bailiff Griswold.

My gloomy deliberation was interrupted by Jip, who rose from his place in the corner and emitting a low growl, went to the door where he stood listening, head tilted to one side and the hackles of his wiry coat raised.

'What is it boy? What have you heard?'

I strained for any sound but there was silence. Quietly I picked up the wooden bar and slipped it across the door. I took my skinning knife from its sheath at my belt and pressed my face against one of the gaps in the boards. I could see nothing but still Jip maintained his quiet growl; clearly something had alerted him. It could not be my father – too early for that, and besides, Jip would have recognised his step.

The gentle tap on the other side of the door startled me in spite of my state of alertness. Whoever was there had moved with the lightness of tread that was the accomplishment of a forest dweller.

'Tom? Are you there?' The voice of Godwin Lightfoot was hushed and hesitant from the darkness beyond. 'Are you alone? Is he back yet?'

'Quiet Jip! It's Godwin. It's alright.' With relief, I lifted the latch and opened the door to greet my friend. Godwin ducked his head beneath the lintel and the dull glow from the fire illuminated his large frame.

'It's alright, he won't be back for another hour yet.'

Godwin grinned and bent to stroke Jip who was fussing around his ankles. Godwin was a year older than me and a head taller. His black hair and thick beard hinted at a forceful character, but the truth was very different. Godwin was a gentle giant and spoke only to say what was necessary. His simplicity hid no guile or sophistication and he had been my friend since our earliest days. He worked at the tannery at the edge of the village, and its pungency had followed him into the room. Godwin's father had died in the same year as my mother, another victim of the deadly sweating sickness of 1456.

'Here. From mother,' and he produced an earthenware bowl from under his jerkin whilst in his big hand was a chunk of rough bread. I smiled gratefully and taking a spoon, I started on the bowl of pottage, stopping to dip a lump of bread in the steaming contents and feed it to Jip. Godwin watched me eat with an expression of satisfaction tempered with anxiety. Only when the bowl was empty and wiped clean with the last of the bread did he speak.

'Mother worries about you.'

I smiled 'I think I would be dead if it was not for your mother. She is so good to me.'

'Her Christian duty she says. "Have to look after Maggie's boy. Owe it to her." Have you to stay with us if not for him. Black Bear again is he?'

I remained silent hoping that by choosing not to answer, Godwin would drop the subject. Talking of my father pained me; hearing others criticise him was hurtful, but Godwin was not to be deflected; once he started on a topic, he was hard to shift.

'Mother says, "One day he'll go too far and kill that poor boy, see if he don't. Then they'll drag the worthless bugger off and hang him." - that's what she says, Tom. Frets over you.' Godwin's voice was slow and deliberate, failing to see the sadness in my face.

'She's very kind, your mother, but tell her there's no need.'

Godwin's mother, Martha, was my godmother and lived on the other side of the green here in Upper Broomfield. She had been close friends with my mother, Maggie, and had nursed her throughout that June day when the Lord took her. "Fine at breakfast, dead by supper-time," that's what they say about the Sweat. The following day she had continued her vigil with my ten year old sister, Molly, and laid them both out for burial. Martha's own husband followed them only a few days later, leaving her to manage as best she could from her earnings as a midwife.

'He wasn't always like this you know,' I offered lamely. 'He has always had a temper on him, but he never raised his hand to mother once. Molly and me were always a bit wary of him ... tried not to cross him, but he never hit us. When mother was alive he was so different. He had plans, hopes for the future. But now ...' my voice trailed off to silence.

'Now he kicks the shit out of you and brings home any old strumpet he can find. What do you do then?'

'I sleep in the woodshed with Jip. I can't bear it for other women to be here instead of mother.'

'So why stay? Get away from him. Run. Go to Gilmortain. Work to be had there. Only a day's walk from here. Go to the castle, offer your services as an archer to the Nevilles.'

'Because he is my father,' I snapped, 'and I can't just abandon him.'

There was a silence while Godwin took in this piece of information, considering it in the same way that my father would examine a piece of stone, turning it over and over in his callused hands, checking for flaws.

'Don't you think I'd love to leave?' I reprimanded, my pain and frustration turning to anger. 'To get away from here and perhaps make something of myself; earn a good living and be free of ...' I faltered, instantly regretting my flash of temper. 'I owe him my loyalty for mother's sake,' I finished in a quieter voice.

'Why does he treat you so bad then?' Godwin's unshakable sense of justice was offended. 'Mother says you wouldn't treat a dog like he treats you.'

'I think he blames me for their death.'

'How so? That's mad! T'weren't your fault they died!'

'I think he blames me for still being alive when they are dead. Like I said, he wasn't always like this and most of the time he puts up with me. It's when he goes to the Black Bear - that's when he loses his temper. "Why are you still here boy? Why couldn't God have taken you and left them alone?" And then he either starts to cry or ...'

'That ain't fair!' Godwin interrupted angrily. 'That ain't bloody fair! He can't say that - it's cruel!'

'He doesn't mean it. The drink makes him like that. I just have to keep out of his way when things are really bad.'

I paused to consider the implications of my words. Would he come home raging tonight? Should I take Godwin's advice and save myself another beating?

We sat gazing into the fire, each following our own thoughts, weighing up the realities of the situation as the steelyard struggled to find a balance; loyalty in one scale pan and injustice in the other.

At last, Godwin stirred himself and rose to his feet with a sigh.

'Well, I had better get back before he comes home.' He gathered up the empty bowl and tucked it under the folds of his thick leather jerkin. As he reached the door he turned. 'Don't take on too badly Tom. I know he's all you've got left.' As he lifted the latch, an afterthought brightened his face 'Anyway, it'll soon be Shrove Tuesday and there's the ball game to look forward to. Always fun to be had then!' and he smiled as he ducked under the doorframe, closing the door behind him with a click, and slipped away into the darkness.

***

The sound of the latch woke me: I had fallen asleep by the remains of the fire with Jip curled up beside me, and as I blinked, rubbing the sleep from my eyes, I could see my father framed against the night sky beyond, as he leaned against the doorpost for support.

'Get up boy,' he slurred. He half-walked, half-stumbled into the firelight's dying glow. 'Wake up! God's bones, is this all I have to come home to?'

I tried to see his face, to read his expression and from it, what might happen next.

'Wake up, God damn you! I have things to tell you.'

‘What is it?’ I asked as I raised myself to a sitting position, all the while watching his boots carefully.

‘Ha! You would like to know wouldn’t you! Like to know what I know, eh?’

As his voice rose, the familiar belligerence began to scorch the air around him. His temper could rise from nothing, like the forge responds to the blacksmith’s bellows, white hot and blistering in moments. Jip ducked away and I put my hand on him, feeling him shake beneath his rough, wiry coat. I stayed silent, tensing myself, ready to roll out of the way. I had learned that safety lay in silence; no matter what I said it would be wrong. Stay silent, watch, wait.

‘What, nothing to say boy? No greeting for your father?’

His question was flung at me; a challenge to which, I had discovered, it was better not to respond. How would this play out? Unexpectedly, he drew up a stool and balanced on it unsteadily, looking sideways at me. His expression in the dull glow of the embers was partly defiant, but I could see guilt and self-pity there also.

‘Rouse that fire. There are things for you to hear.’

Obediently, I threw on a few twigs until they kindled and then added small branches. Bright flame leapt up, sending the shadows dancing on the rough stone walls, and casting a flickering light on my father’s square face. I had expected it to be angry and embittered, but this time it was different; he looked tired, but he had the beginnings of a smile on his lips; more, he seemed almost pleased with himself.

‘I expect you’re wondering what it is, are you?’ When I still did not reply he glared at me in frustration. ‘Right, well if you’re not interested you can bloody well stay in ignorance, and serve you right. Don’t say I haven’t tried.’

‘What is it father?’ I asked warily.

‘Ha! At last he manages to speak. Sulking are you?’

‘What is it that you want to tell me.’

‘That’s more like it. Well, it’s two things if you can be bothered to listen.’ He lurched and almost fell from the stool. ‘Been talking to William Langley. You know him? The new land agent for his lordship at the manor?’

I nodded. Like everyone else in the village, we owed our fealty and the roof over our heads to Hugh Thain, Lord of the Manor of Upper Broomfield. I had heard of this recent arrival, but had not met him.

‘He needs a new well digging at Hagg Farm. Wants me to do the job properly – stone lined shaft, head stock, everything. It will bring us a tidy sum because he has promised me extra payment if I get the job done quickly. That’s where you come in. There is digging to be done.’

As he finished, he looked at me hopefully. His expression bore so much pathos, as if he was trying to please me by delivering good news at last. I risked a smile.

‘When do we start? Tomorrow?’

‘Course not, it’s no bloody good starting yet. Don’t you know anything? It’s February. The land’s wet through and we can’t line the shaft with stone because the mortar won’t set in winter. No, we start in spring when the weather warms up – probably early May.’

‘Does this mean we can eat better?’

‘Course it does. We can live like lords!– especially if we can get it done by midsummer quarter day.’

‘That’s impossible - by the end of June – can it be done in such a short time?’

I should have known better than to doubt him. His expression changed in an instant.

'Are you calling me a liar? Saying I don't know what I'm talking about? Course it can be bloody well done!'

'Then we will do it but ...' I hesitated, not knowing if I dared continue.

'But what? Eh? What now? Nothing seems to bloody suit you boy. What is it this time?'

'It is going to be hard work. We will need feeding – you can't do that kind of work on an empty stomach, father.'

He calmed on the instant and a sly look crept across his face as his eyes levelled on me.

'Don't worry about that. I said there were two things I had to tell you. Well, here is the second bit of news – you can expect company!'

'What?'

I tried hard to control my expression and hoped that my feelings remained hidden. Surely he was not planning to set up another woman in my mother's place? To take her in as a replacement?

'We will have company. Ursula Gurnard is moving in with us. You know her?'

'Widow from Lower Broomfield? Husband was hanged for sheep stealing last assize? That one?'

'Aye, that's her. She needs a place to stay, and she can cook and clean. She's strong and healthy and she'll earn the roof over her head. She'll do well.'

He sounded as though he was completing a transaction at the horse fair.

In spite of my fear of him I heard myself blurt out: 'She might do well for you, but I don't want her here. What about mother? You can't just forget her as if she hasn't existed.' I was on dangerous ground now, but my anger had made me reckless.

'Your mother's been dead these four years come midsummer so don't get high and mighty with me. She will be here tomorrow so you can like it, or bugger off.' Each word was delivered like a chisel blow. 'Your choice, but I tell you this, you will bloody well respect her, or I'll teach *you* some respect,' and he raised a huge fist in front of my face. I did not flinch or give him the satisfaction of thinking that he had scared me.

'You can do what you like,' I retorted, 'but there is one thing you will never do ... you will never get me to call her mother!'

***

Chapter 2

February 1460

Sunday the fifth of February was a bright, clear day with a slight westerly breeze that gave an edge to the air in spite of the weak winter sun. Above me there were mare's tails forming a delicate tracery in the fragile blue sky. I stood where the road turned a corner out of the village to begin its descent to the river, and awaited the arrival of Ursula.

Since father's announcement three days ago, I had thought of little else. Of course I had heard of Ursula Gurnard; she had put up a spirited defence when the constables dragged her husband away for trial and by all accounts, was lucky to escape arrest herself, having wielded a fencing mell and threatened to assault the officers with it. His offence of sheep stealing was proven, and he was hanged after the quarterly assize had found him guilty. Ursula had no man to protect her and the certainty that she would be evicted from her home at Lower Broomfield, where she had friends but none that was prepared to take her in. The men of the parish regarded her with interest, since she still retained the remnants of her youthful good looks; the women were wary of her and perceived her as a threat.

I was expected to welcome her into our lives and I was not sure I could do it. I could already feel antipathy building in me against this person who would drive away the last cherished wisps of the memory of mother. Yet I had no choice but to act out the part; make her welcome and give no hint of hesitation or reserve. I could be sure that he would be watching my every gesture, alert for the slightest insinuation of resentment.

From my vantage point I could see a small two wheeled cart make its way up the long gentle slope towards Upper Broomfield. I watched it cross the stone bridge that spanned the Howlbeck in the deep valley that separated the two villages, and now it slowed as the driver set the single horse at the slope. There were two figures on the box seat, side by side and as they drew closer I could see they were deep in conversation. Closer now, and I could faintly hear the horse's hooves on the gravel and the crunch and rumble of the wheels of the cart that he had borrowed. I walked back to our door with a sick feeling in my stomach as I struggled to accept the change that had been forced upon me, and turned to face their arrival.

The cart emerged onto the green and slowed to a halt, the horse snorting with exertion after the pull uphill. I took its head as the two prepared to step down. Now she was here, I realised that my father must have presented her with an opportunity that was not to be missed even though he was a good twelve years her senior.

'Leave the horse and help her down,' he ordered, and I reluctantly released the bridle and went to the side of the cart to assist.

'Lift me down, there's a good lad,' she instructed, ignoring the hand I had offered.

Obediently, I reached up and, putting my hands round her waist, lifted her to the ground. She had a slim waist, and was so light that it was like lifting a child.

'Well you are a big fellow! John, you didn't tell me he was such a strong boy.'

She spoke in a clear, confident voice with an accent that I had never heard before, and certainly was not from our small part of the world. This was the first time I had set eyes on the woman who was going to be sharing our home and as she held my arm, she seemed reluctant to let go. It gave me chance to look at her properly. I had braced myself to receive a tavern whore; what stood before me was a pleasant surprise. She was younger than father and I estimated her to be in her early thirties. So this was Ursula Gurnard. She was slightly built with blond hair plaited into a bun at the back of her head and covered with a brown headdress. She was an attractive woman and I understood at once why the goodwives of the parish were wary of her. Life had not been kind to her though, and whilst she still kept the last vestiges of her youth, her face was lined with hardship.

Her appearance had surprised and unsettled me, and it was several moments before I could make sense of my first impression. As last it came to me: her features were those of a refined woman; the bone structure of her face presented an almost cultured appearance, showing none of the coarse qualities of a labourer. Her eyes were evenly spaced, her nose small and delicate, whilst her high cheekbones were sophisticated, ladylike. When she smiled, she revealed small, evenly spaced teeth, but I noticed that the smile on her lips did not transfer to her pale blue eyes. They were alert, searching and evaluating. I broke away from her gaze, and turned to father who had come round to stand beside me.

'Don't just stand there gawping. Get her bags boy.'

I went to the rear of the cart and began to lift down the few things she had brought.

'Don't drop any of those,' she ordered, as we went inside, our every movement being scrutinised by people who had emerged from neighbouring cottages around the green to study this new arrival.

'So you are Tom,' she said as the door closed. 'I have heard about you from your father, and now I get to meet you in person.'

I remained silent, uncertain of myself. Her voice was unhurried and even; she was not in the least disquieted by her new circumstances.

'Well go on then - answer her.' I could hear the beginnings of annoyance in his voice.

'Good afternoon Miss,' I mumbled, diffidently.

'And a good afternoon to you too, Thomas Gifford,' she answered brightly, 'and there is no need to call me "Miss" – I am Ursula so please call me by my given name.'

I was puzzled by her tone and the friendliness of her reply. I had expected coldness, resentment even, but not this, and it had thrown me off balance.

'Thank you Miss ... Ursula,' I stuttered uncertainly, 'I am Tom, Miss. Please call me Tom.'

She laughed then. My confusion must have been obvious, and she seemed to find her effect on me amusing. Laughter was never heard under our roof or at least not for the last four years when mother ...

my train of thought ended abruptly. I had learned not to be vulnerable. I could not allow myself to be anything other than the civility that courtesy demanded.

She put down the small bag that she had been carrying and began to look around her, still smiling. Her expression should have been horrified as she took in the squalor that we had lived in for so long, yet the smile never left her lips.

'I can see I have some work to do here, so the sooner the better. I'm going to need your help Tom. That is if you don't mind?'

The choice I was being offered was confusing. To be consulted like this was certainly not what I had expected. She emanated reassurance and kindness, and I began to warm to her in spite of my instincts urging me to be cautious.

'If you don't mind? He won't bloody mind I can tell you – not if he knows what's good for him.'

'And that will be enough of that, John Gifford, or I will set upon you with a broom and leave the door open so all your neighbours can see!'

Nobody spoke to him like that, and I braced myself, waiting for him to give her the back of his hand and knock her to the floor; to hear her cry out in pain and anger; to see her pick herself up wiping blood from her mouth where her lip had split. Instead, he smiled, slowly at first, as if he had forgotten how to shape the expression. I could not remember the last time I had seen him smile, but he was smiling now. A silly, sheepish grin had spread across his face, and for the second time since her arrival, Ursula had bewildered me. Perhaps I had misjudged her and formed an opinion too early. Now that I had met her, my certainty had been disturbed and left precariously balanced, like a fledgling poised for flight.

'Tom will you bring the rest of my things from the cart. I have brought food and after we have eaten we will *all* ...' she said this while pointedly looking at father ... 'we will all start to put this place to rights. I want every stick of furniture taken outside and the floor swept. John, you will fetch firewood and set water to boil. Tom, will you be so kind as to put my bags up there?'

She pointed at the ladder that led to the raised loft at one end of the room, where my father slept when he was sober. He went out obediently to do her bidding, and I was alone with her. I paused with my foot on the first rung; this was where my mother had slept. Again I experienced a pang of resentment, and she seemed to sense it, because she turned briskly.

'I know what you must think - I am intruding, but life has to move on. I am sure we will get along well, but you can expect things to be different from now on.'

The smile had gone, replaced by a look that was not exactly hostile but very determined. I began to climb the wooden ladder to the sleeping platform with one hand holding the loosely tied bundle that contained her things. I felt nervous and as she watched from below, my foot slipped. I was only on the third rung, but it startled me and I grabbed for the ladder with both hands. In the process, the bundle fell open and discharged its contents onto the floor. With the speed of a weasel taking a rabbit, she was on her knees, scooping the few possessions back into the cloth, but not before I had seen it lying there, partly covered by a shawl.

'You careless young bugger. Now look what you have done!' The façade had dropped and she was furious.

'I am so sorry,' I began, 'I slipped. Please don't tell father.'

This was likely to end in a beating if she made a fuss, particularly when she had only just arrived and he was anxious to impress her. She finished replacing the fallen items and tied the cord round the top with a savage twist of her wrist. Then she stood and confronted me, her face close to mine, her eyes simmering with anger.

'What did you see?' she demanded.

'Nothing, Miss Ursula.'

'Don't lie, boy. What did you see?'

The truth was that I had seen something. It was something that was completely out of place, and surely could not belong to her. At any moment, my father might return in the midst of this confrontation.

'I ... I saw ...'

'Go on,' she hissed.

'I saw a book, Miss,' I reluctantly stammered, flinching before the force of her anger.

'No, you did not. You did not see anything, do you understand me?'

'Yes Ursula, I understand. I saw nothing at all.'

She stood glaring at me, then seeming to make up her mind, she calmed. 'Then all is well. You saw nothing, and I have nothing to complain about to your father.'

***

I was able to resume my bird scaring duties, keeping rooks and pigeons off the turnips and kale that had fed our village through the winter. I took my bow and a few old arrows because it gave me chance to practise, and hopefully bring back some pigeons or a couple of crows for the pot. It was on my return that I encountered Jasper Griswold.

Jasper was the son of Ranulf Griswold, bailiff of Upper Broomfield. As the lord of the manor's direct representative, Ranulf held a great deal of authority. He could be ruthless in the way that he governed the demesne, and his brutal enforcement made him unpopular. His eighteen year old son, Jasper, took pleasure from the authority he usurped from his father. Where Ranulf was burly and ruddy cheeked, Jasper was tall and wiry with an arrogant swagger that echoed his father's status.

'I hope you intend paying for those,' nodding at the brace of pigeons I was carrying.

'They're vermin, free to anyone. Besides, it's proof that I've been doing my job properly.'

'And of course, I'm forgetting, you couldn't pay for them even if you wanted to. Your father drinks all your money away, doesn't he!' He was smirking now, confident of his superiority.

I glared at him. It was true and it shamed me to offer no defence. He was relishing this moment of dominance and he saw that his barb had found its mark.

'What, nothing to say? Well, you had better listen then. They want you out of here, both of you. They know that you won't be able to pay your quarterly rent and they want shot of you, and get somebody here who will look after the place and pay up on time.'

'Don't you worry, you'll get your money.'

'Then you won't object to giving me half of what's due right now as a sign of good will. It will stand in your favour and give his lordship confidence that you can be trusted.'

I had not heard our door open, but suddenly Ursula was standing beside me.

'He will not give you a single penny and you have no right to ask. I know you, Jasper Griswold. You would take his money and then deny that he had paid at all,' she paused, staring him out; her eyes probed him like a physician's knife, and he weakened. 'There you are! I can tell from the look on your face. That is exactly what you had intended. Don't deny it. The truth is written all over you!'

'And who the hell are you to say you know me?' Jasper was thrown by her appearance beside me and the coldness of her gaze.

'You know fine well who I am. On your way or I will report you for attempting to steal from us. Thief!' she screeched at him.

'We'll see who gets reported to who,' he blustered, clearly rattled by Ursula's fury. His nerve broke, and with a long look at me he turned to leave. 'You haven't heard the last of this, Gifford!' he muttered over his shoulder.

He was the sort to hold a grudge, and I knew there would be trouble ahead. Ursula stood and watched him go, hands on her hips, her eyes still blazing their defiance at his retreating back.

'Thank you Ursula,' I said, grateful for this unexpected alliance.

'Don't thank me boy. Just looking out for myself, that's all,' she said crisply. 'Last thing I need is to be homeless again just because your father's too feckless to pay the rent.' She turned on her heel, leaving me in a flutter of uncertainty.

***

Chapter 3

14th. February 1460. Shrove Tuesday

The two parishes of Upper and Lower Broomfield stood roughly a mile apart and were separated by a valley containing a watercourse. The slope from Lower Broomfield was steep, leading down to the Howlbeck which wound its way along the valley floor. The beck was wide in places and deep where its banks narrowed – too big to be called a stream, yet not quite a river. A ford crossed the beck at one of the wide, shallow places, and beside the ford was a narrow stone bridge, soaring high in a steep arc as a precaution against winter floods. From there, the road carried on across and up the gentler side of the valley, reaching Upper Broomfield at the summit. A long-standing rivalry smouldered between the two parishes of St. Mary Magdalene at Upper Broomfield, and St. Cuthbert's at Lower Broomfield. The two communities identified themselves as "Uppers" and "Lowers" and usually, the practical necessity of collaborative existence prevailed. Today it would erupt into open warfare in the guise of the Shrove Tuesday ball game.

'Looks like most of the village has turned out,' I observed as the crowds began to gather in the weak sunshine of the February morning. Ranks were swelled by men from neighbouring villages who aligned their loyalties with one or other of the two sides until several hundred men faced each other across the ford.

'Where's your father?' Godwin asked. 'I thought he would be joining in the fun.'

'A drain culvert has collapsed at the manor, and it will flood the home pasture if it isn't fixed. His lordship wants it done without delay.'

'But today is a holiday for everyone. It always is on Shrove Tuesday.'

'Ursula has made sure he goes. Besides, our rent is due soon.'

'How is it going with her? Is she alright?'

I paused, before replying. 'Tell you the truth, I can't make my mind up. She seems to be friendly enough, but I don't know. There is just something about her that comes to the surface for a second or two every once in a while.'

'Probably just settling in.' Typical of Godwin, always seeing the best in people.

'Perhaps. One thing is for sure, she has father under control. He can't do enough to please her. She has put paid to his visits to the Black Bear, and now we seem to be able to eat properly. She bakes bread and cooks good stew and pottage.'

'So why do you doubt her? Sounds good to me. Sounds as if ... '

'Look, there she is,' I interrupted, pointing across the shallow water of the ford, where Ursula could just be seen mingling with the Lower Broomfield crowd. 'Now that's interesting. She has sided with the Lowers and not with us.'

'Well, that's where she's from isn't it? Only natural that she goes to her own people.'

'Is it where she is from? How much do we know about her?' I found that I was becoming curious about Ursula, now that I had seen more of her. She was definitely not born in our area – her accent told me that.

'Anyway, we're her own people now!' I exclaimed. 'She should be with us! That's where her loyalties should be.'

Above the restless mob, in his exalted position as lord of the manors of both villages, the gangly figure of Hugh Thain stood behind the parapet of the bridge with two other men beside him; one was his bailiff, Ranulf Griswold, and the other his new land agent, William Langley. Hugh Thain's pinched face and aquiline nose, turning blue with the cold, was contrasted by the burly outline and florid features of his bailiff. As lord of the manor, his duty was to start the proceedings with a blast of a hunting horn. Then he would hurl the ball into the centre of the stream, and chaos would be unleashed.

He had donned a grey woollen cap against the chill air of early spring, but now he removed it, revealing his thinning brown hair. Cap in hand, he waved it to one side of the beck and then the other, and from each in turn issued a loud cheer, indicating their eagerness to engage.

'Ready with the horn Ranulf?' he asked, turning to his bailiff.

William Langley stood mystified. As a relative stranger, he had never witnessed the Shrove Tuesday game and his bewildered expression made Hugh laugh.

'This is foreign to you I expect. You are a newcomer, so watch and learn!'

That was quite true; William Langley had moved from his previous employment near Coventry and had not experienced this kind of event before.

'Why do they do it?' he asked in bewilderment.

'Because it's a tradition. It is as old as the hills. It will go on all day, and they will be roaring drunk by the end of it.'

'Why do you allow it then?'

Ranulf laughed: 'They get to let off steam, sort out old rivalries, settle scores between each other instead of bothering me with their complaints at the manorial court. Besides, I would rather they work out their grievances on each other than turn their resentment on me.'

'Looks like they're lining up for battle,' William observed in disbelief.

'Well, that is another point in its favour. If these men are issued with orders to muster and bear arms for the king, they have already experienced close quarters skirmishing!' Hugh said, smiling.

'Are there any rules at all? How does one side win?'

'There are a few rules – no weapons are allowed for one thing. When the horn blows, I throw this ball – here , have a look.'

William was handed a battered leather ball; just a simple bag stuffed with sheep wool. It was the length of a man's arm from wrist to elbow, roughly stitched and surprisingly heavy.

Hugh continued: 'There is a post set up in the centre of each village and what they try to do is to get into the opposing village. The women decorate their post with greenery and ribbons and try to outdo their rival women on the opposing side to see whose decoration is the finest

... you can judge that for me if you like. I give a prize of a goose to the winner.'

'But how does a team win?' William still looked baffled.

If they manage to fight their way to their opponents post, they have to bang the ball against it three times to score a goal. They are not allowed into houses, gardens or the churchyard. Apart from that, anything goes! Now, it's time to make a start.'

After a nod from Hugh, bailiff Ranulf raised a horn to his lips and blew a long blast. Hundreds of faces looked up expectantly as their lord stood above them, the ball raised in his hands. It flew outwards and downwards in a graceful parabola, landing in the centre of the beck. The splash it might have made was inaudible, drowned by the roar as both sides closed on each other.

***

'Are you ready for the fun?' Godwin beamed as he emptied the last of his ale in a gulp. I grinned in return, barely able to make myself heard above the insults being traded between the rival parishes, and the chanting battle cry of "Upp-er! Upp-er!"

'Bloody Cuthbert! He was carted all over the north country because nobody wanted him!' I yelled, shamefully directing my abuse against the patron saint of their parish church.

'At least our church isn't named after a whore!' came the repost, sullying the reputation of Mary Magdalene, referring to her supposed occupation before she became a disciple. Then the horn blew, the ball landed, and we were off, up to our knees in water, struggling to keep our feet in the melee.

***

After an early success, the Lowers had lost possession and the Uppers were in a tight pack, slowly heading up from the beck and ascending the steep slope towards the centre of Lower Broomfield. Somewhere in the midst was the ball, closely guarded against any flanking incursion.

'Can you see it?' I gasped, my feet slipping on the grassy slope. We had reached the top of the ascent where the ground flattened into level pasture, and the cottages of Lower Broomfield could be seen about half a mile away in the distance. Light flurries of snow had begun to fall, adding to the confusion, and making the ground even more treacherous. Before Godwin could answer, the ball sailed high in the air, emerging from the sweating, steaming pack. He jumped and scooped it into his big right hand, and then all chance to speak had gone as we found ourselves in the middle of the fray. Heads were down, shoulders interlocked as, little by little, our progress resumed. Godwin had managed to relinquish custody of the ball and together we eased ourselves to the outer edge where the press of bodies lessened, and we could breathe again. It was then that I felt a hand grab my shoulder, spinning me to my right and the sneering face of Jasper Griswold appeared inches away from mine.

'This is a game for good folk, not paupers like you.' His words drew a ripple of laughter from his friends. 'What, nothing to say? Words don't cost money so that's one thing you won't be in our debt for.'

'I have no quarrel with you, Jasper,' I replied. 'I do not see it is any concern of yours. Lord Thain gives this day for everyone to enjoy.' He had been drinking and was not going to let things rest.

'Free day eh? Everything has to be free for you doesn't it! Free rent too by the looks of things. Well I can tell you something – you will be turned out of that house when you fail with your payment. You and your drunk of a father and his new woman.' He staggered as a man barged past him heading for the mob. I stood, facing up to him, angry now and working out my chances. He was two years older, taller than me, and he was drunk, yet I knew I must not touch him. To allow him to provoke me would be madness and probably end with our eviction.

'Even the new woman doesn't want you... Ursula... She told me so.'

'That's a lie! She sent *you* packing soon enough.' A ripple of laughter from my friends who knew what had happened. 'She soon made you turn tail and run!'

'That means nothing. You think you have her loyalty do you?' he scoffed. 'You do not! She told me as much half an hour ago. She wants you gone – just like your mother,' His spite and triumph were still not enough. 'She didn't stay around long did she. Better off in the churchyard where she is now, I reckon.'

'No, Tom ...' but Godwin's warning was lost to me.

Four years of grief and loneliness translated to fury; I lost my senses to the rage that overwhelmed me, and I hit him with all the strength I could muster. He tottered, a startled expression giving way to fear as I caught him with a second upward blow under the side of his jaw. He fell to the ground, and I was on him in an instant, my hands round his throat, choking the life out of him. I felt myself being lifted up, dragged away, for I would surely have killed him. They pulled me to a safe distance and slowly, reason began to return.

'Steady lad; he isn't worth hanging for.' I recognised the voice of the ploughman, Solomon Green.

'He should not have said those things. He should never have said anything about my mother.'

'He's no good, that one. Nasty piece of work. Heaven help us if he ever takes over ...' Solomon was cut short by a warning shout from behind. I whirled round to see Jasper advancing towards me, covered in mud and slush. In his right hand was a short dagger.

'I'm going to gut you, you hedgerow bastard!' he shouted with a face that was twisted into a grimace of hatred. I backed away, but he kept coming, a smile of anticipation beginning to form on his lips. All about us, the commotion of the game continued, oblivious to this other drama being played out among the churning mass of bodies. I was just beginning to realise the seriousness of my situation when Godwin appeared behind him. Seizing Jasper's wrist, he slowly applied his enormous strength and began to twist his hand backwards until it seemed likely that his wrist would break. There was a look of calm, unstoppable determination on Godwin's face as the knife fell to the floor. Wrapping his arms round Jasper, Godwin picked him up, effortlessly, as he would lift a sheave of corn in a harvest field. He threw him to the ground, and stood looking down on him with a mixture of sadness and contempt.

Jasper stood slowly, spitting grass and wiping his mouth. 'Watch your back, pauper. Your dull-witted friend might have saved you this time, but next time you won't be so lucky.' He turned and vanished into the crowd.

***

A shout: a roar of triumph swelled high above the pack of steaming bodies, as a runner broke free and headed back towards the valley. He was flanked by a posse of Lower Broomfield men, and it was clear that this breakout had successfully outwitted their opponents; a hue and cry burst from them as several hundred set off pell-mell in pursuit, heading for the steep sided ravine, the Howlbeck waiting for them at the foot of the slope. The snow flurries that had continued into the late morning had made the ground slippery; mud and snow combined to challenge the chase as they poured over the rim at the end of the pasture.

Godwin gave me a huge lop-sided grin, accompanied by a slap on the back that made me stagger. 'Come on,' he shouted. 'We're missing the fun!' Before I could answer, he had broken into a run, and we were soon caught up in the mixed horde of supporters. As we reached the rim, he stopped. 'Christ's holy nails! Look at that lot!' and before us was a scene of confusion as hundreds streamed down the treacherous ground in pursuit of the breakaways who had by now crossed the beck and begun their ascent up the gentler gradient of the far bank.

The slope was black with figures, slipping and falling in the snow and slush as they gave chase. The bridge below us was choked with spectators, leaving no room for the pursuing horde who plunged into the icy water up to their knees and scrambled up the opposite bank. We paused there to take it in, gasping for breath, and our hearts beating wildly. How little I knew that this was a scene I would bitterly recall under very different circumstances.

***

Chapter 4

May, 1460

'Do you miss your other husband?' My question should never have been asked and I had no idea why I had blurted it out.

'What do you want to know about him for? He's dead and gone this past six months.'

Ursula straightened her apron as she stood up to face me. Her expression was both puzzled and annoyed; her eyes probed me cautiously, trying to discover the reason behind my question.

I shrugged. 'Just curious I suppose,' I said, feigning indifference. The whole parish knew that he had been hanged after a bungled attempt to steal a sheep from the far pasture at Lower Broomfield. He had put the sheep across his shoulders and set off to meet his associates when the bailiff's men had captured him.

'I'm sorry Ursula. I should not have asked. It is none of my business.'

'That's right. It is none of your business. But since you have asked, I don't mind telling you. No, I don't miss him. He was a useless no-good wastrel. Always dodging the law, dealing with thieves and gutter-mongers.'

'Why did you stick with him then? If he kept such bad company why did you stay?'

She threw her head back and laughed. 'You don't know much about life do you? Because he gave me food and shelter and didn't ask much in return.'

'But you could have left him – set up on your own,' I persisted in my naivety.

'Doing what? Earning a living on my back like a street whore? Is that what you think of me?' My question had annoyed her. I was furious with myself; here was my chance to find out more about her and my clumsy attempt had raised her defences. I decided to take a safer route.

'Where did you meet him?' This might be the only time that she would speak openly about her former life: I had to seize the moment.

'I met him at York,' she answered in a calmer voice. 'I was born near there, and I met him at one of the street fairs. He told such lively tales, and I was young and stupid enough to listen.' She paused, her eyes seeking the distance as if the past could be found there. 'He was a pedlar and he had been all over the country, stealing, buying, selling. He was full of stories about places he had been, people he knew. I took up with him and that was my big mistake, although I never properly married him or took his name. He was soon in trouble with the law, and we had to make a run for it. Somehow, we ended up down here, but it wasn't long before he was in trouble again.'

'What happened this time?'

'Went to steal a sheep to pay back a debt and couldn't even do that right!' she snorted with disdain, 'and because they hanged him, everything he owned was taken by the Crown. Well, nearly everything,' she added with a sly smile and a sideways glance. 'I managed to hide something from them – not much, but enough to get by. Even his home was forfeit and I was turned out to live in the hedgerows,'

'So my father must have come along at just the right time.' My careless observation did not please her. The smile fell in an instant, replaced by a look of wariness like a vixen that has just heard the distant note of the huntsman's horn. Her blue eyes fixed on me, searching out the inference behind my comment.

'Your father offered me a home, a roof over my head when I was desperate,' she paused, still unsure of my intent. 'He has changed his ways and through my hard work, we were able to meet the rent last Lady Day.'

And it was true, he had changed. He seemed to have become more calm, less unpredictable and even anxious to please her. All of this was undeniably due to Ursula's influence, and yet...

'What's the matter then?' she demanded. 'Not satisfied with the way things are? Well, I'm very sorry if I don't come up to your standards.'

Again her mood had changed and unexpectedly, she gave a sob, wiping her eye with the corner of her apron. I shuffled, unsure how to respond.

'I'm sorry, Ursula. I didn't mean to give offence.'

'How old are you now Tom?' Tears were dispelled and her change of direction threw me for a moment.

'Sixteen. Seventeen next Easter.' I studied her face, wondering what would come next.

'No young woman that catches your eye then?' she teased. The smile was back; a fragile interlude that made her face softer, her blue eyes gentler. 'Surely you ought to be thinking about setting up on your own now? What if I spoke to our bailiff? He would give you work. He was saying only the other day that he needs a forester.'

When I did not reply, she put her arm round my shoulder. 'As for a girl, I could help you there too. A few words in the right ear, a nudge or two – what do you think?' She could see me redden and she laughed out loud; 'Too shy to ask are you? Well let me do the asking for you, I'm not shy!'

I was taken by surprise and quietly flattered that she should take such an interest in me. Perhaps beneath her hardness there was a softer side; perhaps she felt that she had known me long enough to give me encouragement.

'It's quite alright,' I mumbled, 'plenty of time yet.'

I thought I saw a look of disappointment at my reply, and instantly I wished that I had been more receptive to her offer. She was right – I was shy, and her help could be a good thing. She would never replace my mother, but having no child of her own, perhaps she had a sympathy for me that drew on a natural instinct to nurture, or perhaps a need to please my father and prove her worth. Maybe my spontaneous resentment of Ursula had been misguided and she only had my best interests at heart after all. She had improved our lives and I had repaid her with suspicion. A surge of guilt shamed me, and I resolved to try and have more faith in her, but I had no sooner made my decision than I began to question its wisdom. No matter how much I wanted to accept her presence in our household, my mind returned to the day in early February when she moved in, the book spilled out of her belongings and her fury at its discovery. People like her do not own books, in fact I doubted whether she could even read. Either she had stolen it, or there was something in her past that she had chosen to conceal. I knew that the story that she had told me about her first partner was true: the trial and execution of Stephen Fulford was common knowledge, and the parish talked of little else for days. She said she had come from somewhere near York, so that would explain her accent, but what of her life there? Before I could allow myself to place my trust in Ursula, I had to know more, and the obvious place to start was the book.

***

The town of Ravengill lay three miles from Upper and Lower Broomfield, at the confluence of the Howlbeck and the River Raven. It was a bustling community, representing an eclectic mix of religious, agricultural and industrial concerns. The town had grown in both size and population, due to its position where two valleys met at a strategic crossing point that led towards the fortress of Gilmortain. Prosperity was clear to see in the affluent style of housing; single storey hovels gave way to grand two, and sometimes three storied timber framed buildings with jettied extensions projecting into the narrow, crowded streets.

Ravengill held a weekly market which was the hub of commerce for the surrounding parishes. Twice a year however, the market was transformed; in May and November on St. Boniface's Day and Martinmas, a holiday was declared, and the town was bedecked in fête day regalia announcing the arrival of the fair.

Today, on the fourteenth of May and the feast of St. Boniface, I found myself with Godwin, having walked into Ravengill, marvelling at the sights, sounds and aromas that greeted us. I had a few coins in my purse and ahead lay the prospect of a day filled with festivity and entertainment. My thoughts were focussed on something else – an opportunity that rarely arose - to win a sum of money. There was always an archery competition at the fair, which was a tradition at most gatherings, but today was different: today, a gold mark would be given to the winner. This was a huge sum of money, as much as I could earn in four months by toiling on the land.

'Keep your hand on your money, Godwin,' I warned. 'The place is full of cutpurses and vagabonds. We must be on our guard.'

'Don't fear, my eyes are everywhere,' he said, smiling. 'Did you see our Lord of the Manor back there? No? Well maybe I'm the one who should be warning you! He was near the White Boar in the corner of the marketplace, and Griswold was with him.'

'Ranulf – the bailiff do you mean?'

'Jasper.' His economical reply articulately expressed contempt. 'Better watch out for him today.'

My thoughts immediately returned to the confrontation at the Shrove Tuesday ball game three months ago in the mud and slush of that cold February day. By now it was mid-morning, and the sun was beating down from a dappled sky. It seemed like a different world, and there had been no further incident in spite of his threat. Nonetheless, Godwin was right.

The sights and smells were overwhelming, and we lingered, taking in the magicians, jugglers and performing players that drew crowds to watch, listen and spend. There was a carnival atmosphere as families with their children enjoyed a rare day free from the relentless toil of everyday existence.

'Stop Tom!' Godwin's face was a picture of concentration as he listened to a wiry, dark skinned storyteller.

'... and God had endowed Samson with mighty strength, so great that no man could overcome him. He led his people and fought the Philistines who were occupying the land of Israel...'

Godwin was transfixed now, his face like that of a child at his mother's knee. A crowd had gathered around us, and the little storyteller rose to the occasion, embellishing his tale with theatrical gestures.

'And Samson led his people to great victories for twenty years until ...'

A dramatic pause held the audience spellbound in silence.

'until ...' he continued, playing his audience with the skill of a minstrel picking out a madrigal on the lute ... 'he was betrayed!'

Loud booing and shouts of "shame" issued from the throats of the crowd.

'He was betrayed by his *wife*, his very own wife Delilah who caused him to be captured by the Philistines. They put out his eyes and blinded him and mocked him, but he was not yet beaten ...' he paused for effect.

'What happened next?' shouted Godwin, thoroughly captivated by the skill of the storyteller.

'He used his great strength, took hold of the pillars that he was chained to, and with a mighty heave he pulled them down, bringing down the roof and killing himself and hundreds of Philistines inside.'

A roar of approval was accompanied by the chink of coins in the basket at the storyteller's feet.

We meandered further through the stalls, past furs, perfumes, spices, wine and meat. The wrestling booth had drawn a crowd with wagering taking place on each bout. Godwin was inspired as he entered the ring. In his mind, he was the mighty Samson and overpowered his Philistine opponent in moments. He emerged victorious with a few coins as his reward, resisting the pleas of the booth master who scampered after him, tugging at his tunic like an abandoned lover and begging him to stay and be his resident champion.

After we treated ourselves to a pie from a stall on the corner of the marketplace, we arrived at the archery competition, waiting for the event to begin. There were targets set up at different ranges but that was not what I wanted. On the outer edge of town was the lob shooting contest and here I entered for my turn.

'What sort of contest is this, then,' enquired Godwin. 'There are no targets to shoot at.'

'You just can't see them, that's all. See the posts in the distance over there?' I pointed to three posts driven into the ground at intervals from us. 'There are targets lying flat on the floor next to each one. They start at a hundred yards, then one hundred and fifty and two hundred yards. I have to shoot into the air and drop the arrow onto the target.'

We were standing on pasture outside the edge of town with woodland bordering its eastern edge. Already a crowd was gathering, and several dignitaries had assembled.

'Can you do it?' Godwin sounded doubtful. 'How do you hit a target that you cannot see?'

'It's easy.' I replied. 'I have had so much practise shooting crows and pigeons in the fields; they are much smaller, and I get them often enough.'

A blast on a horn and an announcement gathered the competitors together. It was then that I saw Jasper Griswold watching me, almost hidden by the jostling onlookers. Why was he here, and what new malice was he planning? I tried to put him from my mind, but he had unsettled me. A large crowd had gathered before a marquee displaying the Neville colours. Within its red and white striped interior were the aldermen and an official wearing the Neville livery.

'We are honoured by the presence of Sir Richard de Coverdale, representative of Gilmortain Castle and of our lord Sir Richard Neville. Thanks to our lord's generosity, today's contest will be rewarded by the payment of one gold mark to the winner.'

'We get three arrows to shoot at each target,' I explained to Godwin.

'So that is nine arrows altogether?' he queried, the effort of his calculation aided by the fingers of his huge hands.

I smiled at his painstaking logic. 'Yes, and they use a glass to time it, so it has to be quick, before the sand runs through.'

As each competitor took his place at the mark, the glass was turned, and some were eliminated. When my turn came, I felt the draw weight of the bow with anxiety; it was a heavier bow than my own and I would need to pull it to its limit to reach the furthest post. At a hundred yards I managed the first target easily: the second was more challenging; at a hundred and fifty yards I watched my three arrows fall in a tight group around the peg. Try as I might, I could not reach the third target and saw all three fall disappointingly short.

'Too bad!' The final competitor spoke to me as he brushed past. He was not someone I recognised as he took up his stance, but his physique told all: he was a seasoned bowman. I could hear mutterings from the other men as they waited for the outcome.

'Bloody cheats! We have no chance.'

'That man in the livery, do you know who he is? I asked.

'Sir Richard de Coverdale? He is the garrison commander at Gilmortain Castle, and he has sent his best archer to make sure we don't win. Didn't you see him? That big bugger who shot last, just after you? Just typical – offers money with one hand and takes it away with the other!'

'Then what is the point of this contest?'

'Because there is trouble coming. His master, Sir Richard Neville, the Earl of Warwick, means to be on the winning side and this way he gets a good look at men he might muster when needed. More than that, there are some who will be hand-picked to form the core of his company of archers. In combat he needs men who can mark down the nobility and their commanders – shoot down their leaders.'

'But what trouble is coming? There is no sign of trouble breaking out up here. Surely, all that sort of quarrel happens among the nobility at court?' I asked him. Everyone knew of the ongoing rivalry between the cousins of York and Lancaster. Pedlars and postriders brought news of bitter conflict from places I had not heard of. Tales of the mad king who stared blankly without seeing or speaking had travelled far and wide.

'His grace our king Henry VI may be ill, but the she-wolf that he married is fighting his cause. Margaret of Anjou will never allow her son Edward of Lancaster to be disinherited and so the Crown is the prize they fight for. That is why our Earl of Warwick has pledged himself to Edward March, and *that* is why he is strengthening his forces here. It will reach us sooner or later, just mark my words.'

***

The officials had judged the final fall of arrows and predictably, the prize went to the man who shot last – Sir Richard's man.

'You two!' We were being addressed by the adjudicator of the contest, a pompous little man with a blustering sense of his own importance. 'Yes, you,' he repeated in irritation. 'Go down the field and collect the posts and targets.'

Sir Richard de Coverdale congratulated his man. Turning to the adjudicator he asked, 'Who are those two? The big one and the smaller man beside him?' pointing at our departing figures.

'I don't know, Sir Richard. They are not Ravengill men, but I can find out for you.'

'I want them,' he replied, pointing in our direction. 'The smaller one has the makings of an outstanding bowman. He would have won today if he had been stronger, and the big one would be a man I would choose to stand beside in the battle line. I want them both!'

***

I sighed as we set off dutifully to gather in the flat sheets of sacking and the post that was driven through the centre of each. The first at one hundred yards was liberally pitted with holes. The second, at one hundred and fifty yards had fewer marks, and I noticed three bodkin holes near the peg.

'I'm sure those are mine,' I told Godwin, with a hint of pride.

The final target was at the far edge of the field and enclosed on two sides by woodland. Godwin carried the other posts and I tugged at the marker stake which stubbornly resisted my efforts.

'Come here, let me do it,' Godwin threw down his burden as I stood aside.

At the fringe of the wood, where trees gave way to scrub and bushes, something drew my attention. It was the merest hint of movement, something I would have missed had I still been struggling to withdraw the marker. Then there was no doubt; a flicker of light on an arrow shaft as it left the edge of the wood and arced inexorably towards us. With no time to shout a warning, I pushed Godwin, who was bent double and off balance. The shaft fizzed harmlessly overhead, bedding itself in the turf a few yards away. Already, another arrow could be nocked and ready for us, but before a second shaft could follow, we ran.

'Bloody hell, that was close!'

We had covered the distance to safety at such speed that we were both sucking in huge gasps of air and our hearts were beating wildly.

'Griswold.' I panted.

***

Chapter 5

Summer 1460

Sinking a well was a slow, arduous and often dangerous venture. The joyous song of the cuckoo heralded finer weather and longer days, and May saw work begin while the ground was soft but not waterlogged. Hagg Farm was a short walk from our house and was a tenancy of the manor at Upper Broomfield. There was a sense of immediacy about the job now; the old well which had served the farm for years had failed last summer, probably due to a change in an underground watercourse. It had sufficed over the winter months when the ground was saturated but now, all water was being carried on a cart in barrels from a stream that ran several hundred yards away.

Father touched his forehead with his knuckles in deference to Bailiff Griswold.

'The sooner the better, Gifford. The weather has picked up and we cannot wait any longer. Besides, carting water like this costs time and money.'

'I'll start straight away, as soon as Adam Cooper has been to show me where to dig.'

'I expect your boy will work with you?'

'Aye, he will do a lot of the digging and then help me with the masonry to line the shaft.'

'Best get to it then. I expect to see progress next time I am passing.'

I watched fascinated while Adam Cooper searched for the best site on the side of the farm nearest the village.

'How's that work then?' I asked as he studied the slope of the field.

'You have to look at the shape of the land first. Narrow it down a bit by finding the most likely place.' Adam was an elderly man and looked like an Old Testament prophet. His battered felt hat and long grey beard seemed to blend into one with a wizened brown face peering out like a weasel looking out of a stook of corn.

'Water likes hollows, so start by looking for a bowl in the land. There's a likely place by the byre wall. Don't want to have to carry buckets of water too far, do you?'

He stopped and lay down, examining the shape of the land. 'Ah, this'll do for a start,' and he unslung a long, 'Y' shaped hazel rod that he had carried over his shoulder.

I watched as he took hold of the two 'Y' shaped ends in his fists, holding it lightly with his thumbs pointing inwards, toward his chest. I had heard of this, but never seen it in action.

'So what is that thing then, Adam?'

'This is what tells us where the water is; tells you where to dig.'

I watched, fascinated as he began to walk back and forth with the rod extended at waist height pointing forward. Suddenly I saw it twitch, and then dip strongly towards the ground.

'Hammer that peg in boy,' as he kicked a sod out of the grass.

'How did that work? Can I try it?'

'Walk alongside me and put your hand on top of mine.'

He retraced his steps and took a line at ninety degrees to the one he had just walked. Sure enough, as we came to the peg, I felt his hand jerk downwards.

'Is it witchcraft?' I asked in awe.

'No, and don't you go saying that it is! Words like that can get me into trouble.' He was momentarily angry, and glared at me. 'Perhaps a little magic is all ... good magic ... earth magic.'

And so we began digging; slowly, the circular shape of the shaft began to form, and over days it deepened. When we had reached a depth where our heads were almost below the level of the ground, it was time for father to start lining the walls of the well with stone. At the bottom of the shaft, strong metal pegs were driven into the earth round the sides of the well at intervals to take the weight of the first course of stone. The blocks were mortared into place, then the next course until the masonry formed a tube that rose steadily up to the surface. Then we would repeat the process as the shaft went deeper.

***

Ursula had been sharing our home for three months now. It seemed longer.

'Why can't you get the simplest things right?' she scolded. 'Is it too much to expect dry firewood? And the last lot was so green that the smoke reeked us out. What is the matter with you?' Once again I had displeased her, something that seemed to happen often.

'Sorry Ursula, I'll spread it out and the fire will dry it.'

She grunted an acknowledgement as she sat on a stool outside our door, plucking and dressing a brace of woodpigeons. She paused with a handful of feathers. 'Thought any more about finding a girl and setting up on your own?'

I shook my head, avoiding her gaze.

'You don't want to leave it too long or they'll all be spoken for.'

I laughed. 'Don't have time. Too busy digging at Hagg Farm.'

'When I was a young maid I would have been flattered to be asked by a fine young fellow like you,' she smiled up at me; her blue eyes flashed but her smile did not reach them. 'You need to be bolder, chance your arm. "Don't ask, don't get." That's my motto.'

'It seems to have served you well enough,' I replied without thinking, and instantly regretted my careless words.

'And what is that supposed to mean? What are you suggesting?' The smile was gone and her brow furrowed as she stiffened and stared at me.

'Oh, nothing Ursula.' I saw her mood change. 'It's just that things seem to work out for you. You get what you want.' I knew I had stumbled into dangerous territory.

'You think I get what I want? Really?' Her body tensed. 'Well, that just shows how wrong you can be! Do you think I want you?' She dropped the partly plucked bird and stood to face me, her pointed chin thrust forward. 'I have tried being patient, being kind. Even offered to help you find someone, but my patience has its limits. Your father and

I have a life here together. It's time you moved on. You say I get what I want ...' she pointed a bloodstained finger at me. 'You would do well to remember that!' She did not raise her voice, but somehow her words carried a potency that chilled me.

When father returned at dusk, Ursula had prepared a meal. She had baked bread in the parish oven with the other Broomfield women, and we sat to eat with a rushlight burning a sooty flame in its holder in the centre of the table, casting an uneasy light on our faces.

'Tom has been a good help to me today,' she said, smiling. 'He's a willing lad and no mistake.' Father nodded at me without comment as he spooned stew into his bowl and tore a chunk of bread from the loaf.

Ursula could alter her appearance to suit her circumstances with a swiftness that came from practise. That in itself was alarming. She reminded me of a stoat that changes its coat in winter to become as white as the December snow that drifts against the walls and hedgerows; the white of the ermine that trims the robes of royalty. Her skill for deception worried me and I knew that I had to find out more about this woman whose true origins were so elusive. Her name for example: Gurnard was an unusual family name. It was not local, and I had never heard it before. There was something about her; something that she did not want us to see.

***

Martinmas would soon be here and there was no doubt that my father had changed. His violent temper still lurked just out of sight, waiting in ambush for the day he could no longer subdue it; a beast straining at the chains that held it in check, and yet since that day in February when

Ursula arrived, he had altered. Like a calm zephyr, she had soothed his anger, dissipated his rages and brought an uneasy peace to our household. Yet, I could not forget the day when her temper had flared and for a moment, she had dropped all pretence. It had worried me to think that this woman might mean to harm me. Maybe she was right after all and it really was time to move away. I was desperate for a different life and perhaps the moment had come. But where would I go and how would I keep myself?

***

'Ursula, have you seen Jip?' I shouted through the door as I returned at the end of the day.

'He's about somewhere. Saw him on the green a while ago,' came the reply. 'Probably gone ratting at Home Farm. They were taking a rick down today.'

It was unusual and not like him. The wiry haired terrier always greeted me when I returned at the end of the day. He would bark and make a fuss – but not today. It was uncomfortably quiet and empty. I knew that Jip was a ferocious ratter, and like the rest of his breed, he was quick and nimble. I had once seen him kill three rats in as many seconds when a rick was being dismantled on threshing day.

'I'll have to go and look for him,' and without waiting for a reply I set off in the failing light. I did not have to go to Home Farm; I found him at the edge of the green, lying partly covered by bushes. Vomit had issued from his mouth, and he was quite dead.

'He has been poisoned, Ursula,' I said, carrying his lifeless body. 'Somebody has poisoned him.'

'Nonsense.' She looked away. 'Probably picked up some rat bait. People should be more careful. Poison is a dangerous thing ...' she turned and stared at me ... 'and it can kill people as well as animals.'

Her voice chilled me like an east wind on a grey January day. Had she really just threatened me? Perhaps the words came out wrongly and there was no malice behind them. I could quite easily have attached more meaning than was intended, simply because I was suspicious of her. It was her face that gave her away; that cold matter-of-factness delivered a message beyond words. She wanted my father to herself; she wanted the house to herself, and I was something that she had not bargained on. I was an imposition and of no consequence to her. At last I began to understand that perhaps this woman did mean to harm me. I had to find out more about her background, but where to start, and how to avoid arousing her suspicion? I knew where the answer might be found, but just the thought of it made my stomach churn and I gasped for breath like a drowning man in a cold torrent.

I thought back to the day when she moved in, how my clumsiness had spilled the book out of her bundle; her anger and resentment that I had seen it, and how quickly she covered her tracks. I knew I had to find that book and see if it gave me any insight into Ursula's past, but how to achieve that without being caught? The possibility of being discovered was terrifying, but I could think of no other way.

The opportunity presented itself two days later when Ursula announced that she was going to market at Ravengill. It was a good hour's walk each way, and although she wanted to be back before nightfall, I would have plenty of time.

***

As she tied the ribbon on her bonnet, Ursula looked around the room as if to satisfy herself that all was in order.

'Your father needs help when you have finished here,' she said with one hand on the latch.

'I have firewood to collect but I will go as soon as I can,' I replied vaguely.

She turned, her eyes narrowed and looked at me closely. Was it my imagination or did she suspect that I was trying to deceive her? Those cold blue eyes were so intense that it felt as if they were probing my very soul and looking for a weakness that might betray me. I did my best to remain calm although my breath caught in my throat, and I thought that I heard a slight tremor in my voice as I spoke when she turned to go.

'God grant you a safe journey.'

Then she swept up her basket and closed the door behind her: the house was empty.

I waited for some time after she had gone, resisting the temptation to go outside and watch to see her figure disappear over the green. If she had looked back then and seen me, it might have made her suspicious enough to return. At last, I judged it safe to begin, and breathing hard, I went over to the rickety wooden ladder that leaned against the sleeping platform. I put my foot on the first rung and halted. I was unable to climb: my foot seemed to be glued to the ladder and I was a captive there as if a sorcerer had placed an enchantment upon me. With a shudder, I shook off my misgiving and continued upward, listening all the while for the slightest sound that could indicate her return.

It took very little time to search her few belonging. Her clothes were folded neatly, and safely stored beside the straw mattress that they shared. To my surprise, I found that she had a brush and mirror, and a comb made from carefully worked bone with a fine silver inlay. These were expensive items and I wondered how she had come by them, but of the book there was no trace. I took the greatest care to replace everything as I had found it, but I could not help feeling a sense of guilt that I had resorted to the behaviour of a common thief by violating her privacy. I understood now how poor she was and how desperately she needed this roof over her head.

As I gathered an armful of the dry ash logs from the woodshed, my mind was working on the problem that I had set myself. There was no trace of the book anywhere and it certainly was not in our main room where anyone might find it. I still had to gather small birch twigs, birchbark for lighting the fire and a faggot of sticks for the bread oven. A foraging trip into the wood behind the manor house would take an hour or more, and then father needed my help. I made my way across the green and entered the forest beyond, pausing to wave to Martha as I passed her door. There was a plentiful supply of small branches that had fallen during the autumn gales, and as I wielded my billhook I piled them in lengths to form a bundle which I secured with cord to sling over my back.

As I reached the edge of the village, a thought pricked me as sharply as a rose thorn. Suppose she had hidden it in the roof? There was enough space between the oak roof beams and the thatch to conceal a small package. As I thought about it, this would be a perfect hiding place; well out of sight and warm enough to keep such a delicate object dry. I had to look, but did I have time? I reasoned that Ursula would be on her way home now, and to search again risked discovery. Although I knew that she could appear at any moment, I had no choice. After all, I had looked everywhere else, and to search the tiny space above the rafters would take seconds. I threw down my bundle and ran.

The house was empty when I reached our door. I looked around furtively, checking for her to appear on the path from Ravengill but there was no sign of her. I plunged inside, scrambling up the ladder, panting in my haste. I looked up and saw where there was an obvious space above me; where the thatch did not quite reach the blackened oak purlin, and I cursed myself for not having noticed it before. I stretched up, and as my hand explored the cavity, I touched a package. Lifting it down, I found a small bundle of coarse cloth, and when I opened it, there was the book.

There was so little time. I knew she could return at any moment, but I also realised that this opportunity might not present itself again for several weeks. I found that my hands were shaking as I withdrew the book from its covering, dreading to hear the sound of her hand on the latch. The tiny volume was as I remembered it on the day that she moved in. It was not much bigger than my hand, and bound in soft, brown leather with a gilded cross embossed on the front. It was clearly old and well used, judging by the darkened cover, stained by frequent handling until it was the colour of walnut and worn smooth by the passage of time.

I was helpless with indecision. My instinct was to stuff it back where it came from and run, but having come this far, I knew I must open it and look for any clue that it might contain. With the reverence of a priest handling the sacred host, I folded back the stiff outer binding, The first two pages were blank, but my eyes were drawn to several lines of carefully written script on the fly leaf and a sort of diagram – a picture of a tree, hand drawn in ink on the second leaf.

Then the stupidity of my actions became abundantly clear: I could not read. How had I ever expected to make sense of anything that I found here? I knew I had to continue and look at the other pages, if only to get a general impression of what lay inside.

The next leaf was a beautifully illustrated picture of a saint or perhaps a bishop, holding a crozier and with his hand raised in blessing. The crozier was gilded, and the gold leaf shone as brightly as the day it was applied. Next came a series of unadorned pages, each had a title and a prayer written beneath it, but what the words said I could not tell. The final pages were a surprise; they had a sequence of letters, which I recognised as the letters you would use to teach a child to read. And that was it – there was nothing more that could give me the slightest insight into Ursula's past. I realised that if anything was contained here, it would be in the handwritten script at the beginning, but I could make no sense of it.

Something made me stop with a jolt and cock my head to one side. With dismay I heard Ursula's voice: she was back, and I was going to be caught. I pushed the book back into its cloth cover and on impulse, I hid it inside my jacket. Martha could read and my only chance was to let her see it. Voices were right outside the door now.

'I have baked too much. You are welcome to have some,' I heard from outside, and I recognised the voice of Elizabeth Weaver.

'Thank you Mistress Weaver and I have eggs to spare. I will bring you some.' As she finished speaking, Ursula came into the room below. I had flattened myself to the floor and lay there, my face in the dust trying not to breathe for fear of sneezing. Then the door opened again, and

Ursula was outside, walking away with Elizabeth Weaver to exchange their goods. I raced down the ladder and fled, the book still inside my jacket.

***

Chapter 6

Autumn 1460

My father was well-matched to the life of a stonemason, and he was never short of employment. Other men knew of his reputation and that he was handy with his fists; although courteous enough to him as a fellow labourer, they gave him a wide berth. Working alone suited his surly nature. There were always buildings to repair, walls to remake and occasionally there were new barns to erect for the manorial demesne at Upper Broomfield. I had never intended to follow him in his trade, and he would have been a poor tutor. His short temper, intolerance of mistakes and simmering violence would have seen to that. Although I helped when I was needed, I knew that it was not for me. I had an intuition, a sort of voice in my head that told me that something else was waiting, but what that might be, I had no idea.

***

Our work on the well was nearing completion and as we had gone deeper, our progress had slowed. 'Pull it up when I shout,' and I hoisted the bucket of water up the shaft, emptied it and returned it to father who was bailing out below. This was how a day's work started, with the laborious business of draining the well. The task was building the muscles in my arms and shoulders with each bucket that I hauled. If only I could shoot in the archery contest now! I could feel the increased power in my upper body. and knew that I would certainly reach the two hundred yard target with ease.

'Are you daydreaming up there? Send it down boy.' I jumped out of my reverie to see father's head appear at the top of the ladder as he climbed back up onto level ground. I awaited a clout from his fist, but instead he seemed pleased.

'We're nearly there. One more week will see it done, just in time with winter coming on.'

'We have not managed to finish by the midsummer quarter day as we had hoped. I suppose we can say goodbye to any extra payment.'

'I have to attend his lordship today and give him a progress report. I will explain how much work it has been. You never know, he might be generous. Meanwhile, keep digging for the last two courses of stone. That will be enough.'

He began to pick up blocks for the parapet that extended above ground level. They were already dressed in readiness, and now he assembled them loosely in position, checking their fit.

'I will mortar these in before we finish today.' With that he was off, leaving me the task of digging and bailing out water on my own, as the well continued to fill. I returned home at noon to find something to eat, but paused as I turned the corner of the track that entered the village. Ursula was standing outside the blacksmith's yard with a basket over her arm, and she was talking intently with Jasper Griswold. Curious, I watched from behind the shelter of the pinfold and studied them. They were deep in conversation and occasionally, Ursula would look around her almost as if she was checking to see if she was being observed. Then I saw Jasper nod as they parted company.

I dismissed the thought that first came to my mind; she would know Jasper as an acquaintance. They were both from Lower Broomfield, and would be on speaking terms and yet this did not appear to have been a casual conversation. I had no doubt that Ursula still owed some loyalty to the village that had been her home. She had never been fully accepted by the women in Upper Broomfield, and although they were superficially polite, they regarded her with a degree of suspicion that excluded her from their more private conversations.

***

It was early in the afternoon and father still had not returned from his meeting with Lord Thain. I needed his help now; I had removed enough material for him to set the last two courses in place and I was filling the last bucket with mud when I straightened for breath. The air was foul down here, and I had heard of people who had suffocated whilst doing this kind of deep digging. As I stood, I saw a shadow cross the bright circle of light high above me. At the same time, one of the loosely placed parapet stones came crashing down, bouncing and skipping as it clattered off the sides of the shaft. I pressed myself as tightly as I could with my back against the damp masonry and my eyes clamped shut as the big stone hit the bottom of the well with a huge, echoing crash. The bucket splintered into fragments, soaking me with muddy water.

I was transfixed for a moment, my heart racing, legs shaking. Gathering myself, I brushed the stone chips from my hair and face, and climbed the ladder, up into fresh air and safety. I looked around but there was nobody in sight. Even when I searched behind the walls and in the farm buildings, the place was deserted and yet this was no accident: somebody had just tried to kill me.

***

I made no mention of it when I returned at the end of the day. Instead, I went to speak to Martha, with the book still wrapped in its rough cloth cover, tucked inside my jerkin. Martha could perhaps read what the handwritten words said, and make sense of what I had found. Night had fallen and they had closed the shutters and barred the door, so that when I knocked, my godmother's voice sounded wary.

'Who is it? What do you want?' I could hear her nervousness. Then Godwin's deep tone: 'Who are you?'

'It's me Godwin. It's Tom.'

I could hear the sound of the bar being drawn and a moment later I was made comfortable on a chair by their fire with a mug of ale.

'He was never much of a husband, even when your mother was alive, may she rest in peace,' Martha said, crossing herself. 'I always thought she deserved better. She was such a kind, gentle soul was Maggie. Always saw the best in people.' She paused and looked across the blue smoke that spiralled up from the fire. 'And what about you? How are you doing, now that she's moved in?' she asked with a jerk of her head to indicate Ursula.

'Well, we are eating better, I'll give her that. She has stopped him drinking all his money away.'

'Yes, I have seen her baking bread and buying food at Ravengill market. She never has much to say, and to tell you the truth, I don't think that the village women are easy in her company. They say she is too young for him for one thing. They don't trust her much, and they are careful what they say in front of her. Still, at least you are getting fed properly now. I was really worried about you.'

'Tell him the story about the old woman and the donkey,' Godwin suggested. I looked up, waiting for him to expand, but there was no hurrying Godwin. Instead, he looked to his mother with a smile of childlike expectation, while she shuffled her feet in embarrassment.

'This is from when I was a girl, growing up at Raventhorpe – do you know it? Just a tiny place.'

'Mother liked it at Raventhorpe. Happy days there,' Godwin interrupted.

'Yes, but the story?' I asked, seeing that he had broken her concentration.

'Oh well,' Martha said with a sigh, 'If I must. It's a silly story but it reminded me of you when you were not getting enough to eat. Made me worry that I was not doing enough to help you. I am your godmother after all.' She cleared her throat and began. 'At Raventhorpe there lived an old lady who owned a donkey, and she rode it to market each week.'

'A nice donkey it was, a holy donkey with a cross on its back,' Godwin elaborated, but my look reduced him to silence.

'Anyway, times were hard, and they didn't have enough to eat so she decided to cut down the donkey's rations.'

'Is that it? Is that the story?'

'No, course not. She hasn't got to the important bit yet! Carry on mother.' Godwin was aggrieved at my impatience.

Martha continued. 'Well, cutting down his rations seemed to work, so after a while when times got harder still, she did it again. And then she did it once more. She was so pleased with herself that she decided not to give it any food at all because it seemed to be able to manage. She had just got it used to living on nothing and the damned thing went and died!' Martha concluded with a smile.

'She said that you reminded her of that donkey. There!' Godwin announced triumphantly. I smiled at his obvious enjoyment at the re-telling of a story he must have heard many times. For a bittersweet moment, I had travelled back through the years; this was just the sort of story that mother used to tell us, and the pain of her memory burned brightly.

'I think she wants rid of me. I think she tried to kill me today.' There was a stunned silence. The smile on Martha's face had frozen with disbelief, while Godwin looked at me open mouthed.

'*What*?' Martha asked.

I went on to describe recent events: the warnings she had given; Jip being poisoned; the stone down the well.

'Is it her or Jasper Griswold? He threatened you at the Shrove Tuesday game. Even pulled a knife. And don't forget the arrow at the St. Boniface Fair.' Godwin reminded.

'There is something else,' I began. They both waited expectantly while I looked down at my feet, uncertain what they would make of me searching through her things.

'Well go on then!' Godwin leaned forward, eager to hear more.

I reached inside my jerkin and produced the rough cloth parcel. Godwin's eyes lit up with excitement. 'What is it?' he asked, full of innocent curiosity.

Rather than answer, I drew the book out of its cover and set it on my knee. The leather looked black in the firelight and the cross gleamed as an occasional flicker caught the gold ornamentation. This was the last thing they had expected, and they seemed to be afraid of it, denied the power of speech as they stared at it.

It was Martha who spoke: 'Where did you get that?' she asked in a hushed voice.

'It was in Ursula's belongings,' and I explained how it had come to my attention. 'Trouble is, I can't read. I hoped you might make something of it. Thought it might tell us a bit more about her. She was blazing angry when I found it, so it must be important.'

Martha held out her hand and took the book, turning it over, examining the leather cover. Very delicately, she opened it and studied the handwritten inscriptions, then proceeded to look at each page in turn, while Godwin and I sat in silence, waiting for her to finish. Finally, she closed the book and passed it back to me.

'Well? What is it mother?' Godwin's patience had failed him.

'I can tell you what it is, but I can't explain why she has got it. It is valuable, that is certain. This is called a Book of Hours - it is a prayer book - the sort of thing a fine lady might own.' She reached over and took the book again and turning to the first printed page, pointed to the top. 'See the title "Matins?" that is the first service of the day, and there is a prayer to go with it. The next page says "Prime". Each page is given over to a special time of day when prayers are said, right through to "Compline" which is the last service of the day. Then there are some pages that you would use to teach a child if it is learning to read. See, "A" followed by "B" and so on.'

'And is that it?' I asked in disappointment. 'Is there nothing else? What about the writing at the front – does that give any help?'

Martha turned to the blank flyleaf, shaking her head. 'There is a name written here: "Rosegill Priory", but I have no idea where that is.'

'Perhaps that is where she stole it from,' Godwin suggested. 'Bad luck that, stealing from a church.'

'What about the other page?' I asked.

'It is a picture or a diagram of something. It looks a bit like a tree with fruit hanging from its branches, and there is a prayer to Saint Egina written beneath it, although I've never heard of her.'

'She must have stolen it, Tom. Probably wants to sell it I expect.' Godwin's interpretation seemed unlikely.

'I don't think so,' I replied. 'She treasures it too much, and if she was going to sell it, she would have done so by now.'

'Then it is urgent that you return it as quickly as possible. It is the sort of thing that she might look at often. It is her most precious possession and it will be missed.'

I replaced the book into my jerkin and stood to leave.

'You must get away from here.' Martha's voice betrayed her concern. 'You are not safe. Is there nowhere else for you to go ... no other family you could turn to?'

'I have an aunt, my mother's older sister, Aunt Anne, but she lives miles away, outside York at a place called Thorpe Greenhow. I have decided to go in the spring, when travelling is easier.'

'I will write to her for you, explain the situation. It's better if she knows what is happening.' She paused, then ... 'Tell Ursula that you are going. It may just keep you safe if she knows that you are planning to leave.' She put her hand on my arm and with a look that conveyed her concern, added, 'Return that book to its hiding place without being discovered, and for the love of God do it quickly.'

***

Chapter 7

20$^{th.}$ March, 1461

Upper Broomfield rested below the summit of a gentle incline, as though its founders had run out of breath in their attempt to crest the brow and chosen the site as a compromise. The cottages were of similar appearance – low, single storied dwellings with a thatch of blackened wheat straw and a hole where smoke issued from the central hearth beneath. On the upper edge of the village, in superiority, the manor house stood exalted above its demesne where geese grazed noisily on the green. To the north of the manor was woodland, a rich resource of revenue, while stretching away to the south were the field systems and common land spreading down the banks of the Howlbeck, to Lower Broomfield and ever southwards over the gentler plains that extended into open country.

Broomfield Manor stood in dominance over all; a sombre presence that kept the commoners in their place by its position above the village. Sir Hugh Thain's hall was busy today; the feast of St. Agatha had been celebrated by the Abbot of St. Wilfrid's, Father Gervase Porteous, who had said mass for the assembled household. A temporary wooden altar had been placed on the dais, fresh rushes scattered on the floor and trestle tables cleared aside to make space for the service. After mass was concluded, the household had dined together with the abbot as their guest of honour.

'I am so glad you were able to join us at dinner, Father Abbot,' Lady Edith smiled as she ushered Gervase Porteous to a seat in their solar. Comfortable chairs were arranged around a table that held two bottles of wine and a selection of glasses. Gervase settled his generous frame with a sigh. The ruby set in the gold band on his index finger gleamed opulently, as he clasped his hands comfortably across his midriff.

'That was an excellent goose Lady Edith, and Lent will soon be here so we did well to enjoy its bounty while we may.'

He took a glass of malmsey offered by Sir Hugh and sipped it appreciatively. Sir Hugh took his own glass and settled facing the abbot. Candles had been brought and their soft light played upon the faces of the small gathering. Sir Hugh Thain's tall bony figure, with his aquiline nose that dripped constantly, was an odd juxtaposition to Abbot Gervase.

'My land agent, William Langley, may join us shortly. He has been negotiating a contract for our timber with the woodyard at the cathedral.'

'Then he will be exhausted. Two days ride in this weather!' Gervase observed.

Lady Edith signalled to her maid, Mary Conyer, to be seated in a corner of the room, while she chose a place in the centre of the semicircle and picked up her embroidery. She was a lady of indefinable age; her face with its fine bone structure carried all the warmth and generosity of spirit that her husband's expression failed to achieve. While he was gaunt, hawklike and severe, she was demure and considerate. Although she showed a superficial interest in her embroidery, it was merely a convenience that enabled her to listen to the men's conversation while maintaining an appearance of disinterest. Lady Edith was an intelligent woman, both astute and politically aware. Events in the south of the country gave her cause for serious concern and she intended to be alert to the implications for her world at the manor. Political allegiances were fickle here in the subservience of Gilmortain Castle, and the affinity of the Neville family dictated all their futures.

'Have you news from your sources in the south, Gervase?' Sir Hugh had placed his glass on a side table and turned to face the abbot.

'None of the news is good these days,' he replied with a sigh. 'After the great battle at Wakefield at Christmas, the cause of the Yorkists is in a sorry plight. Richard Plantagenet dead, his son killed, and our own Earl of Salisbury, Richard Neville also fallen. Such a bitter harvest of our nobility.'

'And their heads placed on spikes above the Micklelith Bar in York, I hear,' Sir Hugh added.

'Such vengeance has no place before God – to place a paper crown on the Duke of York's head was unseemly mockery. "York may look upon York," it said. It does Margaret of Anjou's cause no credit. They would do well to read Deuteronomy; Our Lord's words to Moses: "Vengeance is mine, I will repay" It should shame them all in their spiteful brutality, and lust for revenge.'

'I fear there are many scores to settle.' Lady Edith observed with a note of sadness.

'Certainly Edward, Earl of March will seek revenge for the execution of his father and his older brother after their capture at Wakefield. As the oldest surviving son, I suppose he is the next Duke of York, and the next claimant to the throne,' Sir Hugh concluded.

'He may claim what he likes, but only Henry VI is our king and anointed before God,' Gervase snorted. 'Besides, the Yorkist cause has been badly weakened after their second defeat at St. Albans.'

'That means Margaret is in control again. Although Henry is king, she is the monarch.' Hugh observed wryly. 'He is so feeble minded that he is incapable of making a decision ...' the Abbot coughed uncomfortably and shuffled in his chair at Sir Hugh's observation.

'I beg your pardon, Gervase, I do not mean to cause offence or to question God's judgement, but it is a fact that he has never been suited to the role of king.'

'He is still our monarch,' he paused for reflection. 'although better that he had gone into the church, perhaps,' Gervase acquiesced. 'He is not a strong person. It is true that his mind is delicate, and he appears ... ahem ... somewhat distracted at times.'

'I believe that his "distraction" makes him stare blankly at the wall, renders him unable to speak; makes him seem like a sleepwalker who is dead to us for month after month. The people tire of his inability to govern. They do not care for the queen and her French ancestry, and yet it is she who is leading the country.' Sir Hugh's voice revealed his frustration. He stood and refilled his glass, clattering the bottle down as a mark of his annoyance. 'Margaret of Anjou... the one they call "the she-wolf", she has recruited an army in Scotland and the borders, which is little more than a band of outlaws – reivers, cattle thieves, ruffians of every sort, and what is worse, she has offered them no pay for their service.'

Abbot Gervase raised an eyebrow: 'Then why do they follow her? What possible motivation can they have?'

'She has told them that they may exact their wages in plunder, and men like those need no second bidding. They have pillaged and thieved their way down the country – with such a degree of enthusiasm that their reputation has gone before them. And this band of brigands has been given the blessing of Queen Margaret.'

'Perhaps the people do not care to be led by a woman?' questioned Lady Edith, laying aside her stitching. 'I think, if I have understood correctly, that her son would become king after the death of her husband, Henry, but he will be disinherited by the Act of Accord. She would never allow Edward March to brush her own son, Edward of Lancaster, aside.' Both men turned to look at her in surprise. They had not expected to hear such clarity of observation. 'But what do I know?' She smiled sweetly. 'I am just a woman, unversed in such matters.' She signalled to Mary to bring her a glass of wine, delighting inwardly at the discomfort that her accuracy had engendered.

A disturbance from below caused Sir Hugh to rise and walk to the small window that looked down from the solar to the great hall beneath. The familiar figure of his land agent could be seen as he strode to the fire, dripping water on the rushes from his sodden riding cloak.

'Eat, then come up to join us, William,' he called down. His wave sent servants scurrying to the kitchen and setting a place for William Langley, who looked weary after a long journey in such poor weather.

***

'What news from Lincoln, William?' Sir Hugh placed a glass in his land agent's hand and ushered him to a seat.

'We have a fair price for our oak from the last felling. We agreed tenpence per foot on the smaller stuff and a shilling for the bigger timber. The longest baulks are double that.'

'I'm sure that can wait for now Will,' Hugh said, smiling. 'I meant, what other news have you gleaned from all your contacts? Father Abbot does not want to know about the price of our timber!'

'Then I have much to tell you. Nottingham is buzzing with expectation and gossip is flying round every street corner.' Lady Edith turned to face him and inclined her head with interest. 'They say the king and queen have been there, on their way northwards to York. The city is like an ants nest with messengers scurrying to and fro, and dispatch riders galloping through Vault Lane Bar from the south. Troops loyal to Edward March were setting up temporary camp and gathering outside the walls; everywhere you look there are preparations being made to equip an army for battle. The forges are burning night and day as they make ready for a great confrontation. Trouble is brewing and from what I have heard, it is not far away.'

He paused to take a draught from his glass, allowing Sir Hugh to frame the question that they all were thinking: 'But what are the king and queen doing up here? Why are they heading north at all speed, and what is the cause of all the panic?'

'All I can tell you is the snippets that I have been able to pick up as I went around Nottingham. It may just be tavern gossip, but there seems to be a ring of truth to it. After her victory over the Earl of Warwick at St. Albans, Queen Margaret took possession of her husband the king, who the Yorkists had abandoned on the battlefield when they fled, and there her army halted. They say she should have marched straight to London and taken the Tower and all its arsenal of weapons under her control, but for some reason she hesitated. Perhaps she just took it for granted that she would be welcomed and his grace, her royal husband, restored within his own great city. Perhaps she wanted to rest her troops after the long march down from Scotland and fighting the Yorkists. Only she can say.'

'But you still have not told us what they were doing in Nottingham. What has happened to bring Margaret's army so far up the country? Are they on the run?' Sir Hugh's curiosity was bordering on irritation.

'From what I can understand, Margaret's army had behaved so badly that their reputation was their undoing. The Londoners were afraid that they would ransack the city, so they barred the gates and denied them entry. She had no choice but to retreat; to regroup and provision her army from the Lancastrian estates up north, so she is setting up her power base at York. Meanwhile, Edward Earl of March was welcomed into London. They adore him there. The Londoners have been so won over by his good looks and his profligate spending that they have invited him to replace his grace Henry VI as monarch. They are calling him Edward IV now.'

'But how can that be?' Lady Edith looked puzzled. 'Surely we cannot have two kings?'

Gervase had remained silent, turning the ring on his index finger thoughtfully, so that the ruby gleamed in the candlelight. Now he spoke: 'You say trouble is on the way. What gives you reason to make such a prediction? What kind of trouble are we to expect?'

'Edward has moved up quickly from the south, recruiting troops as he goes. He intends to catch the Lancastrians and bring them to battle.'

'And that battle will be at York.' Gervase concluded sadly.

'He will attempt to take the city, that much seems clear. He is sworn to avenge the deaths of his father and brother, and placing their heads on spikes has given him extra determination,' William replied.

There was a long moment while each absorbed the situation that faced them. Lady Edith's quiet voice broke the silence: 'And how will this affect us at Upper Broomfield?'

'Yes, how indeed?' Gervase was prompted by her question. 'Will there be a Commission of Array issued and will you have to supply fighting men from the estates up here?'

'I think that may well already have been done,' William said, 'but it is my understanding that Gilmortain has been asked to supply a company of five hundred archers to be drawn from the garrison and the surrounding area, so we may well be given a quota.'

'In that case, I already know who we will send. Sir Richard de Coverdale, garrison commander at Gilmortain, wants the two who he watched at the fair on St. Boniface's day, the Lightfoot boy and our stonemason's lad, Tom Gifford. They are chosen men. The Gifford boy's skill with the bow drew special praise.'

Lady Edith's maid, Mary Conyer had been seated all the while, staring abstractedly at the pattern in her mistress's gown, but she jolted to attention at the mention of two names that she recognised.

As the gathering drew to a close, William Langley turned to Sir Hugh: 'There is one thing I forgot to tell you that may be of interest; I saw Ranulf Griswold's son in Nottingham. He was drinking in one of the low taverns with a group of soldiers, I recognised their colours – they were wearing the red and yellow sashes of Northumberland's men.'

'Lancastrians. Henry Percy – the Earl of Northumberland. Bitter rival of the Neville family of course. Well, it seems Jasper Griswold has chosen his allegiance already. You had better make sure his father is aware of this. He will not be pleased. Father Abbot, I shall send an escort with you back to St. Wilfrid's. Tonight's news must put us all on our guard.'

'Thank you Hugh. Ordinarily I would not dream of putting you to the trouble. I wonder if I might beg one more favour? There is a statue in a niche on the west side of the bell tower which has been loosened by the wind. It has slipped and tilted to one side most alarmingly… '

'Leave it to me. I shall send our stonemason to attend to it at the earliest opportunity.'

As the guests departed, Lady Edith dismissed her maid, and they resumed their seats. 'This is grave news husband.' Now they were alone, Lady Edith's face had lost its composure.

'Do not fear, we are safe here, my dear,' he reassured her with a pat on the arm.

'On the contrary, I would say that we are most certainly *not* safe. We are caught between the hammer and the anvil, can you not see it? Queen

Margaret's forces are raiding the countryside to the north of us, while to the south, we hear that another army, Edward March's army, is heading towards us, bent on bloody revenge, and you say we are safe!' She had raised her voice, so great was her agitation. 'How are we "safe?" How can we be sure of anything when our small world is caught up in such disorder?' Her cheeks had flushed with anger at her husband's inability to read the situation.

'We have always been within the protection of the castle at Gilmortain. If we are given a quota to fill, then we have no choice. We must obey.'

'Then think carefully, husband, for soon it may be time to choose your allegiance, and pray God that you choose wisely. Send only the two men who have been named and no more. There may come a time when our actions are held to account, and whichever side emerges as the victor will treat those who supported their enemy with the harshness due to the vanquished.'

Below, in the darkness of the courtyard, Mary Conyer had pulled her cloak about her shoulders and set her hood so that her face was in deep shadow as she slipped out of the fortified gateway that led from the outer wall of the manor and made her way quickly into the night.

***

Chapter 8

March 1461

'Godwin, we must think quickly.' It was early morning as Martha Lightfoot stood by her door looking across the green towards the house where Tom Gifford lived. She wavered restlessly, knowing that her godson was unaware of the huge events that were unfolding about them and that threatened to overwhelm them in a confrontation that was beyond imagination. In truth she had not slept, so she scarcely noticed as the wind caught the corner of her surcoat, tugging it playfully, oblivious to her turmoil of indecision. As she hesitated, Ursula Gurnard came out with a bowl and threw its contents onto the grass, then turned without greeting, and closed the door behind her.

'Mary Conyer is a good girl. I delivered her sister's baby last year and the little mite nearly died. Perhaps this was her way of saying thank you.'

As midwife for her surrounding area, Martha had assisted at many difficult birthings, each presenting its own challenge, but what she faced now scared her more than the long hours of labour at the childbed had ever done. If she was to avoid her son and godson being slaughtered in the madness that lay ahead, she must act swiftly, but cleverly.

'Her warning has given us a moment of precious time. Nobody else knows of the muster and you must be long gone before they do. If it is true that they have issued a Commission of Array, then you cannot refuse it.'

'Why, what would happen if we refused to go?' Godwin asked, more out of curiosity than any inclination to stand his ground in defiance.

'To refuse is treason, and they would hang you both as traitors ... but if you were already gone ... if you were already miles away for a genuine reason before the call to arms had been given, they would have to get somebody else to fill their quota. They would be none the wiser, and you would both be safe.'

'You know people will call us cowards, don't you?' Godwin was slowly turning over the implications of his mother's suggestion.

'No! No they won't! Not if you are long gone before word of this gets out. I have a plan which will work, but only if we act now. You need to see Tom. Explain the situation and make sure he understands that he must keep his mouth shut. Tell him to come tonight and by then I will have thought it through properly. Go and see him now and remember, not a word to a soul. Your life may depend on it.'

***

As I strapped on my boots, I was already thinking about father's instruction. I was to go to St. Wilfrid's and conduct an inspection of the work on the statue. I was to see how urgent it was, how much scaffolding was needed and if possible estimate the height of the plinth by counting the courses of masonry beneath it. Godwin's knock was a surprise, even more so because of his uncharacteristic shiftiness.

'Tom, need to speak outside,' he muttered. Godwin was not his usual phlegmatic self, and I could see there was a problem.

We stood away from the cottage. In the growing light of the rising winter sun I read the urgency in my friend's face, so I leaned nonchalantly against the woodshed door, hoping my casual manner might convey some reassurance and sooth his agitation. It seemed to have the opposite effect and my apparent lack of concern only served to make him more distressed, as he divulged his confidences.

'... need to get away quickly, probably tonight.' Godwin finished in a rush of words that tumbled from him in escalating urgency and volume.

'But what about food? What about explaining where we have gone?'

'Mother will see to all that. She has a plan. Bring a warm cloak and anything else you can think of, and remember, if they catch us, they will hang us, so not a word.'

'Tonight then,' I replied, and with my thoughts in confusion, I set off for St. Wilfrid's.

***

Inside the darkness of the woodshed, Ursula released the breath she had been holding in a long, shivering sigh. She leaned back against the woven wall of hazel rods, and tilted her head back so her sharp chin pointed up to the roof, eyes closed in relief. Her arms ached from the burden of wood that she was holding; her muscles burned with the strain of keeping it secure without dropping a single stick that would have betrayed her presence. She put the firewood down, and flexed her arms to restore the circulation. Her quick mind was already actively exploring the potential of the information that she had just overheard.

'He said he was leaving in the spring but yet he is still here. He shows no sign of going. He seems to be able to work with his father now. Perhaps he will never go. Well this will take care of things once and for all,' and she allowed herself to smile, just briefly, before she picked up her bundle, closing the woodshed door behind her.

***

The monastery of St. Wilfrid's was half a mile to the east of Upper Broomfield where the Howlbeck valley broadened into a wide plain. It was an unostentatious collection of buildings fashioned from the grey local limestone that made it seem as if it had sprouted from the ground upon which it rested. As I made my way along the narrow path towards the monastery, I heard a bell announcing Terce, a brief service before the morning's work would begin.

I made my way to the gatekeeper's lodge where I found a small bell with a short length of plaited cord. I gave a vigorous pull, which set it dancing on its spindle, and announcing my presence with its clear, bright clanging. The stout oak door was studded with iron nails, and beneath each, ran a stain of rust like Calvary tears. In its upper portion was a metal grill, covering a tiny, hinged flap that allowed the gatekeeper to assess any callers in safety, before admitting them.

The flap swung open, and a face peered cautiously through the grill. 'Yes?' enquired a nervous voice.

'Tom Gifford, sir. Stonemason's assistant required by Father Abbot to look at the statue on the bell tower.'

'Ah yes, you are expected. Wait one moment,' and the flap shut again with a snap. Then there was the sound of heavy bolts being drawn before the main door swung open, its considerable weight moving surprisingly easily on well-greased hinges. Before me stood a lay brother, a man of about my own age and height, dressed in a plain grey woollen robe, tied at the waist with a length of rope.

'I am Tom Gifford, here on behalf of my father, John Gifford the stonemason.'

'And I am Brother Mark. I apologise for my delay in admitting you. Father Abbot has insisted on extreme caution after some bad news he received yesterday.'

I thought that I could guess the nature of that news and why Brother Mark had been told to exert great vigilance. The gate was closed and secured behind me with a series of heavy thuds as the bolts were pushed home. If that was not enough, a stout wooden bar was placed in metal hasps to brace it across the opening.

'I have instructions to take you to Father Stephen. Now that Terce is over, he will be in the scriptorium,' and with that, he set off, taking long strides that set his sandals flapping on the flagstones, and his robe fluttering about his bony frame. I was led through a small door from the outer courtyard to the cloister. We skirted round two sides of the square under a colonnaded and roofed walkway, finally arriving at a door on our left. We entered and I found myself in a large room filled with shelves of leather bound books and rolls of manuscript. The air was heavy with the smell of old leather and dry parchment.

'This is the library,' explained Brother Mark. 'We must go up the stairs to the scriptorium and we should find Father Stephen waiting for us.'

As we climbed the creaking flight of wooden stairs, I could hear someone moving across the floor, and the thud as a heavy volume was placed upon a table. I entered the room and saw a number of writing desks with their angled surfaces turned to catch the benefit of the light that flooded in through a large window at the end of the room. Father Stephen was seated at a desk, pen in hand and engaged in copying a text from a volume beside him. He was an elderly monk with a grey complexion that suggested that he must spend much of his time indoors as a concession to his advancing years.

'Please bear with me for a moment while I finish this,' his quiet voice seemed entirely fitting for his scholarly occupation, where the loudest sound was the rustle of parchment or the scratch of a quill.

I stood and watched him in fascination; his pen strokes so sure and delicate, as the words revealed themselves in a dancing tracery of swirls and curlicues. He looked up and noted my interest. 'Can you write Tom?' he enquired.

'I have never mastered it fully yet, Father. My mother taught me a little before she died.'

'I am sad to hear of her death. May God bless her and keep her,' he said and made the sign of the cross. 'Perhaps we may resume her lessons? Would you like that?'

‘Indeed Father, I would be honoured to learn.’

‘Then while I complete this line, let me find you a scrap of paper and you can try your hand here and now.’ He searched his desk and found a torn piece of paper which he placed on the table in front of me. ‘Here, write what you can. Copy a few words from the manuscript in front of you if you wish.’

I was at a loss to know how to resume; my efforts had been on a stone slate with a piece of limestone to make the letters – never with a quill and paper. I looked at the richly illustrated page, twirling the pen round in my hands in hesitation. I decided that rather than write, I would draw, and with a sense of trepidation, I began. Time seemed to vanish as I worked, and I became aware that Father Stephen had stopped what he was doing to watch me. I had drawn a picture about the height of my hand: the crucified Christ looked out on the figures of his mother and Mary Magdalene as they knelt beneath him.

‘That is extraordinary!’ murmured Father Stephen in a voice that expressed both surprise and delight. ‘Where did you learn such skill?’

‘I ... I don’t know father’ I stammered in embarrassment. ‘I have never learned it. I can just do it I suppose.’

‘Then you have a gift that should be used to the glory of God!’ he exclaimed. ‘Wait, let me add something.’ He took my paper to his own desk and began to write. When he had finished he beckoned me over and he read to me:

“Pater noster, qui es in coelis, sanctificetur nomen tuum”

‘It is the first part of the Lord’s prayer,’ he explained, although I recognised the words from the mass as soon as he read them. He had written it beneath my drawing as a kind of dedication. He sanded the ink and folded the paper carefully. 'Keep this safe, and if ever you decide to enter the Lord's service, bring it with you.'

'Thank you Father,' I said as I took the paper and placed it safely in the purse at my belt.

'Now, let us take a look at this statue,' he said with a smile. 'We seem to have become distracted somehow!'

***

The sky had changed from lapis blue to rich amethyst and finally to jet black: the moon had not yet risen, and the last of the seeping twilight had yielded to night-time's cloak of sombre shadows as I knocked on Martha Lightfoot's door. It was opened immediately by Godwin who ushered me swiftly inside without ceremony. 'Did anybody see you?' he asked, a note of anxiety in his voice.

'Nobody,' I replied.

'What did you tell them?' he asked, nodding in the direction of my home.

'Said I was going to be away for a few days. Had a job to do. Helping you with something.'

'Didn't they ask what it was? Where you were going?'

'Not interested. Pleased to see the back of me more like.'

'Come, you two. Time is too precious for gossiping,' Martha ordered.

She had assembled a pile of essentials on the table and began packing them into two satchels.

'If you are still here when the commissioner's messenger delivers news of the muster, then you will have no choice. As it is, this way you stand a chance. If I tell them a good story, they will go elsewhere for their quota. I will not send you to be butchered in a quarrel that is not our own. We don't even know which king has the just cause, Henry or Edward. I cannot lose either of you just because the nobility choose to fight amongst themselves.'

'But they will ask where we have gone. We will be hunted down.' Now that the moment had come I was full of uncertainty; could it be right to run from the muster like a coward? What would people say? How would I feel if Martha's plan worked and I was safe but another was killed in my place? She was protecting us both in the only way she knew how, and I understood how precious Godwin, her only son, was to her. Her answer was strong and determined:

'I am sending you to my brother's farm at Greenhurst. We can say he has been taken ill and needs help urgently with the spring sowing. I have written a letter for you to take, explaining everything so he will get the story right, should anybody ask. It could be days before you are summoned and nobody else knows that this is happening. Mary might just have saved your lives!'

'Uncle Matthew lives miles away. It must be three days walk from here,' Godwin looked puzzled. 'I don't even know how to get there!'

'It couldn't be easier.' Martha replied. 'Go from here to Lower Broomfield, then just head west. Follow the corpse road ...'

'The what?' I interrupted.

'The corpse road ... the road that the country people use to bring their coffins over for burial in the churchyard. Follow it to the hills, then ask for directions.' She handed us each a satchel: 'This should last you for the journey, but now you must be on your way. You have to be well clear of here before daybreak. It is a young moon so there will be just enough light to see by and enough darkness to hide you from view.' She held us both in a long embrace, then pushed us to the door. 'Now go! And God protect you both.'

***

We skirted the village green, taking care to seek out the shadows. We had just left the safety of the last house when a dog began to bark fiercely.

'Quick, run!' whispered Godwin, and we raced for the cover of the trees before anyone might look to see what had unsettled the dog. Having left the village behind, our eyes began to adjust to the night sky. The moon was in its first quarter, lighting our way as we set off to follow the road to Lower Broomfield. We split up, one on each side of the track, keeping to the verges where our shapes would not be so noticeable against the lighter colour of the road, should anyone be watching. Soon we began to feel the gentle slope fall away from us as we headed down to the bridge over the Howlbeck.

'One at a time,' I whispered to Godwin as we reached the stone parapet.

'You first!' He replied nervously.

Keeping my head low, I scurried to the other side, then waved silently for Godwin to follow. He came at a clumsy, scuttling run, his large bulk clearly visible above the high arch of the bridge. He reached me and we stood, breathing heavily, when a command came from the blackness, fixing me with the gut-wrenching chill of discovery.

'Stop there both of you! Stay where you are!'

The voice made us whirl round in panic, incapable of flight. My heart raced and I thought that this must be the feeling of the condemned man as he stood on the gallows, knowing that all hope was gone.

A single figure emerged from the deep shadow of the bridge where it had concealed itself, and climbed up onto the road. Surely there must be more men in hiding if this was a robbery or an attempt to stop us from escaping; did I dare to hope? As the figure took on shape, I recognised Solomon Green, the man who had saved me once, when he thought I was about to throttle Jasper Griswold at the Shrove Tuesday ball game.

'Solomon!' I exclaimed in a mixture of fear and relief as my bowels churned with shock. 'What are you doing here?'

'Well, I think I am saving you both from the hangman!' came his low reply. 'Ranulf Griswold was given warning that you were on the run from the Commissioners Officers. He has set a trap for you. If you had tried to go through the village, you would have been ambushed. Badly beaten too I should think. He was going to take you prisoner and hand you over to the constables. I don't like that Griswold bugger, nor his nasty little son, so when Mary's message reached me ...'

'What? Mary Conyer? She saved us?' I interrupted.

'Overheard him planning it at the manor, she did.'

'But why would he do this? What possible reason could he have to turn on us like this?' I asked.

'Because if they caught you, they could collect the bounty, and if you had escaped, then every villager would have to pay the fine that would follow. As it is, there's nobody any the wiser. Just get yourselves back home before dawn and nobody can prove a thing. If anyone makes an accusation, you can dismiss it as malicious gossip.'

'How did Ranulf know anything about this? How could he possibly have known?'

'It was your father's woman who told him. She belonged to Lower Broomfield, don't forget. Hoping for a share of the reward I suppose.'

'Ursula!' I spat the name out. 'She would have seen me hang. I knew she wanted rid of me, but I didn't think even she was capable of this.'

'She would have had me hanged too.' Godwin's voice sounded puzzled and bewildered; more offended than angry.

'We have no choice now, we must go back. Thank you Solomon. You have put yourself at risk to help us. We are in your debt.'

***

Martha's astonishment was equally mixed with outrage when she heard our story. We had manged to slip back unnoticed, just before dawn that same night.

'That woman is evil!' she raged. 'She has never belonged here, and never will now, when I let people know just what she has done.'

'That's just what you must *not* do.' I advised hurriedly. 'I don't think people would like it if they found out that we had tried to save our own skins last night, so that others would have to go in our place. We must hope that what Mary heard was incorrect; we may be spared the muster after all.'

***

Chapter 9

March 1461

A troop of mounted men swept into our village at noon, delivering the call to arms for both of us, just as we had feared. They had clearly ridden hard, and were mud spattered from the rutted lanes between the various parishes where they had delivered their message. Their officer was purposeful and direct.

'I am looking for a man called Gifford, and another called Lightfoot.'

'That is me, I am Tom Gifford,' I replied, surprised at being summoned by name.

'Your service is required by our master, Lord Fauconberg. Here, you are to wear these,' and he took two red and white tabards from his saddlebag. 'Bring provisions for three days, your bows, jacks, sallets and billhooks,' the officer ordered brusquely. He was dressed in the Neville household blazon, and his mounted escort carried lances with red and white pennants.

'But where are we to go?' I asked. The officer looked down on me in irritation. He had not dismounted and was clearly in a hurry.

'Travel due east from here. When you reach the great north road, go to a place called Brampton. It is a small village but easy enough to find. The manor there is owned by the Nevilles, and we muster on the common outside its gates. Look for the tents and household banners.'

'When do we need to be there?'

His horse fretted to be off, as impatient as its master. 'Make what preparations you need. Be there in three days' time,' and he twisted in the saddle, heels poised, wheeling his horse as he prepared to leave. Unexpectedly he paused, 'Oh, one last thing,' he shouted over his shoulder. 'You are to report in person to Sir Richard de Coverdale. He has asked for you by name – Gifford isn't it?'

'Yes,' I shouted, 'but why does ...' my words were wasted as the troop splashed their way out of the village, horses snorting and hooves clashing on stone.

'Well that settles it,' Godwin's voice was quiet and resigned. 'We are going to fight.'

***

'I do not possess a jack,' I explained to Martha. 'If we ever had such a thing I expect my father will have sold it.'

'Godwin has something that I made – just a thick doublet with extra padding sewn in. It doesn't have metal plates or a mail collar as it should do. I would not have time to make one for you before you go. I fear you are poorly prepared for what lies ahead, Tom.'

Over the next day, I spent my time at practise with my bow. The hard days of labouring to dig the well had strengthened me, and I found that I could draw the full weight of the bow with ease; my arrows were reaching two hundred paces, and sometimes further with advantage of the wind. In the short time at my disposal before our departure, father spoke very little. Ursula too, had kept her distance, saying nothing about the night when she betrayed us.

'So you are finally going,' she said. 'Decided to do the decent thing at last.' She stood with her head raised, chin thrust forward to provoke me.

'What do you mean? I am not leaving because of you. Don't think that you have managed to drive me out. I do as I am ordered by our lords at Gilmortain. Is that what you mean Ursula? Or perhaps you would rather that I refused and was hanged as a traitor!' I had not confronted her with her treachery, but her expression told me that she was startled. She had not expected this, and her certainty wavered.

'You may not survive this battle,' she countered, 'but if you do, then don't expect to come back here. It is time you were gone ... one way or another.' Her blue eyes glittered like dagger points as she glared her contempt into my face. I dropped all pretence:

'It was you, wasn't it? You poisoned my dog. You tried to kill me by dropping a stone down the well.'

'A dog? Who cares about a dog, but I had nothing to do with any stone. That must have been somebody else who hates you.' A sly expression shaped itself insidiously on her upturned face. 'Perhaps I might have let something slip to the wrong person ...' She stopped short of the name, but I knew it already. 'Griswold! You told Jasper Griswold where I'd be.'

She laughed openly then, defiant, with her hands on her hips enjoying her moment of triumph. 'Now go, or I will tell him that you have laid hands on me and tried it on; fancied your chances with an older woman!'

I stood, shocked by her callousness. I found myself engaging in a ridiculous train of thought: as I looked at this attractive, blonde haired woman, I wondered what bitter treatment she had endured to make her so vicious; how could someone so superficially personable store up such malice?

Without another word, I collected my bow and arrow bag from the woodshed, knowing that I would never return.

***

John Harper, the smith at Upper Broomfield had abandoned his day's work under orders from his Lord, Hugh Thain to attend to us as we presented him with our requests; my billhook, modified to include a short spike at the end, and mounted on a stout ash pole. He had also rivetted a metal spike on the bottom of the shaft so the weapon could be more versatile. With Godwin, he attached a meat cleaver and spike to a similar ash shaft. Then he forged more arrow heads and sharpened them till we each had a bag of twenty four arrows, as was required of us by the law. Even though it was a cold March day and the wind chafed through the open door of the forge, the sweat stood out on John Harper's forehead as he beat out the hot iron, and hammered, shaped and quenched it to his satisfaction.

The morning of our departure was clear and bright. We waited for Martha to be finished, but she seemed to take an age, fussing over this and that, reluctant to let us go and fearful of the moment of our leave-taking.

She reluctantly handed us our satchel of provisions and stood looking at us. She enfolded Godwin in a mother's parting embrace. 'May God keep you safe and return you to me, my precious son,' she murmured.

'Tom, I have nothing to give you to protect you, no harness or coat of mail, but I do have this,' and she reached into the pocket of her apron. She withdrew her hand and when she opened it, I saw a beautiful teardrop-shaped stone with a cord threaded through it, to wear round my neck.

'Here, take this,' she said. 'It will keep you safe. I call it the sunstone, and it has helped many a young woman through a difficult birthing. They say it has special powers of healing, and gives whoever wears it strength and endurance.'

I took the stone and understood at once how it got its name: it was about the size of a pigeon egg and was a deep, glorious amber. I held it to the light and watched as the sun danced through its iridescent heart. It seemed to contain sparkling chips of fire that caught the light playfully as I turned it in my hand. It put me in mind of the tall windows in our church of St. Mary Magdalene, that depicted the faces of saints; the windows that lit up our drab world with their brilliant colours and scattered a mosaic of exotic splendour across the grey floor when the sun gave them life.

'Thank you my lady godmother,' I managed, as I held her in a close embrace. 'I shall return it to you, I promise.'

We knelt for her blessing and she placed her hand on our heads in turn, murmuring the words with a catch in her voice. As we reached the edge of the green, I glanced back to see Martha standing motionless, fixing the sight of her beloved Godwin in her memory.

***

We were silent as we left the village. For once we chose not to speak, and our mood was downcast, each wrapped in his thoughts of what might lie in store for us. The truth was, that this was beyond what we could imagine, and the prospect of men fighting to the death was terrifying. One or two workers in the home fields wished us luck but our replies were short and reserved. It was only after we had walked for the first mile that either of us felt inclined to talk.

'Tom, what do you reckon it's like?'

Godwin's question had framed the exact thought that had been running through my own mind. How would it feel to stand in the line of battle, where huge numbers face each other, trying to hack each other to pieces? How could Lord Thain command our loyalty to a king we had hardly heard of?

'Don't know. Noisy I expect. Confusing I suppose.' I tried to answer in a neutral voice to spare his worry. Godwin did not have the imagination to picture the hellish vision that was beginning to shape itself in my mind.

He seemed satisfied with that, and we continued eastwards at a steady pace hoping we might meet others who were answering the muster, but the track wound on ahead and we met no one. As the sun started to dip towards the horizon, we reached the great north road.

'Is this it, Tom?' Godwin sounded doubtful as he regarded the broad muddy track that was the main thoroughfare up and down the country. 'Doesn't look very special to me.'

'It was built by the ancient people long ago as a way to travel quickly. You had better get used to it because we will be walking miles of it as we head northwards.'

As we neared the village of Brampton, the fading light caught the tents and banners of the encampment that was our destination. We found a large pavilion that flew a red and white flag and guessed it was there that we should report. We entered to see a desk with rolls of paper, scrawled messages and a candle burning to melt the sealing wax for outgoing letters. Several clerks were busy with dispatches and ledgers. A man seated at the centre of the table beckoned us over. Unlike the others, he was dressed in military clothing, with a red and white sash across a long white tunic. He took our names and peered by the flickering candle light to check us against a muster roll as darkness began to fall.

'Ah, you two have been expected. You are late. The roll is almost complete, and Sir Richard de Coverdale left word that he wants you in his own division. Says you impressed him with the bow, is that right?' My puzzled expression and lack of response prompted him to continue.

'Our officers are not here at camp. They have billeted themselves at the manor until we march north. Well, you will be in the thick of it soon enough. You have tabards ?' I nodded. 'Get them on, they show your authority to the other men.'

'Authority?' I asked. 'We are not soldiers. We have no authority.'

'Sir Richard has marked you out with his colours. You are chosen men and will fight beside him.' He looked at our makeshift weapons and shouted for one of the guards outside the tent. 'Take these two and arm them properly. They look as if they have come from the harvest field. Feed them and show them where to sleep. One more day and we leave for the north, no matter if the roll is complete or not. We are already two days behind and at this rate it will be over before we get there. Those who have not arrived here yet will pay a heavy price for their mistake.'

With a nod to his officer, the guard took us to a cart and selected a poleaxe for Godwin and passed me a halberd. Then he lifted the lid of a wooden case and after moving the straw aside, produced two swords. 'Here, take these falchions,' he ordered. 'When you get to close quarters, there is nothing like them.' I was handed a short, single edged sword with a slightly curved blade. With its hilt caught into in my belt, the tip reached my knee..

Before he left us, the guard looked us up and down. He was dressed in knee length mail and wore a sallet with a sweeping brim; clearly a man who had fought before.

'We have a day to get some sort of order into you,' he muttered. 'The whole company will report to the butts tomorrow. They will work you hard, so be ready. When we join King Edward's army, he will expect fighting men, not farmers: we want you to break heads, not clods of earth!'

'Where are we going? What is the plan for us?' I asked quickly, before he could go.

'Do you not know?' he asked in surprise. Our blank faces answered his question. 'We are to form the King's rear guard while he is headed for York, to take back our country from the French she-wolf who thinks she can deny Edward his throne.'

'But isn't Henry our king?' Godwin asked in a slow, puzzled voice.

'Used to be, but the London people have declared Edward to be king now. They want a proper leader, not that grabbing bitch of Anjou and her witless husband who called himself our king. They wouldn't let them into London – barred the gates against her, and the murdering rapists that she calls an army. She has had no choice but to run back up north. She knows that Edward is chasing her up from London and gathering his army as he comes. Margaret has summoned all Henry's Lancastrian affinity and is ready to make a stand at York, but it won't be in the city, she will meet us in the open fields. Her scouts will be out choosing the ground now, so that's where we are heading – north with our Edward to break the House of Lancaster once and for all.'

***

The following morning saw a turmoil of activity; orders bawled, men shoved into groups, lined up, reorganised again, then marched to the practise butts. Here, officers watched and noted, advising and coaching where they could, as group by group, we were put through our paces. We practised for speed first, shooting twenty arrows as quickly as possible. On that cold March morning, we worked harder than any Sunday practise at home. Here we began to realise that our lives depended on each other; on command, we threw down our bows and formed into fighting groups of twenty under a single officer. In the afternoon, the entire company of five hundred men lined up, as if to face the enemy, arrayed in an extended line. This time there were no targets, just marker flags to show distance. We were to loose five arrows at fifty yards, then increase to one hundred, then two hundred yards. Then, when all the arrows were retrieved by the runners, we were to unleash our deadliest onslaught – unrestrained continuous fire at maximum range.

We waited as our officers went around, checking their groups – showing how to stick spare arrows into the ground, push some through our belts, all in preparation for speed, jostling us into the required chequerboard formation; 'So one of their arrows can only kill one of you at a time!' they joked. 'To make sure you don't shoot each other by accident is more likely.'

'The first group to shoot all their arrows will win a barrel of strong beer,' declared the company commander, raising a loud cheer. 'Every man shoots every last arrow – all twenty four of them.'

Godwin and I exchanged glances as we stood in readiness, listening for the command that would let loose an arrow storm to darken the skies in a deadly cloud.

'Ready your bows. Knock ...' and arrows were fitted on bowstrings.

'Draw ...' We braced our shoulders, holding the huge draw weight of seasoned yew under tension for what seemed like an age.

'Loose! ...' with a resounding thrumming sound, arrows were released with a sigh like a playful wind through leaves in woodland at springtime. We continued as fast as we could go, muscles straining, shoulders burning; bodies steaming in the cold air from the effort of our exertions. I had time to notice that my range had increased, and I was reaching the two hundred yard marker consistently; even my last arrows when my muscles were all but spent, still kept the distance. As I relaxed, watching the flight of my last shaft, a voice behind me made me start: 'Good work, my lad.' Sir Richard de Coverdale had appeared un-noticed to watch me shoot.

***

A brittle dawn light was seeping into the eastern horizon, as a messenger dressed in royal livery galloped into camp. After a hurried consultation with Sir Richard, there was a blaring of trumpets as our encampment was roused to action. Tents were packed into the baggage carts and our entire company lined up for the long march ahead.

'We have received news that King Edward is approaching the River Aire at Ferrybridge. We are his rearguard, and we will join his main force once they have crossed. We are commanded to meet at a village called Saxton while battle plans are being drawn up.'

***

Chapter 10

Saturday 28$^{th.}$ March, 1461

Footweary hours, ever northward, while chaffinches and yellowhammers sang from the hedgerows, oblivious of our deadly purpose. Stories were told, laughter, even, as we tried to bolster our resolve. Mile after muddy mile of ground churned up by the passage of thousands of men, horses and wagons in the main force ahead of us.

'Make haste, we are already a day behind.' Orders relayed back from the head of the column resulted in an increase of pace to a fast walk.

Everywhere, doors were barred; not a living soul was to be seen. Even the livestock was missing, either looted or hidden away for safety.

'They are an unfriendly lot, and no mistake,' Godwin observed.

'They have had the pleasure of French Margaret's army through here,' came the voice of a man walking in front of us. 'That wolf-headed demon gave her men permission to rob and rape and plunder their way from the top of the country to the bottom and back again. You would be unfriendly after you had that lot past your door, not just once but twice. There's no wonder that the Londoners shut her out.'

'What has made them so bad? Why has she not controlled them?' I asked.

'Because they are from the north. They are a different breed up there. Folks say they are not normal – more animals than people, not humans at all. But don't worry, when we catch up with them we will slaughter them like the beasts that they are. There is no mercy for the likes of them. We will have our revenge for all the harm they have caused down here.'

Another man joined in, from behind us this time, anxious to make his contribution: 'They say that they have roasted babies on their cooking fires and eaten them.'

And another: 'They have broken into convents and raped the nuns, even the elderly ones.' Cries of anger. Voices eager with their lust for retaliation. 'For shame!'

'But don't worry, we will punish them. They shall not expect any mercy from us. We are the Lord's right arm; we are His avenging angels, and our Edward shall deliver His justice.' Shouts of agreement; cries of outrage, and our pace quickened again.

As we drew near our meeting point at Ferrybridge, silence fell on our number like a marsh mist seeping up from the frozen ground on a raw day. It was time to exercise caution, and a mounted scouting party hurried ahead to seek out the lie of the land and discover what news was available of Edward's main force. Soon our outriders returned, announcing that our army had already fought a skirmish when they tried to cross the River Aire. When we reached the crossing point at a place called Ferrybridge, it was clear that it had been more than a skirmish. Bodies were being thrown into hastily dug pits by a burial detachment of sweating, swearing soldiers. Some of the diggers had minor wounds dressed in bandages. I could see that the bridge had undergone makeshift repairs to allow our company to cross. On the other side, the bodies of Lancastrian soldiers were still strewn over the ground where they had fallen. Many of them had been stripped down to their braes. Any armour, weapons or valuables had long since been looted.

'What do you think has happened here?' Godwin asked, as he took in the grim scene.

He was answered by a soldier who had been hauling a body clear of the roadway. He dropped the legs of the man he was dragging, straightened up and regarded us with hostility.

'You took your bloody time getting here didn't you?' he growled and spat on the ground.

'Got held up, friend. Still, better late than never, eh?' I replied with a smile.

'Thought they could stop us by breaking the bridge. We tried to cross but their archers shot down anyone who got near. In the end, our cavalry crossed at the ford upstream at Castleford and chased the buggers off. I pity them when they are caught. They have killed a lot of our men. Even the great Warwick himself has been injured – got an arrow through his leg so they say.'

***

It was drawing to the end of a cheerless day as we reached our destination at Saxton, collapsing wearily on the cold ground, as the bell of the village church rang to announce Vespers. It was almost April, when Spring sunshine should be reawakening the earth, yet still it felt like winter's talons gripped our world.

Saxton was a tiny village, and reminded me of my home at Upper Broomfield. It sat in a natural hollow in the rolling, undulating countryside. There was a church and a small cluster of houses where officers were billeted. We would have to find what shelter we could behind hedges, in barns or huddled round camp fires. As darkness began to descend, I caught a glimpse of a well-equipped troop of cavalry with lances and banners. They halted by the church, and I guessed that they must be King Edward's personal guard.

'I think I might have seen the king,' I told Godwin as we found a place that offered some degree of shelter from a chill southerly breeze.

'Did he have a crown?' he enquired hopefully.

'Too far away to see.' I replied.

'He'll have a crown tomorrow, right enough. He'll take Henry's crown from him!' The voice came from a sergeant at arms, supervising our efforts. 'I see you are chosen men,' nodding at our tabards and introducing himself. 'Roland Green, the man who has to form you up tomorrow.' He spoke with a strange accent that did not belong in our parts.

'What do you mean, "chosen?" Chosen for what?'

'You must have impressed somebody important. Those tabards set you out for special work. You will fight in the vanguard tomorrow as the close escort to Lord Fauconberg. He is our field commander.' When he saw our blank expressions, he added, 'You are in good hands there.

He's not much to look at, not like our Edward. Now there's a man you can't mistake. He is well over six feet tall. Six foot four somebody told me. Lord Fauconberg might be short in height, but he is a brilliant commander. If anyone can win the day for us, it will be him.'

Godwin and I looked at each other in disbelief. This was beyond us; there was no point in arguing and we had no other choice but to comply. As I looked southward towards the place where our enemy must be encamped, all I could see was a gentle hillside rising above us in a rolling incline, and I wondered what lay in wait for us tomorrow on the other side, when we crested the ridge. Roland Green settled himself beside me with a grunt of resignation.

'Going to be a long night. I have men out gathering wood, so we shall at least have a fire to sit by.'

It was obvious that Roland was not a conscripted soldier; his arms and expensive coat of mail showed that he was a veteran of other conflicts. From what I could tell in the half light, he was in his thirties, stockily built and powerful. He eased his sallet off, laying it beside him, and before he replaced it with a woollen cap, I had time to notice the long blue scar that ran from his brow to the top of his head. When he saw me looking he pointed to it with a grim smile. 'Got that at Mortimer's Cross from a Lancastrian cavalry officer. Lucky! His blade caught the rim of my helmet and just nicked me.'

'What is it like?' Godwin asked.

'Being in battle you mean?' Roland laughed humourlessly. 'Well, if you are still alive this time tomorrow, I'll tell you!' He looked more closely at Godwin's expression, reading the guileless nature of his question. 'Well,' he said more seriously, 'it all comes down to luck in the end, but one or two things might help you. For a start, keep your eyes open and your wits about you. Conserve your strength: some of them fight like madmen and are spent in half an hour. That's when they get killed – too tired to dodge. Another thing; don't get isolated from your mates; don't chase after your man if he runs, or they'll close in on you like hounds round a stag.'

'That is a lot to think about,' replied Godwin, in a subdued voice.

'Well, here is the most important piece of advice I can give you. Remember this above all else; whatever happens, stay on your feet. If you go down, you will be dead in seconds.'

We were silent then, each drawn within the shroud of his own thoughts until men arrived with wood and a fire was lit. We were joined by a great number of others of our company, and we huddled together in a dry ditch with the hedge at our backs offering some degree of protection. It was dark now, and bitterly cold. The stars were beginning to be obscured by clouds that were driven in on a southerly breeze. We would not sleep much tonight.

Dozens of men had gathered to share our fire. The blaze crackled, and golden sparks embroidered the velvet sky. The flicker from the dancing flames illuminated their faces into uneven patches of light and grotesque shadow, turning eyes and mouths into pools of fathomless blackness. I had never felt so much in need of comfort, and in a moment's recollection, I reached for my purse and took out the stone that my lady godmother, Martha, had given to me for protection. I remembered her tenderness, and I wondered if Godwin was thinking of her too; how I wished that it could have been my own mother who had embraced me and given me her blessing before our departure. "I call it the sunstone. It will keep you safe," she had said. "They say it has special powers of healing, and gives whoever wears it strength and endurance."

Holding it to my lips for a second, I slipped the cord round my neck and tucked it down into my shirt. Perhaps it would give me the fortune to survive what horrors the morning might bring. There was something else in my purse, and as my reaching fingers found it, I remembered the piece of paper that Father Stephen had given me at St. Wilfrid's. I took it out and unfolded it in my lap. My careful drawing of the crucifixion shaded wanly in the firelight's glimmer; black ink on white paper; good and evil; darkness and light; damnation or eternal life.

'What is that?' Godwin broke my wandering thoughts, looking over my shoulder at the simple line drawing.

'It is a drawing that I made for a priest back home at the abbey.'

He considered it for a moment. 'It is a good drawing Tom. Good enough for a church wall, like the one we have at home with Christ rising up to heaven. What does the writing say?'

In the distance, the bell sounded for Compline and its sonorous tone gave tongue across the still air. I looked again at the crumpled paper, but I knew the words by heart:

'*Pater noster* ...' I began, reading aloud to him. '... *qui es in coelis* ...' several men on either side of us joined in. '... *sanctificetur nomen tuum*...' I continued, recognising a solemn, unbidden moment when these men had followed me in prayer. I spoke more loudly, and our encampment became a murmur of voices reciting the Lord's Prayer; some faces were illuminated in the yellow firelight, dozens more were unseen supplicants from the anonymous darkness beyond. Men standing by the fire had sunk to their knees, some had clasped their hands before them; all had responded to the powerful bidding that my scrap of paper had prompted; the spontaneous entreaty of soldiers on the eve of a great battle, craving comfort from the familiar words. Many crossed themselves, and after a humble 'Amen', all was silence but for the crackling of the fire and the ethereal cry of an owl from a distant woodland.

***

Chapter 11

29th. March 1461. Palm Sunday

The first hint of a bleak dawn revealed a grey world. I had not slept; dozed a little perhaps, but the cold made true sleep impossible. A light powdering of snow had sifted down, undetected in the hours of darkness, but now it covered the many resting figures that had spent the night in the open. It was a slow, saturating cold that crept up from the chilled earth and steeped our bodies with its pitiless torpor. I nudged Godwin and he stirred with a grunt.

'It's time Godwin.'

'But it is Palm Sunday,' he objected.

'Nonetheless, we must be about the king's bidding.'

All around us, men were stirring; massaging cramped limbs, stretching and stamping in an effort to restore their protesting bodies to a state where movement did not bring pain. Some cursed volubly as the agony of returning circulation made them cry out in anger. It seemed as though the snow-scattered landscape had burst into activity; an ants' nest when the stone has been lifted. It was sunrise; the sixth hour; the start of a new day as I heard the church bell announce Matins to thousands of men arising with no certainty of seeing sunset. Some were quiet; clearly the sense of foreboding had robbed them of any inclination to speak; some were forcefully loud, seeking comfort through bluster and bravado. Others worked patiently with whetstones, honing and burnishing their blades. Carts had arrived, laden with barrels of ale and bread and we took what refreshment we could. All the while, scouts were being dispatched to find intelligence of the enemy's intentions.

The pewter grey of early dawn began to lighten reluctantly, revealing the gently sloping hillside that rolled lazily up ahead of us, and across its wide brow and beyond that, lay the unknown. Our force was beginning to gather now, hundreds upon hundreds of them; men appeared from the barns and hedgerows where they had sheltered; cavalry soldiers led their brightly caparisoned horses, awaiting the order to mount; knights and nobles followed behind their squires who carried flags and pennants to rally their divisions. A southerly wind had sprung up at daybreak, streaming out the banners and battle standards with a rattling, fluttering confusion of colour. Now occasional flakes of snow began to fall, whipped away by the strengthening wind. It was not long before the scouting parties began to return, clattering into the village to report; shortly after their arrival. Roland Green appeared, eager to take charge of his detachment of archers.

'Well, it seems that our reckoning with the House of Lancaster is about to begin, be it Palm Sunday or not,' he said to our group as he regarded the faces waiting for news. 'The scouts have come back saying the enemy are taking the field. They are forming up into their three groups, and goading us to action.'

'Where are they?' I asked.

'You will see them soon enough,' he replied. 'When we cross the brow of that hill in front of us, they will be straight ahead. You two are to stay by me. We will be at the van of our force so you will have no doubt where they are!' He paused, then added, 'His grace has ordered that no quarter shall be given, and that we should expect none either. While the heads of his father and brother are on spikes in York, he has no mind for mercy.'

I turned to look at Godwin. 'We stay together, no matter what happens.'

***

As our force moved forward, we were already roughly formed into three 'battles' or divisions, and streamed across the slope in our thousands, with cavalry on our left wing. It was as we crested the incline that we saw them: a great host of men gathered on the opposite hilltop like flocks of rooks, blackening an August stubble field after the last stooks of corn had been cleared. There they shuffled and manoeuvred into their three battles, each division adjusting position while facing us across a shallow depression scarcely deep enough to be called a valley. As the two armies caught sight of each other, a great roar was emitted by both sides, eager for the engagement to begin.

'It always begins the same way,' Roland explained in a subdued voice. 'A meeting of heralds to negotiate terms, only today there will be no terms. Then it's down to us poor bloody archers. It starts with an exchange of arrows. Get your two dozen away as quickly as you can, then retreat behind the fighting men – if you are still able,' he added grimly.

We took up our position at the front in a long row, many men deep and in our thousands we straddled the field from left to right. Our line sloped downhill below me, whilst to my right the land sloped gradually up until it reached the limit of our ground, which seemed to be a narrow plateau. From our position slightly to the right of the centre, we were set out in chequerboard formation as we had practised, and looking back, I saw that Sir Richard de Coverdale, in the ranks of knights behind me, had dismounted, ready to fight on foot. He beckoned Roland over, and after a brief word and a nod in our direction, Roland returned. 'Sir Richard wants you close by him. He has a use for you both when the time comes.'

'Who is the mounted knight in the bright armour and a red plume on his helmet?' Godwin asked.

'That is Lord Fauconberg.' Roland pointed to a resplendent figure surrounded by knights and messengers, riding the length of the battlefront, shouting orders. 'He is the field commander for our whole army. He will be close to the king today.'

Runners came down the line, repeating instructions to officers as they went.

'He's a crafty bugger, that one!' Roland shouted, pointing to Lord Fauconberg. 'He's waiting for the weather!'

Looking up, I could see the sky had turned a dull, leaden colour and the wind had strengthened at our backs.

'It's going to snow. Those clouds are full of it,' Godwin observed.

'Right you whoreson buggers!' Roland shouted to the group under his command. 'One arrow only, then withdraw. *One*!' he yelled in emphasis. The snow had started with blinding ferocity and was driving across the gap that separated the two armies, full in the faces of the Lancastrian archers. We knocked an arrow and waited: from somewhere in the white obscurity, a trumpet blared a single note, and we released our first flight of arrows, then withdrew as instructed.

'Wait for it! Say your prayers now.' muttered Roland as he braced himself for the return shafts to begin raining down, striking and killing at random. Men huddled under the rims of their helmets, held their breath and waited. I screwed my eyes shut and clenched my teeth in fearful anticipation. I found myself praying to be spared; 'Not me, not me!' I heard myself, shamelessly wishing another to be skewered in my place. With soundless approach, arrows began to fall faster than the snowflakes but to our astonishment, none reached us; the spent shafts fell harmlessly a good forty yards ahead of our line. Men looked at each other in amazement and relief; the strength of the wind had reduced the enemy's range. A great cry of derision went up; some danced and capered around; some turned their backs to the enemy and bared their arses in contempt.

'Forward to the nearest arrows.' And we marched forty paces down the slope until we reached the limit of the carpet of spent shafts. One or two were still falling harmlessly as we lined up again.

'They have shot the lot,' I shouted to Godwin. 'They didn't know that we had stopped.'

'I told you he was a sly old fox,' Roland joined in.

Another trumpet blast, and we began, rapid shooting of all the arrows in our bags. When they were used, we pulled the Lancastrian arrows out of the ground and returned them to slaughter their masters. Although the blizzard stopped us from seeing the deadly effect of our onslaught, we could hear what it had done; screams and cries of wounded men and horses were plain to hear; the strong wind had given us such range that we had caused havoc deep into their packed ranks. The ground was covered in snow, and across it, as their lines began to advance came a chorus of voices from our line.

'Here they come boys!' I heard a shout from behind me.

Another: 'They can't stand and take such losses. We have forced them off the higher ground to fight us at close quarters. Now we'll see what they're made of!'

To our right, the Lancastrian battle commanded by the Earl of Northumberland had started to move forward and it was then that I saw ... but no, surely that was impossible ... he could not be here!

'Back now lads. Drop your bows and grab your halberds.' And we ran back up the slope through the ranks of our armoured men, who now held the higher ground. I was troubled by the brief glimpse of a figure in the enemy ranks.

'Godwin, did you see ...' but there was no time.

'Look at them, tripping over their own arrows!' interrupted Godwin, and indeed they were; stumbling and falling over the remaining shafts that were as thick as the spines on a hedgehog.

I pushed my hand down inside my jacket and touched the sunstone, holding it and praying for its protection.

When the two armies met, there was a sound like a winter wave rolling along a rocky shoreline, as heavily armoured men crashed into each other. It was not long before we were slowly being driven back by the weight of superior numbers. A yard at a time we retraced our steps up the slope towards our starting point. A commotion had broken out down the left flank, where a cavalry charge had scattered our men and the line had broken.

'That's Edward himself!' pointed Godwin. 'Look, he has a sword in his hand. He is fighting with the men.'

He had taken charge and slowly began to regain control where our line had failed. His tall figure, surrounded by his personal guard laid into the enemy and they began to falter. Reinforcements had followed King Edward and the danger had passed.

'Now that's a leader for you!' exclaimed Roland in admiration. 'You won't see Henry here; he'll be safe in York; probably on his knees in the minster with his French wife beside him.'

The sun was at its zenith, and I estimated it was mid-day; the fight had continued unabated for three hours and still there was no easing of the ferocity of combat. A runner arrived and delivered a hurried message to Roland.

'Sir Richard has summoned you both. He wants you with your bow,' he shouted, nodding to me. 'He orders you to him with all speed.' Roland was breathless with exertion. Godwin gripped his poleaxe, I found a bag of arrows, and we struggled through the ranks of reserves till we reached Sir Richard, who had now been joined by Lord Fauconberg himself.

'He can do it, my lord,' Sir Richard promised.

He grabbed my shoulder and pointed to the enemy's left division.

'I saw you shoot at the butts. Now is the time to make it count. I want that man,' he indicated a knight at the rear of his force sitting astride a destrier. He was surrounded by mounted messengers, runners and an escort arrayed with a yellow and red battle standard. 'That is Henry Percy, Earl of Northumberland. Mark him down!'

I drew a bodkin headed arrow and examined it, running my eye along its slender length, ensuring the shaft was straight. The range was fair; at a hundred and fifty paces I had hit crows in the fields like this many times. I waited for a lull in the wind, drew and released the arrow in one swift movement. I watched its flight, saw it begin to drop and nodded to myself, knowing that my aim was true. It struck the man on the left shoulder, and I saw him clutch his arm and slump forward towards his horse's neck, to be hurriedly led away by his standard bearer.

'By Christ's holy blood!' roared Sir Richard. 'By all the saints and angels, you have dropped the bugger!'

A ragged cheer went up from the men around us who had witnessed the event.

'That man is the enemy of my family as well as a traitor to his grace our king. If we both survive this day, you must find me.' Lord Fauconberg had eased his horse until it stood beside me. 'I will reward your skill, archer. Your name?'

'Tom Gifford, my lord,' and I bowed in subordination.

'No need to bow to me, brave lad.' He looked at me steadily, memorising my face and nodded. Then to Sir Richard: 'Where *are* Norfolk's men? He is sorely needed.' wheeling his horse he cantered up the slight slope to our right flank.

'John Mowbray should have joined us with his men a day ago, and still no sign. The Duke of Norfolk he might be, the Duke of tardiness he certainly is! You have done well goodman Gifford. You have won favour for us both.'

***

'We are losing this fight,' Rowland said grimly as we stood in readiness, waiting to be called forward to relieve exhausted men.

The field of combat was narrow and the intensity of the battle was fierce; men were pulled back as they became spent, to be replaced by fresh troops from the reserves. Soon it was our turn, and we joined the battle line. Ahead and all about us, men were locked in struggle and the noise was fearsome. I stood beside Godwin, and we slowly worked through the press of hacking, screaming men till we faced our enemy. The ground was slippery with slush and blood, churned up by horses into a filthy mire. A short, thick-set man in a leather jerkin confronted me, and thrust his sword at my neck. His breath smelled sour in my face as I grabbed his blazon with my left hand and pushed him away, the long reach of my halberd keeping me clear of his flailing sword. As a man to my left dodged a sword thrust, his shoulder crashed into me, sending me reeling, and to my horror I felt my feet slip. Down, half-smothered in gore-laden slurry, I braced myself for the killing blow; instead my opponent drew his foot back and took a vicious kick with the point of his metal sabaton aimed for my head. Dodging my father's boots served me well, and I rolled quickly aside. I saw Godwin hold him off with the point of his poleaxe, giving me sufficient time to struggle to my feet. I thrust my halberd under the collar of his mail and felt the crunch of bone as it passed through his neck. There was no pause to draw breath; the next man was stepping forward, armed with a flail. I slid the hook of my halberd behind his ankle and pulled; he fell backwards swiftly dispatched by a sword thrust from a man to my right.

I could see the tall figure of Godwin, wielding his poleaxe, his great strength combined with the effectiveness of the deadly weapon driving a gap through their lines. Gasping for breath, we found ourselves in a space, and that was when I saw him, and this time there was no doubt. Dressed in a hauberk with a yellow and red sash over his shoulder, the figure of Jasper Griswold was unmistakable. He was some distance away, standing with a troop of men who were waiting to be brought forward. He looked across the fifty yards that separated us, and his look of recognition turned into a grimace of dislike. He had a bow in hand, and now he drew and released the shaft that would surely kill me. It seemed that the arrow flew slowly, and the sounds of battle dimmed as I found myself unable to move, braced for the inevitable.

From somewhere to my left, a riderless horse screamed with pain. It plunged through the ranks of men, scattering them like skittles in its death agony, an arrow sticking out from its flank. With its eyes rolled up and foam flying from its mouth, its charge was irresistible, and it caught Godwin a glancing blow sending him reeling across me. The arrow struck Godwin in the centre of his chest, and he sank to his knees with the arrowhead protruding from between his shoulder blades. A look of surprise and disappointment registered briefly before his lifeless body fell forward.

'No!' The word was torn out of me in anguish as I saw him collapse. This giant of a man had never harmed a soul and loved nothing better than to listen to a familiar story by his own hearth; my only friend and lifelong companion, slain at my feet. I had only one purpose then; it burned my mind and scalded my thoughts with vicious intensity - to reach Griswold and wreak my bitter vengeance on him.

'Leave him lad.' I heard Rowland's voice, but his words seemed to come from a distance. 'There will be time enough to mourn him. Right now, you need to stay alive.'

All sense of personal danger had gone, and I laid about me with Godwin's poleaxe, thrusting and smashing my vengeance into one man after another. There seemed no limit to my anger, and it was only when Rowland grabbed my jacket and pulled me back that my reason began to return. Fresh men took our place, and we drew to the rear, joining the groups of exhausted men too tired to be thankful for the respite. A cart had been driven up with barrels of ale and we both drank gratefully for the first time since morning.

It was late afternoon and still the battle raged as the sun dipped towards the horizon. I noticed that we had regained some ground and the Lancastrians had been pushed back down the slope and slewed slightly back on their left flank, slanting the battle line at an angle. As unexpectedly as thunder from a cloudless summer sky, a great shout came from the men on our right flank; a triumphant, exuberant roar of victory. Casting caution to the wind, Rowland jumped on the back of the cart to gain a better view.

'It's Norfolk!' he yelled. 'It's bloody Norfolk at last. Now the sparks will fly!'

Norfolk's division with knights already mounted and in full battle array, pitched themselves straight at the Lancastrian left, and even though they resisted, fresh men against those who had fought all day was no match.

'Look, see over there?' Rowland pointed to the rear of the enemy ranks. 'It's Henry Beaufort. He has sent for his horse.'

'Is he going to lead a charge?' I asked.

'He's going to save his skin, more like. The Duke of bloody Somerset! He is their field commander, and he is running for his life.'

All across the field I could see mounts being brought for noblemen. The whole shape of the battle had changed and what was left of the fighting line had been turned westward; the organised combat began to break down as I watched, and scattered companies of men clustered into desperate groups, fighting without order or cohesion. I saw one or two men turn to run. They were soon joined by others, dispirited by the sight of their officers deserting them. Soon, the battlefield had become a rout; a scene of bloody carnage as thousands of men turned to run for their lives. A troop of Norfolk's cavalry galloped past. They had abandoned their lances and carried maces and horse hammers 'No quarter! No quarter!' their battle cry rang out as they hunted down fleeing men and clubbed them to death.

***

The thunder of hooves behind us made us whirl round in alarm; I stood with Godwin's poleaxe raised to deliver a blow, only to see the red and white pennant of Sir Richard de Coverdale's troop, as he reined in, pulling his horse's head back and bringing the protesting animal to a skittering halt.

'Get me a score of bowmen. Get full bags of arrows and follow me,' he ordered Roland. They galloped off to the lower limit of the field, where the trampled furlongs and headlands gave way to a steep slope. Casting our eyes around for familiar faces, we quickly assembled a detachment of archers and set off at a run. On reaching Sir Richard, we looked down on a massacre. The steep, almost precipitous slope plunged unforgivingly towards the bottom of the valley, where winding through the twisting terrain, was a torrent. The River Cock was in flood, barring the way to a host of panic stricken men, fleeing for their lives. The scene was black with thousands of figures who slithered and fell down the snow-covered slope; most had thrown away their weapons and were defenceless against the pursuit that followed them down.

'Set your men in a line on this ridge. Mark down any that cross the river. There is no mercy to be shown, so choose your targets well.'

There was something about the scene before me; suddenly my recollection became vividly clear. 'Christ, it's Shrove Tuesday!'

Roland was nocking an arrow on his bow but stopped and turned.

'What?' he asked in disbelief.

'It's like the bloody Shrove Tuesday ball game at home,' I said with a shake of my head at the stupidity of my own words. Yet there it was: a steep hillside leading sharply down to a river and everywhere a scene of flailing limbs and thrashing bodies.

The carnage continued as hundreds of men threw themselves towards the safety of the rolling plains that led back to York. The River Cock was not wide, but made unusually deep by the floodwater that brimmed its banks. Men in full harness were swept away, those attempting to ford were caught by the strength of the current and all the while, they were clubbed and butchered by the pursuit. The bridge which had been destroyed by the Lancastrians to protect their flank was now their undoing as I watched the bodies of dead and drowning men carried away to my right, following the downstream flow. The fight had spilled into the water's edge where desperate battles were being fought; foemen locked together as they drowned in a raft of grotesquely embracing corpses, piling up against the bridge abutments, blocking the river and damming it. The foam-garnished, burgundy gruel became deeper and more impassable; men scrambled over the dead and drowning bodies of their comrades, using them in desperation as a bridge to the relative safety of the opposite bank, and all the while the killing continued in an endless craving for revenge.

The light was failing now, and we abandoned our position on the ridge line, moving to a knoll halfway down the slope. The shorter range compensated for the poor light, and it was then that I caught sight of a figure wearing a red and yellow sash scrambling over the human bridge. I knew it was Jasper and the desire to avenge Godwin filled me with a glittering anger that my grief had burnished until it dazzled my senses. At first I thought he had gone; run for safety in the half light, but there he was again; he had gained the far bank and was preparing to run. The only shaft I had left was a hunting arrow with a broad, leaf-shaped head. I drew, and with careful aim, felt the bow release. A dying man grabbed his ankle, pleading for help, and as Jasper turned to kick the man's hand away, my arrow took him in the face. He fell, but somehow dragged himself upright again with the arrow protruding from either side of his mouth. He took the shaft, broke it and pulled the arrow clear. Then he was gone, running south.

***

Chapter 12

Towton Field, nightfall, Palm Sunday

The sky was a cloak of purple twilight, its draping folds like the shrouded wings of a falcon as it stood victor over its prey: the stealth of advancing darkness concealed the worst reprisals that were being delivered to the remnants of what had been a vast host.

'Our arrow bags are empty - we can do no more here. Back up the slope,' ordered Roland, and we began to climb the treacherous incline, trying to avoid the rush of men still pouring over the ridge, oblivious of our presence as their fear deprived them of reason. As we crested the summit, we were challenged by a troop of mounted men who at first mistook us for escaping Lancastrians. Thankfully I recognised Sir Richard's voice in the half light.

'You men, return to our lines, take a mount each and what arrows you need.'

They accompanied us through the body strewn landscape that once had grown crops in its winding ploughlands, and now grew corpses; we stepped over the remains of what had been men, some still alive and crying out for mercy as rondel daggers explored the gaps in their armour.

'Mount up, we head for York.'

I found myself in the company of half a dozen of our archers, following Sir Richard de Coverdale and his men at arms. One of the troop carried a lance with pennant to identify us as victors to any other Yorkist cavalry. The others had abandoned their lances in favour of a mace or a horse hammer. Our small group of archers had become known to me although none were men from the Ravengill area. Beside me rode tall outline of John the thatcher, and on my right, the slouched figure of William Kirkham was silhouetted against the night sky. We were silenced by what we had seen, although ahead, the group of men at arms were loudly recalling their individual triumphs in feat of arms, exalting in the death of their adversaries.

'Nightfall doesn't seem to stop this does it Will?' I asked, turning in the saddle to look at the faintest afterglow of a sun long since set. I found the silence oppressive and needed the comfort of conversation, no matter how trivial to take my mind off the things I had seen.

'This has been a long day indeed Tom.' Will Kirkham seemed relieved that I had spoken. 'No need to fear that we might get lost - we can find our way by following the bodies.'

We had taken a direct line towards Tadcaster, the landscape occasionally interrupted by corpses; waymarkers of the relentless pursuit that had hunted men down over the open fields as the bloody conclusion continued. Our escort rode ahead, occasionally stopping to search a barn, dividing to scour each side of the hedgerows in an attempt to flush out stragglers to be dispatched.

'It is a day I would like to forget, but I fear we are not finished yet.' John the thatcher seemed equally pleased to seek some comfort in conversation.

'Surely this must stop soon,' I replied.

I was begging inwardly that we would turn back. The heat of battle had died in me and what was happening now was vengeance served up like cold gruel. Unarmed men who had lost the will to fight were no threat: they deserved the right to return to their hearth and family; these were ordinary people who had not chosen this fight as their own. I wanted to voice my revulsion, but dared not.

Instead, I asked: 'How long has this day's work lasted would you say?'

'How long now?' John considered for a moment. 'The battle started at the sixth hour, just as the bell sounded for Matins. Compline must have been sung hours ago, probably as the rout began, so nine hours, perhaps ten hours?' His question was more to continue the comfort of conversation than any real desire for an answer.

Still I did not feel tired. My veins coursed with energy so generously furnished by the things I had seen and heard in this blasphemous sacrament of death. Our progress halted suddenly as our leading knights spread into a line, A small church lay ahead, and clustered by were a few dwellings. All was in darkness, the houses hunch shouldered as though they too were trying to press themselves into the landscape to evade detection. Our men at arms had dismounted now, and were walking cautiously over the fifty yards that separated us from the open field to the churchyard.

'Did you see it Will?' I whispered. I had noticed the faintest candle glimmer in the church, hastily extinguished as we approached.

'I think we have caught some of our rabbits,' Sir Richard muttered as the men at arms loosened their swords in anticipation.

'Some of them seem to have sought shelter in the church,' Will relayed to us in a hushed voice. I almost pleaded for their pardon. These were no longer our enemy. I could imagine the thoughts running through their heads, praying for the protection of the Church.

'Here, you, archer, hold our mounts!'

Obediently, John took the reins of their horses and watched as they surrounded the church. Three knights were in readiness by the door, and at a signal, began to hammer on it.

'Open for King Edward. Open up!' When there was no response, a knight stepped forward with a mace and began to beat on the door. 'Open, or we will break it down!'

After a drawing of bolts, the door was pushed open a crack and the frightened face of a priest could just be seen, peering out from the darkness within.

'This is God's house,' he began nervously. 'You have no business to treat it with disrespect.'

'Stand aside, Father. We mean you no harm but if you are sheltering our enemy, we want them out here.'

Sir Richard stepped forward. 'Open the door, priest. If you refuse, you will be sorry.'

The heavy wooden door crashed open, catching the priest in the face and making him stagger back under the impact. It revealed a group of twelve or thirteen men cowering inside by the altar. They were a mixture of ages, and I noted that two of them were younger than me – perhaps only fourteen. Just boys. One of them began to whimper with fear.

'Outside all of you!' but they did not move, knowing the fate that awaited them.

The priest had resumed his place in the doorway; his eye was starting to swell from the force of the blow; his arms were outstretched in a messianic posture.

'These men have sought sanctuary. You may not touch them. They are protected by the power of the holy cross!' With a pale hand that trembled like a man with a great fever, he held forward the silver crucifix on the end of his rosary, daring them to challenge its authority.

'Step aside, priest, if you do not wish to be hurt.'

'This is blasphemy! You may not break the sacred law of sanctuary. By your actions, you proclaim yourselves to be more powerful than God and he will damn you for all eternity. Your wicked souls will burn in Hell!'

'The laws of sanctuary do not apply here. There is no sanctuary for traitors!'

They pushed him roughly aside and the men were dragged out of the church screaming for mercy that they knew would not be granted. I watched powerlessly as they were lined up on their knees to be killed; some were belching with fear, others pissed their braes as throats were cut, or they were struck on the head with a mace or war hammer. I looked on horrified, and as I retched in the darkness, I knew that I could never do this again. Even if Griswold was on his knees before me, I could not bring myself so low as to slaughter him in cold blood, and I knew that Godwin would not have thanked me for it.

'Do you want one boy?' the knight's mailed hand was bloodstained, and he offered me an ear. 'Here! Take it.' but I could not. I looked away as ears and noses were hacked off and displayed as trophies.

'Fix it on your belt to show you are one of us. His grace, our Edward said: "No mercy"; no prisoners to be taken here.'

'But ...' I stopped myself just in time. I wanted to say that this was not war, this was murder; committing such an act of mutilation was against all the teachings of the church. I hoped that whatever the consequences of their actions, I was not equally damned alongside the perpetrators of such a sacrilege simply by being unable to prevent it. How I longed to be away from this sickening place. My face must have betrayed my feelings.

'What? No stomach for it? You'll learn. This is what would have happened to us if our circumstances were reversed, never doubt it.'

The knights stood back and regarded their work: helmeted black silhouettes starkly outlined against the night sky, appearing to me like ancient chessmen regarding a long abandoned game as they leaned on their swords and casually looked upon their discarded opponents with indifference. The pawns in this game had been removed from the board and we left them to the caprices of nature.

***

The stars were fading as we approached York in the late hours of this seemingly endless night. By the fragmented light of a quarter moon that slipped in and out behind high clouds, we abandoned the fields and picked up the well-made road that took us to the city walls of York. We had not found any more fugitives and to my relief I realised that the killing was over. The towers of Micklelith Bar loomed above us, and in the turrets I could see sentries looking down, assessing if we were a threat to their great bastion. Sir Richard rapped loudly with his mace, and after a short conversation, the huge double gates swung open to admit our detachment into the sleeping city.

It was approaching Matins when we were directed through the narrow streets by the officer of the watch. There were few signs of life in the sleeping city as we threaded our way down the sloping Mickleway, our horses' hooves clattering loudly on the cobbled street. Here and there, a dog barked but there was no sign of life: people remained behind their doors, barred tightly after the retreating Lancastrians had fled. They had no reason to expect the victorious army to be kindly disposed to them: Edward, as he entered England's second city in triumph as its king would not easily forgive the sight of the heads of his father and older brother on spikes over the Royal Gate, waiting to greet him.

As we crossed the River Ouse, I could see a slight mist rising from the swirling surface as it slapped and eddied around the wooden piles that formed the staithes on either bank. An early ferryman was steering his boat away from us down the centre of the channel, a black shape on the inky, stygian waters, with a lighted lantern swinging gently from side to side on a pole at the stern. We had been directed to St. Sampson's, a church close by the river, where we were to be billeted. I heard the minster bell chime for Matins, its message picked up by bells from other parishes across the city as we dismounted wearily and handed our horses over to grooms who had been recruited from citizens willing to please and perhaps earn a coin or two.

The cavernous interior of St. Sampson's was dark, and I noticed there was still a slight fragrance of incense that hung in melancholy recollection of the Palm Sunday masses that must have been said here whilst two armies butchered each other only ten miles away. Even that was not strong enough to overwhelm the stink of the sleeping soldiery who filled the church, leaning against the walls and pillars of the aisles, or simply prone on the hard floor. Many were bloodstained and all were muddied by the treacherous, sucking mire that the battlefield had become; all shared the profound and total exhaustion of men returning from battle after they have fought for their lives.

'We must rest Tom.' Will's voice echoed in the nave as we threaded our way through prone figures. 'I swear I was asleep when I rode the last two miles.'

We found a space beside the altar and settled thankfully, our bodies numb with exhaustion. John the thatcher stretched out his long limbs and was snoring in seconds. Will Kirkham unbuckled his sword and lay it beside him with a clatter on the stone floor. He sat gratefully on the chancel steps, reflecting for a moment.

'What do you suppose we will do next, Tom? Is this it? Are we free men again now that we have won the king such a great victory?'

'I expect we will get our orders from Sir Richard tomorrow.' I replied. As soon as I said the words they made no sense – it already was tomorrow. Matins had been sung and it was the start of a new day; it was Holy Monday when Jesus entered the Temple and found it full of money changers and thieves. I wondered what he would think of this temple and the things we had done. Will fell asleep in an instant, sweet oblivion wiping out the sights and sounds of the brutal events of the day, but for me the blessing of sleep would not come. Each time I closed my eyes, visions of the dead and dying tormented me. Hacked-off limbs and faces battered beyond recognition would give me no rest.

I sat partly upright, leaning my back against the cold stone of the altar. My mind was tormented by the loss of Godwin. Till this moment, I had not had the luxury of time to think of him, but now I could see his face, hear his voice. How I would miss his good nature and generosity of spirit; his lop sided grin and his love of listening to a story being told, no matter how familiar it was. I had known Godwin all my life: we had grown up together as young children, sharing adventures and secrets. The reaching arms of grief began to find me then, creeping through the darkness and enfolding me in their cold embrace, and I wept silently. I discovered I was holding the sunstone which had remained secured round my neck throughout. I could not see its colours, but I could imagine the gold and amber, glowing opulently in my hand. I could feel its smooth, rounded shape as my fingers turned it over and over in the darkness, and its touch brought me comfort.

I was overwhelmed by guilt. Godwin's mother, Martha, had insisted that I took it to keep me safe. How I wished she had given it to Godwin. What had she said? "They say it has special powers of healing, and gives whoever wears it strength and endurance." He should have had it, not me, and perhaps he would still be alive. He had saved my life: he held my opponent off when I had fallen helplessly to the ground, protecting me until I could regain my feet. When the dying horse had knocked him aside in its headlong rush, Godwin had been killed by the arrow that Jasper Griswold had intended for me. While I rested here, back at home Martha's hope burned a bright candle for her son, longing for his return and unaware of his fate. Tears misted my eyes as I thought of him, lying there cold and alone, abandoned in the filth of death. It was then that I knew with certainty what I must do, and without delay.

***

Chapter 13

March – April 1461

'The king has no time for common soldiers, he is busy with his commanders. Be gone with you!' I could see that this officious, self-important little man was not going to be easily persuaded.

I stood in the guildhall where all was a scene of great activity. This was the grandest building I had ever seen, and it made the great hall at our manor at Upper Broomfield look insignificant by comparison; vast oak timbers soared upwards, framing a huge, vaulted roof, and windows of the most exquisitely coloured glass added to its magnificence. Messengers came and went, scurrying through the doorways and passages, scarcely pausing to remove their helmets in their haste. The outer room in which I found myself was being used by clerks to filter the rush of despatches that had followed an overwhelming victory. It was a tiny room into which, somehow, they had managed to cram three tables with hardly a scrap of space for the black robed clerks stationed behind them. The surface of each table was buried beneath a covering of letters and notes which the clerks were desperately trying to assemble into some kind of order. Inks and quills were in danger of being sent flying in the haste to impose organisation, their efforts denied by the sheer volume of material and the speed of its arrival. It was not yet good daylight and fluttering candles on the tables only added to the confusion.

'What, are you still here? Do I have to send for guards to have you removed?'

The short, bespectacled man pointed an ink-stained finger and glared at me in annoyance.

'I have business with Lord Fauconberg. You may send for the guards by all means, but you might find that it is you they are escorting away.' He stood blinking at me in uncertainty; my boldness had created doubt. At that point, Sir Richard de Coverdale came towards us from the inner reaches of the hall.

'What, not asleep? Surely you must need rest.'

'More than rest, my lord, I need to speak to Lord Fauconberg.'

He beckoned me and I followed, leaving the clerk wearing an anxious expression as he returned to his papers, wondering who this common soldier was and what repercussions might arise after he had obstructed me.

We found a quiet place and Sir Richard drew me aside. 'Lord Fauconberg is with the king. Is this a matter that I can attend to?'

'I wish to ask for his generosity, as he promised on the battlefield.'

Sir Richard threw his head back and laughed. 'The archer that felled the whoremonger Percy! I said we had both gained favour from your skill and so it has proven. He has promoted me to his campaign secretary after your lesson in archery. Wait here,' and he disappeared in the throng of people who crowded the great room. In a while, he returned, smiling. 'Lord Fauconberg has a brief moment to see you. Follow me.'

We threaded our way to the far corner, where a table with food and wine had been set with dishes of meat and pastries. I saw Lord Fauconberg spear a slice of meat with his eating knife. He had removed his harness and was dressed in a plain green doublet and brown hose. He looked up and after a momentary look of confusion, he smiled.

'I know this man!' he paused, 'Griffin!' he announced triumphantly.

I removed my cap and bowed. 'Gifford, my lord,' I replied as humbly as I could.

He ignored my correction and turned to address a man seated in the corner who I had not noticed. 'This is the man I spoke of your grace. This is the archer who knocked Henry Percy off his perch!'

A figure rose from his chair, and I realised to my astonishment that it was the king. I fell to my knees, bowing so low that my forehead almost touched the floor.

'Rise up goodman Gifford. You have served us well, by all accounts. You must not kneel to me.' I stood uncertainly, amazed by the glorious man who was now the king of England. He was dressed simply in a blue doublet with grey worsted hose, and a black, fur-lined cape around his shoulders. This was a handsome man indeed, with collar length blond hair and finely formed features. He seemed to radiate a golden aura about him, like the saints in a church window. It was easy to understand why his men adored him and ladies rivalled each other for his attention.

His unusual height and sheer physical presence left no doubt that here was a great monarch. He towered over Lord Fauconberg, and I gaped in awe.

'So this is the man who unhorsed the great Harry Percy! You are my talisman of good fortune, archer Gifford. Have you heard the saying "contra felicem vix deus vires habet"?' I looked blankly at him, and he laughed at my incomprehension. "Against the lucky even the gods are powerless!" You have brought me luck. You may even have turned the tide of battle with that arrow, even though it did not kill him.'

'He is dead, you know,' Lord Fauconberg commented. 'The heralds recorded him amongst the fallen within the hour. He died fighting on foot amongst his men.'

'So I believe, but archer Gifford's dart will not have improved his sword arm, hey?' the king announced with a broad smile. 'You are here for reward, I expect.'

'I gave him my promise,' Lord Fauconberg interrupted. 'What is it that you want?'

I knew that this was my moment: hesitate now and my chance would be gone. Taking a deep breath, I replied as confidently as I could: 'I would like your authority to recover my friend's body and to give him a Christian burial in hallowed ground at the churchyard at Saxton, your grace.'

'That is hardly a reward. Granted.' The king was smiling. 'Your loyalty to your friend does you great credit. There must be more? This is scarcely what I expected.'

Plucking up my courage, I continued, 'Your grace, I would further ask that I may keep a horse to make my way home. I must inform his mother that he has died in your service.'

'We have horses by the hundred, most of them have seemingly lost their Lancastrian masters. Attend to it Richard – and give him coin from my privy coffer. He asks too little of us.'

I bowed low, and taking several shuffled steps backwards, I left the presence of my king, escorted by Sir Richard. 'As you see, I am promoted now,' he announced with an air of satisfaction. 'His grace has won a great victory on the field at Towton, and at the moment, his mood is so joyous that he would grant anybody anything. His only regret is that he has failed to capture King Henry and Queen Margaret. While they remain at liberty, the Lancastrian cause is still alive. The pair of them had been sheltering here at York whilst they awaited news of the battle, but the birds had flown when we looked for them. They had their horses saddled and ready and their escort standing by. As soon as they heard that the field was lost, they fled north with as many of their troops as they could gather. I expect they will be in Scotland by nightfall.'

We had re-crossed the crowded hall and returned to the outer office.

'Now, I will instruct the clerks to write you an order for the burial of your friend and authorisation for the allocation of a horse. While that is being attended to, We will visit the comptroller of the royal purse and see to it that you are properly rewarded. I shall make it clear that you are to be given a warrant of safe conduct and made free from any further service to his grace. You may return home.'

***

A feeling of utter exhaustion began to set in, numbing my mind, and it was only then that I realised that I had not eaten or slept for a day and a half. Had it not been for my determination to bury my friend, I think I might well have fallen to the floor and slept where I landed. As I rode alone towards Saxton retracing the journey we had made in pursuit of runaways, I was challenged several times by mounted men: troops of cavalry were still looking for Lancastrian soldiers who might be in hiding, awaiting chance to escape. I carried a satchel containing the highest authority in the land and when I showed the king's warrant with his personal seal, all suspicion vanished. They recommended that they should escort me, and some even offered ale from their own costrels but I declined and continued on my way, following the highway until I neared the fields of Towton. The call of carrion crows and magpies became louder as I took the lane to Saxton.

A tented encampment had appeared, and it was clear that the baggage train had caught up at last. As I dismounted and gave my horse to a groom, I was almost immediately hailed by Roland Green.

'Well met, Tom!' His greeting was accompanied by a slap on the shoulder. 'I feared you were lost in the skirmishes last night.'

'I see you have not escaped untouched,' I replied, looking at the blood stained bandage wrapped around his right hand.

'An unlucky encounter with a halberd. Lost a couple of fingers but the rest of the hand is sound enough. What news do you carry?'

I explained the events of the last evening, the pursuit to York and the meeting with the king. 'Have you eaten?' I shook my head wearily. 'We must put that right straight away.'

He led me to the large cauldrons where the cooks had made stew. I ate ravenously, scarcely pausing to look up until I had wiped my bowl with bread and swallowed a jugful of ale.

'I need your help Roland. I must find the body of my friend.'

'The big fellow who was with you?'

I nodded. 'I have authority for his burial in the churchyard, signed by the king.'

His eyebrows shot up and he looked at me afresh. 'As you can see, the main part of our army have either moved on or been disbanded, but there are plenty here who can help with your task. Signed by the king himself you say?' and he shook his head in amazement.

We took a small cart, and with two other men, returned to the battlefield to begin the grisly task of finding Godwin. A light mist shrouded the ground, and as we approached, the air was filled with the sound of beating wings as carrion crows rose above the haze like the spirits of the dead departing their broken bodies.

The sight that greeted me was one I shall never forget: it was a sleeping army, covering acre after acre with the prone figures of the slain. All lay where they had fallen, or where the looters had left them. Harness had been stripped away, even clothing had been taken, leaving naked bodies exposed to the bitter wind. Crows flew up in a raucous cloud of whirling black wings: to chase them off was futile for they only settled further away and continued their feasting.

'The heralds were here at first light,' Roland explained. 'They have identified the noblemen by their shields and devices. The bodies were taken away on carts for better identification, and their names have been added to the roll of the dead. There was a large number of great gentlemen on that list by the time that they were finished. It seems that the flower of the Lancastrian nobility was cut down yesterday.'

I found that I could take no satisfaction from the news. 'So many dead. How many gave their lives yesterday do you think?'

'The heralds are still working to try and arrive at a number, but it will be many. I have heard talk of twenty thousand or more slain. Today I have set men to work digging burial pits, so we must find your friend without delay. I have sent ahead to Saxton and a grave is being prepared for him in readiness.'

It was a difficult and arduous task to find one body among so many, especially where the dead were piled high or where the carcases of horses made it hard to see those buried beneath. I was shocked to realise the extent of the injuries especially to heads and faces – almost as if the victors had wanted to destroy the identity of their foe, with features smashed by mace or hammer until they were unrecognisable.

It was with a mixture of relief and great sadness that I found Godwin. He lay as he had fallen, face down in the soil. His expression was peaceful, almost as if he was dreaming of home, and mercifully, the crows and foxes had not found him. We raised him up, and I snapped off Griswold's arrow which still protruded from his chest. I threw it aside angrily, and with surprising tenderness, Roland's men carried him to the waiting cart.

***

Godwin's final resting place was in a corner of the churchyard at Saxton, where the sun would find it on a spring morning. When the priest had pronounced his final "requiscat in pace" I returned to our encampment, and finding a space in one of the tents, I fell into the kind of sleep that only complete exhaustion could bring. It was late into the forenoon when Roland woke me with a bowl of stew and a loaf of bread.

'Thought you might be ready for this,' he said, sitting beside me while I ate. 'I have orders to move on after the burials are finished. What are your plans now?'

For the first time in many days I found myself in a position of being able to choose my own destiny. There was only one thought uppermost in my mind. 'I have to go home. I have to bring the news of Godwin's death to his mother. After that I do not know.'

'You carry the king's warrant for safe passage and discharge from his service. You have fought well, Tom. I feel sure that you could find a place in his grace's permanent service if you chose.'

How could I tell him what I really felt, when he meant so well. I knew I could never again witness the kind of events that had happened here on Palm Sunday. The sight of unrestrained bloodlust had sickened me to the core, and all I knew was that I had to get away from this place.

'I think my time in the king's service is over now, and besides, I expect my father will want me to help him – he is a journeyman stonemason you know. I looked at my left forearm and realised that the leather bracer that all archers wear, was still strapped to it. I unfastened the thonging and threw it across the tent.

'That looks as if you have made up your mind,' he said with a smile. 'I will be away from camp now, so I will wish you God speed and the safety of the road.'

I began my return journey the following day, saddle bag filled with any provisions that the camp could spare, and a purse of the king's coin stored safely out of view. I had already decided that I would give this to Martha with the king's blessing, scant compensation for the loss of her only son.

The journey south seemed to pass quickly. I rode steadily away from the northern country always with the sun rising on my left shoulder. I stayed at inns if necessary, but by preference at monasteries, where it was safer. As I rode, I began to wonder how I would break the news to Martha: how do I begin to tell her that her only child is dead, and worse, his death should have been mine. As the countryside became familiar and I recognised landmarks, I knew that the moment when I must say the words that would break her heart could be delayed no longer. It was early evening when I followed the lane round the final bend and entered Upper Broomfield, just as the hens were being fastened in and the first shutters closed. My horse somehow seemed to know that this was journey's end, for she gave a little whinny and shook her head as we stepped onto the green. I looked across the open grassy space and saw Martha waiting for me, standing by her cottage door where I guessed she must have waited, night after night. She stood, motionless and watched me approach, knowing that I was alone.

***

Chapter 14

Spring 1461

'Come in Tom.' Her face was composed, accepting. 'I knew he was dead. I knew when I watched you leave that I would not see him again.' As I entered the familiar, comfortable surroundings of Martha's room, a fresh wave of grief swept over me as I realised that Godwin was not here. I had somehow stupidly half-expected to see him waiting for me where I had always seen him, in a chair by the fire. In an attempt to cover my sadness, I showed her the king's warrant, authorising Godwin's burial. She read the letter briefly, nodded in approval and handed it back to me.

'He has a proper grave in a churchyard, and a burial service conducted by a priest.' She sat silently with her hands folded in her lap. I did not tell her of the alternative burials that were taking place as I left – bodies thrown carelessly into huge pits, anonymous and undignified, friend and foeman united in death until the last trumpet sounds.

'You have done well by him, Tom ... by both of us, and I am grateful. I will be able to think of him now, and picture his grave just as you have described it to me, and when the day comes that we all meet again, I am sure he will thank you himself.' She got up, suddenly old and weary and went to a cupboard. 'This was his rosary. You take it Tom. Say a prayer for him when you can.'

She handed me a set of beads, hand carved from sections of a hazel rod, their core hollowed out and joined by twine with a simple hand-made rood hanging beneath the lower decade. I took the rosary and put it around my neck. We sat in silence then, each with our thoughts. At last, Martha lit a rush light and placed it on the table beside her, its smoky glim painting her face in light and shadow. As the fire crackled, she brought food and I ate a little rough bread and cheese. When I had finished, she placed a flagon of ale beside me, and looked hard into my eyes.

'This has damaged you Tom, hasn't it? I can see the hurt in your face. You can tell me about it if it will help.'

I could not bring myself to think about some of the sickening events that I had seen in the bloodbath called Towton. It would not help, and she need not know the depths of savagery that we had been forced to endure.

After a long pause, I murmured 'I could never answer the muster again, even if they arrested me as a traitor, I could not do it,' and then blurted out, 'If only you had given Godwin the sunstone!' I took it out from my purse and held it out to her. 'If only he had kept this, he might have lived. Please Martha, take it back.'

As I offered it to her, the firelight caught its colours, amber and gold melding into a richness that kindled a recognition that I could not place; as the light gleamed through its heart there was something calling to me...

'No Tom.'

She took my outstretched palm and folded my fingers back around the stone's smooth surface, enveloping it tightly, and wrapping both her roughened hands around mine.

'No, that would be wrong. It has accepted you. It has kept you safe and you belong together. Remember when I told you that I used it for difficult birthings? How it gives strength and endurance and healing? You need all those things to bring you back to us. Keep it safe and let its healing power help you.' Her grip was firm and as she held my hand in hers, it was as if something had passed between us that could not be reversed and I knew without question that it was part of me now.

***

The following morning when I awoke, I struggled to make sense of my surroundings. At first I thought I was on the floor of the tented encampment at Saxton. Then, as wakefulness begrudgingly replaced sleep, I realised it was daylight and Martha was busy at the fire, stirring the contents of her cooking pot with a long wooden ladle.

'I thought you would sleep the whole day through,' She said in mock annoyance. 'Here, eat,' and she spooned some of the steaming contents onto a wooden platter. 'Sleep is a great healer, and you need much of it.' As she placed the bowl on the table I had a pang of conscience.

'I have not been home yet, Martha. What news do you have of father and Ursula? Did he finish the well?'

She stopped, half-straightened as I spoke, then said 'Of course, you don't know,' and stood beside me, her hand resting on my shoulder. 'It seems we must bear each other bad news. Your father is dead, Tom.' The words seemed to hang in the air like the fading reverberations of a sexton's bell.

'What?' I asked softly, unable to reconcile what she had told me with my memory of the man who I had called father. I thought of the quickness of his temper; the beatings I had endured, and the hardness of his boot. This slab of a man was made of the living stone with which he worked; his powerful bulk was a cliff of adamantine rock that no storm could weather. It was impossible to think of him dying.

'How can that be?' I managed at last.

She sat down beside me. 'It happened just a couple of days after you left. He was ...'

'Was he down the well?' I broke in, remembering the incident with the coping stone when I had such a lucky escape.

'No, not the well. He was at St. Wilfrid's, working for the abbot.' It was then that I remembered the morning before I left, and the statue that the winter storms had loosened.

'The statue?'

'Yes, well ,,, no, not directly. He had set up scaffolding against the wall so he could take the statue down, clean it and re-set it in new mortar. He had everything in place so he climbed his ladder, and just as he was stepping onto the planks at the top, the statue fell, destroyed the scaffolding and took him with it. The fall killed him I'm afraid. Father

Stephen was there when it happened and he gave him the last rites, may God rest his soul.' Martha finished, and crossed herself.

'Then what of Ursula? What has become of her?'

'Gone.'

'What? Gone where?'

'Gone back up north where she came from, so they say. Your father was the third man she has buried, so nobody would have her round here now, not after that. They said she was cursed, and that bad luck followed her around. She was never popular and one or two women who she had offended started to spread the word that she was a witch. That sort of talk is malicious, but gossip travels quickly, and she fled to escape being arrested and put to the question.'

'What has happened to our things?'

'Ursula took anything she could carry I suppose. Anything of value that was small enough for her to pack into a bag.'

'What of my home? What has happened to it?'

'All boarded up now. The bailiffs men came and emptied it. They took anything that they could sell – to pay outstanding rent, they said. Ranulf Griswold came to supervise in person. All the rest was burned, and the house was nailed up tight.'

'But our rent was paid. We were not in debt. How can they do this and get away with it?' I was suddenly faced with the injustice of what had been done to me. 'I shall go to Lord Thain, tell him what has been done. Ask for his justice at the manor court.'

'You would be wasting your time I'm afraid, Tom. You have no trade or steady income to give him surety. He will put somebody in as a tenant who has the money to pay his rent regularly, on time and in full ,,, something that your father could not manage after your mother died.'

I was at a loss. So much had changed in the short time that I had been away. I had made up my mind to leave, even without Ursula's threats but now it had become a reality I found myself unable to think clearly.

'What will you do, Tom?'

I shook my head. 'I don't know. I hadn't expected this.'

'You can always stay here with me,' Martha said with a note of optimism. 'I am your godmother after all. I feel that it should be my duty to look after Maggie's boy. Why not stay here? There is room, now that Godwin ...' She trailed off, unwilling to say the words.

She looked hopefully at me as I sat quietly, wondering how to answer.

'I cannot stay here, Martha. So much has happened; so many unhappy memories. If mother or Molly were still here, of course I would stay, but they are gone. As for father ...' I thought for a moment of the man with fists like mason's mallets. 'I think I have done my duty by him. I would like to get to know my Aunt Anne. She is my mother's sister, and yet I have never met her.'

Martha tried hard to disguise the look of disappointment that my decision had brought. She sighed: 'I can quite understand that. It might make you feel comforted by being near her, perhaps remind you of Maggie, just hearing her voice. Well, if that is your decision, I will write to her and let her know that you are coming.'

She sat gazing into the fire, then: 'If it is not to your liking, you can always come back here to me,' she added with a smile.

***

It was with a heavy heart that I saddled my little mare and bade goodbye to Martha. I knelt for her blessing, and she stood and watched me leave, a lonely figure by the doorway of her cottage. My stay had distracted her but now that I was going, I knew she would feel the loss of Godwin more keenly. After much argument, she had accepted two gold half angels from the king's purse, sending me on my journey with the rest. 'You will need all that and more to set yourself up in a trade,' she insisted. So it was in mid-April, a week after Easter Sunday, that I retraced my journey northwards, hoping that Martha's letter of introduction had reached its destination.

The year was just starting to open out before me as I made my way up the great northern road. The days were longer, and I was able to make slow but easy progress on horseback. I was grateful that I was not travelling on foot as I had last done, in the company of hundreds of fighting men: I found it difficult to remember that barely a month ago, I stood on the snow covered killing field of Towton.

The favourable weather brought more travellers: drovers with their cattle heading for markets in the south; girls driving flocks of geese to the shambles in nearby towns; all variety of people were moving up or down the great highway on foot, driving carts and a few on horseback. It was not until I drew nearer to York that I saw the first body. It was the corpse of a man who had been hanged from a roadside tree. The grim remains were decomposing, and the stench was dreadful. As the bodies became more frequent, I realised that these were the victims of Yorkist vengeance; those who had fled the rout at Towton, only to be hunted down by the pursuit.

Where possible I stayed at monasteries, but occasionally, when circumstances dictated, I had to sleep at an inn. I was within a day's travel of York when I caught up with a group of fifteen or so, walking together and enjoying their easy companionship. I realised that parting from Martha had left me feeling empty and alone. I craved friendship and distraction so I dismounted and walked along beside them.

'Where are you bound, brother?' The man beside me was pleased to allow me to join their group, and was probably looking forward to some new conversation. He was a tall, grey-bearded man who walked with a slight stoop and relied on a staff to keep his balance on the uneven surface.

'I am visiting my family near York,' I explained. 'My aunt is expecting me.'

'Then join our fellowship friend, even if only for a short while. I am Samuel Miller and pleased to make your acquaintance.'

'I am Tom Gifford, and thank you for your offer. Conversation makes the miles seem shorter – but why are there so many of you in your group?'

'We are pilgrims, heading for the shrine of St. Cuthbert in Durham. We have many days travelling ahead of us but for today at least, our walk is over. We shall stay at the Golden Lion tonight. You must join us.'

The prospect of a night with good company decided the matter, and as the sun dropped lower, we found the inn at the next village. It was a big building with two stories of windows and no doubt more rooms up in the thatched roof. The Golden Lion was clearly used to providing accommodation for large groups; as we arrived, its kitchens were a scene of great activity with scullions and servers rushing through our assembling crowd with trays of hot food. The milling band of pilgrims were soon allocated to their rooms, six or eight to a room, and sleeping on straw mattresses. I stabled my horse, and she whinnied with pleasure to be in the company of other horses at the large stable. I gave the groom a coin to make sure she was rubbed down and properly fed. Then I took my saddlebag and found a space on the floor of a small room at the top of the first flight of stairs.

After a generous supper, we gathered by the fire and chatted in small groups while candles were brought. After a while, one of the men looked about to find Samuel Miller. He was seated next to me, and we had chatted for a while before a call summoned Samuel from my side.

'Come on Sam. It's time you entertained us. Tell us one of your stories.'

'Oh very well,' he acknowledged, and a cheer went up. Rather reluctantly he rose and made his way to the fire, where he stood with his flagon of ale. A hush had fallen on his audience and taking a long draught, he wiped his mouth on his sleeve, and clearing his throat, he began:

'A long time ago, in a land far away called Greece, there was a king called Midas. He was very fond of gold and could never get enough of it ...'

'They're all the bloody same then!' heckled a voice, quickly silenced by shushing from all around. Sam continued:

'No matter how much gold he had, he always wanted more. One day, when he was counting his gold coins, a Greek God appeared before him and granted him a wish as a reward for his good deeds. King Midas thought quickly: "I wish that everything that I touch would to turn to gold".'

Murmurs of approval and admiration issued from the audience.

'The Greek God granted Midas the wish of the golden touch and vanished. Sometime later, when the king was seated under a huge apple tree in his garden, an apple fell beside him. The king picked it up, and the apple immediately turned into gold – the king could not believe his eyes. Whatever Midas touched turned into gold. The king was filled with joy and was beside himself with excitement…'

Sam paused to take another drink. His audience waited, captured by the tale, and in that unguarded moment, my eyes misted over as I found myself thinking of Godwin. How he would have loved this.

'Soon, the king was hungry but whatever food he touched turned into gold. Midas realised that, even though he was starving, he could not eat anything.'

Sam paused, looking at the sea of faces, pale in the candlelight, eager for the story to continue.

'King Midas had a daughter. She loved her father dearly and came running to him and threw her arms around him. But to his horror, even his daughter turned into gold as he hugged her back. Then at last, Midas saw the error of his ways. His innocent little girl was a lifeless golden statue and his greed had placed a curse upon him.'

'Go on! What happened next?'

Sam pointed a finger. 'Just you be careful what you wish for, next time you meet a Greek God, John Saddler!'

Raucous guffaws were followed by bawdy suggestions of what John Saddler might ask for from the next Greek God that he happened to meet.

'He ain't done any good deeds to be rewarded for!' Goodwife Saddler roared, strong beer encouraging her bravado. 'He certainly hasn't done *me* any good deeds lately. I think he's forgotten how!' Cheers and shouts of laughter filled the room.

'Never mind asking for gold, I'd ask for a wife who doesn't have a shrewish tongue!' John replied, grinning with embarrassment. 'Finish the story Sam.'

Sam resumed: 'Soon, the Greek God reappeared before the king and took pity on his condition ...' Loud cheers and banging of flagons showed their approval.

The door burst open with a crash, soldiers entered the room, and a chilling silence fell on the company. Their officer strode forward, looking intently at the faces before him.

'What insurrection is being hatched here?' he demanded.

'There is no cause to be concerned, sir,' Sam stood and bowed to the officer. 'We are pilgrims heading north to worship at the shrine of St. Cuthbert at Durham Cathedral. We are enjoying a little merriment on our way. If our laughter has caused offence, then we are sorry for it. I am Samuel Miller at your service sir.'

'Richard Fisher, Captain of Horse. We are still hunting for any rebel Lancastrians who may be at large, hiding in barns and byres and hoping to escape the king's justice. Who can be vouched for here?' he asked Sam, while his eyes roved round the faces before him. He walked slowly among us and stopped in front of me.

'You!' he pointed. 'You are not dressed like the others. Who are you?'

'I am a traveller heading to York to visit my aunt, sir,' I replied. Having seen the bodies of those who had been caught and hanged, I was under no illusion of this man's capability.

'Name?'

'Thomas Gifford, sir.'

'Where have you come from?'

'Broomfield,' I replied. I was tiring of this man.

'Where?' he demanded, rudely.

'Broom Field,' I answered in exaggerated precision. 'It is far south of here.'

'Is this true?' he demanded of Sam. 'He was heading north with you? His direction of travel may just have saved his neck.' He stared hard at me, his unblinking gaze seeking out any hint of deceit.

'Clear a table by the fire,' Sam ordered and a space was vacated hastily. 'Please sir, warm yourself. Innkeeper, ale for our brave officer.'

'All in good time. It seems you are in a hurry to end my questions and that makes me wonder why. Draycott, a word with you outside. Watch these people,' he instructed the remaining soldiers.

They stepped out into the darkness. 'Sir?' enquired Draycott.

'Find out about that young man Gifford. Search his belongings. Ask the master of the house what he knows and if he has seen him before.'

Captain Fisher returned to the warm interior and sat by the fire, where a leather tankard of ale awaited him. After a while, he was joined by trooper Draycott, who looked agitated and ill at ease.

'Sir, I must speak to you in private.'

As they stepped outside and the door closed behind them, Draycott waited for his eyes to adjust to the darkness. 'Well? What is it man?' Captain Fisher asked impatiently. Draycott looked about them to make sure they were alone before answering:

'Do you know who this *is*, sir ?'

'God's holy bones! Of course not. That is what you are supposed to find out.'

'Then let me tell you. He carries the king's warrant.'

'What?'

'More than that, his saddle bag is embossed with King Edward's insignia. He is a royal messenger!'

There was a moment of stunned silence. 'Satan's hairy arse! We nearly strung him up. I knew he was different and didn't belong with that lot. Wait, let me think...' Captain Fisher paused, frantically trying to make sense of something that had been nagging at the back of his mind - an elusive detail that he could not quite put into place.

'Mary, Jesus and Joseph! That's it. Broomfield. Do you remember when I asked him where he was from he said Broomfield?'

'Yes, but he said it differently the second time.'

'Yes, God save us. Our liege lord King Edward – his lineage is Plantagenet, and their emblem is the broom plant. His grace is said to have declared that now he is king, all this realm will be a glorious field of broom. BROOM FIELD. Now do you see?'

Again a look of incomprehension.

'Christ's nails, Draycott. Do I have to carve it into your sorry hide? He was giving us a code word. He is an intelligencer, probably one of Warwick's network, here to meet someone. If we have fouled his plans, Warwick will have our arses on a spit.'

'All we have done is question him, sir. No rough treatment. All should be well.'

'Let us hope you are right. Bloody Warwick of all people. Apart from the king he is the most powerful man in the land – and probably the most ruthless. We must report what has happened here at York tomorrow. In the meantime, Draycott, not a word to anyone if you value your bollocks.'

***

After we had broken our fast, I went to the stable to find that one of Fisher's troopers had already saddled my mare and was waiting for me, holding the bridle and stroking her nose. I was taken completely by surprise.

'Good morning sir,' he said deferentially. 'All ready for you, sir.'

'Thank you, but why have you gone to this trouble? Last night I thought you were going to arrest me.'

'Captain Fisher's orders, sir. He wishes us to escort you to York to guarantee you a safe journey.'

We mounted up and soon left the Golden Lion far behind. Captain Fisher was courteous to a fault, and seemed interested in my family, talking casually but trying to coax as much from me as he could while not directly questioning me. I was in no doubt that he was still suspicious of me. Nonetheless, the conversation was a pleasant diversion and soon our route took us close by the fields at Towton, now just furlongs and scarred acres where the skylark sang.

Captain Fisher leaned across towards me. 'There was a great battle fought here Tom. His grace Edward our new sovereign has destroyed King Henry's army, and with it the Lancastrian hope of ruling the country. Edward and Lord Fauconberg have driven them out for good.'

'Where are they now, Henry and the Wolf Queen?' Draycott's voice came from beside his captain.

'They are both in Scotland.' I replied without thinking.

'Back where they came from, hey? And how would you know that, may I ask?'

'King Edward and Lord Fauconberg both said so...'

'You have spoken with the king?' he asked, incredulously.

I chose not to elaborate and continued: 'They said that what is left of their army has run north with them.' I was confused by Captain Fisher, and particularly by his sudden change of attitude towards me. Perhaps I should have kept my own counsel. I looked away to try and discourage further questions, but when I looked back, I was just in time to see that Captain Fisher and Draycott had turned to each other and exchanged glances.

We passed through the barbican of Micklelith Bar and into the city, where we parted company. Captain Fisher wished me a safe journey, and I thanked him for his trouble. As I rode away, I shrugged to myself, still unable to make sense of recent events.

After a brief respite in the bustling city of York, I headed north, through the Monk Bar and onwards towards the great Forest of Galtres. My Aunt lived some thirty miles further at a village called Thorpe Greenhow. I hoped that Martha's letter had found its way ahead of me and that I would be welcome. I had no knowledge of my Aunt, but she was my mother's sister and that alone filled me with hope. Of one thing I was certain – this was where my future lay now.

***

I had such hopes when I arrived at Aunt Anne's home. We had never met before, and I was in a turmoil of nervousness when she answered the door. She was my mother's older sister, but how two sisters could be so different dismayed me. My mother was warmth and laughter; Aunt Anne was dour, resentful and sharp tongued. As her door opened and we eyed each other, I knew this had been a mistake.

'You would be Magdalene's boy I suppose,' she greeted me coldly.

'God give you good day Aunt,' I replied. 'My godmother, Martha Lightfoot said she would write to you and ...'

'Yes, I have her letter,' she snapped. 'Well, since you are here you had better come in.'

I had expected her to offer a heartfelt welcome and show pleasure at finally meeting me, but her welcome was as warm as a fish on a stone slab at the Friday market.

'Your mother was too soft hearted and I knew that no good would come of marrying that man. She followed him down to the middle of the country because he said that was where he could get the most work. I warned her against him, and it seems I was right. Well, our home is already crowded. My son and his wife live here, and she is with child. Whatever possessed your godmother to send you here I do not know. We will soon have another mouth to feed when the child arrives, and now it seems we have you.'

I was shocked at her callousness. If it had been my mother in her circumstances, she would have embraced me, made a huge fuss and made me feel as welcome as the first cuckoo in May.

'I can give you money for my keep, aunt. I never meant to stay without paying my way.'

'And where are you going to get money?' She looked disdainfully at my appearance, shook her head and turned away.

'I will sell my horse. That will help until I can find work.'

I was sad to part company with the little chestnut mare who had been my companion through hard and dangerous times. I rode her to the horsemarket and stroked her nose fondly before I left her, hoping that she would be well cared for. My aunt took the money with a grunt of acknowledgement.

'I have found you a place as an apprentice with man called Martin Garnett. He is a master glazier at York Minster. You are lucky because he will give you lodging and a good trade if you work hard.'

'I will try to do you credit, Aunt Anne.'

'Thank you, but I do not need your good wishes. My conscience is clear and I have done my duty by my sister. The rest is up to you, but if it is not to your liking you must look to your own salvation. It is no good thinking that you can come back here. How old are you now?' she peered at me, estimating my chances of success.

'I was seventeen last Eastertide.'

'Quite old enough to find your way in the world. We leave for York tomorrow.'

***

Chapter 15

York. July, 1461

For the third time that morning, Alice Garnett went to her door and glanced expectantly up and down Stonegate. The centre of York was busy with the usual bustle of tradesmen, messengers and travellers, and as Stonegate led directly to the minster, pilgrims and those with business with the Dean and Chapter swelled the numbers further. The booming note of the minster bell announced the hour for morning mass at Terce as Alice paused indecisively with her hand on the latch.

'Are you expecting news Alice? You have been back and forth to your doorstep. It must be something important.'

Margery Brandsby threw her bucket of slop into the runnel in the centre of the street before straightening painfully and wiped her hands on her apron. She was an elderly, wizened woman with grey hair tucked haphazardly under a brown headdress. She smiled at her neighbour and paused, catching her breath.

'I am waiting for a visitor Margery,' Alice replied, smiling inwardly at her friend's inquisitive nature. 'Martin has taken on an apprentice, and he should have been here by now. He is being delivered by his aunt, and he will lodge with us.'

'Will you not find it strange having a young lad to stay?'

'To tell you the truth, I am rather looking forward to it. Martin is not getting any younger and he needs somebody who can ease his burden. Besides, we have no child of our own and it will be nice to have his company.'

In the later years of their life, Martin and Alice had resigned themselves to a childless marriage though not by choice; they loved children but somehow, nature had not worked in their favour. Alice still yearned for a family, but she knew that it could not be.

'Who is he then?' Margery lived alone, and gathered gossip with the vigour of a goodwife whose coins have fallen from a broken purse in a crowded marketplace.

'His name is Tom – Tom Gifford. I don't know too much about his background, but life has not been kind to him.'

Margery put her bucket down with a loud thud, and stretched, rubbing her aching back with both hands. 'Huh!' she exclaimed, 'when is life ever kind to anyone of our sort? What do you know of him?'

'It is a rather sad story. His mother and sister died when he was quite young. The sweat took them I believe. Since then he has lived with his father - that is until his father died in an accident. He was taken in by his aunt, but he was only there for a short time and now he is coming to us.'

'Sounds like they didn't take to each other. Does he have a trade?'

'His father was a stonemason, and a thoroughly bad lot by what I can tell. The lad has some skills as a mason, which will come in handy. He is seventeen now and Martin wants to train him as a glazier.'

The sight of a small cart approaching, weaving tentatively through the crowded street brought their conversation to an end. A prim, severe woman stared fixedly ahead, while an anxious looking young man climbed down and turned to greet Alice.

'Good luck!' shouted Margery. 'Let's hope he's a hard worker.'

***

Aunt Anne chose to remain seated on the cart she had hired. I had assumed that she would have joined me to speak with the small lady who was standing waiting for me.

'Drive on!' she ordered curtly, and without a word being exchanged I was dumped in the street like a parcel of baggage.

I heard the carter flick his whip and the cart rumbled off, leaving me without the least idea of what I might expect. I had resolved not to raise my hopes as I had done when I first knocked on my aunt's door, and yet here in front of me on her doorstep stood a smiling lady who had watched as I dismounted. In three strides, she had thrown her arms round me, and was giving me a hug.

'You must be Thomas. Let me look at you. You need feeding. You are as thin as a stick of rhubarb!' Her delight in my arrival made words spill out of her like rain from a summer cloudburst. 'I am Alice, and my husband is Martin. You will meet him later. In the meantime, come in, come in!'

'Well, he looks alright.' Margery Brandsby's observation went unheeded as the door closed behind them.

***

The house was much grander than I had expected. It had an upstairs, which was unusual, but I reasoned that because Martin was a master craftsman, this house must fit his status. The windows that looked out onto Stonegate had small, diamond shaped panes of glass, and the floor of the fire room was made of flagstones and covered with rushes. In one corner was a large wooden desk, strewn with sheets of paper, scrolls of various sizes, and ledgers which I assumed must contain business accounts. Quills and inkpots occupied what little space remained. There was a large oak table placed by the window, while chairs were arranged round the fire, which to my surprise, had a stone hearth against the wall so that the smoke vanished up a hidden channel. I reasoned that in a big city, things were done differently, but I thought that my master must be an important person. Finally, much later that day I met the man who was both my host and my tutor.

Martin Garnett was a stockily built man with hands that were hardened by work. They were scarred from small cuts and nicks where the sharp edges of glass had caught him. His hair was short-cropped and greying at the temples, giving him an air of distinction and seniority. He had a cheerful smile and a deep, booming laugh that I found infectious. By comparison, his wife, Alice was tiny. She was two years younger than her husband and looked small and birdlike next to his burly bulk. Her dark hair was swept back behind her head and plaited into a single long strand that she curled up into a tight bun and pinned at the back. Alice was a bundle of vigour and determination, and managed the household with boundless energy. As the evening drew in, she closed the shutters and made herself comfortable.

'Tom, tell me how you come to be here with us. Your aunt didn't say much in her letter.'

'Now then Alice, let the lad settle in before you interrogate him!' Martin's cheerful reprimand did nothing to deter Alice's curiosity. I felt obliged to tell these kind people as much as they wanted to know about my mother, and my sister Molly. I told them about my father, leaving out much of the less pleasant side of his nature. Instead I explained how he had died.

'Falls from scaffolding are not uncommon, Tom. I must teach you how to stay safe. A man died at the minster last Eastertide from a fall. We don't want you having an accident.'

Outside, I heard a bell ringing in the distance.

'What is that bell ringing for?' I noticed that it was not a regular ring as for a church service, but came in groups of two chimes, followed by a silence, then another two chimes.

'That is the curfew bell Tom,' Alice explained. 'If you have never lived in a city you will not know. It tells us that it is time to be indoors. Only the watchmen and the gentry are allowed out now. It is to keep the streets safe from robbers, but there are so many of them at the moment. They say that they are the deserters from the Lancastrian army who have found easy pickings round our streets and taverns.'

'The gaols are full of them,' Martin agreed. 'There are regular hangings, but it doesn't seem to deter them. We will be given our chance to keep the city safe sooner or later. Everyone has to take a turn at the nightwatch. Now, on to pleasanter things. Tomorrow, we shall start your apprenticeship. I believe that you have gained some training from your father?'

'A little sir, but it was rough work - bridges, barns, that sort of thing.' I was tempted to say just what "rough" meant where my father was concerned, but thought it wiser to keep that to myself.

'Well that will certainly be useful - and you must call me Martin. Have you any other talents that we might be grateful for?'

I thought hard. Bird scaring and working on the land would hardly be relevant here. I was at a loss, but I so much wanted to impress him.

'No? Well no matter, You seem a bright fellow and hopefully a quick learner.'

'Well, there is this...' I added, doubtfully. Something had just fallen into place in my memory. 'I have this,' I said, opening my purse. I produced a very crumpled piece of paper. I had last shown it to Godwin on the eve of battle, and the memory of that moment was still raw. Father Stephen had been pleased with my efforts, so I hoped it might interest Martin. Dismissing my sadness, I smoothed it out and passed it to him.

'Did you draw this? ... Alice look,' and he passed the grubby paper to her.

'Wait, give me a moment,' and he went to his desk where after some rummaging and shuffling, he produced a sheet of clean paper, a quill and an inkpot. Laying them on the table, he invited me to sit.

'Here, draw anything you like.'

After a moment's thought, I dipped the quill in the ink and began.

Alice passed my drawing of the crucifixion back to her husband, and they exchanged glances. The room was silent, save for the scratching of pen on paper, as I drew the Blessed Virgin holding the Christ child in her arms. Eventually when the last pen stroke had dried, I handed the paper to Martin. He looked at it for a moment, then passed it to Alice without a word while I scanned their faces anxiously to see if they were pleased.

'Well!' Martin exhaled deeply. 'It seems to be my lucky day!'

***

I had not expected to have my own sleeping room, but Alice showed me to a door at the top of the stairs that opened into a room that was for me. It had a bed, a chest and a small table pushed up to a tiny window that peeped out through the thatch. It had been a long day and I was tired. As I settled down for the night, I could hear the owls calling outside and sleepily thought of my mother and her sister, Aunt Anne. How could two sisters be so different? I fought back a wave of sadness as I thought that mother would never see how well I was doing in my new life. In spite of Aunt Anne's failings, I knew just how lucky I had been on the day that she had introduced me to Martin and Alice.

The following morning, Martin took me to his workshop near the minster. It was in a corner of a large yard that opened off a street running behind the minster gates. The yard had huge wooden doors that stood open to reveal a cobbled courtyard with a series of small workshops opening off it. Already it was a scene of activity, with apprentices busy about their tasks at the start of another working day. Martin showed me his workshop, and though he was a modest man, I could feel the pride he took in showing me round.

'Here we are Tom. This is where you will learn your craft. Here is a furnace where we heat the glass to melt the different colours that we use in our drawings, and these are the tools we use when we cut and shape the small pieces of glass.' He directed me to a workbench where an assortment of tools were laid out neatly, ready for the day's work.

Over the months that followed, I watched Martin as he created scenes from the Bible in glass that was coloured in the most beautiful shades of yellow and red, green and blue. He drew the faces of the characters in special paint which contained expensive metals, giving each colour a different tint. After the pieces of glass were prepared, he showed me how to load them into the furnace so that the colour fused onto the plain glass beneath. It was when the firing had cooled, and it was safe to handle that I took up a piece of amber coloured glass and looked at it carefully. I marvelled at the way that the light gave it richness; the way it came to life as I turned it this way and that, and I realised with a jolt of surprise, that it was the same glowing colour as the sunstone. I had always known that something was waiting for me, and it was as if I had been gently led here, not knowing that I could learn to create such beauty. In truth, the things that I had been forced to see and do on that snowy wasteland called Towton had sickened me. Perhaps there was peace to be found here.

Finally, I was allowed to try my hand at painting the face of an angel on a piece of old glass. My efforts were clumsy at first, but Martin was patient, showing me how to draw the fine lines and delicate shading that brought faces to life as they showed joy and sadness, agony and rapture to those who read their message.

Chapter 16

Spring 1462

Morton on the Forest was a small community of ten or a dozen houses, clustered round a central green. Travellers journeying south towards York, would find themselves passing through light woodland, mainly of beech and hornbeam. At last, after taking a left turn, the road dropped down a gentle slope until the village seemed to appear, as if by magic, out of the trees. During the day, the barking of dogs and the smell of woodsmoke would give the only indication of its existence. At night, the village was in darkness and seemed to disappear off the face of the earth, save for the occasional glimmer of a rushlight seen through a chink in the shutters. The houses were the homes of working people and whilst one or two were built of stone, the majority were single storey timber-framed dwellings with wattle and daub walls and roofs made of straw thatch. Most had two rooms with a central hearth that was shared by the whole household.

At six feet in height John Cooper was a tall man by comparison to the other villagers, and his ginger hair and beard contributed to an imposing presence that commanded respect. He was as timeless as the gnarled old oak trees that he nurtured; sinewy, tough and enduring, with callused hands that bore testimony to a lifetime of hard work. At the age of forty nine, he had much to be grateful for and he took his duties seriously. His position as one of the four Royal Verderers came with status and responsibility, and he even had a green and gold livery to wear on ceremonial occasions: he was in charge of the enforcement of forest law that covered wood and timber; he also reported directly to Hugh St. Claire, steward at Sheriff Hutton Castle in all matters that related to the welfare and protection of the king's deer that roamed the vast acres of the forest. John was awarded a comfortable home as part of the living paid by the castle: the Verderer's House was placed centrally on the edge of the village green and beside the main road that lead to York. It reinforced John's position in the hierarchy of their small society, boasting a staircase and an upper floor, jettied out in replication of the grander town houses in York. His hall served as a meeting place for the village to assemble if proclamations needed to be read, and as a courtroom both for administration and the hearing of disputes. John was answerable indirectly to the king himself for the wellbeing and good management of the vast royal hunting ground north of York, known as the Forest of Galtres.

His relationship with his superiors at Sheriff Hutton Castle was conducted on quarter days, when John would give a report of his work and take orders for the next quarter. The majority of John's dealings with the gentry at the castle was through the Constable's steward, Hugh St. Claire. Hugh was a cold, penny pinching man; a hard taskmaster with a sense of compassion like ice on a midwinter pond. Hugh's son, Steven, was serving with forces in the northern marches. John had only met him once, but his reputation for drunkenness and brutality was well earned, according to gossip. John had found that Hugh was a stickler for discipline, supporting John's adjudication in the enforcement of the matters that came before the local jurisdiction in the courtroom at his home. Misdemeanours and minor breaches of forest law were tried by John, and usually ended with a warning or a fine. More serious matters were referred to the magistrates at York, and punishment could be severe. Like all stewards, Hugh's overriding preoccupation was with his ledgers; the reckoning of money and punishment of miscreants were treated with equal vigour. Fines and enforcement were always sources of conflict with tenants. While complying with the demands of his overlords, John lived amongst the forest dwellers and worked alongside them; much as he might like to be an intercessor to mitigate the severity of punishment, John Cooper had learned not to contradict his masters. It was a difficult path to tread, and he knew that he relied considerably on his wife Mary.

They had met when he was twenty two and she was nineteen at one of the Martinmas fairs. They had been married for twenty seven years, with one child: although John had longed for a son to follow him, Rose was his delight. She was a young woman now, with a lively, active intellect and was not easily discouraged once she had made her mind up – strengths that she drew from her mother. After barely a year together, John had become aware of the qualities that his young wife brought to their marriage and how it supported him. Mary Cooper was a skilled healer and had a knowledge of treating illness that had earned her respect both in their small village community and wider afield. Her skills had helped to ease the ailments of most of the families under John's purview. She had gained repute as a midwife; her knowledge and the ability to be calm under trying circumstances brought confidence, particularly to younger women having their firstborn. Mary was in demand because of the reassurance that her presence provided to a frightened young woman; simply by attending them, she seemed to ease their birth pangs and help them to negotiate the dangers of childbed. Her skills were highly regarded and much sought-after in times of crisis, and although John had to enforce the law, Mary was the one who won the hearts of a community that trusted and valued her. He often reflected how much he owed to his wife's mediation when the more difficult judgements such as mutilation or a hanging could have roused the forest dwellers to anger or violent disorder.

***

'Bring the candle closer Rose. We need to take a better look at this.'

Mary Cooper bent forward to inspect the injury, as her daughter brought the candle from the table. Its flickering yellow light revealed the deterioration in the wound to the left leg of a young man who lay gazing anxiously up at her.

'Hmm. It is worse than yesterday. Closer still Rose,' and by the flickering light, Mary could see that the stitches that she had inserted a week ago were straining at the flesh, which was angry and inflamed. Clear liquid seeped from the horsehair sutures and the area around the wound felt hot to the touch. She placed her hand on

Stephen Bowyer's forehead; it was feverish and damp with perspiration. Stephen's wife Elizabeth was seated quietly on a chair by the table where she had watched Mary working, nervously twisting her apron into tight corkscrews. Stephen was in his late twenties and had never had a day's illness in all their eleven years of marriage as far as Elizabeth could remember. His dark beard formed a contrast against the pallor of his face as he lay helpless, with his left leg in bandages. The accident had happened eight days ago when Stephen had been felling a rowan tree for John Cooper. It was a small tree and he had used an axe rather than the saw which would have normally been his choice. Stephen had measured his swing, but inexplicably on the first stroke, the axe had rebounded and struck his leading leg, laying his shin open to the bone. 'I told you to be careful.' Liz had said. 'Rowan is a special tree. It has to be treated with respect. My mother says it should only be felled at dawn on the morning after a full moon.'

'Your mother says a lot of things!' he had replied. Nonetheless, the power of the rowan was not to be ignored. 'I spoke to it, and begged its pardon. I promised to plant another rowan in a better place, so it would live on.'

'Then you should have taken her advice and followed ancient ways, because this is what you get for offending it. This is its revenge!' she had said angrily when he was brought home on a litter.

'How long has he felt hot like this. Liz?'

'Since this morning. I have bathed his forehead, but it did no good, so I sent for you.' Her voice betrayed her anxiety.

'Is it bad, mistress?' a wavering voice asked anxiously from the shadows cast by the candle flame.

Bending her face down to the wound, she sniffed deeply like a hound trailing a fox through a thicket.

'That's a good sign anyway. There is no smell. Now you rest easy Stephen. Rose and I will have you put to rights.' Then, in an attempt to reassure him, she added, 'Besides, John wants you fit and well as soon as can be. There's all the spring coppicing to start!'

Turning away to her daughter she said quietly, 'We can't leave it another day, or it will start to fester. It needs cauterising.'

Rose suppressed a gasp. She had heard her mother describe the process before, but had never seen it done, let alone help to perform it.

'Now listen carefully. Go home and fetch my roll of equipment from the shelf. Bring the dark brown bottle, and a jug with some vinegar. We need clean bandages and the jar of honey.'

Rose Cooper had lived in the village of Morton on the Forest with her parents all the sixteen years of her life. She was tall, slender as a willow wand and had an effortless grace of movement that conveyed poise and confidence. Her self-assurance was superficial however, and masked inner misgivings; despite her outward appearance, Rose was acutely aware of her left foot which had been slightly twisted since birth. She hated its imperfection but it rarely troubled her in other ways, and she could run like the wind. She had detected the note of urgency in her mother's voice and knew that there was need for haste.

'Liz, I want you to make up this fire. Get it glowing hot and keep it like that. Use small branches or charcoal if you have any... oh, and I want the contents of your piss pot.'

'You aren't going to cut it off are you?' Stephen's trembling voice had a note of rising panic.

'No, God bless you. No. Nothing like that.' At least, not yet Mary thought grimly to herself.

Rose closed the door behind her with a click. Allowing herself a second to let her eyes adjust to the darkness, she hitched up her kirtle and sped off on long slender legs that carried her with the speed and certainty of a deer in the forest. She ran down the lane and turned right, by the green until she reached her own door. As she burst in, her father looked up.

'No better then?'

Rather than stop to answer, Rose began gathering the items her mother had requested.

When she returned, she found that the fire was glowing red hot, and the heat in the small room was oppressive. She laid her bundle on the table where her mother set out the jars and removed their lids. Then she unfolded the roll that contained her equipment and set it out on the table in readiness.

'Have you a spoon Liz?' as she uncorked the small brown bottle containing a dark viscous liquid. 'Lift his head Rose.' She gently gave Stephen a spoonful, followed by a second. He grimaced at the bitter taste.

'What is that?' Liz asked.

'Nothing for you to be feared of. It is an old medicine called dwale; it will help him to bear the pain while I clean his leg. He will be asleep in a few moments, and I promise you he will not suffer.'

Mary took two pieces of medical equipment from her bundle. Each had a wooden handle attached to a short, chisel-shaped metal blade, which she doused in vinegar. Then she placed them on the glowing fire and waited for them to heat up. She turned to her patient who had now lapsed into a state of unconsciousness. He looked a deathly white and murmured occasionally in his stupor.

'Is he ... is he dying?' Liz looked at her husband's corpse-like appearance in dismay.

'No, just deeply asleep,' Mary answered shortly, irritated by the interruption. Above all, she needed to be allowed to concentrate. 'Now I need both of you to help. Liz, come to his head and get ready to hold his shoulders. Rose, I need you to hold this leg steady. He may try to thrash about, even though he is asleep, and I have to work quickly, so be ready.'

Mary took a sharp blade and began to cut the sutures one by one. As she did so, the suppurating wound opened, its edges forced apart by the inflammation within. Rose turned her face away as she felt her stomach churn.

'Now, both of you take hold.' Mary took the first cauterising tool out of the fire and inspected it, blowing lightly to remove any flakes of ash. Then she turned and laid it firmly on the wound. There was a sizzling and stench of burning flesh. Stephen cried out and squirmed in the depths of his sleep, but they held him down.

'Now again. Ready?'

Mary took the second tool and repeated the process, catching the edges of the flaps of flesh until she was satisfied that all the surfaces had been treated. Then she tipped urine over the wound and dabbed off the excess before taking a fine needle and fresh horsehair to close it up. Finally she smeared the site with honey and made a poultice of honey and wild garlic which she bound lightly on Stephen's leg.

'There, that is all I can do for now. If he wakes, give him a spoon of this in milk. It will hurt tomorrow, and this tincture will help to lower his fever. Keep damping his forehead with a cloth. You will not be able to sleep tonight but I will come in the morning so you can get some rest. Come Rose.'

***

Rose Cooper had reached an age where she had begun to give serious consideration to her future. She knew that the time when she should marry was drawing near, yet she had such misgivings about what lay ahead. In her mind, she had evaluated the local young men and the possible choices that her father might make for her; she dismissed them all outright. She could not see herself filling the traditional role for which young women of her age seemed destined, and she vowed that she would never become another man's property. She took stock of herself from time to time and was modestly content with herself in general. 'I can read and write,' she noted with satisfaction, 'and I can keep father's accounts and ledgers in good order. I have much help to offer a man with his business dealings if he would allow it.' Rose accepted that she could never be described as a beauty; plain to look at, with a pointed chin, snub nose and freckles ... that is, until you saw her eyes. They were clear green, like spangled chips of glass from a sunlit church window. Her long, auburn hair shone when she brushed it out and she wore it plaited and pinned into place so that her coif would cover it whilst she worked. Perhaps it was as a result of her twisted foot that Rose felt imperfect, and she resented the abnormality deeply. When she was alone, she would pull up her smock and her underskirt, and look down at her legs. The right leg was perfect but her left foot was twisted inwards. Sometimes as she compared her legs, she tried to wish the foot to become straight by the power of her will. She said decades of her rosary to the Blessed Virgin, begging her intercession to make the foot correct itself. Recently, Rose had found herself praying that if she had children of her own, they would not bear the same affliction. She resented her deformity for the way it threatened her future happiness: 'No man will want me like this,' she thought in moments of bitterness. The older she had become, the more self-conscious it had made her, until at sixteen, she had developed a natural reserve that to others made her seem cool and remote. Rose was critically aware that her body had changed shape from her thin, girlish appearance to that of a young woman. Men were beginning to notice her, but she was not flattered by their attention, seemingly indifferent to their interest and preferring to keep her distance. In her mind, it was safer to be detached from their clumsy overtures and remain independent for as long as possible rather than face rejection, or worse still ridicule, because of her foot.

There was, however, another, much darker legacy on the female side of her family which mother and daughter kept to themselves. It was a knowledge so dangerous that they never spoke of it except to each other and even then only behind locked doors and bolted shutters.

***

'How was he this morning?' Rose walked beside her mother as she returned from her visit to check on her patient.

'Much better, it seems. The fever has eased, and he was awake and able to take a little broth. Liz said that he was grumbling about the pain, so she knew that was a good sign.'

'It is only thanks to your knowledge that he still has a leg to grumble about!' Rose added wryly. 'I must try to learn all I can from you.'

'You know a great deal already, probably more than you think. Tell me, what would you give to someone with a stomach ache?'

'That is an easy one. I would give boiled mint, and sip the liquid as it cooled.'

'And what of my aches and pains as I grow older? What will you give me?'

'Nettles, of course.'

'There, you have learned much, and I can teach you so much more, given time.'

'How would I make someone love me?' The question tumbled from Rose's lips before she could stop herself.

Her mother smiled. 'So that's it! It's a love potion you're after. Well I can't say that I'm surprised – you are of the age to be thinking such thoughts. Who is the lucky young man? Someone I know?' She paused but Rose did not answer straight away.

'There is no-one that I would choose here at Morton. I have grown up with them and I know them for what they are – nice enough as friends but they have no spark about them, no wish to be anything other than what they are now. I want more than that. I want a husband who has plans; someone who has the strength to make his plans work and ...' she paused, suddenly realising what it was that she yearned for ... 'somebody who would let me share his ambition and let me help him to achieve it. How would I find him. How would I know he is the right one? How would I draw him to me?'

She laughed: 'So many questions daughter. The restlessness of the young – everything must be done in a hurry. Perhaps what you really need to do is to ask God for the gift of patience!'

Mary smiled when she saw the frown of annoyance cross Rose's face. 'I see that patience is not your greatest strength, so heed me now. You have no need of potions, for he is coming.'

Rose paused in her stride to look at her mother. 'Have you seen him? Has the Sight been visited upon you?' She searched her mother's face.

'Hush child. Not so loud. You are forgetting yourself.'

'Then tell me!' Rose ordered in a fierce whisper, seizing her mother's arm.

'Later. In two days' time it will be the feast of Imbolc.'

'What is that?' enquired Rose suspiciously. 'I have never heard of such a feast.'

Mary Cooper smiled. 'You have heard it called Candlemas I expect. It was a special day for the old religion but taken over by the Church. It is the day when the earth arises from winter; a time of awakening, new life and visions of the future. When the twilight comes and the world slips into night-time we will go to the sican stone and then we will see what we will see.'

***

Chapter 17

Spring 1462

Rose closed the wicket gate with a quiet click. She lingered for a moment, watching the retreating figure of Beth Sawyer as she made her way home in the twilight along the lane that ran beside the green. It had been a settled warm day, unusual for February, and the two had been enjoying the last of the sunshine as they sat on a bench beneath the overhanging thatch of Rose's home. The closeness of their friendship had encouraged their conversation to stray into raucous speculation. What was it that Beth had said?

'It's time you were looking for a lad,' she had remarked. 'You will be a wrinkly old maid if you don't hurry up. It is time you were wedded and bedded girl!' And it was true, Rose knew that at the age of 16, she could have been betrothed long before now if her father had insisted.

'Plenty of time yet. I'm not in any rush,' Rose had replied, smiling at her friend's well-meaning concern. She had no intention of being pressed into a marriage that she would later regret. She was more worried about Beth's reckless interest in Robert Askham, a local man who Rose disliked. He was older than Beth but perversely, it seemed that his reputation for leading a dangerous life was the very thing that kindled Beth's interest. His disregard for the law sparked rumours that he was a poacher, and Rose prayed that he was never brought before the verderers court for trial by her father. It could mean the end of Beth's friendship. She had responded to Rose's concern with a typical salacious dismissal:

'Don't worry, he's not the only fish in the pond – when you have duckies like these you can get anyone you want!' She had grinned wickedly, hitching up the bodice of her gown with a generous flourish. 'You wait, spring fever should get your sap rising ready for a roll in the hay when the warmer weather gets here,' and gave Rose a sharp nudge with her elbow. Rose giggled in spite of herself. Beth's bawdy sense of humour was very direct and part of her charm. You always knew where you stood with Beth. With all her faults, she was a good friend and had been Rose's close confidant since childhood. She was a year older than Rose, and certainly more worldly-wise; her dark hair and generous figure drew the eye of the men around her, and she responded to their comments with mischievous glee.

'And that Maude Chapman can keep her eyes off him,' Beth announced spiritedly. 'Just because her father owns the ale house she thinks her generosity will win him over.'

'She's very generous by all accounts,' Rose had heard herself reply. 'She distributes more alms than the parish poor box!' Discretion gained control as she regretted her unkind remark 'Beth Sawyer, you are a disgrace... you have made me blush!'

They sat for a while enjoying each other's companionship as the day drew to a close and a chill crept into the air.

'Have you heard there is to be a new chapel built here?' Rose asked at length. '... a chantry chapel with a priest to pray for our master at Sheriff Hutton Castle, so my father says. He is to supply the timbers for the roof.'

'Huh,' retorted Beth. 'It's alright for some to buy their way into heaven. What about the rest of us poor buggers who haven't got two pennies to scratch our arses with?'

The daylight was fading as they stood and embraced before Beth took her leave. If by any chance she were to marry soon, Rose would miss her dreadfully. She would miss her ready laughter and her earthy sense of humour.

As the wicket gate closed, Rose lingered, deep in thought. Tomorrow was Candlemas and the day when her mother had promised to take her to the Sican stone. The thought both frightened and excited her; what would she discover? It was dusk, and a chill had crept into the air. Rose gave an involuntary shiver. The sun had dipped towards the horizon and was painting the clouds in delicate shades of pink and lemon yellow. There was not a breath of wind and she saw that the smoke from their fire was rising straight up to the darkening sky. The day seemed to be holding its breath before the world was plunged into night-time. As she turned to go in, a sound caught her attention and looking up she saw a flight of wild geese passing overhead, calling to each other as they went. There were about a score or more in a closely grouped V formation. As she watched them head west into the sunset, they constantly shifted position, swapping places and changing the leader as if by some carefully laid plan. Rose's laughter had deserted her, leaving her feeling a little melancholy, and she looked longingly up towards the geese that were now dwindling to tiny specks against the light of the dying sun.

'I wonder what it's like,' she mused to herself. 'What must it be like to be as free as that? Just to be able to go where you want and follow your wishes wherever it takes you. Beth says that I need to find myself a husband – well, I will, one day. And when I see him, I'll know he's the one and he won't get away like those geese!'

***

It was the second of February, the feast of Candlemas. For Rose the time had dragged as she waited for evening when her mother had promised to help her. She knew of the great stone that her mother called the sican stone, but which others referred to as the sighing stone. She had often walked past it, glancing incuriously at its tall shape as she went on her way. Today it had assumed a significance that held an element of the unknown: no longer a familiar feature or a waymarker, it had become a living thing, a Wakeman; brooding and powerful as time itself. Rose realised with increasing anxiety that the stone was the guardian of the gateway to the ageless wisdom of the ancient ones. She had no idea how her mother planned to use her gift, but she hoped that her courage did not fail as darkness transformed the landscape into an ominous watchfulness.

A soft dusk was falling when Rose and her mother set off across the green. They had their winter cloaks pulled tightly about them, for the sky was clear, and there was a chill in the late afternoon air.

'How did it get its name?' Rose asked as she followed her mother along the narrow path into the scrubland at the edge of the wood.

'Nobody can say for sure – perhaps it is the sound that the wind makes when it blows through the hole in the centre. It is such an ancient stone, and it has been important since the time of the old ones. It has been a place where lovers have met – and parted - so maybe it holds the echoes of sadness from times long ago. It is next to one of the burial sites of the old people, so perhaps their spirits still live there, and it is their voices you can hear, calling across the ages.'

Rose gave an involuntary shiver. 'I am frightened, mother. Is this a good thing to do? Is there evil in the stone that might be awakened by us?'

'I would not bring you here if I thought that. You wanted to know more about the Sight, and it is time that you learned some of the wisdom that has been gifted to our womenfolk. The stone is a guardian to another world, and it stands here waiting. It is like the pointer on a sundial, ready to answer what you ask of it – if you know how to ask. You wanted to know about your future husband. Do you still want to know?'

Rose nodded, taking in the importance of what she had heard as she stooped to free the hem of her cloak from a briar that had encroached on the path. 'How does the Sight come to you, mother? What makes it happen?' she asked at length.

Mary walked for a while before answering. 'You have never experienced it yet? The women of our affinity have the gift, and almost always by the time that their first course has finished, yet you have not been visited by it?' Rose shook her head. 'Well ...' she began, gathering her thoughts '... it is rather like being asleep and awake all at the same time. Dreaming while you are awake – that's what it is, and you can't stop it once it starts – and you can't force it to happen either, but sometimes ...' she looked up into the darkening sky. '... sometimes you can give it a little nudge.'

The path they were following opened out into a grassy clearing about a hundred paces across where two footpaths met. As they approached, Rose began to understand the significance of the place: in the centre of the clearing was a low mound rising just above head height which must be the burial site of the old ones; close by, at the junction of the paths was an ancient standing stone. Mary led her daughter up to the stone and laid her hand on its pitted, age-worn surface. Patches of lichen mottled the grey pillar, making it seem as though it had emerged from the earth as a living being but was now petrified for all eternity.

'Here it is – the sican stone. There is an old story that my mother – your grandmother Jane told me. She said that long ago, in the days when the earth was younger and the faerie people were greater in number, they used to mix with humans quite freely. One of the local young men fell in love with a faerie princess and decided to follow her to her home deep in the woods, to ask her father for her hand in marriage. The faerie people are too clever to be hoodwinked by mere mortals: when the young man was discovered, the faerie king was so angry at his deception that he changed him into stone.' They stood side by side, looking up at the towering pillar of rock. 'You may not believe the story, but mark well when I tell you that this is sacred ground. It guards a special place; forces meet here beneath the earth. The old ones called it the “sican stone” for that was the old word for ‘sigh.’ It is a focus of great energy and power for those who know how to use it.’

Rose stood uncertainly before the stone and looked at its grey shape. It was a thin, flat upright slab about a clothyard across and higher than her head. There was an oval shaped hole through the centre of it, and when the wind blew strongly, it emitted a sound that varied between a sigh and a moan.

Rose had heard tales of women passing their babies through the hole if they were ill, hoping the earth magic would help to heal them. ‘You must leave a small gift – a piece of cheese or bread. Something small to show you are respectful.’ In the grey half-light Rose understood the plight of a desperate mother trying to save the life of her child, and how the ancient power of the stone could be her last chance.

Mary turned to face Rose, her solemn face conveying the significance of the moment. ‘Now daughter, it is time for you to see into the future, if that is still your wish.’

Rose was filled with reservation and gave an involuntary shiver, but she nodded and stood waiting for instruction.

‘First, take a pinch of salt and lay it on the floor. That is our gift. Now, stand by the edge of the stone, facing the sunset. Reach your arms round, one at either side and clasp your hands together through the hole in the centre.’ Rose found that she was afraid and unwilling to touch the stone. In daytime it was just another piece of rock, no more threatening than a tree trunk or a gatepost. Now, in the eerie half-light, it seemed to be waiting for her, sensing her vulnerability and feeding on her fear. With a great effort of will she did as she was told. ‘Now, lay your face against it and close your eyes.’

Again, Rose did as her mother instructed and waited. The stone felt rough and cold against her cheek, and as the wind soughed through the woodland at the fringes of the glade, she knew it was in vain. She felt nothing: no tingling in her hands and face, no whispered message, no vision of things to come revealed behind her tightly shut eyelids.

'Nothing?' Mary's voice came from the shadows.

'Nothing, sorry.' Rose replied apologetically.

'No matter.' Her mother sounded disappointed. 'I will try instead.'

The sun had dipped below the trees now, and in its wake, the sky was a deep shade of tangerine, fading to lemon yellow at its lower edge near the horizon. Mary Cooper clasped her hands through the stone, placed her cheek against it and waited. Suddenly, she stiffened and opened her eyes with a start. Before her was revealed a glorious deep amber sky. The dying embers of the sun seemed to contain sparkling chips of fire that caught the light playfully and danced through the iridescent afterglow.

'What do you see, mother?' Rose's anxious voice brought Mary back from her dream.

'Have you ever seen such colour?' Mary asked, her voice trembling slightly, and ignoring Rose's question.

'It reminds me of the pictures in the church window when we go to mass,' Rose replied. 'But I don't understand. What have you seen? How can this tell you anything?'

'All things in their due time. Be patient child.'

'Then please let us leave this place; it frightens me.'

They walked the short distance back to the village, at first in silence, but as they left the stone behind, a sense of relief compelled Rose to talk.

'You saw something, didn't you? I tried but there was nothing. What did you see?'

'You saw the same as I did, but you could not understand its significance. Our women draw their answers from the sky above us, and the wind is our messenger. The answer was revealed in the wind and the clouds. He is coming for you.'

'But who is it?' Rose's voice betrayed a hint of exasperation. Her mother held up one hand to silence her, and Rose knew it was pointless to question her further.

They reached the green and soon were safely home. As she turned with her hand on the latch of the cottage door, Rose had the strangest feeling that her life had just changed in a way that she did not yet understand.

***

Chapter 18

York. March 1462

'He is there again.' Alice took Martin's arm and drew him towards the window of their home in Stonegate. She stood, partly obscured by the heavy drapes and peered cautiously out into the street beyond. Martin walked clumsily up to join her.

'Not in the open, Martin. Use a bit of sense. Hide round the side of the drape or he will see you.'

'What am I supposed to be looking for?' Martin was impatient and had no time for playing games.

'There! In the doorway just down the street. See him?'

Martin allowed his eyes to take in the bustling citizens, hurrying about their business. Beyond their to-and-fro he finally saw a figure.

'Yes, now I can see someone. Is he leaning against the doorway across the street? Short with a cloak and a deep-brimmed hat?'

'Yes!' Alice replied in exasperation. 'He has been there all morning, just standing and watching.'

'Probably waiting for a friend or a business contact. I can't see what you are making such a fuss about.'

'Yesterday there was a girl selling posies in exactly the same doorway. The day before that it was a blind beggar.'

'And what is so suspicious about that Alice? This is not like you – jumping at shadows. If you are worried, I will go and challenge him – threaten him with a lesson in manners!'

'No. That would be the very last thing I would want you to do. I will keep my eyes on him and see what happens.'

The daylight was fading as the Vespers bell began to chime and the late afternoon sun dipped behind the rooftops, casting Stonegate into deep shadow. There were few passers-by at this hour, and yet a figure remained in the doorway. It was hard to distinguish details as Alice kept her vigil from the window. Then, appearing from her right was Tom, walking unsuspectingly past the doorway. As he reached the point where she had seen the figure, an arm reached out and dragged Tom to one side. Alice put her hand to her mouth with fright, unable to warn him. After a few moments she saw Tom being escorted away by the stranger to a fate that she dared not think about.

***

I heard the Vespers bell begin to send its message across the smoky rooftops as I made my way to our home on a chilly March afternoon.

‘Tom Gifford?’ The voice came out of the shadows of a doorway. I started with alarm and recoiled but a hand had whipped out from the recess and held my arm in a firm grasp A man with a grip as powerful as that was not someone that I could fight off.

He emerged from the doorway and released my arm.

‘Stand away!’ I shouted. ‘Stand away or I will call the constables.’

‘Then I am here already, and calling out would be pointless. I am a constable sent by the authorities to collect you. Your presence is required elsewhere. There is no need to fear – you are in no danger, nor are you being arrested. My master needs your help.’

‘Who is your master?’ I asked suspiciously. ‘What help can he possibly need from me?’ My first reaction of fear had changed to one of annoyance at this intrusion. ‘What if I refuse to go?’

‘I beg you, sir, lower your voice. My orders are to escort you to him as quietly as possible and without drawing the attention of onlookers. My master will be known to you, but I cannot say his name here. Trust me. You will come to no harm.’

It was clear that I had no choice but to comply, and we walked without further conversation through the centre of the market. The traders were beginning to clear their stalls, packing unsold wares into wicker baskets and covering them with cloths. There was still half an hour of good daylight left, and my irritation was replaced by curiosity. Who was this person that had sent for me, and what could he want?

At first I thought we were heading towards the castle, but then my guide changed direction, doubling back, working his way through narrow passages and stopping occasionally to look around. It was clear that he was making sure that we were not being followed; that in itself was worrying. Finally, we began to take a more direct route and I realised that our destination was somewhere by the river. Here, the air was damp and smelled strongly of mud, offal and excrement from the great waterway that carried the waste of the city out towards the sea.

The buildings were low, poor houses that I guessed were the dwelling places of the river folk – the boatmen, ferrymen and shore workers who manned the staithes on either bank. As we neared the landing area of the quay I saw piles of wooden crates, anonymous mounds of objects covered with tarpaulin, and hawsers coiled for storage; everywhere was the stench of the river, mixed with tarred rope. It was the perfect place for a thief to conduct an attack, emerging from behind a stack of goods, wielding a knife and escaping undetected. I glanced anxiously at my escort who sensed my misgiving.

'Not far now, sir. Nearly there,' he reassured me.

We arrived at a warehouse with living quarters above it, and my guide indicated a rickety wooden staircase that led onto a balcony. He indicated for me to go up and he followed. The balcony looked out over the quayside, and we stopped at a low door. The constable gave two sharp knocks followed by two more. There was the sound of heavy metal bolts being withdrawn through their staples, and the door was opened to admit us. A servant in a dark full length robe stood aside as we entered, and closed the door quickly behind us.

I entered a low-ceilinged room which had a single window that looked out over the river. There was a table in front of the window that was almost entirely clear, apart from a pile of paper, an ink pot and some quills. A click made me look round quickly and a small door in the back wall, which I had not previously noticed, opened, and a figure entered. In the gloomy depths of the room I could not make him out, but as he came nearer to the window, his face was caught in the dwindling daylight.

'Tom Gifford! It is good to see you.'

It was a face that I recognised with a rush of relief.

'Roland Green!' I replied. 'The last time we stood together was at Towton.'

With a nod, the constable and the servant were dismissed to wait outside and he gave me a welcoming handshake, while exchanging reminiscences. I was offered a seat and a cup of wine, and we chatted for a while until Roland called us to business.

'Tom, you are wondering why I have called you here and I must give you an explanation. Much has changed since we helped our king to victory. I am promoted to garrison commander here in recognition of services on that day. We thought our triumph over the house of Lancaster was complete, but it was not so simple. In spite of King Edward and his cavalry racing here to York, he was not in time to capture Henry.'

'Yes, I had heard that.'

'Once Henry's messengers brought news to him here that the field was lost, he fled north with whatever remained of his army. They have taken refuge with their allies in Scotland, where they continue to pose a threat.' He paused, gathering his thoughts for a moment. 'You will remember Sir Richard de Coverdale?'

'Our field commander? The aide to Lord Fauconberg?'

'The same. What I tell you now must remain a close secret, and to disclose anything that follows would be an act of treason.' He looked at me and I nodded my assent.

'There are always rumours of discontent at court. Each week there is fresh gossip of one plot or another, and such talk has to be investigated.

Sir Richard's loyalty has also been rewarded; he is now one of the king's spymasters here in the north. It has come to his notice that a credible plot exists. There is a move afoot to enlist help from abroad and here at home to gather funds and support for a rising to reinstate Henry VI to the throne and to overthrow Edward.'

I was completely puzzled. 'But what is this to do with me?'

'Do you remember a Captain of Horse called Robert Fisher?'

I shook my head. 'Sorry, the name means nothing to me.'

'Just over a year ago he nearly hanged you on the road south. He thought you were a Lancastrian escaping from Towton. He had your possessions searched and found a royal warrant with the king's personal seal. He said your saddlebag bore the royal stamp and so he escorted you here because he thought you were a king's messenger. He reported it directly to Sir Richard, fearing that he had committed an offence. He said you told him you were from Broomfield. He thought you were using the Plantagenet emblem as a codeword and that you were Warwick's spy.'

I laughed incredulously: 'But that was over a year ago! The king granted me safe passage that is true, and he rewarded me for my action on the battlefield, but I am not his messenger, and I am not Warwick's agent either! The only thing he got right is that I am from Upper Broomfield.'

'But you have met his grace? Spoken to him in person? Carried his seal?'

'Yes, but ...'

'Sir Richard is satisfied that you are in a position of trust to follow his orders. Besides, you are uniquely placed to carry out this task.'

'You had better explain. What task?'

'Does the name Hugh Thain mean anything to you?'

'He was Lord of the Manors of Upper and Lower Broomfield.' I replied.

'Does he know you by sight? Could he recognise you, and more importantly, could you recognise him?'

I thought back to the Shrove Tuesday ball game that Hugh Thain had set in progress, and the milling crowds; we would just be anonymous faces to him. 'I know him, but he would not know me,' I answered.

'Then come Tom. We are comrades in arms and have stood one beside the other through the long day at Towton. Will you do this one last service for our king?'

I paused, looking out over the river, watching a wherry hoist sail and set off downstream for Hull. I nodded. 'Yes, but arrangements must be made. I am apprenticed and my master needs me. He knows nothing of this, and he cannot be placed in danger.'

'If that is your only concern, then be assured that he will be amply compensated and given a limited explanation of why you must be absent.'

He looked expectantly at me, and I found myself nodding in agreement. 'Very well,' I heard myself say.

'Then, to business. We have it on good authority that Hugh Thain is using his manor as a rallying point for supporters of Henry, or to be more precise, for Henry's wife Margaret of Anjou. He is due to meet an envoy from France tomorrow night, who we believe is a priest called Father William Burley. He is bringing information for Hugh Thain about the progress of their plan to raise an army; he may even be carrying written orders for his followers. We know that the manor at Upper Broomfield is a safe house for conspirators.'

My brow furrowed. 'Then why not simply arrest him? Capture his messages and discover the details of the conspiracy?' I asked.

'It is not as simple as that. For a start, we don't know the full extent of his network so at this stage we will watch him closely and learn what we can. That is where your help will be invaluable. We have arranged lodgings for you at Hull in a tavern that overlooks the quayside. We know the ship he will use and when she should dock. Watch for the priest - it will be easy to identify him because he will meet Hugh Thain, and you know him already. Follow them, observe from a distance, find out all you can and then tell us what you have seen.'

***

Chapter 19

June 1462

The road from York ran northwards through the great forest of Galtres and passed through the centre of Morton on the Forest. There were always travellers heading to and from York and so the largest building in the village was an inn. The Star offered food and accommodation to passing trade, and it boasted its own brewhouse with a reputation for good ale. There were great wagons loaded with timber that creaked and rumbled past its door, drawn by teams of oxen that laboured under the heavy load. There were travellers on horseback, journeymen on foot and even the occasional arrival of men at arms on their way to Sheriff Hutton Castle. Rose was made to stay indoors when armed men were passing through because they could be dangerous and unpredictable, especially when they had stopped for refreshment at the Star.

It was towards the end of the afternoon when John Cooper adjourned the Verderers Court. Mary attended the court hearings because she could read and write. Minor infringements were entered in a heavy ledger, bound in green leather, where date, description of offence and fine imposed were neatly recorded. She kept a record of the more serious cases on a sheet of paper for referral to the magistrates in York for confirmation. The case before him had been one of poaching. A young man from a neighbouring village had been caught two days previously and brought before John for a hearing.

'Is there no way of avoiding this John? I know the Bolton family. There are young children and no father to provide for them. Sarah Bolton relies on her son because he is the oldest. Noah has no real harm in him, and it was only a rabbit after all. Can we not settle for a fine just this once?' Mary Cooper looked to her husband, hoping her intercession might moderate his judgement.

'This is not his only offence, Mary. The first time he came before our court, I let him off with a warning. I fined him on the second occasion and hoped that would stop him, but he has been caught a third time now, and I cannot ignore it. I have recommended that he lose two fingers on his left hand which is the most lenient that I dare to be. I quite expect that the magistrate may overrule me and he will lose a hand – still better than being hanged. If it had been a deer he had taken, that would have been his fate.'

'Surely there must be something you can do?'

John's stern countenance told her that she was wasting her breath and testing his patience.

'You know perfectly well that I have no choice. Do you want me to look weak?'

'No, of course not – but perhaps you could send a written plea to the magistrate – explain his circumstances and ask for clemency?'

'That will only encourage others to try their luck, or worse still, open me to accusations of favouritism. You know as well as I do that the law must be seen to be maintained. No, and that is my final word.'

Mary's expression hardened and her lips compressed into a tight line.

'He will be sent to York tomorrow for confirmation of my judgement. If he is lucky, he will get away with losing just the fingers, but in my opinion, they will insist on a tougher punishment. He can make his case to them, but I doubt it will do him any good. Sentence will be carried out. Then you may wish to help him when he returns by dressing his stump. The lad will be kept here overnight and in the morning escorted to York, and that is that.'

She turned away to hide her anger. This was harsh justice and if she had not stayed her tongue, she would have expressed an opinion that would have landed her in trouble. Her scratching quill angrily confirmed the sentence on a sheet of paper, which she now sanded and placed in a brown folder. After laying the quill aside, she stalked out of the room without a word.

The following morning, Mary took bread and cheese with a mug of ale for the prisoner, who was shackled to an iron staple in the wall of the store room. His frightened face looked up at Mary as she unbolted the door.

'Here Noah, you will need this today.'

'What is to happen to me? I thought I would just get a fine.'

Mary sat on a box beside him. She was unable to answer his question with the truth. He was just a boy. 'They will take you to York this morning where you will see a magistrate. You can explain your situation – tell him that your father is dead and that your mother relies on you because you are the oldest son. Plead with him for leniency.'

'What will happen if he doesn't listen? What will they do to me? Will they hang me?' Noah's voice became desperate, and he clung to Mary's arm as though she was his mother.

Mary wanted to hold him like a frightened child but to do so would be disloyal and undermine her husband's authority. Instead she turned away, unable to face him. 'They will not hang you for a rabbit, Noah,' was all she could say as she rose to leave, trying not to see the desperation in his eyes.

***

It was a bright morning as Rose closed the door of Elizabeth Bowyer's cottage. She had carried a basket with a jar of salve for Liz to rub on her husband's leg wound. In return, Liz had given Rose some eggs to show her gratitude for her mother's continued care. The leg was healing nicely, and all trace of infection had gone.

The sound of horses made Rose look around quickly. Men on horseback could mean trouble and she was caught in the open. They rounded the corner at the top of the green at a canter, scattering geese left and right. Their hooves kicked up turf as they headed straight for her.

Rose's heart sank as she realised she was trapped: if she ran, they would hunt her down for sport. Her only chance was to stand still and hope they would go by. She froze, clenching her eyes shut, not wanting to look at the three mounted men who were bearing down on her. They reined in their horses sharply, bringing them to a skittering stop and surrounded her, their mounts blowing hard and throwing their heads impatiently.

'Well now. This is a stroke of good fortune. Here we were setting off for a day's hunting and it seems we have found our quarry without the thrill of the chase. This little hind seems to be waiting for us, ready to be caught.'

Rose remained still, praying under her breath that they would go, or that her father would come to her aid.

'Open your eyes and look at me girl!'

Reluctantly, Rose did as she was told and saw the man who had spoken. He was stockily built with short-cropped hair and carried a boar spear. He was young, possibly in his early twenties with small closely set weasel eyes. His round face, bristling stubble and the coldness of his expression told Rose that this man was dangerous, and she was in trouble. The man stared down, running his eyes greedily over her body, taking in the curve of her hips and the thrust of her small breasts beneath her tunic. Rose shuffled uneasily as the horses were manoeuvred to pen her in so she could not run, obscuring her from the view of any villager who might be reckless enough to intervene.

'It seems that our prize is poised for flight. Perhaps she was not waiting to be caught so easily after all – perhaps she means to tease us into greater pleasure by running!' Laughter from the other two men as they anticipated what would come next.

He swung his leg over his horse's neck and slid to the ground, the corners of his thin mouth twisted into a humourless smile. He grabbed Rose's chin roughly, turning her face up to his.

'I know you!' he smirked, 'You work at the Star. I have seen you waiting on gentlemen's pleasure ... well this gentleman will take his pleasure now,' and he bent forward and kissed Rose roughly on the mouth, forcing his tongue between her lips.

Angrily, she broke away, wiping her mouth with her hand and spitting the taste of him onto the floor.

'Spirited little filly, aren't you? Perhaps you are not broken to be ridden yet...' As he spoke he reached down and squeezed Rose's breast with such force that she cried out. She pushed him away and in a moment of outrage, slapped him hard across the face, heedless of the consequences.

'You will regret that, you vixen. Do you know who I am?' he shouted. Silence as Rose glared back furiously at him. Then she spat once again, but this time full into his face.

The speed of the blow was like a striking snake as he smashed the back of his hand across her face, knocking her to the floor.

'I am Steven St. Claire. My father is Steward at Sheriff Hutton Castle. All this village and its people are in his demesne,' he growled as he wiped the spittle from his cheek. 'You are his vassal and that makes you mine to use as I wish.'

The other two companions shifted uneasily in their saddles. They knew what he was capable of and the kind of depravity that he could inflict on this young woman, if he chose.

'Steven, enough. We have a hunt to attend. This is too public and will bring trouble for us all.'

Steven stood glaring down at Rose's body as she lay on the grass, motionless with fear. 'You have not heard the end of this,' he hissed, breathing heavily. 'You will learn not to cross me. I shall teach you what respect means to a little nobody like you.'

He swung back into his saddle and the group gathered their reins and prepared to ride off. As they wheeled their horses, the door to the Verderer's house opened, and Noah Bolton was led out by John Cooper. His hands were bound, and they awaited horses to be brought round from the stable at the back. Steven had an instinct for trouble and his attention focussed on the prisoner. He kicked his heels into his horse's flank and cantered across the green.

'What mischief is this? You have a prisoner there. What has he done?'

'You are Hugh St. Claire's son?' John Cooper knew the man before he asked the question, and sensed that his interest was not merely casual.

'And you are John Cooper, my father's Verderer, and I ask again, what has this man done? Why is he bound?'

'He has been found in breach of forest law and is on his way to the magistrate in York for confirmation of punishment. He has been found guilty of poaching.'

'Poaching,' Steven said thoughtfully. 'So he is to be strung up?'

'Less severe, because only a rabbit was taken.'

'A hand then?' Noah gave a whimper as he realised what lay ahead.

John Cooper nodded curtly. He resented this interference and was beginning to wonder why a man like Steven should be interested in his dealing with a minor crime.

'It is your lucky day, Verderer Cooper. I can save you the time and trouble of a journey to York. Why waste your day and wear out good horses for no reason? Punishment is so much more effective if it is carried out where all can see, don't you think?' He turned to his two companions. 'Take hold of him. Bring him to the smithy.'

Noah Bolton was dragged to the front of the smithy where a large tree stump was used as a soft anvil for delicate work. Noah was wailing pitifully and begging for mercy. His legs had buckled, and he was held upright by Steven's companions where he trembled like a man with a fever. Mary Cooper had seen the exchange, and worked out what was taking place. She grabbed her husband by the arm and shook it. 'John, you must stop this!'

She spoke loudly, and Steven turned to her with a smile.

'Your husband has passed judgement and found this man guilty. We are merely carrying out his sentence. You surely are not challenging his authority are you?' Turning to Noah he asked: 'Which hand do you favour churl?' but Noah was incapable of answering. 'Which hand do you work with?' he shouted again.

Thinking quickly, Mary shouted out 'His left hand. He is left handed,' she lied, hoping that if he survived he could earn a living.

'There seems to be confusion,' Steven's voice was playful, enjoying the moment. He took his gauntlet and threw it on the floor in front of Noah. 'Pick it up!' he ordered. Instinctively, Noah picked up the glove with his right hand, too frightened to think clearly. 'I see we have our answer,' he said coldly, glaring at Mary as he realised her attempted deception.

Rose had joined them, still shaken and tearful. She clutched her mother's arm. 'Mother, please stop this. You must not let this happen.'

'Go inside Rose. You shall not see this. Fetch bandage and as much cloth as you can find. Bring it to me when this is done.'

'So this is your daughter, is it?' Steven looked at John Cooper with interest. 'There are things concerning her that I wish to discuss, Verderer Cooper, but we shall attend to the king's justice first.' He nodded to the smith 'Bring a stout nail, a hammer and an axe.'

Noah was dragged to the block where his right hand was held and a heavy iron nail was driven through it, fixing it to the wood. He screamed with pain, trying to pull free. Steven took the axe and looked at it admiringly, feeling its edge and smiling at Noah, who was pleading for mercy, wetting himself in terror. With a deft downward stroke, the blade fell, severing Noah's hand in a single blow. Instantly, blood spurted forth in a torrent, while Noah fell insensible to the floor.

'Quickly Rose.' Mary knew that time was everything now. 'Get him up!' she ordered her husband. Noah was raised to a sitting position, collapsed against the tree stump. 'Raise his arm above his head Rose.' Other villagers had gathered, muttering their disapproval of the brutality that had been inflicted on one of their own. Rose soon found there were willing helpers while Mary staunched the flow of blood and wrapped bandage tightly round the shattered wrist.

Steven St. Claire drove the axe violently into the tree stump beside the severed hand, and motioned to his companions to follow as he re-mounted in readiness to leave.

'Let that remain here till it rots,' gesturing to the testimony of his justice. 'It seems that he has no further use for it.' He glared around at the sullen faces before him. 'It will serve as a reminder to others who may feel tempted to help themselves to what is not theirs.'

He leaned down towards Rose, who shrank back and turned her head away.

'Mistress Rose I believe? I admire a woman with spirit! It arouses feelings in me that you could scarcely imagine. How unlucky for you that I have to return north to my duties in the border country – there is so much we could have enjoyed together, but no matter, we shall meet again, and when we do, I promise I will give you my undivided attention.'

As the horsemen rode away, loud jeering broke out as the small crowd expressed their anger and contempt.

***

Chapter 20

July 1462

It was a warm clear day on the second of July, just a few days after Pentecost, when I took ship from York. My instructions from Roland Green were fresh in my memory, having met that morning. I was to find a man called Robert Shap on the quayside at Hull. He would identify himself to me when I disembarked, so I assumed he knew of my travel plan and would be waiting, with further arrangements already made, to enable us to keep watch for Hugh Thain and any of his associates.

I waited on the staithe beside the river, standing in the shadow of the arch of the bridge that brought the main highway from the south into the city. I was feeling a mixture of emotions, not least of them guilt at deserting Martin, repaying his kindness with my disappearance.

Although Roland had compensated him generously for the lack of my services, he could not give Martin a full explanation of the purpose of my absence, saying only that I was carrying out duties ordered by the king. Martin had never heard any of the details of my encounter with King Edward at Towton, or the events that followed after; I found the memory of those days was painful and better left unsaid. I knew that I would have to talk to him more fully when I returned.

I was beginning to worry about the nature of the task ahead. I had no experience of the sort of clandestine work that Sir Richard had in mind for me. I assumed he had control of spy networks all over the north, and certainly around the ports where enemy agents might come and go. This sort of work was his trade – but it certainly was not mine, and the safety of Martin's workshop and the sound of his patient voice suddenly felt very attractive. I had been assured by Roland Green that my only function was to identify Hugh Thain and thereby to uncover the agent he was meeting. "We are expecting an envoy from France tomorrow night, who we believe might be a priest called Father William Burley", was all I had been told. I hoped that the task was just as simple as it had been described to me, and not one that might end up in violent confrontation. The very thought of a brutal hand-to-hand struggle to stay alive rekindled too many memories and set my stomach churning.

In spite of myself, I reluctantly acknowledged that I had a feeling of excitement; I could not help it - a tingle of the unknown set my sense of adventure alive and the thought of identifying the mysterious enemy of our king was justification enough for me to ignore my guilty conscience and help to unmask a traitor.

I was a passenger on a low hulled river barge that plied to and from Hull with cargo for York. It had a crew of two and when I tried to pay its master, I was told abruptly, 'Already paid,' So I reasoned that preparations were well organised in advance. The master was a dour mariner, who refused all efforts at conversation. His pale eyes seemed bleached by the sun and the wind, with the air of detachment of one who is always seeking distant horizons. I could tell by his leathery brown skin that he must have spent his life on the water, becoming tanned to the same colour as the worn canvas sail that flapped in readiness on the single mast. As his deckhand cast off the last cable that bound us to the shore, I felt my heart leap with a surge of anticipation. He nodded to a bench seat that ran athwart a small cabin at the stern, motioning me to sit while we got underway.

Then we were in the middle of the channel, and with a rattle of iron hoops and pulleys, the boom paid over with a speed that would have sent me flying had I not been seated. Stays creaked and sheets were tightened as the great full-bellied sail caught the wind with a thump and we were on our way. The deck was piled with what seemed to be empty boxes and crates that must be making the return journey, to be filled again. They were tightly lashed down to iron fixings on the deck, a precaution against the rougher water where the river widened and became tidal. Our steady progress brought us to the quayside at Hull by late evening and as we made fast, I stood to thank the master for a safe passage.

'No need. Doing my job, that's all. A bit of extra pay always comes in handy.'

I smiled to myself at his unexpected eloquence. I suspected that he had used up a full day's ration of words in one brief burst.

'He'll be wanting to talk to you.' He nodded to his deckhand who now came forward.

I had taken no notice of the man during our short voyage, but now he came up and shook my hand.

'Time we were off,' he said, winking.

'Are you …' but he held up a hand to silence me. 'When we are ashore,' he said with a grin.

***

'Robert Shap... Rob.' He held his hand out and introduced himself once we were safely away from the people who bustled round the wharf. 'Sorry for the small deception but caution buys safety in this work.'

'You knew who I was yet didn't let on?' I questioned in surprise.

'Yes, sorry but I needed to have a good look at you first to be sure you were who you said you were.' He slapped me on the shoulder. 'Supper is waiting for us at the Mermaid just along the dock. We have a room there where we can watch what goes on. You are my guest!'

I could not help but like this man, in spite of his minor deception. He was slightly older than me – I guessed him to be in his mid-twenties with shoulder length blonde hair. He was clean shaven and wiry. By the way he had managed himself on the barge, I concluded that he was no stranger to life onboard ship. There was something about him that was hard to define – confidence and certainty in the way he conducted himself that gave the feeling that he could be relied upon in a crisis. After a brief walk along the busy quay, dodging porters and nets of cargo being swung ashore, we found ourselves before a harbourside tavern, with the busty effigy of a long-haired siren jutting out above the door.

'Here is the Mermaid. Let us go and eat.'

The tavern was in the middle of a row of buildings set back from the waterfront and separated from it by a narrow road. There was a mixture of warehouses and low dwellings clustered tightly along the wharf and extending round a curve, hiding the full extent of the frontage from view. Ships of various descriptions were berthed along the wall of the quay, some unloading, others apparently idle with no sign of life. The calling of the cargo handlers and the clatter of horses hooves on the cobbled road showed how busy a port this was, even later in the day. Overhead, gulls wheeled and cried, looking for a fishing boat that might put in to land its catch.

Rob opened the door and we ducked below the low lintel to enter the ale room. The generous figure of the alewife came to meet us. She had rolled up the sleeves of her smock, revealing powerful forearms, her grey hair tied back and fastened beneath a grubby white headdress. Wiping her hands on her apron, she showed us to a table by the only window in the room. A jug with two leather flagons was put in front of us and we had chance to relax for a while. Very soon, the woman reappeared with two platters piled with mutton pie, and we ate gratefully. Pushing his platter away, Rob wiped his mouth and took a long draught of ale.

'Well, here we are, fed and watered,' he announced. 'Just got to wait for a while now.'

'What is to happen?' I asked in a low voice. 'How will we find him?'

Looking around and checking that we could not be overheard, Rob leaned across the table.

'It is high water at sunset today. There is a ship anchored out in the lanes, waiting to come in on the tide. She is a two masted carrack called the Hirondelle, newly arrived from France, and our friend should be aboard. All we have to do is wait.'

'What about the man I know – Hugh Thain? Where do you think he is at the moment?'

'Don't worry, he will come to us. We must make sure that when the Hirondelle docks, we are close by.'

Rob looked up sharply as the door opened and a man entered. His eyes searched the room quickly and seeing Rob, gestured for him to meet outside.

'Wait here,' Rob instructed. His face showed concern; clearly he had not expected this interruption. He left to join the stranger outside. After a few moments he returned.

'Change of plan,' he announced briskly as he sat down. 'Our friend is not going to meet us here after all. The Hirondelle is making ready to raise anchor. Her topmen are working on her sails, and she will be underway in a short while.'

'What are we to do?' I asked in dismay. 'We will lose them.'

'Then come quickly. If our luck is in, all may not be lost. No time to explain – just follow me.'

We hurried out of the ale house and found the messenger waiting for us. He looked suspiciously at me, then turned to Rob.

'Quickly, the Aurora is just along the wharf and her master will take you, but you must run, or he will leave without you.'

Casting caution aside, we raced along the quay in the half-light; our boots clattering on the cobbles, attracting curious glances as we dodged the porters still working as the sun began to set. There before us was the Aurora, a single masted cog, straining at her spring line and her master pacing the deck impatiently. As we jumped onboard, the gap between quay and the vessel began to widen; her sails filled and started to pull her out into the channel,

We stood beside the gunwale, gasping for breath and grinning like boys who have narrowly escaped being caught raiding apples.

'That was not in the plan,' Rob said as his breathing steadied. 'We must look to our own devices now. Goodness knows where the Hirondelle is bound but we must follow. We cannot lose this man or who knows what the consequences might be. I will speak with the ship's master.'

Rob returned several minutes later with two heavy sea coats. As we donned them he explained: 'He is bound up the coast for Whitby, but he will put us ashore wherever Hirondelle is heading. I have had to tell him more than I would have liked, and it has cost me deep in my purse to gain his cooperation. He knows we are on the king's business.'

***

This was the first time I had ever seen the sea, let alone travelled on it, and my stomach was beginning to churn as we left the estuary, and the water became more broken. We had spotted the Hirondelle as we left the calm river mouth behind and she was now under way, her white sails catching the light from a moon that was nearly full. Her wake glowed with a pale phosphorescence, and it looked as if she was trailing a ribbon of moonlight in the swell behind her, as she headed northwards.

'We will trail her like this, keeping a safe distance,' Rob said, staring ahead. 'Can you see her, Tom?'

'I risked a quick look ahead, and could just make out the faint glimmer of her stern lantern as she crested and dived in the undulating sea. The mere sight of it was enough to make me stagger, with my hand over my mouth.

'Lucky that it's not rough – just a gentle swell so we should be able to keep her in view till daybreak if need be.' The rest of Rob's conversation was lost to me as I dived for the side and threw up violently. I raised my head, wiping my mouth and regarded Rob, who seemed to be oblivious to the ship's wallowing progress, and deeply amused by my discomfort. I put my hand inside my shirt from force of habit and clutched the sunstone where it hung from its leather thong around my neck. Putting my trust in its protection, I found myself praying aloud: 'Jesus, Mary and Joseph, make this end.'

'Don't worry, you will soon get used to it!' he laughed, patting me on the back as I reached for the side again in a state of abject misery.

Our pursuit lasted through the night, our course only changing once as we tacked to starboard, gaining sea room to avoid the jagged teeth of the Rocks off Flamborough Head. Then as the first pink light of dawn drew a rose petal path across the sea, the master came up to speak with Rob.

'Seems like she is putting in to Scarborough.' The Aurora's master had risen to the challenge of following Hirondelle, and seemed to have enjoyed the chase. 'She has taken in sail and should soon alter course for the harbour. I'll not follow her in, or I will have to pay harbour dues, but I can set you on the beach in our shore boat,' then added with a hint of amusement, 'I fear your friend is no sailor!'

'I think he will greet dry land like a priest greets the collection plate!' Rob laughed.

***

We sat in the stern of the small boat, leaving the Aurora which had hove to in the bay. Two sailors rowed us ashore, riding through the breakers and grounding on a shallow, sandy beach. As the boat's crew pulled away, cutting into the surf with steady splash and stroke of the oars, we turned and headed up the gently sloping sand. The port of Scarborough was only half a mile away, tucked in the shelter of the bay with buildings crammed into the hillside. Both harbour and town were dominated by the great grey fortress that stood as a stern guardian on the promontory overlooking the bay. In the early morning light I could see thatched roofs on the sloping ground that rose from the quayside. There was no time to lose if we were to keep in touch with our quarry. The Hirondelle had entered the mouth of the harbour, and as we hurried along on the shoreline, we could see her being warped in, her masts just visible as she neared her berth. We were fortunate that it took time for her to be positioned alongside the quay, and it gave us the chance to get our breath back.

'Wait here and keep out of sight,' Rob ordered. 'I have someone I need to see. Meanwhile, keep watch. It will be some time before they can be put ashore, so keep your eyes open for Hugh Thain. I shall be at the Dolphin, just across the road.' He headed for an alehouse on the harbour side which boasted a sign showing a sea creature.

I watched him walking hurriedly towards the Dolphin, and I turned to my task, wondering just how big the network of Sir Richard's intelligencers could be. I took up my position in an alleyway that ran between two warehouses. It looked little used, and from where I stood in the shadows of the early morning sun, I watched the Hirondelle make final berthing arrangements before a walkway was lowered across the gap to the quayside. I began to wonder what I should do if our enemy left the ship before Rob had returned. There was no need to fear; Rob appeared silently from behind me and took up his position by my side.

'All taken care of,' he said in a low voice. 'No sign of any activity yet?'

'Nothing yet,' I replied. 'I expect he is staying aboard out of sight until Hugh Thain turns up to escort him.'

We waited, with only the restless calling of the gulls to break the silence. Some movement was beginning to catch our attention; porters had appeared with carts laden with boxes that were clearly destined for the Hirondelle. They were heavy and each took two men to lift it down from the cart, and carry it to the end of the gangway. A small pile began to be assembled, and crew from the Hirondelle gathered on deck ready to begin loading. I searched for any sign of Hugh Thain, taking in every corner, shady recess and refuge point.

'Anything?' questioned Rob.

''Nothing,' I replied, 'and I'm sure I have not missed anything. He is not here ...' I stopped in mid-sentence.

'What is it?' Rob's voice was urgent as he craned his neck to see past me.

'It's him!' I exclaimed. 'But it can't be him. I thought he was dead.'

'For the love of the Blessed Virgin!' Rob exclaimed. 'What have you seen?'

'Look at the two men carrying the box. Now look at the taller one of the two. See him? I swear that he is the man we are after, but it is not Hugh Thain – it is Jasper Griswold!'

It quite astounded me to see this man again. I had hoped that my arrow had killed him in the rout after Towton. Clearly he still supported the Lancastrian cause and was actively working to foment rebellion. After fleeing the battlefield, he had thrown in his lot with the old king and was part of the conspiracy to restore him to the throne. I did not care at that moment for secrecy or the need for subtlety; no matter how much the reprisals after Towton had sickened me, this was the man who had killed Godwin. I thought of the loss of my friend and the sadness of his grieving mother; reason and balanced judgement evaporated as I drew my dagger and tensed myself to dash across the open ground.

'What in God's name are you doing?' Rob grabbed me and pushed me back out of sight against the wall of the building.

As my breathing settled, I recovered from my first instinct and explained briefly.

'Then you would gain a far sweeter revenge by helping me to catch him and have him tried and convicted. I can assure you that the kind of death reserved for traitors is not an easy one. It is slow, brutal and so agonising that he would pray for the swift release of your dagger.'

The dockside workers had all left, gathering their barrows and carts as they went. Only one man was still waiting on the quayside. A figure appeared from a hatch in the bow of the ship, and stepped carefully over the gangway, where he briefly greeted Jasper Griswold with a single word, almost certainly a code. The reply obviously satisfied him, for they shook hands. This must be Father William Burley, but he was too far away to see his features. He had a deep brimmed hat pulled down to obscure his face, and a heavy black cloak that reached to his ankles. The two men turned and walked away from us, heads deep in conversation and making their way slowly along the harbour wall.

We followed at a distance, taking care to stay well back and gain advantage of whatever cover might be available. Soon, they stopped and looked around. After satisfying themselves that they were alone, they entered a livery stable in the yard of a large alehouse.

'They are getting horses. They are going to escape! I should have killed him when I had the chance,' I muttered.

'Stay here and watch. I have horses already saddled at the Dolphin. It will only take a moment to fetch them. They have not escaped us yet.' He turned and ran back the way we had come, while I stood watch from the other side of the street, looking under the archway to the livery yard and hoping that Rob would be in time.

The slow clatter of hooves on the cobbles signified my worst fear as two mounted riders emerged from the yard, one tall, the other with a deep, broad brimmed hat. They paused to exchange a few words, then set off up the street. I was past myself with frustration. After all we had done, they were slipping away.

Rob made no attempt to approach quietly; he cantered up, sending gulls into a panic, leading a second horse by the reins. I jumped on without waiting to speak.

'Which way?' he asked urgently, and I pointed straight ahead.

***

Chapter 21

July 1462

The July sunshine was fierce as it passed midday. We left the cool sea breezes behind, and it became hotter still, yet we dared not ease our pace, even though our horses sweated on the long slow pull uphill from the coast. Speed was essential, but so was caution and we could not risk being detected by travelling too fast. Rob had arranged for saddlebags with food and a costrel of ale for us, and we set off in pursuit.

Rob strained his eyes, looking for any sign of our quarry. 'They don't know we are trailing them so they will not be on their guard. We are travelling faster than they are, so we should be up with them in the next mile.'

We were following a worn track which led steadily uphill, where the outskirts of the town had given way to scrub, and the call of the gulls was replaced by the stuttering song of the lark. At the top of the hill with the sea left far behind, the track levelled out. Our route took us along the side of a broad, flat bottomed valley; to our left in the far distance, purple and blue shaded hills formed the other side of the vale. Between the two sets of flanking shoulders, the bottom of the valley was flat and waterlogged, even in the summer heat. It appeared to be a vast tract of marsh, where the curlew called amongst the reedbeds. Looking ahead, our road followed a level course along the side of the hill where the ground was dry. There were gentle undulations which could easily hide a horse and rider from view, and sure enough, we sighted our two riders about half a mile ahead, riding side by side and heading steadily west.

'See them?' Rob asked, as if to confirm the testimony of his own eyes.

'They haven't got much of a lead. We could easily catch them.' I replied, squinting in the glare of the sun.

'No need. We can ease our pace now and spare the horses. Who knows how far they are going. As long as we can keep them in sight it is better to stay back. If we are still following as the sun goes down, we will need to get closer.'

'What are we hoping to gain by this , Rob?'

'My instructions are simply to find out as much as I can about their movements and the identity of anybody that they contact. We know their intention is to start another rising. It is up to us to nip it in the bud.'

I thought of the consequences of this; another bloodbath like Towton; thousands more ordinary men killed; families destroyed, and homes wrecked. It must not be allowed to happen.

Rob continued: 'This time it looks as if he is gathering pledges of troops from abroad, the funding to pay for mercenaries and the weapons to arm them with. Our priest from the Hirondelle has come from France, probably with promissory notes and assurances of help when the time arrives. Sir Richard is only one of many intelligence gatherers all over the country. He needs to know how widespread is Henry's support, which families give shelter to his agents, and Father William Burley is the key to it all in our part of the world.'

'So we just follow and watch?'

'That is exactly what we do, Tom.'

'Then may I make a suggestion; perhaps we should ride singly for the next hour, then join up again for a while, riding together. That way, if they look back and check, which they are sure to do, it will not alert them; it will not appear as though they are being followed by the same two people.'

'By God Tom, you are right! I would never have thought of that. It seems you are well suited to this line of work.'

***

As the sun began to dip, we shortened our distance, little by little so we could keep them in view in the fading light.

'They must stop soon,' I said, feeling the effects of a day's riding and longing to rest.

‘It is a pleasant evening, and the moon will rise before long. While it is warm and dry, I think they will keep going. Who knows, their destination could be quite near.’

I gathered my thoughts, wondering whether to explain to Rob what was in my mind. After we had covered another half mile, I decided I had to speak. ‘There is something I must tell you Rob.’ He turned in the saddle and looked quizzically at me. ‘When this is over, I mean to kill Jasper Griswold. He caused my friend's death and left my godmother without anyone to care for her. I cannot stand idly by while he escapes in the vague hope that the law may catch up with him. I thought my arrow had killed him as he fled the field, It took him full in the face and I was sure he would die. Now I must finish the job.’

‘But surely, your friend died an honourable death on the battlefield. Sad though it is, he died bravely in combat, fighting for our king.’

‘You do not understand. The arrow that killed Godwin was meant for me. Godwin stepped in front of me. Now he is dead, while I am alive. This is not about justice, Rob it is about revenge.’

‘Then all I ask is that you stay your hand until this is over, and I do not have to bear witness against you.’

We continued in silence then, each considering the implications of our last conversation. The evening was warm as we entered woodland, where the trees packed either side of the road and the darkness made it hard to keep a safe distance. As the moon rose, the road was once again bathed in light, each hollow looking as if it was a puddle of quicksilver.

‘They must stop soon. Their horses will be exhausted.’

‘Perhaps this is their destination,’ I replied. I had detected a thinning of the trees and could swear that my nose had detected the faintest hint of woodsmoke. Sure enough, as we came to the edge of a clearing, a small village emerged from the shadows; it was as if the houses had risen from the ground like mushrooms appear overnight in a lowland pasture. We waited in the cover of the trees and watched as our two riders dismounted, led their horses across the green and vanished behind a small dwelling that stood on its own. They returned and were admitted without knocking; clearly they were expected.

'What now?' I asked, relieved that this journey had finally ended.

'See, yonder?' Rob pointed to a large building on the opposite side of the green. 'That looks like an inn. If so, we are in luck.'

We dismounted and walked cautiously into a wide stable yard at the rear of what was indeed a large inn. Our horses hooves clattered on the cobbles and the commotion roused the groom. Once our mounts were settled, we were admitted to what seemed a spacious and comfortable ale room. Although it was dark, the hour was not late, and Rob explained that we were in need of a room and food.

'We have been given a room that looks out over the green. We can keep watch from there, and I have arranged for food to be brought to us; I have not disclosed our real business, so as far as the alewife is concerned we are travellers who misjudged our journey. She said they are used to late arrivals. People regularly lose their way in the forest as night falls.'

While Rob was making arrangements, I had taken a careful look at the room and its occupants. A large fire blazed in the hearth, even though it was July, and gathered around were several travellers, breaking their journey and enjoying a chance of company. They had given us a casual glance as we came in, then turned their backs and resumed their talk beside the fire. We were in a large, rectangular hall with a stair leading up the wall on the left. To the right was the hearth with chairs pulled around in a circle, while straight ahead was a long trestle table with benches on either side, and behind it, a doorway led to the kitchen and store rooms. As soon as Rob returned, we went upstairs and prepared to sit out our vigil. There was a knock on the door and a young woman entered carrying a tray. She was generously built with a round face that puckered up when she smiled.

'There we are gentlemen. My mother sends her best coney stew with her compliments.'

She adjusted her kirtle slightly and fixed me with a radiant beam. 'Will that be all for tonight?' she enquired with a suggestive tilt of her head.

'That will be all, thank you,' Rob replied, and as she still delayed her departure, he gave her a coin for her trouble. She closed the door behind her, and we heard her descend the stairs.

'There was more than coney stew on offer there, I think.' He smiled, and turned to the small, diamond paned casement. It was a warm night, so he opened the window to gain a better view of the cottage across the green. Smoke could be seen issuing from the smoke hole in the thatch, so clearly the visitors did not intend to sleep just yet.

We took turns to keep watch, sleeping alternately on the truckle bed against the left hand wall and observing the doorway of the cottage. The moon did not set until late into the night and the July sunrise came earlier than we had expected. Still, we had been able to rest and were fully alert to any movement that might show that our traitors were on the move again.

'At the first sign of activity, I will gather our horses while you keep watch here Tom. I have arranged for food to be ready to take with us, so we can leave at a moment's notice.'

The early sun rose high in a dappled sky, and it was not until mid-morning that a figure appeared through the low doorway opposite. Ducking under the thatch, I recognised Jasper, even at this distance, as he disappeared out of sight round the back.

'It seems they are ready to leave Tom. Keep close watch – we must not lose them.'

We waited for what seemed an age. 'He has been a long time – do you think he has given us the slip?'

'He has two horses to saddle remember,' Rob replied, and sure enough, Jasper appeared, leading their mounts, saddled and ready to leave. Without ceremony or farewells, the figure of the priest appeared. He mounted, but Jasper seemed to be having trouble with the girth strap, and dismounted again. I turned to warn Rob, but he had already left. As soon as he appeared from the stable yard with our horses, I went as quickly as I dared without drawing attention, down the stairs and across the big room which was filling with travellers ready to depart. The room was bustling with chatter from those preparing to leave, clamour from the kitchen and exclamations from the cheerful young woman who had brought our supper.

I threaded my way as quickly as I could across the crowded space, making for the door. I was aware of Rob outside with the horses, anxious not to be separated from our two adversaries, so I jostled through as quickly as courtesy would allow. I reached the door and lifting the latch I swung it open, pushing hastily through, just as someone else was entering from the opposite side, equally hurriedly and without care or caution. We bundled into each other, and in her haste, she overbalanced and fell to the floor, dropping the basket of turnips she was carrying.

'I beg your pardon, sir!' she exclaimed in dismay, scrambling to her feet. 'Please forgive me. I am late and I should take better care.' She sounded upset and anxious to know that I was not discomforted by our collision, perhaps fearing a reprimand from her employer.

'The fault was all mine, miss. Please, let me help you,' and bent to gather the spilled contents of her basket. She stood while I collected the last of her vegetables, seeming embarrassed and uneasy at my presence; she adjusted her kirtle to hide her feet, and smoothed her apron nervously. I stood and handed the basket back to her.

'Here miss. No harm done.'

As she took it from me, she looked up. 'Thank you sir, that was kind of you,' bobbing a curtsey. She smiled timidly, holding my gaze briefly before turning to enter. I had time to notice that she walked with a slight limp, and hoped that my clumsiness was not responsible. As the door closed behind her, I stood still for a moment to recover; she had the most remarkable eyes – they were like chips of flawless emerald, and as the morning sun caught them, it made them crackle with colour.

'No time for that sort of thing!' Rob's voice brought me back to reality. 'They left five minutes ago, heading back the way we came.'

I gathered my senses and quickly forced myself back to the task ahead of us.

We kicked our horses into a trot and left the village behind, heading back through the forest and trailing the conspirators discretely to yet another unknown destination. By the time we had ridden for an hour it was clear that their route was taking us over new country. We had left the well-marked road that ran due east to the coast, and were now heading uphill, leaving the pastures and furlongs behind in exchange for wild moorland and heath.

***

Our relentless pursuit took us through the hours of daylight, alternating our positions to make sure that we did not draw suspicion.

'Have you managed to gain anything useful from their assignation Rob?' I asked when we had cleared the village.

'I spent some time talking to the groom last night. It is surprising how much information you can get from unlikely sources. He sees and hears everything and yet manages to remain invisible: nobody takes any notice of a groom, so they talk freely in front of him. He told me that the house where our friends stayed was the home of a chantry priest who has only just arrived in the village. Apparently they are building a chantry chapel under orders from the Neville family. The priest is called Piers Routledge, and it is interesting that he has family in the border country – the northern marches, where Henry hopes to draw support. Whatever business our two had here, it is obvious that Piers Routledge is involved in it.'

'What will happen now, once you report this to your masters?'

'They will watch him closely I expect; intercept his messages, note his comings and goings; that sort of thing, or ...' he paused ominously, '... they may just arrest him and question him closely. Much depends on Sir Richard and what is already known, but it would be difficult to keep watch in such a small place without being discovered. It would need a reliable villager to be recruited to perform the task. Of course, yesterday's visit may have been all the final evidence they needed. Proof of a conspiracy against the crown usually only ends one way, and he may be sent to the Tower for questioning. If that happens, his priestly garb will not protect him against what he may have to face.'

'What was the name of that place where we have just been - or is it too small to have a name?'

'They said it is called Morton on the Forest,' Rob replied. 'Why, are you thinking of paying the alewife's daughter a visit? Her name is Maude, if you need to get as far as knowing names!'

'No, it was not her that I was thinking of,' I replied absently.

***

All day we had followed their trail on a track that wound up and down, sometimes over the high moor top, then plunging down into deep valleys. As daylight was fading, we realised that we were nearing the coast; there was an unmistakable smell of the sea, and the calling of the gulls became more frequent.

'We have only a short while before nightfall,' Rob observed. 'We should shorten our distance to keep better watch on them.'

'They must be heading for the coast,' I reasoned. 'Perhaps they have a boat waiting to pick them up. Perhaps the Hirondelle has returned for them. What do we do if we see them taking a boat? Do we challenge them?'

'We let them go. I want to be certain that they have left, and that they have not taken anyone with them, and that nobody else has been put ashore. Let us close up; I cannot see them in the gloom, and we are only a mile or so from the beach.'

We cautiously closed the gap between us, and to our dismay, realisation came too late.

'How many can you see, Tom?' Rob's anxious voice came out of the semi-darkness.

'Only one. We must have lost one, but it could be some while ago. They have split up.'

'Christ's bloody shroud, they have fooled us! They have waited for nightfall and separated. Perhaps they have known we were here all along, and just played with us. What do you make of it Tom?'

'I think that one of them may have doubled back to check; lain in wait to see who was following. They may have an emergency plan for this situation. The moon will rise soon, and we will be able to see what is happening. Meanwhile, all we can do is keep following whoever that is in front of us.'

We rode together at an unhurried pace for another half mile before the moon appeared from behind the clouds on the horizon to our left, casting a silver mantle over the path we were following. The coast was close now, and soon we would be within sight of the sea. We were high up on a clifftop, where moorland had given way to rough grass and gorse. The track seemed to be leading towards the place where the land ended in a steep drop; where the path must turn and follow the edge of the cliff. The solitary horseman kept his unhurried pace in front of us, but the whereabouts of his partner was uppermost in our minds, and the uncertainty was troubling. I kept looking behind to see if he was following, or worse, had summoned help to attack us. Our confusion was resolved when the second rider appeared from our right, and calmly re-joined his companion as if nothing was amiss.

'What do you make of that, Rob?' I asked in a low voice.

'I can't work out what has happened. If they had discovered us, they would be galloping ahead to escape. It looks as if one of them has had some kind of task to perform. Once we reach the cliff we can watch what happens.'

'Where are they now?' I asked in alarm; both figures disappeared from view with such speed that it seemed as if the ground had opened and swallowed them.

'There must be a track down the cliff. They have gone down to the beach.'

We dismounted for the last hundred yards and left our horses so they would not appear on the clifftop, silhouetted against the skyline. We had reached the edge of a steep drop that descended about a hundred feet to the beach. Below, the tide was in, and the shore was edged with milky surf where the slight swell made the sea foam look like the lacy frills on a fine lady's gown. I could hear the gentle suck and rush of the wavelets as they broke on the sandy beach below. We were looking out over a small, sheltered bay where the high ground at either side formed the shape of a horseshoe, enclosing a natural harbour, and contained by rocky headlands reaching out like fingers at either side. As our eyes adjusted to the brightness of the moon on the water, I pointed out to sea.

'Can you see it?' I whispered.

'Aye, she's there, ready and waiting.'

Clearly visible in the haven of the bay was the black silhouette of the Hirondelle, hove to and preparing to pick up her passengers.

'That explains where the other one went,' Rob said, indicating to the cliff face high to our right, where a niche had been hollowed out in the vertical rock face, and within its secret alcove, a lantern burned brightly, sending a clear signal to the waiting vessel. There was a shallow ravine to our left with a path that led down to the shore, and we followed it, careful not to dislodge a stone that could clatter down and give us away. We had just begun our descent when I grabbed Rob's arm and pointed; a boat had pulled away from the Hirondelle, and was swiftly covering the short distance to the beach. By now, two figures were standing with their backs to us at the edge of the surf, waiting for the boat to ground on the sand so they could embark.

We were at the bottom of the ravine and had taken refuge amongst the boulders on the tideline, watching. They were only fifty yards away from our hiding place, and we had a clear view as they made ready to embark. The oarsmen had driven the boat into the shallow water, where it grounded, rolling gently from side to side in the swell. The priest was in the water first, up to his knees in the surf with his cloak swirling around him; then he clambered over the gunwale and sat on one of the thwarts leaving Jasper remaining on the beach; he seized the prow and braced himself to push the boat out into deeper water. What I would have given for my bow and just one arrow to finish the job; in my mind, I saw Godwin's face as Jasper's arrow struck him, I saw him fall into the filthy slurry of Towton's killing field and I saw Jasper Griswold right before me, getting away. In that moment I lost all restraint and was overwhelmed by an irresistible desire to avenge my friend. Without a word I stood and broke cover. 'Tom, no!' but Rob's hoarse whisper went unheeded. With my dagger in my hand I raced across the sand towards the boat. A warning shout said that my headlong rush was discovered.

Jasper leaped aboard as the boat floated free of the beach and the oarsmen frantically back sculled. They were only feet away, but already I was up to my waist and the gap widened with every stroke of the oars. It was only then that I looked up and saw the face of my enemy, and what I had done to him; it had been a wide-bladed hunting arrow that had caught him in the mouth, slicing both cheeks open. The wound had healed but left jagged scars on either side of his mouth, twisting his face into a crooked leer.

'You are too late,' he shouted over the surge of the breakers. 'You are always too late. Too late to save that want-witted friend of yours!' He threw his head back and laughed at my frustration.

'May you rot in hell Griswold! May God damn you for all eternity!' I screamed my wrath across the widening gap as the rowers took up the stroke and pulled hard. 'I swear by Christ's holy blood that I will kill you when I find you!'

His voice, distant now through the tumble of the surf; 'You will never find me, but I will find you. I will haunt your dreams. You will always look over your shoulder for me. You are a dead man, Gifford!'

***

Chapter 22

August 1462 At Stonegate, York

'Well here you are lad. Back from your adventures!' Martin's beaming face greeted me as I returned to Stonegate, having left Rob on the staithe by the river. 'Alice has been fretting about you and hoping you were not in danger - she has been as prickly as a hedgehog these last few days, so be warned!' I grinned knowingly.

'Don't worry, I'm not going to ask you what you have been up to – they made it very clear that I was not to ask any questions – just that you had been attending to serious matters for the Garrison Commander, no less. How you come to know such mighty people is beyond me, but I won't ask.'

'You said, "they made it clear?" What has happened?' I was starting to fear that Martin and Alice had been threatened to ensure their silence.

'Oh, just after you mysteriously vanished, I had a visit here at home from two men from the castle. They were men of rank, judging by their clothes, one said his name was Fisher, a Captain of Horse, and the other one said he was the Comptroller for Sir Richard de Coverdale. They wanted to make sure of my silence, and to compensate me with coin for the loss of your services for a few days. They gave me far too much, but when I objected they said that you had earned every penny. I don't know what you have been up to lad, but it pays well!'

I laughed. 'I haven't been up to much at all, but I am glad that you have not been forgotten.'

'Oh, that's not the half of it,' Martin continued. 'The other piece of news is that we have received a major commission. We have windows to make for Sir Thomas Gower, the Constable at Sheriff Hutton Castle, under orders from the Neville family. It seems that Sir Richard Neville ...'

'Do you mean the Earl of Warwick?' I asked incredulously.

'The very same,' he continued, brushing aside my interruption as if it were an irritating midge on a summer's evening. 'Sir Richard Neville has commissioned the building of a chantry chapel in a little village just north of here. It is a place called ...'

'Morton on the Forest?' I interrupted, smiling.

Martin looked crestfallen and mildly irritated, like a man who has just discovered a moth in his ale. 'How ever did you know that?'

'Lucky guess!' I replied, but marvelling at the turn of events. It was clear that my service to Sir Richard's intelligence network had been rewarded, but my pleasure at Martin's good fortune was tempered with some anxiety: I could not help wondering whether I had heard the last of Sir Richard or whether I was now caught in his web of intrigue.

***

Once the pattern of life at Stonegate had resumed, I found I began to take stock of myself. At the age of eighteen I had already seen some of the worst of human nature, and in Martin and Alice, the obverse side of the coin; two more kind and honourable people it would be impossible to imagine. Still the thought of the future nagged away at me. What would happen when my apprenticeship was completed? I would have to face the world on my own and leave this place which had been so safe and predictable. Martin had been a wonderful tutor and friend; he was kind, patient and above all, forgiving when I made a mistake. I could not help but compare him to my own father and the kind of lessons he had meted out.

'This work on the chapel is valuable beyond money,' Alice had confided in me one day. 'He is as proud as a peacock to have been chosen, and he knows he has you to thank for it Tom. What ever would he do without you I wonder?'

'Well, he will have to find out one day. Martin has plenty of work to keep us both busy at the moment but whether he could afford to pay me a proper wage once my time is served is another matter.'

'Could you manage to set up on your own do you think?'

'I doubt it, Alice. It would take more money than I could imagine to buy tools, hire premises and stock up with everything that I would need as an independent tradesman. Then there would be taxes to the corporation, and fees to pay to the Guild.'

The more I thought about it, the gloomier I became. Both Martin and Alice were not getting any younger, and yet it was likely that I would have to desert them just when they might really need me. I had a deep affection for Alice which I knew she returned in her maternal way. I had seen her struggle to bring water into the house: when she went to the well, she found carrying the heavy wooden bucket more difficult than it used to be. She tried to hide it from me, but by the end of the day, I could see that she was quite worn out. To leave them would feel as if I was repaying their kindness with disloyalty.

'Can't you get yourself a nice young lass and get married?' Alice was always keen to get me paired off. 'I would like to be a grandmother one day!' she laughed.

'Marriage? I don't know anybody who might ever want to marry me,' I replied.

'Oh get on with you! You are a fine prospect for any lass. Perhaps you might meet a girl from a family that is well-to-do. Perhaps a good dowry might be the answer?'

I had never had much time to make the acquaintance of anyone outside of the small circle of people I encountered in day-to-day friendship. Perhaps Ursula had been right after all. I was shy, and would never manage to meet someone without help.

'I couldn't marry someone just for their money,' I replied. 'It wouldn't be right.'

'You are too honest for your own good, Tom Gifford!' Alice chided me, 'but I wouldn't have you any other way. Your sense of decency does you credit.'

‘I will just have to wait and hope that the right one comes along, I suppose,’ I said, shrugging my shoulders with an air of resignation.

***

The chantry chapel at the tiny village of Morton on the Forest had been commissioned in person by Sir Thomas Gower.

‘I met with Sir Thomas himself, yesterday,’ Martin announced proudly. ‘He explained what was needed, and approved the plans I had drawn for him. They have paid an endowment for a priest - if I remember rightly, he is called Father Piers Routledge.’

‘Is he living there now?’ I asked, although I knew the answer.

‘Yes, he has already moved into the living accommodation. He will be the parish priest when the new chapel is finished. Its other function as a chantry chapel will only be needed when the Earl of Warwick dies, and in these troubled days, who knows when that might happen.’

***

The stonework shell of the chapel had been completed before the winter had set in, but when the days lengthened the roof timbers were delivered. They arrived on a flat wagon, drawn by a team of four horses and supervised by John Cooper himself. The timbers had been smoothed by men with adzes until their dimpled surfaces shone, and the ground lay covered with sweet-smelling oak chippings.

Then came the thatchers with more carts, laden with wheat straw. The new thatch shone yellow and bright, in contrast to the roofs of the village houses which were dark and weathered by years of exposure to the elements. The gaping holes where the windows were to be placed resembled eye sockets in an ancient skull.

'The sooner we get on with it the better Tom,' Martin had said after Sir Thomas' visit. 'The windows in the north and south walls will be straightforward – just plain glass with a central motif.'

'What about the main window in the east wall - the one over the altar?' I asked.

'He wants the crucifixion,' he replied, 'with a roman centurion and the weeping figure of Mary at the foot of the cross.' He paused, and looked at me. 'I shall depict Jesus, but I think you should be the one to create the centurion and Mary.' I was surprised and humbled by his confidence in me, and I wondered how many Guildsmen would have trusted an apprentice with such responsibility.

When Alice stood with Martin to view the completed work, the anguish on the desolate face of Mary as she looked up at her crucified son had moved her, and she dabbed away a tear.

'Look at the sadness in her eyes,' she had said finally. 'See how he has captured a mother's grief.'

'This young man has remarkable talent,' replied Martin softly. 'I remember when we took him in after his aunt dumped him on our doorstep. We had no idea how he would turn out, but his work is already as good as mine – better, probably.'

'And he was so alone,' added Alice. 'He had lost his entire family, then been through God-knows-what horrors at Towton. Poor lamb,' she said with motherly affection. 'He quite tugged at my heart strings.'

'Poor lamb?' questioned Martin with a broad grin. 'Look at the size of him now. You have fed him too well!'

***

'Let's go and speak to him,' Beth Sawyer said with a confident giggle. 'He looks alright to me, what do you think? Time for a bit of fun, girl!'

'Oh, I don't know,' Rose's voice was hesitant. She was never quite sure what Beth would come out with next.

'Well if you don't want him, he could light a candle in my window any day!'

Rose gave an embarrassed laugh. 'Behave yourself Beth! Still,' she conceded, 'I suppose there's no harm in looking.'

Since work had begun on installing the windows, it had been the focus of gossip for the village. Rose's eye had already been drawn to the man working for the master craftsman. He somehow looked familiar, and she had the strangest feeling that she had met him before, but no matter how hard she tried, she could not remember when.

'Look at him Rose, look at the shoulders on him!' Beth sounded as though she was admiring a new plough horse.

'Hush Beth, he'll hear you!'

All the same, after her prompting, Rose looked afresh at him. He was tall with dark wavy hair that reached over his ears, and was powerfully built with wide shoulders; even in his work clothes, she could tell that he was muscular and well proportioned.

***

I was blissfully unaware of their interest as they watched us preparing to install the first window.

'Good morning, sirs, how does your work progress?' It was the shorter of the two who had spoken, a generously proportioned, dark haired young woman with an indescribable expression that hinted at mischief. I waited shyly for Martin to answer.

'God give you good day ladies,' he replied with a grin. 'All seems to be going well thank you.'

I saw them look at each other with impish smiles on their faces. Then the shorter one said, 'and how is your servant today?'

She meant me, and I stopped to look at the two young women who stood on the edge of the green. They were both dressed in plain kirtles, with their hair pinned beneath simple headdresses. One was dark haired and short, with a full figure, whilst the other was taller and thinner. There was something about the taller one though, something I could not place.

'Oh, you mean Tom?' replied Martin with a laugh. 'He is not my servant. When he finishes his apprenticeship he will probably be a better craftsman than I am. I must be careful, or he will put me out of business!'

'So, he is called Tom,' Rose thought to herself.

'What do you say Tom?' It was the taller girl who spoke this time, with an encouraging smile. 'Will you put your master out of business?'

I felt uncomfortable, and was surprised and rather taken aback by her question. Her buxom friend giggled at my discomfort but was given a hefty dig in the ribs to silence her.

'Why, of course not,' I mumbled, 'Martin has taught me everything I know.' I could feel myself going red and knew that I had shown myself up by my clumsy reply.

I estimated she was about sixteen. Her hair was tightly plaited and secured at each side of her head, but I could see where it showed beneath her headdress that it was a beautiful auburn colour that seemed to glow in the sunshine. Her face wore an honest open expression, but where had I seen her before? And then it came to me: this was the maid that I had collided with in the doorway of the Star and sent her flying. It was the colour of her eyes: I had never seen anyone with eyes like these, and in the bright light of this August morning they transfixed me. I became aware that I was staring at her intently. My breathing seemed to be difficult, and I could hear my pulse hammering in my ears.

'Well,' interrupted Martin, 'if you will forgive us, we must be about our work.' I came to my senses with a start.

'Come then, Rose. Let young master Tom get on, and don't delay him any further with your chatter!'

So, she is called Rose, I mused, then instantly rebuked myself for my stupidity. She will be marrying soon, I thought with a sigh. She is probably betrothed to someone already.

'Yes, of course, we have an errand to run, and we must be on our way,' agreed Rose, with some reluctance. 'I hope we have not stopped you for too long,' and stealing a last look at me, she turned and walked away, with her friend smiling mischievously at her side. After she had walked a few yards further, Rose half turned and, looking over her shoulder, gave me a gentle smile and raised her hand in what could have been a wave.

'Well, I'll be buggered! You were flirting with him!' exclaimed Beth when they were out of earshot.

'No I was not!' Rose answered, hotly.

'Yes you were! Well, you're a dark horse and no mistake Rose Cooper!'

Rose looked down at her legs with a subdued expression: 'Anyway, the moment he sees my foot, he will lose interest in me. They all expect perfection. He won't want anything more to do with me.'

'Bollocks! When you sniff a flower, you aren't looking at its roots. Give him a bit of encouragement– they're all the same. By the time he gets round to your feet, he won't bloody care!' Beth turned to face her with a knowing grin, and placing her hands on Rose's arms, added:

'You know what they say ...' Rose held her breath, wondering whatever might come next.

'A silver shilling only shines if you polish it! You go for it girl.'

***

It was on the following day, approaching noon, when I saw her again. She was on her own this time, wearing a russet gown with a white pinafore, and carrying a basket of eggs. We had just finished placing the first window into the north wall and were about to stop at mid-day.

'Good morning Tom,' she called cheerfully. I was both surprised and delighted that she had remembered my name.

'Good morning . . . Rose, isn't it?' I pretended to be indifferent, but already I could feel my mouth dry up and my words tumble over each other. I had thought of nothing else since our first meeting yesterday. I had wondered where she lived; was she already in love with someone, or perhaps even married, so that I had mistaken her motives? Was her interest in me, after all, just honest friendliness?

'I am on my way to deliver some eggs to our neighbour, so I thought I would call by and say hello.'

'We have already met,' I blurted out, carelessly brushing aside her greeting in my haste to jog her memory.

'What?' she replied smiling, with a curious expression on her face.

'We have already met,' I repeated. 'It was about a month ago. You were the maid who I barged into, in the doorway of the Star. You were carrying a basket and I knocked you over. You must have thought me very rude.'

'And you were kind and polite – not like some who would have sworn at me for getting in the way. You even picked everything up for me. Of course! Now I remember.'

She stood, smiling in recollection of the moment that had seemed so insignificant at the time.

'I notice that you are limping. Did I hurt you with my clumsiness? I am deeply sorry if I was the cause.'

'It is nothing. I have twisted my ankle, that is all. Nothing to do with you,' she answered in a rush, colouring up in embarrassment and suddenly defensive. I cursed myself; I had tried to be considerate and my bungling had clearly upset her. How could I be so inept? There was a painful silence. She must have noticed my crestfallen expression because she seemed to collect herself.

'And how is the work going today?'

I breathed a sigh of relief: 'We have nearly finished this window. We should be starting the next one this afternoon.' Again I kicked myself for the stupidity of my answer. What must she think of the tongue-tied mumbling clod that stood before her? Surely I could do better than this.

'It must look wonderful from inside with the light shining through it,' she said, looking expectantly at me. I could hardly believe my luck, so I plucked up my courage;

'Why don't you come and see? It is mid-day so we will be stopping for a while anyway.' My words came out in a nervous gabble. Filled with self-doubt I knew she would just laugh at me now.

'I'd love to!' she replied.

Martin suddenly and very conveniently, remembered a job that he needed to finish at the other side of the chapel and with a discreet wink to me, he disappeared around the corner of the wall, laughing to himself as he went.

***

Chapter 23

Late summer, 1462

I had met Rose's father and was in complete awe of him. He was a tall, sinewy man with cropped red hair and a ginger beard. Yet although he was a man of some influence, he never once tried to intimidate me or warn me off. I could only hope that he approved of my interest in his daughter.

'Would you care to have a look at the window sir?' I enquired. 'I must hand back the key tomorrow.' I needed to impress John Cooper and I hoped I could convince him that I was worthy of Rose's hand in marriage. It was early one Sunday morning when I met him outside the chapel. I had chosen my moment well; a bright day when I knew that the light from the morning sun would show my work to its best advantage. My feeling of excitement was mixed with some trepidation as I produced the key and we prepared to go inside. The chapel door was made of thick oak planks and studded with stout nails; it was so new that the planks still retained their honey colour and the heavy iron hinges stood out in stark contrast against their dimpled surface. I slipped the heavy key into the lock, and it turned easily with a quiet click; the door swung open, and we stepped inside.

From the subdued interior of the chapel, the sunlit window burst upon us in a celebration of glory; the light flooded through the glass, casting pools of colour on the floor; gold blended into blue; green and red set the floor alight with such splintered brilliance that it seemed to take John's breath away. His forest world was a place of natural colours, the browns and greens of the woodland and the mossy grey of the stones.

'And you have done all this Tom?' he asked after a long pause as he took in the riot of colour.

'Not all of it, sir. Mary at the foot of the cross, and the centurion – they are my work.' He went closer and examined each panel in detail.

'Remarkable, quite remarkable to think you could do all this.'

He had always spoken to me kindly, but now he had a different tone of voice; I could hear respect. As we left, I locked the door behind us, daring to hope that I had won him over.

'You will return to York with Martin soon, I expect. What then?'

'Well, sir, as you know, I have another year of my time to serve. After that I am not sure. I'm hoping that Martin will take me into his employment, but really I need to set myself up as an independent glazier. I will receive my Freeman Certificate from the guild at the end of my apprenticeship. Then I will have to try and gather enough money to set up my own workshop.' I paused, knowing that this was my moment.

‘I had hoped to ask you …that is, I wondered if…’ I could hear myself floundering like a horse in a peat bog. He looked at me fiercely and my courage failed.

‘Well?’ he growled. There was a silence when I knew all hope was lost. Suddenly he laughed and I realised he had been teasing me. ‘You wish to pay court to my daughter!’

‘Yes sir.’ I scarcely recognised my own voice. ‘With your permission, sir,’ I mumbled.

‘And how will you be able to see my Rose? She will be quite miserable after you leave. I know York is only a few miles away, but I will not have her travelling through the forest alone. It is far too dangerous.’

‘We have talked about that, sir.’ A glimpse of optimism had encouraged me. ‘I shall hope that I may afford to hire a horse and come to see her each Sunday, if you will permit me.’

When John Cooper smiled, his face took on an entirely different quality; the authority figure of the King’s Verderer softened to become Rose’s concerned father: ‘You must remember that you have only known each other for a very short time. Perhaps it is too soon to be making plans for the future just yet.’ But somehow, despite his understandable note of caution, I was filled with a new confidence to ask what I needed to know. We stopped at the gate, and with my voice slightly breathless, I managed to look him squarely in the eye and put together the words I had rehearsed over and over in private.

‘Sir, I know that this has been a surprise to you and Mistress Cooper. To tell you the truth, it has been a surprise to me too, and I know that the time that we have known each other has been short. But let me tell you this: upon my honour, there will never be anyone else for me.

Whatever we do, it will be with your permission, and I promise you, I will always treat Rose with respect and make her happy.'

I ended with a rush, and the relief that I felt at getting my speech out intact must have showed.

'Well said, lad!' he laughed, giving me a clap on the shoulder that made me wince.

***

Every Sunday I hired a horse from a local stable and travelled to Morton to see Rose. One day, as I set off down Stonegate, I noticed Martin watching me go with a thoughtful expression on his face. When I returned that evening, he sent me out to fetch wood from the stable. To my surprise, the empty stall now had a resident; Martin had bought a horse whilst I had been away. It was an old chestnut mare that was well past her prime of life but was quite capable of the journey to Rose's house. I ran back to Martin and shook his hand vigorously, seeing the delighted smile on his face.

'We can't have you wasting your money on hiring horses. You need every penny you can get to be able to marry that little lass ... and where's that wood that I sent you for?'

***

As 1462 drew to a close, winter came, and with it the Yuletide festivities. Rose had invited me to be a part of their Christmas celebration, and though I could not stay long, Rose's mother, Mary, made me a bed in their hall and insisted that I stay to celebrate twelfth night, the merriest night of all. They had invited Beth Sawyer and her parents to share the evening with them and to act as witnesses to what would take place. Mary and Rose had prepared a feast that was set out on the big oak courtroom table. They had killed a goose and Mary had made a pie with pigeon breasts and herbs. There were sweet pastries and tarts, with a full round cheese for good measure. The centrepiece of the table was a large haunch of venison: in his role as verderer, John was allowed to take one of the king's deer for himself at Christmas and another at Easter, an act that would get a commoner hanged if he were caught. It was not until several weeks later that I found out that he had sent the best cuts of venison to the Bolton family.

Under ordinary circumstances we would have drunk ale but since this was a special day, John had bought a small barrel of good wine and he served it with our meal. Candles were lit as darkness fell and their soft light fell on the faces of the gathered family and friends. The furthest corners of the hall disappeared into shadow, with the occasional crackle of a log sending sparks drifting upwards.

As we sat by the fire, and the food and drink were a comfortable memory, the moment when I must pluck up courage and make a good show of myself was upon me and I could feel my legs trembling. Without realising, I discovered that I was holding the sunstone, turning it, and was rubbing my fingers over its smooth surface. It had kept me safe ever since Martha had pressed it into my hand on the eve of battle, and now I hoped it would give me the courage to overcome my nervousness. I was happy for Rose that she had both her parents to give her their blessing but when I thought of my own mother and my sister Molly, a sadness came over me, even on this happy evening.

I realised that Rose's parents were looking expectantly at me. They knew that she and I would marry in the coming summer and we had chosen this special evening to make our betrothal. I stood, and offering Rose my hand, I gently helped her to her feet where we faced each other, smiling and a little uncomfortable. I took both of Rose's hands in mine, and looking into her eyes, my nervousness subsided.

'Rose Cooper, let it be known that I make you my solemn promise of marriage. I want no other and I pledge in front of witnesses, that before the next year is out, we shall be married. I will treat you with respect and give you the best life that I can give you on this earth.'

In the soft glow of the candlelight, I saw her blush in a mixture of embarrassment and pleasure.

'Tom Gifford, I accept your pledge and now I give you mine. I will marry you and seek no other. I will follow you where you lead me. I will accept good times and bad times with you and give you my promise that we shall never be parted in this life.'

We stood in the firelight, quite spellbound by the moment, still facing each other with arms outstretched, handclasped, unwilling or unable to break free from our moment of happiness. Rose's parents gazed up at the two of us, captivated by the tableau before them. Mary sniffed quietly and wiped away a tear with her kerchief. Beth's mother, too, gave a loud sniffle. Inevitably, it was Beth who broke the silence, prompted by a good quantity of strong wine:

'Go on give her a kiss, you big daft bugger!' she exclaimed. I complied, timidly at first, then with more enthusiasm. There was a loud whispered reprimand from Beth's mother: 'Hush Beth, you will show us up,' but Beth was not to be deterred:

'That'll do for goodness sake,' yelled Beth. 'Don't eat the poor lass!'

In the eyes of the church, now, having declared our betrothal formally and before witnesses, we were as good as married; Rose's parents had been married in church, but they knew of many other couples for whom this simple ceremony had sufficed. When the last story had been told and the fire burned low, it was time for the evening to end. As the household settled into a contented silence, Rose's parents pretended not to hear the click of the latch and the creak of the stair as she crept down to find me.

***

Chapter 24

January 1463

The snow began to fall, gently at first but as daylight faded, the flakes became bigger until, as a gloomy twilight descended, Morton on the Forest became an expanse of white, covering the grey thatch of the cottages in its silent mantle. At the Verderer's House, Mary Cooper waited for her husband's return with mild anxiety; the snow had been known to cause big branches to snap off the trees and plunge to the ground. She would be pleased when he was safely home.

'This looks as if it is going to snow all night,' she observed as Rose put on her winter cloak, ready to take an evening meal to Father Routledge, the young priest who had taken up residence only a few weeks ago. Mary Cooper, and one or two other households had done their best to make sure he had enough to eat. The task was not arduous, and Mary liked to think of their support as an act of Christian charity. Rose picked up her basket and prepared to face the white world of whirling flakes outside the warmth of their home. She pulled on the deep hood, burying her face in its heavy brown woollen fabric.

'Can't imagine that your Tom is going to be able to travel to see you if this keeps up.'

'Oh, I expect he'll manage. It may stop soon.' Rose's optimism was born of wishful thinking; she could not entertain the thought that Tom might be kept from her.

'Straight there and back then. Don't stop to talk.' Mary was still waiting for John to return. 'I shall not rest easily until we are all home, and the door is barred for the night.'

'That will not be a problem – he has never said much more than "Thank you," or "God bless you," each time I have been.' Rose replied in a tone that suggested she was somewhat put out by Father Piers' lack of conversation.

The simple dwelling that had been built to house the chantry priest was opposite their home, some thirty yards away across the green. The world had settled into a dull grey as twilight fell, so that the snow looked like badly polished pewter and the houses were indistinct shapes, swathed beneath the clinging shroud that now obscured even familiar landmarks.

John Cooper appeared as Rose set out; her father was stamping his boots to free them of snow, blowing on is fingers and complaining of the weather.

A last reminder from Mary: 'Hurry back!' and Rose set off, her boots swishing in the deepening snow. She blinked as snowflakes settled on her lashes and pulled her hood further forward to cover her face. All was silent; not a bird sang, nor a dog barked to breach the hushed sweep of the snow. As she reached the furthest edge of the green, she could see a chink of light through the wooden shutter on the single window that peered out from beneath the thatch. Two yards from the cottage, she checked and looked down. She was certain that the priest had not ventured out all afternoon, yet here were fresh footprints leading from the woodland to his door. Rose studied them carefully. She had been brought up in the forest and her father had taught her his skills; she could read tracks with ease, and noticed that these footprints entered the house but that there were none leaving. Father Piers must have a visitor, and by the size of the marks it must be a man.

She approached the door, preparing to knock, yet still she hesitated, her natural curiosity tempting her to find out who the visitor might be. She could hear the low sound of two male voices from within, but could not distinguish a single word. 'Shame on you, Rose Cooper!' she scolded herself, 'Eavesdropping like a common scandalmonger,' and she gave a sharp double knock on the door. Instantly, voices were silenced. There was a sound of scraping furniture, and eventually, the door was unbolted and opened the merest fraction, letting a chink of light escape from within. The face of Father Piers squinted through the narrow gap:

'Yes?' he enquired in a voice that seemed to tremble slightly, perhaps from the cold, Rose thought.

'It is only me Father, it's Rose, with your supper.'

With an abrupt 'Thank you. God bless you,' he reached round the door, and Rose saw a thin, bony hand grasp the basket and whisk it from view as the door closed in her face with a solid thud. She heard the bolts slide back into place, and she was left outside in the falling snow.

'Well, there's gratitude for you!' she grumbled to herself, partly in disbelief and partly in annoyance as she made her way home.

'Thank goodness you are back. It is a poor night out there.' Mary's voice showed relief that her family were safely indoors for the night. Rose shook the snow from her cloak and closed the door.

'What do you know about our priest?' she asked, still confused by his lack of appreciation.

'Not much,' Mary replied. 'Why do you ask?'

'Oh, just curious I suppose. He never speaks much - sometimes manages to say thank you as he closes the door.'

'Perhaps he is shy; he's only young remember. A monastic life would make him like that, especially with a young woman calling on him after dark.'

'He had a visitor tonight, though.' John Cooper's deep voice came from his seat by the hearth where he was thawing out his soaked feet.

'How ever did you know that?' Rose was a little taken aback by her father's observation; she thought she was the only one who knew and had looked forward to sharing this titbit of gossip with her parents.

'I saw a horse tied up, way back in the wood behind his house. It almost looked as if it was being hidden there, out of sight from the road. I went to take a look in case it meant trouble. I tell you what though, it was no common palfrey; this was a gentleman's horse with a military saddle. Whoever owns it is no member of the clergy, that is for sure.'

'He says his first mass at the chapel on Sunday. Perhaps he will be more forthcoming then,' Mary offered. 'We shall have chance to hear him preach and perhaps he will introduce himself properly.'

John rose wearily, stretching his aching joints. 'Bed for me,' he announced. 'I have firewood to deliver to the castle at Sheriff Hutton and that means harnessing up the sledge. It will be an early start and a long day.'

***

Rose sat by the hearth with her mother, enjoying the last flames as the fire settled for the night.

'We should be going soon, Rose. I don't want to disturb him when he is so tired.'

'Before you go mother, I wanted to ask you ...' Rose paused, unsure how to frame the question she held in her mind.

'Ask me what?'

'About the Sighing Stone.' Mary looked across to her daughter and tilted her head quizzically to one side in a gesture that said 'Well, I am waiting.'

'How do you use it? Why can I not get it to help me? When we visited last year at Candlemas, you said it gave you a message... "He is coming for you"... but did you mean Tom?'

'So many questions for such a late hour! Of course I meant Tom. The colours in the sky said that! He has come for you, and you will marry him in a few months from now, so who else could it be?'

'Yes, but why can I not use it? I have tried and failed. You told me that the knowledge is passed from mother to daughter so why is its power denied to me?'

'I cannot answer that. Perhaps you may inherit it later, or perhaps not at all, but it is true that the gift has followed our female bloodline for generations. My mother - your grandmother Jane - she had the Sight; she even foresaw her own death. That must be twenty five years ago now, when the pestilence came up the river from Hull in 1438. If for some reason the gift has not been granted to you, you have been spared a great burden. Who knows, when you are married to Tom and you have children of your own, you might have a daughter and she may surprise you. If that is so, you must watch her carefully at the age when she turns from child to woman; be especially vigilant for any hint that it has awakened in her. Then you must explain the Sight and make sure that she knows the danger that comes with it.'

Rose gave a heavy sigh of tiredness mixed with frustration.

'And now we must both be a' bed.' Mary lit a small candle in a wooden holder and passed it to Rose. She turned and blew out the remaining candles one by one, leaving the dull glow of the embers as the only illumination in the darkened room. 'Tomorrow promises to be a difficult day for all of us if this snow continues.'

***

How I had missed Rose's company. As a sodden February turned into a brighter March, the brisk days began to lengthen, and the streets around York became passable again after the heavy snowfall at the end of January had reduced them to foul, slush laden squalor. The road through the great forest had become a scene of whirling drift: I had to forego my visit to Morton on two successive Sundays, and the week that followed each one found me the loneliest that I had ever been. I longed to be with Rose, and I knew that our enforced separation would be making her miserable too.

'Never mind, lad, just think how pleased she'll be when this lot is gone!' Alice had tried to console me, but it was a lost cause. She looked at my gloomy face and continued, indomitably:

'When you are married, what are your plans?'

'I don't know,' I replied. 'Haven't really thought that far yet.' I knew it sounded inadequate, but I was deeply resentful of the distance between us and would not allow myself to be cheered up, even by Alice.

'Well, I have thought about it for you then,' she said, in a determined voice. 'Martin and I want you both to live here, with us. There is enough room for us all, and it would be such company for me while you and Martin are at the minster workshop.'

'Oh Alice, thank you ...' I began, but before I could say another word, she had caught me up in a firm embrace,

'Well, that's settled then!' She concluded with a smile. 'We all have something to look forward to now.' Once again, I remembered the frosty welcome I had received from Aunt Anne and how lucky I had been to meet Martin and Alice.

The knock on the door came as an intrusion that evening as we sat at table, finishing one of Alice's custard tarts. It was early evening and the bell for Vespers had just sounded when Martin answered the door. 'Friend to see you,' he announced and wiping the last of the crumbs from my mouth, I went to the door.

'God give you good evening Tom.'

My mouth fell open, but no words were forthcoming. 'Rob ...' I finally managed. It had been nearly a year since we had last met and much as I liked him, I knew that this was no social call; it could only mean trouble. 'I would invite you in, but Martin and Alice ...' I floundered, struggling to absorb the unexpectedness of his presence.

'No need. There is an alehouse called the Angel where we can sit and talk over old times.' Taking me by the arm, he led me down the street.

'Rob, if you are here to ask me to join you in another of your escapades, I must tell you ...'

'Wait till we are settled, and you can tell me how life is treating you. Exciting prospects for you this year, I hear.'

He knew about my marriage; he seemed to know everything. He had probably had me followed for days. My heart sank. This must be Sir Richard de Coverdale's doing; I was caught and could not break free.

He leaned across the table and deposited two tankards. 'Well now, how are you Tom?'

'Rob, I ...' but he held up his hand to cut me short.

'As I think you have guessed, I have a favour to ask.' I waited. He looked down at the table as if gathering his thoughts. 'You will remember our little adventure on the Aurora?' He laughed. 'You seemed to find the sea rather disagreeable!'

I waited patiently, wishing he would get to the point. I nodded, unsmiling.

'And you remember I shared a confidence with you about the priest at Morton on the Forest. I may even have explained that to share that information would be an act of treason.' The word 'treason' alone sent a shiver down my spine.

'But I have told no one Rob, I swear before God I have not said a word.' Surely he was not here to arrest me? Then I remembered: "I have a favour to ask you".

'Be calm, Tom. I need your help, or rather, Sir Richard does.' He paused and took a long draught of ale before continuing: 'As you already know, we have reliable information that there is a plot to overthrow our sovereign, King Edward IV. You have seen with your own eyes that the priest at Morton on the Forest, Piers Routledge, is in the thick of it. He is exchanging information from messengers both here at home, and from Scotland and France – you will remember our little encounter on the beach? Well, we have it on good authority that a full scale uprising is being prepared for next year, but we need to be certain.' He looked up at me. 'We need to keep a close watch on his visitors, and learn who else may be involved ... and there lies the problem. Morton is such a tiny village that a stranger would stand out like a turd on a shovel. We need somebody who would not arouse suspicion – somebody who lives there.'

'But I don't live there, I visit Rose for one day a week that is all ...' and I stopped as I realised what he was leading up to. 'No!' I said loudly. 'No you cannot ask it!'

'But she would be ideally placed to watch him. She even takes his meals. He would never suspect her.' How much he knew! The extent of his intelligence gathering was alarming.

'No. I cannot drag her into this and put her in danger.'

'She would be in no danger whatever, I guarantee it. All we ask is that she continues to do exactly as she is now. She does not need to ask questions or show any special interest in him. Just carry on as normal.'

'Then what would she have to do?' Once again I could feel myself being ensnared despite myself.

'She can read and write, can't she?' I nodded warily.

'All we ask is that she makes a record of who visits – just a brief description will do; when they visit - date, time of day and anything else that she thinks worthy of note. I will give her a packet and a seal. She would seal her note, place it in the packet and a post rider will collect it from the Star once a week.'

'That is all?' I asked.

In my mind, I am standing helplessly, waist deep in the surf, watching the mocking face of Jasper Griswold taunt me. as he slips from our hands.

'That is all. I promise you.'

'And in return?'

'You are becoming a man who drives a hard bargain, Tom Gifford! What would you want in return?'

I had already thought this through while he had been talking: 'My indentures. I would like you to buy my indentures from the guild for Martin. I would be free to trade as an independent craftsman, and Martin would be compensated. I would need to talk to Rose first of course.'

'Then I think we have an agreement.'

***

Chapter 25

Spring 1463

The crisply folded paper stared up at Rose and she felt a tremor of excitement. Taking a candle, she melted the stick of dark red sealing wax and dripped several blobs onto the fold to secure the contents. As the wax began to set, she took a small metal seal and pressed it down firmly, leaving an indentation the size of a silver shilling with a crown and a large letter R beneath it. She looked down with a feeling of satisfaction, and once the seal was fully hardened, she slipped the letter into a heavy leather pouch, tied with a thong. This was her first dispatch and she had been told it would be collected at some undisclosed time during the next few days.

Rose had taken no persuading to undertake the task; once Tom had explained the implication of being licensed as a free tradesman by the guild and released from his apprenticeship, she found the assignment exciting. She could support her betrothed, and not only secure their future income but help to expose a traitor.

'You do understand that you may tell no one about this,' Tom had warned her. 'Even your mother must not know.'

'But what will they say at the Star? You know what a gossip Maude Chapman is. It will be all round the village in no time if she thinks there is something unusual going on.'

'We have taken your father into our confidence. As a representative of the Crown, he understands discretion, but even he does not have the full story. He has agreed to say that you are sending bills for timber supplied to the castle. Nobody will question that. Just remember, all you do is watch and take note – you must not ask questions or try to do anything that changes your routine. These are dangerous people who will stop at nothing if they think they have been compromised.'

Rose had at first been excited by the secrecy and danger of what she had undertaken, but it soon became clear that her role was becoming tedious. Each week she took a fresh sheet of paper and annotated it with date and time, being careful not to sign it. She reported any casual conversation she might have had with the priest, but there was precious little of any significance for the first week, when she sent her report. Nor did the second week yield anything more promising; Piers Routledge might as well be a member of a silent order, so keenly did he keep his own counsel.

Rose was fighting back her frustration and beginning to wonder whether there was any substance to Tom's story of a conspiracy, when events removed her doubt. It began in the chapel, as her family attended mass and the sermon was delivered. Rose found Father Piers' thick accent difficult to understand when he switched from Latin to English. He chose for his theme, the life of the Scottish saint, Mungo, telling how Mungo was the illegitimate son of a witch who was thrown from a cliff while he was in her womb. Rose was uneasily aware that Piers was looking directly at her and her mother when he spoke of witchcraft. Surely he could not suspect them. Could he? Their womenfolk had hidden their dangerous knowledge for generations of a secret sisterhood. Had this priest somehow detected an aura of concealment? His eyes seemed to seek her out, probing her thoughts. She dismissed it, determined not to look guilty, but somehow it had shaken her complacency.

That evening she had the first feeling of anxiety as she took her basket and set off on the road around the green. When she passed the wooden block by the forge, she looked away remembering the grisly sight of Noah Bolton's severed hand, left as a warning to others. Although the evening sun was low, it was still good daylight as she followed the path around the top of the green, watching the cottage carefully for anything out of the ordinary. Smoke was issuing from the hole in the thatch, but that was not what had caught her attention; the shutters were closed. Sure enough, as she drew close, she heard voices from inside. She hesitated. She had been clearly told not to put herself in danger, yet how was she ever to find out anything by being too timid?

She stood by the shuttered window and lingered, trying to catch the faintest scrap of conversation; anything at all that she could report to help Tom. There was nothing else for it. Trying to avoid the molehills by the window, she pressed her ear against the shutter. There were two voices, of that she was certain, both men talking in low tones.

'... when can I ...' That was Piers, she was sure.

'... will be here tomorrow...' A reply sounding mildly irritated.

A dog began to bark in the distance, completely drowning any chance of hearing anything more. Rose cursed her luck, but at least she would have something to report; someone or something was expected tomorrow. It must be important, and she knew she must be extra vigilant if she was to discover what was going on.

Her sealed note was collected the following day. In it, she had recorded the few scraps of conversation, including the additional detail that both voices shared a common accent. Rose kept close watch all day, but nothing out of the ordinary happened; Morton went about its business as usual and though she watched each traveller who came by, studying their clothing for anomaly, nobody caught her eye.

As the daylight faded, Rose gave up. Whoever it was that Father Piers expected clearly was not coming today, unless he travelled at night, which was dangerous and unlikely. She gathered up the basket with his supper and set out on her nightly journey. She had taken no more than half a dozen steps when she saw a figure emerge from the wood and glance around. Rose stopped; if she carried on she would alert whoever had arrived. She turned and went back into the house, seeming to have forgotten something. Then after waiting awhile, she continued, going quickly to the shuttered window and listening intently. This time it was a voice she recognised, and the chill of dread grabbed her like a cold hand twisting her gut. The harsh grinding speech of Steven St. Claire was unmistakable.

'Have no doubt, Piers, the Welsh will join us. Then Henry will take back his crown from the Yorkist usurper. Even now he gathers strength in his northern fortresses.'

'And in the meanwhile, it seems that our messenger has been delayed. You may not stay here; you will be seen.'

'I will return tomorrow at nightfall.'

Rose was in a turmoil of indecision, and she knew she must act quickly, yet the sound of Steven St. Claire's voice had terrified her. She must appear normal, or risk detection. With a hand that shook, she tapped lightly on the door. Again, all fell silent, and the sound of the bolts being withdrawn warned her to be ready. With a gabbled 'Your supper Father,' she turned and with a struggle, managed to overcome the urge to run.

When she opened the leather pouch to place her letter inside, Rose found there was a note waiting for her.

'No more timber deliveries are required. We have all that is needed. Cease immediately.'

Rose was crestfallen. Why this sudden stop? She had the best information that she had been able to gather, and they must have it. She decided to ignore the instruction and write one last message, with every detail she had overheard, and identifying Steven St. Claire.

***

'This is the last time I shall deliver his supper,' Rose consoled herself as she made the familiar journey. 'I have done enough to earn Tom's reward. The priest can feed himself from now on.'

She tapped on the door and waited; it seemed he had not heard her, so she knocked again. Then, without warning, a hand was clamped over her mouth by someone who had stolen up behind her, stifling a scream and dragging her head sharply backwards as she was roughly bundled through the door. Whoever had seized her had crept from the edge of the wood in complete silence.

'So it *is* you! You are the one who has been spying on us.' Piers had been waiting, keeping Rose at the door to give his accomplice chance to catch her. 'You have pretended to bring me food and all the while you have been spying on me. Who are you working for, girl? Who is your master?'

The hand gripping Rose's mouth relaxed, and she was thrown on the floor.

'I remember you.' The cold voice of Steven sounded like a butcher's knife being sharpened. He looked down on her as she lay at his feet. 'Who have you contacted?'

'Nobody sir, I do not know what you mean.' She was in tears now, and whimpering with fright.

'Oh, I think you know exactly what he means.' Piers looked on dispassionately. 'I found your footprints in the molehill soil outside my window. I knew then what you had been up to, and this morning I found proof,' and he held out Rose's note. 'Now we have no choice.'

'Father Piers, I beg you. You are a man of God, please let me go.'

'I think God will not want you. You have committed a sacrilege by betraying me. The gates of Hell are waiting for you.'

'We have no time for this, priest. We must leave tonight before her friends come looking for us.'

'And her?' Piers nodded towards the figure that lay before him.

'We bring her with us. There are people who will have questions for her – and believe me, she will answer them – they are very persuasive. And when they are finished, then it will be my turn.'

***

It was nearly dark when John Cooper was disturbed at his meal by a loud knocking at the door. People did not call at this time of night unless it was an emergency.

'I will answer it,' Mary said quickly. 'It may be a birthing that needs my help.'

The knocking came again, and the urgent nature of its summons caused John to shake his head. 'No Mary. I will call you if you are needed.'

As soon as the door was unbarred, a figure burst into the room without waiting for invitation.

'Why Maude, what is it? Whatever is wrong?' Mary had appeared behind her husband and now stepped forward, taking Maude Chapman by the arm.

'They have Rose, mistress. They have taken her. I knew there was something odd when the priest came to collect your package ...' John looked at her, his face grey with anxiety. 'He said it was a business matter for the Dean and Chapter and he would deliver it. He seemed shifty so I watched him until the second man arrived.'

She paused to draw breath and as the torrent of words halted, John thrust his face into hers with uncharacteristic fierceness. 'What have you seen girl? Where is Rose?'

'They have taken her with them. The priest and Steven St. Claire ... they left on horseback, and I came straight here.'

'What does this mean John, why have they taken her?' but he brushed her aside.

'Maude, I need your help. Can you run to Len Brealey's house and rouse him. Tell him to gather as many of our men as he can raise. Tell them Rose is in great danger.'

***

As she slammed the door behind her husband, Mary Cooper felt her fear turn to rage:

'How could you have let our only daughter put her life at risk, passing notes, spying on people; You must have been mad to allow it. Steven St. Claire is a brute. You saw what he did to Noah. God knows what he may be doing to Rose right now.' John raced to saddle his horse. with her parting words still ringing in his ears.

Now she was alone, pacing the floor, in an agony of anxiety. She looked out of the window towards the green: in the darkness she could see pinpoints of lanterns and the shapes of men as they gathered round John. She watched them set off out of the village until they vanished into the darkness of the forest, heading north in a tight group, and still her anger burned brightly within her. She must protect her daughter, and she knew of only one way to do it.

***

Piers and Steven knew that time was of the essence. Steven had hauled Rose roughly up and seated her astride his horse, behind him. Her hands were tied in front of her, and her face was swollen from the blow she had received when she refused to cooperate. They had left the priest's house in such haste that the fire still burned, and the door was open. Pausing only to gather a few essentials they had run for their lives, taking Rose with them. Now, on horseback, they headed north.

'Where are we to go?' Piers had lost all pretence of courage.

'There is a friendly house just a day's ride towards Whitby. Make no mistake priest, they are following us, and you really would not like them to catch us.'

'We could just turn her loose. They might give up the chase and let us go.'

'Caput lupinum!' Steven retorted angrily. 'Wolf's head, that's what you are now – an outlaw. If we are caught alive we would be brought before the king's justice, and if we defend ourselves we may be slain and our heads carried to the king for we are outlaws, and of no more consequence than wolves. Now hold your tongue and ride.'

***

Mary hastened along the path, heedless of the thorns that snagged her cloak or the branches that whipped her face; personal comfort was of no significance to a mother whose child was in deadly peril. Finally she realised that she had reached her destination as a clearing opened before her. There, towering above her in sombre silhouette against the night sky, was the Sighing Stone, impassive and waiting.

Gasping for breath, she halted in front of the great obelisk and composed herself. The air was still and quiet; the sky was a black satin cloth where a silver needlepoint of stars created a celestial tapestry. Calm now, her breathing was under control, but within her, a cold fury drove her on. She lay her cloth bundle on the grass and knelt, as if in prayer.

First she took salt and placed a small pile at the foot of the stone. Next she took bread and placed it beside the salt. Lastly, she took two berries of deadly nightshade in the palm of her hand, where she regarded their black, rounded shapes closely.

'This, for the priest,' she hissed, 'and this for the knight.' She raised the berries to her lips and softly blew across them, sending her exhalation into the darkness of the sky. Carefully, she picked up the first berry and placed it beside the salt, then the second beside the bread, where they stared up at her like the dark eyes of a malevolent serpent.

'Sican,' she breathed, her voice shaking slightly as she surrendered herself to the darkness of her task. 'Sican' again, drawing down the inherited wisdom of so many generations before her; 'Sican' for a third time and she was at one with the awesome power that had embraced her, swirling her into a timeless void where she surrendered to the whispered murmurings that seemed to come from the very air around her.

Standing now, and spreading her arms, she gently placed her face against the rough surface. It felt warm and welcoming on her cheek as she began to murmur an invocation. As she spoke, she swayed from side to side, her arms outspread and palms flat against the obelisk. As if some force had struck her, she staggered back. Slowly, like one in the grip of a mighty enchantment she pointed to the sky with both hands and held herself rigid, as still as the great stone itself, for what seemed an age. Then she turned, gathered up her cloth and quietly left the clearing.

***

Rose thought the night would never end. She was frightened, uncomfortable and wondered what fate might be awaiting her. She was being bounced roughly, and without stirrups it was hard to stay upright. She knew she would have been missed by now, but how would her father know which way she had gone? They would bring dogs of course, but at this pace, they might not catch up in time. She thought of Tom, and how she wished he was part of the rescue party.

She realised that she must look at what choices she had left to save herself. Her hands were tied, and she began to work at the rope to ease the binding enough to slip her hands free. If she could do that, Steven had a dagger at his belt; if she was quick, she could draw it and stab him, or cut his throat if she was brave enough. Failing everything, she could use the dagger on herself.

They paused after an hour to rest the horses and Rose was allowed to dismount. She listened carefully for any sound of pursuit, but the night was quiet, save for a breeze that had sprung up, rustling the branches and sending clouds scudding across the sky.

'Looks like there is a storm coming,' Steven muttered, as he dragged Rose up behind him.

Sure enough, the sky had darkened, and thick clouds had gathered, making the night even blacker. It was unnatural for the weather to change so quickly. The first rumble of thunder rolled menacingly above them, as though the sound was bouncing from one cloud to another. The wind had increased, swaying the tallest treetops and clattering the branches high above their heads. Now it was right above them.

'Mother!' Rose breathed to herself, her despair unbelievably giving way to optimism. 'This is mother's doing! She has magicked the elements; she has raised a storm.'

A flash of lightning flooded the clouds with a flickering bewitchment. For a second, she saw the outlined shape of the priest riding ahead of them. Then all was plunged into a deeper blackness. The air crackled with menace, and Rose could feel her scalp prickling and tingling; her ears hummed with a dull note that rose and fell. Then a brilliant flash and crack of thunder above them dazzled her senses; Steven's horse reared, whinnying with fright and Rose was thrown to the ground with a thud that drove the wind from her lungs. Swearing and kicking its flanks, he brought the frightened animal under control and signalled Rose to get up, but still winded, she could not respond. Angrily, he dismounted and raising his mailed fist, he strode towards her. With another deafening crash, a brilliant blue and white light seemed to trickle out of the sky with a sound like tearing silk, and gathering momentum, it hurled itself in a wicked, flickering serpent's tongue of brilliance onto Steven's outstretched fist. There was a moment while he stood, his hand like the white hot metal from the blacksmith's forge and a sound of sizzling meat. Then he fell, his body convulsing grotesquely as he died.

***

Chapter 26

June 1463

When John Cooper's anger had abated and we were sure that he would allow my betrothal to Rose to continue, Martin and I went to the guildhall to complete the transaction over my indentures. The Glaziers' Guild had already been paid a settlement by Sir Richard de Coverdale and Martin was to collect his portion today.

From the huge space of the guildhall, we had been shown to an inner office where we waited for the guild official to appear to conduct the ceremony.

'What happens now, Martin?'

'I don't know exactly, but I have to present my half of the indentures, to make sure they match with yours.' We both had our scrolls ready for inspection, and I waited nervously. After all Rose had been through, this had to make it worthwhile if I was to regain her father's respect. The door creaked open and an official of the guild entered, wearing a gold chain and robes that showed his rank.

'Papers please, gentlemen,' and he took both halves of the indenture and examined the dog tooth serration that had been cut to separate them. Having satisfied himself that they were a perfect match, he produced a purse. 'Guildsman Garnett, this is your compensation for the early loss of your apprentice.' Turning to me, he reached into a drawer and unfolded a scroll. 'And this is your Journeyman Certificate. You have passed your apprenticeship, but you have not yet produced a master piece that we have accepted as being worthy of the title of master craftsman. You are free to trade and be paid a wage on a daily basis.' With the precious scroll tucked inside my jerkin, we returned to Stonegate.

***

We were to be married in June, when we would become husband and wife officially. The service was to be held in the chantry chapel at Rose's home, and the celebrant would be the new priest, Father Tybalt.

'Your father is an important man, and his status demands a proper wedding. Besides, I dare not risk offending him again.'

'Why Tom, I do believe you are scared of him!' Rose teased.

'Not scared, terrified,' I corrected. 'He is not a man to trifle with.'

'Go on with you, he is a pussycat! I just have to smile at him, and he will do anything I ask!' she said, sweetly.

The weather on the fifteenth day of June was perfect: the sky was a pure azure with mares tails of cloud streaked high above us. Overhead, swallows were swooping and chattering on the wing, as if they too, had come to celebrate our marriage. The entire community had turned out to share in the ceremony, not just the village but people from farms and cottages dotted about in the forest.

When Rose stepped out for the short walk to the chapel with her father, she could not believe her eyes; so many people and all here for her. Cheers and well wishes were shouted all the way to the chapel. Some of the gathered crowd had clearly been sampling the ale at the Star already, judging by the muffled ribaldry that brought howls of laughter from those near enough to hear.

I turned to greet Rose as she entered the chapel, and her beauty made me catch my breath. With her mother's help, she had made a long gown of white linen that reached to the floor. Her auburn hair was washed and brushed till it shone like a golden cascade, spreading in tumbling confusion over her shoulders. Round her head she wore a plaited garland of summer flowers; honeysuckle, cornflower and ragged robin, whilst in her hand was a posy of white roses. With the robust support of Beth Sawyer following cheerfully behind, her face radiated happiness.

Inside the chapel, as she approached the altar, she saw me and smiled, and my heart went out to her. The light flooded through the east window casting a spangled palate of colour on Rose's white dress as she stood before the altar.

'My Tom made that. That's where it all began,' she thought, feeling light-headed with joy.

When Father Tybalt had pronounced his final blessing, we came out of the chapel and were thronged by well-wishers. Rose held my arm, and we were strewn with flower petals as we made our way down the path and finally headed towards the Star.

She looked up at me, and to my surprise, there were tears in her eyes. 'What is it?' I asked anxiously. 'What has upset you?'

'Tom Gifford, you make pretty windows, but you are the most unromantic clod I have ever met. There is nothing the matter with me - I am happy! I don't think I shall ever feel happier than this as long as I live. I want today to last forever.'

As the sun dipped and night began to fall it was time for me to lead my bride away from the inn and make our way home. We received a riotous send-off with the customary advice to newly-weds to help us on our way. The door of the Star closed behind us, extinguishing the pool of light from the crowded tavern. The party would go on long into the night and there would be some sore heads in the morning.

As we stood outside, I gave Rose a tender, lingering kiss and held her close.

'I'm never going to let you go,' I whispered.

'Don't you worry, you won't get chance to!'

Rose smiled at a distant memory that had fleetingly been reawakened, of a flight of wild geese that she had watched disappearing into the sunset, so long ago.

The twilight was gathering as we walked home. The first bats were flitting soundlessly through the air, catching insects on the wing. The festivities at the Star had resumed behind us and I heard a piper strike up a dance tune. Somewhere from in the darkness of the wood, a blackbird trilled out its farewell notes to the happiest day of my life.

***

We returned to York as newlyweds by the end of the week, living with Martin and Alice at Stonegate, beneath the towering edifice of the minster and there we started to find a new life together.

'And thank the Lord for his mercy!' exclaimed Alice on our return. 'Rose, you are an angel sent to me from on high. Welcome to our home – *your* home I should say,' and she embraced Rose with a matronly hug.

'Life can be easier now,' I reassured Alice with a smile. 'Rose is no stranger to hard work, are you Rosie? You can take some of the heavier tasks from Alice.'

'Here, don't you go saying that I can not manage to look after you all, Thomas Gifford!' Alice's indignation was short lived: 'Mind you, the bucket seems to get heavier every time I go to the well. I suppose I must be getting older,' she added with a sigh.

'She loves you as much as if you were her own son,' Rose acknowledged later when we were alone.

'You don't mind doing some of the heavier jobs for her, do you? I cannot bear to see her struggle.'

'Mind? How could I mind? Apart from anything else, it is my duty. She has taken me into her home, made me welcome, offered me her friendship where she could easily have resented me. I am young and strong and have grown up with hard work. Of course I don't mind.'

And so it was settled. We had been allowed to make our private quarters above the stable. It was functional but cramped. Still, we only used this room for sleeping; we ate together and shared the fire until it was time to bring the day to a close. Then, we would make our way across the yard and climb up the ladder to our bed in the hayloft. As we drifted off to sleep, we could hear the mare shuffle occasionally beneath us as she too settled down for the night. It was a comforting sound, with only the cry of an owl breaking the silence outside.

***

It was mid-July, and the feast of St. Mary Magdalene, a day that always reminded me of my mother – Saint Maggie's Day she used to joke. It was late afternoon when Martin received word that a long overdue consignment of lead channelling was at last unloaded and awaiting collection on the staithe by the river,

'Will you go to the wharf and take delivery of the shipment Tom?'

'Is this the lead you ordered from France?'

'Aye, the boat carrying our goods has been held up by unfavourable winds. It is eight days late already. Can you oversee the loading onto a carrier's cart? Oh, and can you call in and tell Alice we will be late.'

I had to pass our door in Stonegate, and giving Martin's message would only take a moment. Alice and Rose were busy, but seeing me, they stopped. Rose was preparing vegetables and helping Alice make a pie for supper.

'The heat has turned the butter rancid. I cannot make pastry with this Rose. Would you go along to the butter market for me, or we shall have nothing to eat.'

'I can walk some of the way with you,' I offered, pleased at the unexpected prospect.

The streets were busy as we made our way towards the market. The air was filled with the calls of the street traders, advertising their wares to the bustle of passers-by. A musician stood on a street corner, playing a pipe and tabor while further down was a man leading a small bear, with a strong chain that was fastened to a belt around the animal's waist. It looked thoroughly dispirited and was given a sharp reminder with a long switch if it showed reluctance to perform. After a rap on the snout, the bear raised itself up on its hind legs and walked a few paces around in a circle to the delight of the small group of people who had stopped to watch. A few coins were thrown on the floor and swiftly gathered up by the showman.

All was noise and bustle. We had reached the market cross where the stalls of the butter market were set out. Here our ways parted, and I would head for the street that led down towards the river. I was about to say goodbye when my attention was caught by a movement to my right. I stopped so abruptly that Rose bundled into me.

'What is it?' she asked, and when I did not answer, 'What is wrong?'

A well-dressed woman in a bright red gown and white bonnet was walking slowly from stall to stall, taking her time and chatting to the traders.

'See the woman near the cheese stall?'

'The one with her back to us? She looks wealthy; only a rich family could afford cloth so brightly dyed. There is something about the style of her gown, too. It is not cut in the English fashion. It looks really expensive.'

'Forget about her clothing. Look carefully - she is being followed.'

The shadowy figure of a man was dodging along the edge of the street, skirting the passers-by, and keeping to the deep shade of the buildings. Every time she moved, he kept pace at a distance, making sure that he stayed in close proximity but avoiding being seen. He was dressed in a dark brown tunic with a deep hood pulled over his head so that his face was hidden. The woman would soon have to pass one of the narrow twisting alleys between buildings that were just wide enough to walk through. Swiftly, the man moved ahead of her and lay in wait, whilst she was oblivious to the trap that was about to be sprung.

'Look - over there.' I pointed to my right.

Rose squinted against the light. 'Do you mean the woman by the stalls?'

'No, look past her. See the man hiding in the alley?'

'No! ... Tom!' Rose called urgently, but I had already set off at a run.

She hurried after me, but I realised that we were already too late. As the unwary woman approached the entrance to the alleyway, the man darted out and grabbed her. With one hand over her mouth and his arm round her waist he half-carried, half-dragged her out of sight. Like a spider that has waited for its prey to be ensnared in its web, his swift rush was well timed and effective; she vanished soundlessly into the dark recess.

I arrived a moment later and plunged headlong into the alley, followed by Rose. I found them a few yards into the passage; the man had pinned the woman against the wall and already forced her to remove the rings from her fingers. He was reaching for her purse, grabbing it from the leather belt with his right arm whilst holding her head pressed against the wall with his left hand when I arrived. With an oath, he released his grip and turning, we faced each other. I was completely unprepared for what I saw.

'Griswold!' I shouted in disbelief, but how he had changed. The shaft that I hoped had killed him as he ran for his life, had left a terrible mark.

His silent rush took me by surprise, and he came at me with alarming speed, a knife appearing in his hand. I just had time to step aside so the blade missed its intended target in my heart, but it caught my left arm and sliced it open just above the elbow. I could feel blood trickling wetly, but strangely, no pain. Somewhere behind me I thought I could hear Rose screaming. I was not armed and had nothing with which to defend myself. I was bigger, and more powerfully built than Jasper so I had to be quick. As he drew back for the next thrust, I sprang, crashing into him and sending us both rolling to the floor. I had hold of Jasper's right arm and worked my grip towards his wrist. I could tell that I was the stronger of us and I was able to smash his hand against the wall. When I heard a clatter as the knife fell to the ground, I realised that I had evened up my chances; I grabbed the knife and threw it behind me. I began to scramble to my feet, but Jasper was quicker, giving me a heavy boot in the face, knocking me back to the floor. Before I could regain my wits and lay hold of him again, he had turned and fled down the alleyway. Thankfully, Rose's scream had brought half a dozen men to come to our aid.

My arm was bleeding heavily and suddenly I realised how much it hurt. My face throbbed, and a black eye was sure to follow. I was surrounded by helpers who got me to my feet and looked anxiously at my wounded arm. As luck would have it, there was an inn close by where I could be taken for my wound to be tended. The Black Bear was a half-timbered market tavern that was busy with traders who had finished for the day and were taking some refreshment before beginning their journey home. News of the skirmish had obviously reached them because my entourage was greeted by enthusiastic cheers from a crowded tap room.

'Bring him through here,' directed the innkeeper.

I was led down a narrow passageway and was taken to a back room with a window that looked out onto a stable yard. I was helped to a small table by the window and after being seated, was served with a mug of strong ale by the innkeeper himself.

'Here, get this down you lad! I reckon you've earned it,' the innkeeper said, then turned to the throng of bystanders that had followed us into the room, jostling and craning their necks to try and get a better view of proceedings.

'And you lot can clear out! The show is over.'

The innkeeper firmly ushered the spectators back out into the passage, closing the door behind them. I was starting to feel a little light-headed as loss of blood and strong ale took their combined effect.

'I have sent for a barber-surgeon who is quite nearby,' said the innkeeper. 'He should be here soon. In the meanwhile, let us have a look at that arm and stop it bleeding if we can.'

He had clearly done this kind of work before, perhaps after similar fights had taken place at the tavern and he worked confidently to help staunch the flow of blood, which, by now, had soaked my sleeve and was beginning to drip onto the floor.

I gingerly removed my tunic, revealing a livid red gash across my upper arm which was bleeding heavily. First, the innkeeper tightened a strap above the wound and secured it. Then he applied a bandage to the gash and soon the flow had stopped.

'There, that'll do for now,' he said as he surveyed his handiwork. 'It will need stitching though, when the barber surgeon gets here. If you can't afford to pay him, I could have a go myself. I've patched up worse than this in my time.'

There was a quiet cough in the background. We had all overlooked the presence of the woman who had been Griswold's intended victim and now she came forward hesitantly. I noticed again the bright red of her gown. I estimated her to be perhaps in her mid-thirties and quite slightly built.

Speaking to the innkeeper she said, 'There is no question of cost. I will pay, and gladly.'

She spoke in good English but with a pronounced accent. Turning to me, she said;

'I cannot begin to find the words to thank you. I could easily have been killed by that wicked man and perhaps robbing me was not the only thing he had planned to do. You risked your life for me and now you are hurt. You were so brave!'

I was embarrassed and was about to protest that I did not want any fuss, when there was a tap at the door and a man entered, carrying a physician's bag. He examined my wound and inserted several fine silk stitches before rebandaging it.

'It is a clean wound,' he said. 'It should heal quickly provided that you rest it and keep it free from dirt. You will not be able to work with that arm for several days, maybe a week. You will also find that by tomorrow it is very stiff. If it becomes hot and angry-looking you must send for me again without delay.'

'Here, this is for your good services, and thank God you were nearby,' she said, pressing money into his hand. 'I will pay for any further treatment if it is needed. Send your bill to the innkeeper and it will be settled immediately.'

She had a brief conversation with the innkeeper who returned to his duties. When we were alone, she turned to us:

'Let me introduce myself. I am Maryke de Haas. I live in Flanders, and I am here with my husband Jan on business.' She shook hands, and then stepped back, as if seeing us properly for the first time. 'And now it is my turn to take care of *you*.'

Her face showed concern. 'Where are your lodgings? Are you able to return there safely? I can engage a linkboy to bear a torch for you.'

'That is kind, but I can assure you we will be perfectly safe,' I replied. By now, I was feeling tired. I just wanted to get away from here, and I needed time to think. What were the consequences of this near-deadly encounter with Griswold likely to be?

'It is not dark yet Mistress. We will not need an escort.' I could tell that Rose wanted to be away from this place too.

'Well, let me tell you that I am staying at the Angel – do you know it? It is a large inn that seems to be used by travelling merchants like us, who visit York on business. My husband will be waiting for me there and I must go, or he will be worried.'

She turned to me, and reaching out, held my hand in both of hers. 'Thank you Tom. I think you saved my life today.' Then she embraced Rose in gratitude. As we parted company: 'You will hear from me again, soon.'

Once outside the Black Bear, I realised that the shipment of lead was still on the wharf, uncollected. Nursing my arm, which by now was throbbing painfully, we set off for home.

'You will have a wonderful black eye,' Rose observed with a smile.

'I will have some explaining to do!' I acknowledged with a grimace of pain.

***

Chapter 27

July 1463

The following day, a boy appeared at Alice's door with an invitation to dine with Jan de Haas and his wife at the Angel that evening. He had been instructed to wait for a reply and an acceptance was sent immediately.

'You had a lucky escape, lad,' Martin's face was grave. 'He could have killed you.'

'You could *both* have been killed.' Alice broke in. 'That woman was very lucky indeed that you helped her in time. Goodness only knows what might have happened if you hadn't been there - and what about the poor woman's rings? If she is staying at the Angel, she must be well-to-do. Perhaps she might give you a reward for your bravery? She should do.' Alice finished her indignant torrent of words with a nod of her head to emphasise the point.

Now it was Rose's turn: 'We only wanted to help. Nobody mentioned a reward and we would be embarrassed if they had. You don't put a price on helping somebody in danger – you just do it.' Then she added with a smile 'But I was very proud of my Tom all the same.'

I shuffled uncomfortably.

'I don't suppose we will ever find out who he was,' Martin observed, 'but perhaps the constables may come across him again sooner or later. You could pick him out if they arrested him, couldn't you Tom?'

'I know who he is.' There was a silence as they looked at me in disbelief. 'He is called Jasper Griswold and he killed my friend on the battlefield at Towton.'

'I heard you shout a name, but it meant nothing at the time,' Rose gasped. 'Whatever is he doing here?'

I wanted to tell them the full story of my hatred of this man; I settled for a simple version instead. 'He fought for Lancaster at Towton and was lucky to escape – I hoped my arrow had killed him. After the battle, the remains of the Lancastrian army fled to Scotland, but he stayed behind – probably thought he could do better for himself here.'

'I remember that the town was plagued with rogues and deserters,' Martin reflected. 'The gaols were full of them,'

'He ended up acting as a messenger, bringing a French spy into the country. Even though she is in Scotland, French Margaret is setting up a network to support a rebellion that would see Henry back in power.'

'Then this Jasper is a traitor as well as a common thief. You must tell the constables, lad. The theft of those rings alone would be enough to get him hanged – anything worth more than a shilling means the noose.' Martin's face was troubled.

'And they would certainly be worth much more than that!' Alice asserted.

'You cannot leave things as they are,' Martin continued. 'Until this man is caught, your life is in danger.'

***

The following morning, Rose and Alice began to examine their shared resources for suitable clothing; the Angel was an inn where only the most prosperous could afford to stay and Rose wanted to make sure that we looked respectable. In the end, a combination of Alice and Rose's clothes was the best they could do. Rose was dressed in a blue gown with long sleeves that tapered outwards at the cuff. The neckline was low-cut and showed a white linen underdress beneath her gown.

Alice pushed, pulled, tugged and smoothed until at last she was satisfied that Rose was at her best.

'Do you think I will do?' she enquired nervously.

'You look beautiful,' Alice reassured her as she admired the result of her handiwork. 'We just have to work a miracle on that husband of yours now – not much we can do with his black eye though!'

After I had returned from the workshop, I was scrubbed, chided, cajoled and complimented until I was fit to burst with exasperation. In my best doublet and clean hose I was quite transformed from the grubby tunic and leather apron that I wore to work. Finally we were both ready, and as we walked along Stonegate and past St. Helen's church, the sun was dipping towards the horizon. We could see the ornate lantern tower of All Saints' silhouetted against the setting sun, its octagonal shape and delicate tracery fading into black relief before a sky that was fiery orange and pink. As we watched, we saw a lantern being hoisted inside the open-worked masonry of the tower. Those travellers making their way to York through the dangerous Forest of Galtres could draw comfort from its beam and know that soon they would be safe within the city walls.

The streets were busy with people making their way home before curfew and the doorways to the taverns and inns were crowded as we passed. At last we reached the Angel where we stood hesitantly. The building was impressive; it was quite recently built and like all prestigious inns, it was three storeys high. The small windows boasted diamond panes of glass, set into delicate leadwork. The spaces between the wooden frames were filled with lime plaster that stood out starkly against the oak timber. Above the level of the ground-floor windows ran a carved wooden frieze with intricate scrolls and interlaced flowers; no expense had been spared in the construction of such a fine building.

We were feeling nervous and out of our depth as I lifted the latch and we went inside. An appetising smell of cooking, a rush of warmth and welcoming light from many candles greeted us as we closed the door and took in the scene before us. The room was busy with newly-arrived travellers who were dispatching servants with bags and strongboxes to their various quarters. From the midst of the confusion appeared a slightly flustered innkeeper. His bald head gleamed in the light from a lantern hanging from the ceiling as he bustled towards us, wiping his hands hurriedly on his apron.

'Excuse me sir, would you be Goodman Gifford?' Before I could reply, the innkeeper continued: 'I have instructions from Mr. de Haas to expect you. He was most insistent that I should inform him of your arrival immediately - Twitcher!' he bellowed across the room and a small ragged boy appeared, looking apprehensively up at his master, ready to dodge the cuff round the ear that he was clearly expecting. The boy looked about eight years old and had a grubby face, streaked with pale lines which Rose hoped had not been caused by tears. He wore no shoes and had only a thin brown tunic, tied at the waist with a cord. As she watched him, Rose noticed that he jerked his head rapidly to the right every few moments and she supposed that that was the origin of his nickname. She smiled gently at him, hoping to bolster his courage and Twitcher looked up gratefully into Rose's face with eyes like a faithful spaniel, perhaps seeing kindness there for the first time in his life.

'Get up to Mr. de Haas' room. Let him know that his guests are here. And don't forget to bloody well knock this time!' he roared at the diminutive figure of Twitcher as he scurried off up the staircase, his tunic flapping around his thin bare legs.

After the briefest of interludes, a gentleman appeared at the head of the staircase and hurried down to meet us, preceded by Twitcher who skipped dutifully in front of him. As he walked briskly towards us he held out his hand with a broad smile of welcome:

'Hello! Hello! Welcome! You must be Tom, the bravest of men who saved Maryke's life.'

He spoke good English with the slightest hint of an accent and was about to embrace me heartily when he remembered the knife wound in my arm. 'Forgive me, I was forgetting your arm. How is it? Is this your wife? How lovely to meet you, I am Jan.'

His enthusiasm and gratitude had clearly overwhelmed him and I was just beginning to wonder how I was ever going to get a chance to speak when a voice from the top of the stairs interrupted Jan's torrent of welcome.

'Jan, have mercy on these good people and bring them to our room.' Maryke stood at the head of the staircase, laughing, as her husband's cascade of words left us struggling for a chance to reply.

We were escorted up the creaking treads of the broad oak staircase where a landing led to rooms to right and left. Maryke stood by an open door and ushered us into their private quarters.

The room had a low beamed ceiling which only just cleared my head. The walls were panelled, with good wax candles placed in sconces at intervals. By their steady light I was able to take in the high quality of Jan's accommodation, and realised that he must indeed be a wealthy man. In one corner, a temporary altar had been made on a side table, supporting a silver crucifix in the centre of which was a precious stone. At the end of the room nearest the window was a long oak table and on it were plates and glasses, laid in preparation for a meal. In the centre was a candlestick with three candles casting a warm light on a well-set board.

As Maryke's maid took our cloaks and she bade us sit down, I got chance to look at our host. Jan de Haas was in his mid fifties and clearly older than his wife. He was slightly built with a pronounced stoop, and grey hair that was almost white, clinging obstinately to the sides of a head that was otherwise completely bald. He had a firm handshake and a face that was kind but shrewd. Years of business had left their mark on him and his countenance was etched with the passage of time.

Maryke's dark hair was brushed out over her shoulders and it gleamed in the candlelight. She wore a light peach gown that was low cut at the front above a white chemise and long sleeves that were edged with the finest lace. Rose had never seen lace so pure and intricate; more than that though, it was white and somehow stiff so that it stood out from her cuffs to show its elegant tracery in perfect detail. It reminded her of the patterns made by the hoar frost on a winter's morning.

When we were seated, our meal was served with ale and a good wine to follow, and we ate and talked. As the evening progressed, we warmed to each other's company. Rose began to lose some of her earlier nervousness, and finally, when the women moved to sit and talk together, she plucked up the courage to ask Maryke about her dress, and especially about the beautiful lace trim.

'Ah, in Flanders where we live, there is a long history of lacemaking. It is a craft that we have developed over many years. Our Flemish lacemakers are the best in the world and our lace is much in demand. We can sell it in many countries and it fetches a very high price.'

'It looks so delicate. I have never seen anything so beautiful. Your cuffs stand out so well, they are so... so crisp,' finished Rose in admiration.

Jan had replenished my wine and we settled to talk. I told Jan about how I had first met Rose and my work as a glass painter. In return, Jan told me about his visit to York.

'I am here on business as you have probably guessed,' Jan explained. 'I buy wool and have it shipped to my home in Bruges for making into garments. This is a perfect part of the world for me. The wool trade is in decline here at York and so much of the business has moved to other towns like Leeds. The wool producers here are desperate to sell their wool and I can buy it cheaply. Because I employ my own weavers in Bruges, I can make a profit.' He paused thoughtfully for a moment.

'Maryke told me about what happened and words can not express how grateful we both are to you. I have told Maryke that she must not go to the market alone. She must take Berta with her for safety. How is your arm faring?'

'Very well, thank you sir. I think it will heal quickly. I am just glad that your wife is safe.'

'Please! You will call me Jan. I am forever in your debt, and now we must talk about that. I must reward your act of bravery. Would you be offended if I offered you money? It would be small compensation for the injury you have sustained.'

'There is really no need, Jan. This will soon heal.'

'Hmm. Then let me try a different approach. How would you feel if I could arrange employment for you in my hometown of Bruges? There is much opportunity for you in such a prosperous city. Skilled craftsmen are always needed, and I know many people of influence in the city who would help to get you started.'

I smiled at his persistence: 'You are too kind, Jan, but I must decline. I am sure Bruges is a beautiful place, but we belong here. Rose would not wish to leave her parents and travel to another country.'

'Then what would you wish for, most in the world? What would help you both with your future together?'

'I think I know.' I had been so intent on listening to Jan that Maryke's voice surprised me. She and Rose had been deep in their own conversation and I had almost forgotten their presence. 'I have been talking to Rose about their plans, and I will explain it to you later. Excuse me for a moment, I must speak to Berta,' and she slipped out to find her maid.

The evening was drawing to a close and it was at last time for us to leave. The wine and the warmth of their friendship were making Rose's eyelids feel heavy, yet she wished that their companionship could last a little longer.

'I have hired a man to escort you home,' said Jan. 'We must be sure that you come to no harm.'

We pulled our cloaks around us, and after a warm embrace, Maryke slipped a small package into Rose's hand with instructions to open it when we were safely home. Jan held my handshake for a long moment and handed me a letter.

'I never forget my gratitude to you. This is a letter of introduction to my agent here in York. He has my address in Bruges if you should change your mind. I have instructed him to keep in contact with you and inform me of your progress. We leave tomorrow for Flanders, but who knows what the future holds, and I am determined to help you both when the opportunity arises.'

As we walked home, Rose held my arm. 'I am feeling a bit tipsy Tom!' she said with a giggle. 'Who could imagine that we could have had such a fine supper, and to think that we were so nervous before we met them. I like Maryke – she is warm and genuine and easy to talk to. She was really interested in us.'

'They are good people,' I replied, 'and who knows, we may meet them again.'

Once we were safely indoors, Rose opened the package that Maryke had given her and I heard her gasp of delight when she found it contained two cuffs of exquisite Flemish lace.

***

Chapter 28

November 1463 – January 1464

Almost four months had passed since my encounter with Jasper and thankfully, the wound on my arm had fully healed. We had not seen or heard of him since that day, and I hoped that he had moved on, perhaps even gone much further north to re-join his former associates.

'Martin still talks about that Jasper and how lucky Tom was to survive his wickedness,' Alice reminded Rose as they worked together in the kitchen.

'Tom thinks we may have seen the back of him, and good riddance,' Rose replied with feeling. 'I think if he was going to cause any more trouble, we would have known about it by now.'

The kitchen was at the rear of the house, but Rose stopped, tipping her head to one side. 'Did you hear something, Alice?' she asked, listening carefully. 'There it is again.'

There was a tentative knock at the door that gave on to Stonegate. It was so slight a sound that they looked quizzically at each other, wondering if they had imagined it. Alice opened the door and looked in surprise at the child who stood there. 'Yes? What do you want?' she asked the boy.

'Please mistress ...' he said timidly.

'Yes, how can I help you?' Alice asked in a kindlier tone. She looked down at the child who stood barefoot on the street. On this November day, his legs looked blue with cold.

'Is the other mistress here?'

Rose appeared behind Alice, intrigued by the conversation she was overhearing. 'Twitcher!' she exclaimed, 'What are you doing here? Can he come in Alice?'

With a little reluctance, Alice ushered the boy in and sat him down. 'Now what can we do for you Twitcher?' asked Rose in some surprise.

'Please don't call me that,' he burst out. 'I hate that name. He calls me that at the Angel and everybody laughs at me. I hate it!' he reiterated angrily. 'My real name is Barnaby, miss ... Barnaby Glover.'

'Well tell me Barnaby,' asked Alice, 'have you eaten today?' Barnaby shook his head silently, not looking up.

'I thought not. Well, let me see if I can find you something,' and she set a bowl of pottage with some bread beside him. Barnaby looked up with wide, beseeching eyes 'Is that for me mistress?' he asked in disbelief.

'It is all for you if you can manage it!'

Without a word, Barnaby fell on the food and did not look up until the last morsel had been wiped up with bread. After a mug of ale, he seemed ready to talk.

The boy eyed Alice uncertainly, and she understood his unkind nickname as his head jerked nervously to one side. She took away the empty bowl, and Rose smiled saying, 'Now, Barnaby, what is troubling you?'

Barnaby did not answer at first, looking down at the floor as if seeking a point from which to begin. 'How is the master?' he asked at last. 'When his arm was hurt, I had to fetch the barber-surgeon for him.'

'Oh, you mean my husband Tom?' said Rose with a smile. 'He is doing well and his arm is almost better. He will have a big scar though. Thank you for getting help for him so quickly. Why were you at the Black Bear? I thought you were employed at the Angel.'

'I had a package to collect from the Black Bear for my master. They sent me to run for help,' he replied.

Barnaby sat silently again for a moment, remembering the kindness Rose had shown him when she came to dine at the Angel. Suddenly he seemed to make up his mind and jumped to his feet, clenching, and unclenching his small fists in anxiety. 'I saw it happen. I know who did it. I was in the market, and I saw the fine lady and I saw the man who attacked her. I know who it was.'

'You mean the man who attacked Tom with a knife? We know his name, but not where to find him.' Rose knelt and held Barnaby's shoulders gently, looking into his eyes. 'He is a wicked, dangerous man and you must stay well clear of him.'

Barnaby nodded.

'We thought he had gone for good, but if you know where he is hiding, we must tell the constables. They will arrest him and send him to the Assizes. He tried to kill my Tom and he will certainly hang when they find him guilty.'

'I daren't tell, mistress. He would kill me if he even knew I had been here. The constables would not believe me and then he would find out who had grassed on him. He would slit my throat and throw me in the river.'

'Then why have you come here?' asked Alice patiently.

'Because the master needs to know he is in danger. He left York after the robbery – went somewhere to lie low until it was safe to come back – but he is here now, and the master must be warned.'

Rose looked searchingly at Barnaby: 'Can you tell us anything that might help us to find him? Where he is hiding so he can be arrested? Tom is in great danger until this man is caught. We know he is called Jasper Griswold. Have you heard that name?'

'No mistress, that name means nothing to me, but I know he goes by the name of 'Smiler'. He has two big scars one on each side of his mouth; the scars have twisted both sides of his face, so he looks like he is smiling.'

'And his hiding place? Where does he live?' asked Rose, really worried now.

Barnaby remained silent in an agony of indecision.

'Please Barnaby! If you know where he can be found, you must tell me so I can warn my Tom.'

'Mistress, if I tell you, you mustn't ever say that I gave him away.' He paused, 'Warehouse,' he said reluctantly. 'The grain warehouse on the staithe by the river.'

‘Thank you, Barnaby. Don’t worry, you will be quite safe as long as you keep this to yourself. Now, as you leave, go quickly and don’t look back at the house in case anybody is watching.’

Alice opened the door and checked up and down the street. She looked carefully in the doorways and yard entrances but could see nothing that seemed out of the ordinary. Finally, when she was satisfied that the coast was clear, she patted Barnaby on the shoulder, saying, ‘It’s safe; go now, and thank you. You’re a good boy!’

He slipped out of the door and darted quickly down Stonegate without a backward glance, melting into the busy street.

‘This Jasper knows that Tom can identify him. He is bound to come looking for him with a view to finishing the job,’ said Rose, her face lined with worry.

‘Then we must make sure that Tom keeps an eye open for him. In the meantime, Martin will go to the magistrate and ask for his arrest,’ replied Alice. ‘Thanks to your little friend, we now know where he can be found.’ Seeing Rose’s expression she added: ‘Don’t you worry, he wouldn’t risk coming anywhere near here, even if he knew where to find us. Martin will put the word out; he’ll get the apprentices to keep a look-out too. Don’t upset yourself, Tom will be well protected.’

***

The Thursday market was in the centre of the city, and on this unforgiving January day, it was bitterly cold with an occasional flurry of snow in the air. It had snowed overnight but what remained had been trampled into brown slush by the passage of many feet.

‘Tom, will you help me at the market this morning before you go to the workshop?’ Alice asked. ‘I need a round of cheese from the brothers from St. Mary’s, but those cheeses are so heavy. Their stall is only by the butter market so it will not take long.’

I was always glad to help with jobs like this; a full cheese was heavy and awkward to carry. It was too much to expect Alice to manage on her own.

‘Either they are making their cheeses heavier, or I am getting old!’ Alice gave a brave smile, but I noticed it was a thought that sometimes made her sad.

The market was busy as we pushed our way through the morning crowds. The tradesmen seemed to group themselves according to their produce; stalls with fresh vegetables lined the first street with bundles of turnips, kale and onions. Then we approached a street corner, where we turned left and the full width of the market square came into view, thronged with traders calling their wares, porters moving goods on handcarts and women on foot weaving their way through the confusion with their baskets of purchases bobbing on their arms.

Above the clatter and hubbub was the all-prevailing smell of the city; rotting offal, human waste and decomposing vegetable matter combined to make a stink that would get more pungent as the weather warmed up. Along the shambles it was worst of all. Here, the butchers displayed meat, hanging it from hooks in the beams that projected over the footway or on open shelves at the front of their shops. Waste and offal were thrown into the channel down the centre of the street and in summer it was alive with flies.

At last, we reached the butter market by the cross. The cheesemongers had their stalls here; some were full round cheeses whilst others were cut into sections. We finally tracked down the stall that was run by the lay brothers from St. Mary's Priory. It was busy and as we waited, my thoughts strayed idly to Jasper Griswold. Why had he returned after our encounter on the coast? He had clearly been employed as part of Queen Margaret's network of support, but how he had stooped to street robbery was a mystery. Perhaps the prospect of easy pickings was too great a temptation, or perhaps ... Here my deliberation was interrupted by Alice's voice beside me:

'What is that man up to?' she asked curiously. 'He has been hanging around behind the stalls.'

And suddenly, there he was. I glanced across and saw him pretending to look at the goods on display, but clearly watching us.

'That's him Alice, that's Jasper.'

'You mean the one who tried to kill you?' Alice's eyes were wide with incredulity.

I watched him, and was rendered helpless by indecision. It was no coincidence that he was here; he had tracked us down by watching the market, knowing he might see me here sooner or later. One thing was certain - I dared not risk another confrontation and put Alice in danger.

'We should get help and have him arrested,' Alice whispered.

'No, he will have gone by the time we could summon help.'

I knew I had to get us both away to safety but just as I had come to the decision, our eyes met, and I saw his look of intense hatred. Never shifting his stare from my face, Jasper slowly drew his finger across his throat.

'Did you see that?' Alice gasped.

As she spoke, he turned and slipped away into the crowd. He had identified Alice, and could follow her home whenever he chose.

'Come Alice, we must leave here quickly.'

I was the only person who could link Jasper to the crime; the key witness and in effect, the person who could put the noose over his head. Finally, I understood the danger that faced me, and I began to feel genuinely afraid.

As I escorted Alice quickly home, I made sure we kept to the centre of the street to avoid the yards and alleyways where an assassin could hide in the shadows. Looking warily about me, and keeping close to other passers-by, I made sure we were not being followed. At last we reached the safety of home.

***

Even though we were away from the danger that might lurk outside, Alice could not settle and insisted that I barred the door for extra security.

'Martin has been to the magistrates office. He went straight away after young Barnaby came to give us the warning. He even took one of the Guild officers with him, so they knew how serious it was.'

'And have they searched the warehouse?'

'Yes, and Martin went with them but there was no sign of him,' she sighed shaking her head. 'I will not rest until he is caught.'

'Is Martin in the workshop?'

'No, he has a panel of glass to repair at St. Cuthbert's this afternoon. He said you should join him when we got back. Martin said Alfred Gott could use the design table whilst the two of you were away.' She paused: 'Are you sure you will be safe now that dreadful man has seen you? Do you think you ought to stay here?'

'Quite sure. He will not trouble us again,' I replied with more conviction than I felt. 'Besides, I shall be with Martin, and we are more than a match for the likes of him,' I put my arm round Alice's shoulder and gave her a hug, 'so have no fear, all will be well.' I smiled down at her, but her face was solemn, and I knew that my false confidence had not comforted her.

As I left the house to set off on the short walk to St. Cuthbert's, I heard the sound of the door being barred behind me. Alice was frightened and I could not tolerate that. This man was affecting our lives and he must be stopped. I needed to have time to think, and talk to Martin: perhaps if we put our heads together we could come up with a plan.

***

Glazier's Yard was reached through a gateway that led in from the road. It housed five other workshops, all of them owned by members of the guild, and Martin's workshop was the first door on the right-hand side. This was his kingdom; here he kept his tools, his glass painting materials, and his stock of lead channelling. When he was assembling a window panel, he lit an iron brazier full of glowing charcoal at the back of the shop. Several soldering irons - long iron rods with a wooden handle and a heavy copper tip- would be thrust into the centre of the heat ready to solder the joints that fixed each piece of glass in place.

The front of the workshop had big double doors that stood open while he worked, and here were two large tables, positioned to catch the strongest light. The left-hand table was the place where the panels were assembled. The one on the right was the design bench. It was a large flat area that had a white plaster mixture spread into a smooth hard drawing surface. Here, designs could be highlighted on the plaster in fine charcoal so each piece of glass could be laid out to check for accuracy before transferring to the assembly bench. For rich customers, Martin copied the design onto paper so that he could take it to show his patron for final approval. This afternoon, Alfred Gott was working there with Martin's permission.

Alfred knew Tom well and both had become good friends when they were apprentices. Tom had occasionally shared his food with Alfred when otherwise he would have gone hungry. He was squarely built and in looks was not dissimilar to Tom, with the same solid set to his shoulders, the same curly dark hair and beard, with eyes that twinkled with merriment when he shared a story.

Today was Thursday and Alfred hoped to complete his design before the light faded. If not, he could light the horn lantern that hung above the bench; daylight was better though. While he was working on his design, Alfred preferred to be alone so he could concentrate on the careful placing of each piece against the next, ensuring the shapes blended together within the outer frame of the panel. There were occasional interruptions from apprentices from other workshops, or messengers from tradesmen trying to find Martin. Each interruption slowed his progress, breaking his train of thought until he found to his frustration that the light was beginning to fade. In the half-light he bent over the bench, totally absorbed by his task.

The January sun began to dip in the sky, and around the yard was the odd glimmer of light as a lantern was lit against the advancing darkness. It was only then that Jasper made his move. He had discovered where Tom worked some time ago, but seeing him at the market had hardened his resolve; Tom was a problem to be dealt with. Jasper had concealed himself in a doorway close by Martin's workshop where he waited and watched. He saw the familiar figure bending over his work and a slow smile of anticipation crept across his twisted features. Every now and again, someone would approach the solitary figure and stay briefly for a chat. There had been nobody near for what seemed quite a while now, and as daylight blended imperceptibly into dusk, it was his time.

Jasper had no reservation about what he was about to do. He had killed before and it had not troubled him. Slowly and stealthily, he emerged from the shadows where he had hidden undetected for the last two hours. As darkness began to fall, the figure in front of him continued to work intently, oblivious to the danger that was stalking him. Jasper crept ever nearer, slowly, quietly and with infinite patience. As he moved, he slipped a dagger from the left sleeve of his tunic. So quietly, an inch at a time, he slid his silent feet over the cobbles until he stood beside the open door but still remained in shadow. Had he been noticed? Was there anyone near? No, it had to be now.

As he came to his decision, the figure that had been hunched forward over the bench stood upright and reached for the lantern above his head. Now! Darting forward, Jasper came up behind him and, grabbing his upturned head with his left hand, drew the knife across his throat in one swift, deadly movement. Without even a cry, Alfred collapsed on the floor, his life ebbing away in gurgling gasps as blood sprayed from his throat.

Jasper looked down with satisfaction at the body at his feet. He saw a darkening puddle of blood slowly spreading across the floor and bent down to wipe the blade of his dagger on the clothing of the prone form that lay before him. It was not until then that he actually looked at the face of his victim, and with a grunt of disappointment and frustration he realised that this was not Gifford; this was somebody else.

***

Chapter 29

January 1464

We finished our work at Saint Cuthbert's as the light was failing, and set off to return our tools to the workshop. The encounter with Jasper at the market had shaken me. I had thought of little else all day, and had begun to come up with the beginnings of a plan to rid myself of Jasper Griswold for good. I was glad of the chance to speak to Martin alone.

'He was at the market today. He had waited for us to appear, and now that he can recognise Alice, he will intend to watch out for her and follow her home so he can find where I live. She is scared, Martin. She has barred herself in and daren't come out of the house.'

'Then we have to do something, Tom. I am not having my Alice frightened by a rogue like him.' He was understandably angry, and I was racked with guilt. I had brought this into their peaceful lives, and I must act quickly.

'I will go to Sir Richard - ask for his help. After all, I have served him well enough in the past. He has ways of dealing with problems that it is better not to know about – ways of making people disappear. He will be all the more willing to help because he knows that Jasper has acted against the king in support of the Lancastrian cause.'

By now we had passed through the minster gates and entered the Glaziers' Yard. In the failing light, a shadowy figure could be seen by the table.

'There's Alfred, still working!' Martin smiled. 'Time for us to lock up. He'll have to leave it for today ...' He stopped, rendered speechless by the tableau before us, its true nature revealed as we drew close: Jasper, half bending over a lifeless body, dagger in hand looking up in shock as his crime was discovered.

'Murder! Murder! Help us. Murder!' I yelled at the top of my voice. Martin added to the cry, his deep booming voice summoning help from all quarters. Doors began to fly open, figures emerged from workshops around the yard, and all was chaos.

'Murder! Murder!' the cry was picked up by one after another of the emerging workmen as they saw Alfred's bloodied corpse lying on the cobbled floor.

With grimace of rage, Jasper took to his heels as the hue and cry was raised, and behind him was a mob; one of their own had been slain, and fellow guildsmen, apprentices and worthy citizens alike were roused to righteous anger. I set off in pursuit amid the panting, jostling pack hot on Jasper's heels, and alongside me was a lad called Simon, one of the apprentices. Doors flew open and women screamed their encouragement whilst dogs rushed out barking and adding to the confusion, running between the legs of the mob and snapping at the heels of the pursuers.

Jasper was a sly quarry and well versed in dodging from pursuit. He was fast on his feet and light of frame; some of the older men began gasping for breath and slowed down. It was only the younger men that could keep pace and risking a glance over his shoulder, Jasper began to hope that he could outrun his pursuit. There were less people near him now although he could hear the shouts and yells of a growing crowd bent on his capture. He knew a place close by, if only he could reach it. There was a doorway with a hidden alcove inside the archway which would conceal a man in its dark recess. He had used this place before and now it was near. Putting on a burst of speed he managed to turn a corner ahead of his pursuers and was out of their sight for a few seconds. That was all he needed: there it was ahead of him, the deep arched doorway with an alcove that was all but invisible unless you knew where to look. Diving inside he pressed himself into the furthest corner, feeling the cold stone at his back and his heart pounding in his chest.

Rounding the corner, I halted with Simon, both of us gasping for breath and uncertain of what had just happened.

'He's gone!' I exclaimed angrily. 'We can't let him get away. Where is he?'

By this time, the others had caught up, gasping, chests heaving. They, too, looked around in disbelief.

'He can't just vanish into thin air.'

'We've checked everywhere – he's not here.'

'He must have carried on further down the road. We had better spread out and keep going.'

Jasper had regained control of his breathing and could think rationally. If he waited too long, they would return and find him. He was certain that he could outrun them now that he had got his wind back. He slipped out of his bolthole and cautiously stepped into the street. Peering around he could not see any of his pursuers and with renewed hope, set off again, running up the street towards safety.

'There he goes!'

The wild yells of the hue and cry resounded in the street behind him as Jasper once more took to his heels in headlong flight. He twisted and turned through alleys and yards but still the stubborn knot of half a dozen fast runners was close behind him. His strength was beginning to falter, and he was sucking in air in huge sobbing gasps. Still he maintained his pace, jinking and diving through shadows and hidden places hoping to confuse his hunters.

At the head of the chase, I ran beside Simon. 'He's tiring,' I gasped. 'If we keep going, we'll have him.'

And then I knew with certainty where Jasper was aiming for, and what he was intending.

'He's heading for the minster,' I yelled. 'He's going for sanctuary.'

Jasper was approaching the great west door of the minster and safety was within reach. Then he would have forty days in which he could legally leave the country to escape punishment, but there in front of him and barring his way stood the solid figure of Martin and a gathering of other men. Not nimble enough to maintain the pursuit, Martin had outguessed him and now the pack closed in. Lashing out left and right with his dagger, Jasper made a last desperate bid for freedom but in vain. He was overpowered and it was only the timely arrival of two constables that saved his life. Battered and bloodied he was led away with the sound of the mob's baying cries of 'Hang him! String him up right now!' ringing in his ears.

***

The murder of Alfred Gott had shocked the community. Although murders were not uncommon, this killing had struck at the heart of the small group of craftsmen that offered their skills to the glory of God: the guild was outraged that a brother had been so cruelly struck down; the clergy were incensed that one of the men who contributed to the magnificence of the great church had been ruthlessly slaughtered. There is no doubt that Jasper would have been lynched on the spot if order had not been restored to the enraged mob. He had been dragged away to safety and incarcerated in the Mayor's prison, set deep beneath a stone guardhouse at the end of the great bridge over the Ouse. The road out of York ran past the prison, across the river and up the steep rise of the Micklelith where it passed under the Micklelith Bar and reached the Tyburn. Condemned criminals were taken from the prison by cart on their final journey, and paraded through the street, some receiving cheers of encouragement and even the occasional drink for courage; others had missiles thrown at them, depending on the nature of their crime.

For the moment, and in the interests of preserving him for the hangman, Jasper was hurried down the steep stone steps and into the depths of the gaol. The walls and steps were green with slime and treacherous underfoot; the gaol was deep underground, and the river Ouse ran alongside it so that the walls dripped with dampness and the air was filled with the stink of the river. Jasper was thrown into one of the two available cells and collapsed on the filthy straw that covered the floor.

'Any nonsense and you'll be shackled to the wall,' warned the gaoler. 'You're lucky to be still alive. Even the monks wanted you dead. Never mind – if the river floods, it will drown you like the rat you are. Save them the trouble of a hanging!' and with a sarcastic grin added: 'Hope you have friends outside with money for food or else your stay could be a short one.'

'If I give you money, can you get a message out to a friend? He will bring food and arrange for me to plead Benefit of Clergy.'

'I'll send your message but what connection have you got with the church to claim that?'

'I have filled plenty of graves,' muttered Jasper, sullenly.

'Just trying to get before a church court for a lighter sentence, eh? Well that won't save you. They'll ask you to read a verse from the Bible, and I don't suppose you can read, can you?'

Jasper had memorised the verse that was always presented as a test. It was commonly known as 'the neck verse' because knowing it could save your neck. He and others like him had rote-learned it for just such an occasion.

'Anyway,' continued the gaoler, 'the church wants to see you swing just as much as the mob did. You have killed one of their own and they don't take that lightly. You have to hope that they don't flay you alive. That's what they do to people who steal from the church, and you have stolen one of their craftsmen.'

The heavy wooden door slammed shut and the cell was in almost total darkness. The only source of light was through the small grill in the door, where a faint glimmer of daylight could be seen from the street above.

***

The Northern Circuit Assize Court was held in the bailey of York Castle. Here a courtroom had been specially built and housed holding cells and accommodation for the Circuit Judges and their recorders for the duration of the Assize. There were two sessions held each year, one at Lent and the other in summer, when prisoners accused of the most serious offences were tried.

Here, on Monday 28th March 1464, I had been called as a witness for the Crown in the case of the Crown versus Jasper Griswold. I had been chosen because of my knowledge of the earlier crime when Maryke de Haas had been robbed. The barber surgeon and the landlord of the Black Bear had been summoned to give evidence along with Simon Metcalfe, the apprentice who had helped to apprehend the fugitive.

Two days before the trial, on Saturday, I had made my way to the castle bailey and stood with Martin, watching the arrival of the two circuit judges with interest. I had never had any contact with the judiciary and the pomp and splendour of their arrival was impressive. The procession was preceded by armed men on horseback with lances from which fluttered the red and white pennants of the Neville family. They clattered past with iron shod hooves making the arched gateway of the barbican ring with the thunder of their passing.

Then came the two judges in their scarlet robes and white sashes, side by side and flanked by more armed soldiers. In their wake was a procession of court officials, attended by their servants and clerks, all dressed in their best robes and finery. It was a spectacle that was intended to impress and intimidate, for here was the full force of the king's law with its dreadful power to punish wrongdoers. The street leading up to the castle was lined with people who stood silently as the cavalcade passed before them, swept through the barbican, and out of sight into the bailey. The two judges had a week to hear a full caseload before moving on to Northumberland and the next venue in the circuit.

Judge John Fairfax was a local man and had been a Serjeant at Law, working mainly in the Court of Common Pleas where he had often represented the poor. He had a reputation for being reasonable and on occasion, quite lenient on those who had broken the law through genuine desperation. Judge Jerome Lasselles was a tall, sharp faced man in his later years, and came originally from Lincoln's Inn in London. He had moved to work on the Northern Circuit as a consequence of his ties to the powerful Percy family in Northumberland. He had thin, greying hair, a hooked nose and eyes that were never still, darting round his courtroom like a hawk that, once freed of the glove, scours the land beneath its wings. He was hard of hearing, short of patience and lacking in any vestige of human compassion.

I made my way with Martin to the court early on the day of the trial. We passed through into the bailey and entered the small hallway reserved for lawyers and witnesses, that led into the court. Gathered in the hallway were lawyers and court officials, dressed in their black robes, chatting to each other in quiet voices before the day's proceedings got underway. Here we were challenged by guards dressed in royal livery, and having satisfied them of our credentials, we made our way into the courtroom. The court was packed with spectators who had used the public entrance, where they had queued and jostled for the few available seats in the public gallery.

The courtroom was square in shape and had a high wooden ceiling that was painted dark blue and decorated with a scattering of gold stars. At one end was a raised dais and in its centre was a carved wooden throne above which was a canopy of scarlet silk. It was designed to create a sense of theatre, making it clear to ordinary citizens that the judge was the king's representative, dispensing royal justice in all its awe and pomp. In front of the judge was a row of desks for the court recorders and officials. To the right, and in two banked rows of benches, sat the jury of twelve men of good character to hear the evidence and pronounce judgement on their fellow citizens. In tiered seating to the left and rear of the room was crammed the clamouring public, eager to watch the drama of each trial as it unfolded; greedy for the salacious details presented as evidence, and taking a spectator's delight in seeing how a condemned prisoner reacted to his or her sentence. Martin and I had seats reserved for witnesses on a bench at the front and we sat quietly to await the start of the trials.

We did not have to wait long; the bailiff entered from a door at the side and in a loud voice, called the court to order.

'In the name of the King and our Sovereign Lord, Edward the Fourth, I declare these Lent Assizes to be in session. All stand!'

High up, from a door that opened onto the dais, entered Judge Jerome Lasselles, dressed in his scarlet robe with a white sash over his right shoulder and attended by the Assize recorder. He seated himself in an unhurried display of authority and there was a murmured shuffle as all the assembly took their seats. Judge Lasselles was formidable; enthroned on his seat of power, he had the thin face and hooked nose of an imperial eagle, sitting in his craggy eyrie and blinking down upon his world with aristocratic cruelty. He brought his gavel down on the table with a crash.

'There will be no disorder here! Anyone who calls out or disturbs the king's justice will be dealt with severely. All those condemned will be hanged on Monday next week. I would advise any such person so sentenced to use the intervening time wisely in making whatever arrangements they need to make in this world, and by attending to the good of their souls in the next.'

He bent over his table and shuffled his papers into order and called: 'Bring on the first case.'

The bailiff rose to his feet: 'The Crown versus Edward Beylby my lord,' as the prisoner was bustled into the dock.

'Edward Beylby aged twenty years, native of Stockton near York, private soldier in the Earl of Northumberland's Light Horse. You are charged with committing rape upon Elizabeth Bowland, aged 22, of Sheriff Hutton, servant at that Castle, as she was coming to York, in a field where she was walking, about 3 miles from Sheriff Hutton, on Monday, 28th October, at 2.00pm.'

The ensuing evidence was presented as depositions and testimony by the woman's father and lasted only twenty minutes. The Foreman of the jury announced his verdict of "Guilty" to a satisfied murmur from the public benches. Judge Lasselles leaned forward, clearly enjoying his moment of ritual in displaying the full majesty of the law: 'Edward Beylby the sentence of this court upon you is that you shall be taken from this place to a lawful prison, thence to the Tyburn without Micklelith Bar and there you suffer death by hanging ...'

The defendant Beylby began shouting abuse at the judge until he was silenced by the constables at either side of him. In response, Judge Lasselles leaned forward, adding, menacingly: '... and after execution, your body shall be hanged upon a gibbet in the field where you committed the crime, in Sheriff Hutton Road, and may God have mercy on your soul.'

At this last pronouncement, Beylby let out a wail of protest. 'No! You can't do that to me. No. In the name of God, no!'

He was still calling out pitifully as he was led away by two constables, past the armed soldiers at the door and back to the gaol at the castle. I whispered to Martin:

'He seemed more afraid of the gibbet than he was of the gallows.'

'That's because when the birds have picked him over and all that is left of him is a few bones, they will throw them on a rubbish heap. You can never get to heaven if your body is not kept in one piece. It is a dreadful sentence. Condemned in this life, and for all eternity in the next,' Martin replied.

'Next case,' ordered Judge Lasselles, with a loud rap of his gavel.

The bailiff rose to his feet once again: 'The Crown versus Jasper Griswold, my lord' The door at the side of the courtroom opened and Jasper was dragged to the dock by two constables.

'Jasper Griswold, you are charged that on Thursday 21st January 1464 you murdered Alfred Gott within the precinct of the minster at York.'

Jasper stood impassively as the charge was read out. He was a filthy bedraggled figure and stank from the squalor of the cell to which he had been confined for several weeks since his arrest. The scars down each side of his face showed white against the grime and gave the appearance of a twisted sneer. Judge Lasselles leaned to one of the court officials and asked in a loud voice:

'Is that knave smiling at me? Eh? By God he won't be smiling soon!'

The landlord of the Black Bear and the barber surgeon gave their evidence. Then Martin and I explained Jasper's motive for wanting me dead, adding our account of how we had returned to find Jasper, dagger in hand, bending over the body of his victim at the minster workshop. Finally, Simon the apprentice described the fugitive's flight from justice and his attempt to gain sanctuary. At this, Judge Lasselles erupted with anger:

'Sanctuary? Sanctuary by God? The church doesn't want you after you murdered one of their craftsmen.'

All the witness' depositions being concluded, the jury turned to discuss among themselves and reach a decision. After a brief interval they nodded to the bailiff that they were agreed upon a verdict. As instructed, the Foreman rose to his feet:

'Guilty, my lord.'

Jasper let out a howl of despair and sank to his knees, only to be roughly hauled upright again by the two constables who escorted him. Then, unexpectedly, a court usher entered through a side door, bearing a letter in his hand. He passed it to an official on the dais, who passed it to the Judge. Jasper looked up disbelievingly. Could this be hope? Judge Lasselles broke the seal and read the letter with a barely disguised look of irritation, then made an announcement:

'The Dean and Chapter have asked me to make an amendment to my usual arrangements, and in deference to them, I am minded to agree.'

Jasper's heart soared with hope. Had his claim of sanctuary been accepted? He held his breath in anticipation of what could come next.

Seeing the beginnings of Jasper's optimism, Judge Lasselles allowed himself the slightest suggestion of a smile.

'The church has specifically asked that you should be executed on their own gallows as an example to all who might harm the servants of God and the church. Therefore, Jasper Griswold, the sentence of this court upon you is that you shall be taken from this place to a lawful prison, thence to the Church gallows at the Horsefair where you shall be hanged by the neck until you are dead and may God have mercy on your soul.'

Jasper's hopes were cruelly dashed as he heard the sentence pronounced. With a moan, he slumped to the floor, almost fainting and was dragged from the dock only half sensible of the courtroom and the people around him.

***

Chapter 30

April 1464

Back once more in his cell at the Mayor's gaol, he had time to collect his thoughts and to realise that his time on earth was limited to a very few days. In exactly one week from now, he would hang, with no chance of a reprieve. Jasper's mind began to ramble in fragmented recollections of how his life had been spent and how he had come to this sorry end. Although he had not attended church for many years, he still believed in heaven and hell, and the dreadful pictures he had seen painted on the church wall showing demons dragging sinners down to hell, tormented his mind.

He thought of the crime that had been his undoing – not the murder of the glazier in the workshop, that had just been the final act. No, he thought about the day he had attempted to rob the rich woman in the market and how it had all gone wrong. Perhaps there was a way that he could gain entry to heaven – by confession of his sins and restoration of some stolen property.

***

Father John Epplewell was not surprised when a messenger asked him to attend at the Mayor's gaol. He was parish priest of St. Michaels, just fifty yards away from the gaol and the messenger had told him that a condemned man wished to make his last confession. He had performed this task before on several occasions; he knew it was his Christian duty to bring what peace he could to a troubled soul awaiting execution, but he found it a distressing experience. He waited now, in the gaoler's office, seated at a desk with pen and paper at the ready, at the request of the wretched prisoner who stood before him.

'I wish to make my confession, Father. I have taken the wrong path in life, but perhaps I may still have hope of redemption if I repent.'

'The Lord will accept your confession if it is sincere. You may still gain the Kingdom of Heaven if you make true repentance,' Father John reassured him.

The gaoler left the room to allow Father John to hear confession in private, and took up his station outside the door.

'Before I make my confession, Father, I must ask you to write my Last Will and Testament. There is one good deed that I can still do. Who knows, it may count in my favour, but I have never learned to read or write.'

Picking up the pen, Father John listened to the details and began to write. It was not a long task, but the request that accompanied it was unusual:

'Please make sure that my Will is taken to the lady that I tried to rob. Tom Gifford, the man who gave evidence against me in court will know how to find her.'

***

The day dawned grey and cold; Monday 4th April was hanging day. The light began to filter faintly through the grill in the cell door of the Mayor's prison. Jasper had watched the grill intently, hoping it was not yet time for the day to begin, but imperceptibly, the faintest hint of daybreak could be seen through the small aperture in the door. In what seemed only moments it was strong enough to make out the shape of the bars that made up the grill. Now he could hear the first sounds of people moving in the street above him. Soon there was the clatter of hooves as the first cart made its way into the city, going about its routine business, its driver unaware that this was the last day on earth for the prisoner in the cell beneath him.

Jasper had slept very little that night and had woken frequently in his cold cell, the horror of his dreams soon to be turned into reality. He had been visited yesterday by two of his associates who had hoped he would impart knowledge of where any valuables were hidden. Jasper had disclosed one of his hiding places, a loose brick in the wall of the stables behind the Blue Boar on the river wharf, and there they would find a bag containing a dozen half nobles. In return, he asked them to stand by him at the gallows and speed his end.

At the castle, crowds had gathered to see the carts with the condemned criminals setting off on their journey to the Micklelith Tyburn. On the flagpole above the barbican, a black flag was flying to indicate that today was hanging day. For the common people of York however, it signified an unofficial public holiday where the entertainment was free, and a raucous good time was guaranteed. There were street sellers with hot pies and pastries, and a plentiful supply of ale to be had. Those who had been able to force their way to the foot of the Tyburn were being held back by constables, supported by armed soldiers from the castle garrison. Odds were being offered and taken on how long each criminal would take to die. It was a riotous scene of drunkenness and vulgarity.

A huge cheer went up from the crowd thronging the road outside the castle, now three or four deep, as the first of three carts rumbled through the barbican and out into the waiting multitude. In the first cart was Edward Beylby, convicted rapist, and beside him were two horse thieves. Then began their slow journey through the city amidst huge crowds of disorderly citizens, making their way to Ouse Bridge and up the Micklelith to where the Tyburn was waiting outside the city walls.

In his cell below street level, Jasper heard the carts go by, knowing what their purpose was. Then he heard his gaoler come down the steps, and with a jangling of keys his door was unlocked and flung open with a loud crash. Two constables entered with the gaoler, and his hands were bound together. He was taken up and escorted through a door to the rear where a cart was waiting for him. With disbelief, Jasper saw that the cart already contained his coffin.

'It's your day to make a name for yourself.' The gaoler's grim humour fell on deaf ears. 'Make a good show of it; lad, they'll think much better of you if you make a good end.'

Jasper could not reply, and shaking with fear, he was hoisted into the cart. His final journey took him past the minster as a reminder of the offence he had committed against the great church, then through Monk Bar and onto Gillygate. On the very edge of the city now, they came past the hospital of St. Mary's to a great open space known as the horsefair. Here, at the junction where the road divided into two, was the gallows where a great crowd gathered.

Simon and I had reluctantly come to watch at the request of the Glaziers' Guild and were expected to report back at the Guildhall afterwards. We stood at the back of the mob by the ale carts and pie sellers, shocked at the display of depravity that accompanied the delivery of justice. As I waited, jostled by the surging of the crowd, I felt a tug at my sleeve.

'Thought I might find you here.'

I turned in surprise which quickly became apprehension. What could he possibly want from me now?

'God give you good day Rob,' I greeted him warily. 'What brings you here to this sad spectacle of humanity?'

'There is no need to look so anxious,' he said with a grin. 'I thought I might share your moment of triumph to see the end of this churl.'

I found myself conflicted: 'Truly, I feel no satisfaction today. There was a time when I would have gladly killed him myself; now I cannot but feel sorry for his plight, even though he killed my friend.' Rob raised a curious eyebrow, but I continued: 'One thing you might explain that has puzzled me: he escorted an agent from France to the priest at

Morton on the Forest and we both saw them escape by boat. He must have been judged as trustworthy and capable of such a responsibility, so how did he fall out of favour with his Lancastrian masters?'

'Ah, well. It seems that greed got the better of him. He was paid for his services but demanded more, threatening to betray their secrets to Sir Richard. The trouble was - he did not know anything to betray – he had just been used as an escort and after that he had no value. When his money ran out he was reduced to a life of petty crime, which is how you came across him I believe. In the meanwhile, his former employers continue to conspire against our king. Queen Margaret has raised enough support from James III to challenge us once again. Her army has left Scotland and is moving south through the marches.'

'You are surely not here to ask me to take up arms again?' I asked with a feeling of dread.

'I think you have done enough in the service of his grace. You must spend time with your new wife! I hear that she has had an unfortunate experience at the hand of our enemies, and for that I am truly sorry. She was never expected to put herself in danger – she took risks that we begged her not to take.'

He paused for a moment, gazing at the crowd as if gathering his thoughts. Then, turning to me and looking into my eyes, continued: 'But here's a conundrum. Both her abductors died in a freak storm, and both struck by lightning. Yet the weather had been fine all that day and the sky was clear. Strange, don't you think? It feels uncomfortable to realise that a freak storm appeared out of a clear sky and took the lives of Rose's abductors, yet she was spared. If I did not know better, I could be tempted to think that unholy forces had been summoned and some kind of dark enchantment had brought about their deaths.'

This was new to me. Rose had seen Steven St. Claire die, but we assumed that Piers Routledge had escaped. How should I answer Rob, because it was indeed strange, and my mind had immediately turned to Rose's mother. Certainly she had skills and talents for healing, and was at one with the old ways, but to conjure up a storm? To magick a dreadful revenge on those who would threaten her daughter's life? Surely this was beyond even her powers of wisdom. This was sorcery and witchery beyond the ability of the shrewdest of cunning women - yet, when I had asked Rose's opinion, she had been tight lipped and dismissive.

Hearing it now, laid out almost as an accusation, my stomach felt as though a hand had gripped it and twisted my entrails in a lurching, heaving panic. Surely Rob was not here to make an accusation of witchcraft against Rose or her mother? We had been through a lot together, and I had counted him as a friend, but Rob lived in a world of shadows; his whole life was a masquerade and a deception; perhaps I had fallen victim to his natural charm and convinced myself of his friendship. I forced a smile and put my hand on his shoulder:

'I can quite see your point, and I agree, it is strange, but who are we to understand the ways of nature? Perhaps it was God's will, and it was His omnipotence that punished the wrongdoers while the righteous were spared? When Moses parted the red sea, the Israelites were saved but the Egyptians drowned. Who are we to know His ways?'

The hangman's cart began forcing its way through the crowd, avoiding the necessity of any further explanation.

***

'They've all come to see you turned off,' said the carter scornfully. 'Are you going to give them a show?'

'That's enough of that!' one of the constables interrupted angrily. 'We don't want him giving trouble.'

The cart halted beneath the beam of the gallows where the hangman was waiting. Jasper was placed at the rear of the cart and stood shivering with cold and fear. He wore an old shirt and ragged hose; a dark stain was spreading down the front where he had wet himself.

The executioner was a convicted murderer who had assumed the role of hangman in exchange for a reprieve. Over the last two years he had carried out the work as required; a refusal would result in the original sentence of death being carried out according to law. He had found that his duties preyed on his mind and his dreams were filled with the sights and sounds that accompanied his occupation. He had found peace of a sort through drink and today he could hardly stand.

'Come on then!' he bellowed at the crowd, holding the noose in his hand and waving it at them. 'You come up here and try it for size!'

Simon leaned over to me: 'He's drunk!' he exclaimed in disgust.

The hangman tried to put the noose over Jasper's neck but after several attempts and failing each time, one of the sheriff's officers had to help him. By now, his victim was staring wildly about at the spectators, insensible with terror. The mood of the crowd was beginning to turn to anger against the bungling efforts of the executioner. The rope being finally in place, the sheriff's officer turned to the driver of the cart.

'Quickly now or we'll have a riot on our hands.'

The carter gave a sharp flick of his whip and the horse moved forward, taking the cart away from under Jasper's feet so that he swung out kicking and struggling at the end of the rope. A great cheer went up from the crowd as he jerked and writhed, his feet flailing in the air. It was then that his two assistants stepped forward. By common assent, the crowd parted, and the constables let them through, for they knew what was to happen. Jasper had paid them to speed his end; they grabbed his thrashing legs and pulled them downwards to mercifully quicken his departure. After several minutes when the choking sounds had stopped. they let go and walked away, leaving the lifeless body hanging silent and unmoving beneath the gallows.

***

Chapter 31

May 1464

It was Pentecost, the seventh Sunday after Easter and we had attended mass at St. Helen's earlier that morning. It was a warm and pleasant evening in mid-May, and the events of early April that had brought about the demise of Jasper Griswold seemed to belong to another age as we took supper together. It was surprising to think that we had been married for almost a year, and so much had happened in the intervening months.

We sat at table in comfortable companionship, Rose and Alice planning ahead for their tasks next day. I looked at Alice fondly: she had taken me in when my own family had rejected me; she had accepted Rose as my wife, and I knew that she placed increasing reliance on her. I could see the passage of time was beginning to make its mark on Alice.

She had always been so active, such a bundle of energy, but when I looked at her as the evening sun caught her face, it looked lined and tired. Her hair, once glossy black, was now blended with grey and her shoulders had the first hint of a stoop. It saddened me to see her now, where once she had worked from dawn till the shadows gathered at the close of the day. The hand of time had been laid even more heavily on Martin's shoulder. His tiredness at the end of each day saw him retire to his chair after supper, and often fall asleep. More worrying though was the racking cough he seemed to have developed. 'Glazier's cough,' he called it. 'Breathing in lead fumes from too much soldering.'

The minster bell had rung for Compline as Rose went to fetch the egg custard she had made for our dessert. A knock at the door startled her and she hurriedly put down the dish. Straightening her hair and smoothing down her kirtle, she went to investigate who could be calling at this hour.

'Come in, Father.' Her voice showed her surprise at this unexpected visit.

'We have not met before, and I will not stay long as I see you are at supper. I am Father John Epplewell, parish priest from St. Michael's, beside the river.' He sat at table with us but refused our offer of refreshment. 'I am intruding, and I will not detain you long. I am here in my role as confessor to a recently hanged murderer – Jasper Griswold. Do you recognise the name?'

Rose dropped the spoon she was holding with a clatter. 'What can it be this time? Will this man never leave our lives in peace?' she asked.

In reply, he took out a sheet of paper from in his robe. 'There is no need to be alarmed. This is a copy of his Will which he dictated to me two days before his execution. I attended him at his request, and I am satisfied that he had made true repentance. In fear for his immortal soul, he wished to make amends. I managed to track you down through the details of depositions in the Assize records.' Unrolling the paper, he read:

'This is the Last Will and Testament of… etcetera …' and skimming over the introductory details he continued:

'In atonement for my many sins and offences against God and in the certain knowledge of my imminent death, I wish to return that which I stole from the lady in the market. I hope that by this one good act I may shrive my soul …'

There followed a description of the hiding place of the stolen possessions - a box hidden beneath a loose paving stone in the livery stable behind the Sun Inn.

'How you act upon this information, I cannot advise you. I have fulfilled my obligation to Jasper Griswold, so my duty is done. I shall leave this with you to do as you see fit.' Making the sign of the cross, he stood, and Rose showed him out.

'The rings that he stole from Maryke?' I suggested as the door closed behind him.

'I know the Sun – it's near the Angel where you met Maryke and her husband,' Martin said. 'I expect that he couldn't fence them, so he hid them away for safe keeping.'

Rose smoothed out the sheet of paper and read it again. 'No matter what we think of this rogue, he has tried to make amends. This is a condemned man's last wish and I think we are morally obliged to do as he asks, and restore them to their rightful owner – and besides, Maryke would be thrilled to have them back.'

Martin looked thoughtful. 'And how would we do that exactly? If we go round to the Sun and ask for them, they will demand to know the details and then refuse permission, and retrieve the rings for themselves. If we go to the Sheriff to explain and ask for his help, he will say that they are the illegal proceeds of crime and confiscate them for the Crown. No, there has to be another way.'

'You are right,' Rose said with a sigh. 'but I don't know how. Is there no end to this business?'

***

Rose was in the market when she saw a familiar figure coming towards her, and recognised him with a smile:

'Barnaby! I am delighted to see you again and to find you are safe. Have you eaten today?' Rose bought him a pie from a passing trader, and he demolished it hungrily.

'Thank you, Mistress,' said Barnaby, wiping the last of the pastry crumbs from his mouth. 'You are always so kind to me.'

'You deserve kindness,' said Rose, smiling down at the diminutive figure. 'Thanks to your brave help, that wicked man cannot hurt anyone ever again.' She paused for a long moment and then, hesitantly, said 'Barnaby, there is an inn called the Sun close by the Angel. How well do you know it?'

'I know it well enough mistress Rose. I work there sometimes.'

'If I wanted to get something back that was left hidden in the stables, how would I go about it?'

‘Oh, that’s easy,’ replied Barnaby. ‘I work in the stables. I’m good with horses, you see.’

***

It was early in the afternoon when Barnaby went round to the stables at the Sun. With a careful description of where to look, he vowed that he would find the hiding place and bring the box to Rose without delay.

He passed through an archway and into a wide courtyard with stabling on each side. Several grooms were busy in the yard, brushing down newly arrived horses or shovelling straw out of loose boxes into a cart. As Barnaby walked through the passage under the arch, he followed the farrier who had been summoned to attend to a horse that had thrown a shoe.

‘Perfect,’ he thought. ‘They will be busy for an hour with this. Nobody will take any notice of me, and anyway they all know me, so they won’t wonder what I’m up to.’

He found the stable without difficulty; Rose’s description had been quite clear, the right-hand side loosebox in the block opposite the archway. The box was occupied by a large bay gelding with white socks and a white blaze down its face. It was skittish and unsettled in unfamiliar surroundings. Without attracting attention, Barnaby unlatched the door and slipped inside. He soon calmed the horse, stroking its neck and murmuring a few soothing words. Then he began to explore the floor by stamping his foot and listening for a hollow sound. He found a loose paving stone almost immediately beneath the hay rack at the front of the stall. Sweeping the bedding straw aside, he uncovered a small square stone that wobbled when he tested it with his foot. Using a hayfork, he prised up the stone and saw that beneath it was a small wooden box. Quickly, he tucked the box inside his jerkin, replaced the stone and spread the straw back over it; nobody could tell that it had been disturbed. He was just about to turn and leave when a voice challenged him from the doorway.

'What have we here then?' It was Gerard, one of the grooms. He was a bully and had never missed a chance to poke fun at Barnaby. 'What are you up to Twitcher?' he sneered, crudely mimicking Barnaby's nervous affliction.

'Come on you wantwit, what have you been doing?' he demanded as he unlatched the door and stepped inside. Barnaby's heart sank. This was the end of everything. Gerard would take the box and kind mistress Rose would be upset. He had just decided to shout for help when the bay gelding intervened. Already unsettled, he took a dislike to the newcomer who had appeared behind him and lashed out with both hind legs. Gerard was caught unawares; the blow lifted him off his feet and threw him backwards through the open door. Not stopping to see if he was hurt, Barnaby took off at full tilt and was out of the stable yard before anyone was alerted to the accident.

He twisted and turned through the busy streets, avoiding the gaze of passers-by and hugging the small box tightly under his jerkin. It was a small, cheaply made wooden box about five inches long and two inches deep with a hinged lid that had once had a picture painted on it although the surface now was badly scratched and grubby. More worryingly, though, the box rattled when he ran, so Barnaby decided to stop running in order to avoid drawing attention to himself. He had made such a hasty escape that he had not looked inside, nor would he have done so even if he had had time; this was his beloved Mistress

Rose's box and by recovering it, he had been able to repay her kindness. It was clearly important, so he must find her straight away. Down Stonegate he went and reaching Martin's door, he knocked and was quickly admitted. Alice and Rose were surprised to see him.

'That was quickly done, young Barnaby,' Rose said with a smile. Turning to Alice; 'I only spoke to him a while ago and here he is already! Well done Barnaby. I hope you did not have any trouble when you collected it for us?'

'Oh, no. No trouble at all. It was easy.' Barnaby did not want to spoil the moment by saying anything about his incident with Gerard. 'Here mistress,' and he handed the box to Rose with obvious pleasure.

Rose checked with Alice: 'I suppose we had better have a look then,' and opening the clasp, she lifted the lid. There lay the two rings that had nearly cost Tom his life. Taking them out she passed them to Alice.

'These are expensive – gold settings, see?' Alice held them to catch the light: 'One looks like a ruby and the other is a diamond I am sure.'

Rose reached inside the box again and took out the last of its contents. There were five gold nobles that gleamed in her hand. The gold was bright and felt slightly greasy in her fingers. Turning the coin over she saw the figure of the king on board a ship, armed with his sword and shield. Each coin was worth half a years' wages for a maid or a servant and the three of them looked in silence.

'This has cost a man his life; it is dirty money, but we shall not waste what has been given to us.' Taking the coins, Rose gave two to Alice, ignoring her protests, and took two for herself. Turning to Barnaby, she gave him the last coin. His eyes opened wide, then filled with tears.

'Mistress Rose, you are so kind, but I can't take it. I can never spend it because people will say I have stolen it - they will hang me!'

'Don't worry, I have thought of that! I know some people who will change it into smaller coins that you *can* spend,' she said, laughing and giving him a hug.

***

The next day was Friday, and Rose, dressed in a smart brown kirtle with her cloak wrapped about her, set out to call at the offices of the agents for Jan and Maryke de Haas. Even in May, the wind had a chilly edge to it, and it tugged playfully at her hood as she walked down Davygate until finally she stood outside the door of a small two storey building that had 'J. Brigg' written on a sign above it. Stepping inside hesitantly, Rose was met by a small, balding man wearing a black lawyer's robe who peered myopically at her. 'Yes?' he enquired.

She began hesitantly: 'My husband, Tom Gifford, brought you a letter of introduction from one of your clients – Jan de Haas.'

'Yes, I vaguely remember. It was several months ago. How may I help you?'

Rose explained her connection with the de Haas family, then launched into her tale. Mr. Brigg listened carefully, his eyebrows shooting up in surprise at every twist of the story. Finally, she produced the two rings and gave them into Mr. Brigg's custody. He took them in his ink-stained fingers and examined them closely.

'These are indeed valuable. I shall write to my client immediately. He will be most grateful to you.'

As Rose returned home, she began to feel a sense of satisfaction that a distressing episode in all their lives was ended by this small act. She had returned something of considerable value to a lady whom she had grown to think of as a friend. She remembered the expensive Flemish lace cuffs that Maryke had given her as a present. Now she had been able to show Maryke her gratitude.

***

I could hardly wait for the end of the day when Martin and I could return home. It had been a day like no other and we were in high spirits as we hung up our aprons on the pegs beside the big wooden door, and locked the workshop.

'Now remember, not a word!' I instructed Martin, as we tried our best to compose ourselves. We entered as we always did at the end of the day, hanging our bags up before greeting Alice and Rose.

'Whatever is the matter with you both?' Alice demanded with a frown.

'Yes, look at them, grinning like cats that have raided the milk jug. What have you got to be so pleased about, Thomas Gifford?' Rose eyed me suspiciously.

I could hardly contain myself. 'It's no good Martin, we can't deceive them even for a moment, can we?'

'We had a visitor today!' Martin announced, beaming broadly. 'Tell her, Tom.'

'Well?' Rose could not decide whether to trust them. They looked like boys who had been given a new puppy.

'A clerk came from the Dean's office, and he brought this.' I produced a letter out of my jerkin with the triumphant air of a conjurer discovering a dove in his hat, and passed it to Rose. She read the letter and then re-read it to be quite sure she was not mistaken.

'Well, go on, read it to us,' Alice ordered.

Rose cleared her throat and read:

"It is with sadness that the Dean and Chapter acknowledge that the death of Alfred Gott, at the hands of the convicted felon, Jasper Griswold, has left a vacancy. In response to the part you played in bringing the said felon to justice, and in recognition of the high quality of your work, the Dean and Chapter wish to offer you employment as a glazier."

'This is it, Rose, we shall have a steady income. It is the start of better things,' I laughed.

Alice remained unmoved, looking crestfallen. 'I suppose this means you will leave here – find a house of your own.'

'Not a bit of it!' Rose retorted. 'At least not unless you want rid of us. But what it *does* mean is that we can afford to employ a maid and make things a little easier for you.'

***

It was barely two weeks later that Martin fell ill, and in spite of her optimism Alice began to realise that things could not continue as they were.

'He coughed up blood this morning.' Alice's expression conveyed her concern. 'He coughed all night,' she added. He hasn't slept properly for two days now, and he seems so tired and listless.'

'Then let me send to St. Mary's for the physician.' I too was worried about him. I had seen how he had struggled with tasks that had once been easy, and how much he had slowed down in his daily life. It was so unlike him to be ill; his burly strength had made him seem somehow indestructible, yet his grey face told a different story. In spite of Martin's protests, I sent a messenger to St. Mary's Abbey and requested that their physician should attend without delay.

It was after mid-day when a knock at the door announced the arrival of Father Jerome, accompanied by a younger novice who carried a bag containing his equipment, salves and potions. Jerome was an elderly monk with a grey cowl and scapula, which he wore as a working apron, and which showed traces of the herbs and ingredients of the medicines he had made.

'It is an ill humour of the chest,' Father Jerome announced after a lengthy examination. 'He must rest for several days and not consider returning to his work for the time being.'

'With respect, Father, that is not possible. I cannot lie here idle while ...' Martin's protest was interrupted by another bout of coughing.

'Quod erat demonstrandum - I think you have proved me right,' concluded Jerome as he left. 'Put lavender beneath his pillow, and rub the salve on his chest. I will call tomorrow.'

***

After a week of rest, Martin began to show improvement, but he continued to cough frequently and was unable to walk more than a few steps.

'He can't be going to the workshop like this Tom,' Rose concluded. 'A day there will kill him.'

'Then he must stay here until he is properly recovered,' I answered. 'I am quite able to keep things going for as long as is necessary. We have been talking about taking on an apprentice, and this could be the time. Speak to Alice – see what she thinks.'

My worst fear was becoming a reality; I had seen the changes in Martin over a long enough period to realise that he would soon have to stop working altogether.

'If Martin cannot continue, what then?' I could tell from her face that she already knew the answer to her own question.

'He would have to sell his business and I would be out of employment.'

'Perhaps the person who buys the workshop would need your services?' she speculated.

'Perhaps,' I replied, 'but even if that were the case, we could no longer live here.'

***

By the middle of May, Martin was well enough to accompany me to the workshop. The warmer weather had helped his recovery and a return to work had lifted his spirits. As we locked the massive double doors on Wednesday afternoon, I was filled with a feeling of optimism. I glanced up towards the great towers of the minster; swallows were jinking and twittering in their flight, whilst around and about them, swifts carved through the air on their scimitar wings.

As we turned down Stonegate, I could see a figure at our door, and as we drew nearer, I saw it was Rose. My heart sank: she never waited for our return, and it could only mean that something was wrong. I quickened my step, leaving Martin as I hurried forward, fearing that Alice must be ill.

‘What is it, Rose? What has happened?’ I had covered the last few yards at a run and was breathing heavily.

Rose looked puzzled by my anxiety: ‘Calm yourself Tom, nothing is amiss.’ By this time, Martin had reached us, badly out of breath and coughing continuously. ‘Look!’ she scolded, ‘you have made Martin cough with all your running. Come inside and rest, Martin. Tom should not have hurried you like that!’ She helped Martin inside while I followed, bewildered.

‘I was waiting to tell you that we have had a visitor. A messenger came to the door this afternoon with a note from Joshua Brigg asking us to visit him at his office on Davygate. We are to go now, without delay.’

***

On entering the outer office, we were met by a clerk who announced our arrival, and showed us into Mr. Brigg’s inner office. He was seated at a large desk that was covered with papers, with a pervading smell of fusty documents. Some were loose whilst others were in disorderly piles or rolled up and tied with pink ribbon.

‘I have notified Mr. de Haas of his good fortune after your praiseworthy return of their property. He has written to me by immediate reply and instructed me to meet with you. They intend to come to England again in a few weeks, after shearing time when the wool fair is held here. In the meantime, Mr. de Haas has sent the following instruction.’

There was a long pause as he rummaged through the pile of papers in front of him, then with a grunt of triumph he found the letter he needed, and began to read from it:

"With regard to our loyal friends, Tom Gifford and his goodwife Rose: I am twice in their debt; Tom saved my wife from attack by a murderer, and now they have recovered valuable property which they could easily have kept for their own gain had they been less honest ..."

Here, Mr. Brigg paused dramatically, peering short-sightedly at us to gauge the effect his reading of the letter was having. Clearing his throat, he continued:

"It is my privilege to offer my service to them, in an attempt in some small way to express my gratitude. You are requested to make such funds available to Tom that will enable him to establish his own premises, stock in trade, tools and materials such as are necessary for his craft. Settlements are to be made 'in privatis' from my account, as bills of trade."

Mr. Brigg put the letter down and beamed at us, his triumphant smile turning to an expression of concern as Rose burst into tears.

'My dear lady, whatever is it? Have I caused offence?' Mr. Brigg asked in alarm.

Dabbing her eyes, and after a moment to regain her composure Rose gave an embarrassed smile.

'Don't worry sir,' I reassured him. 'She always cries when she is happy.'

***

Chapter 32

Late summer 1465

It was hard to believe that a year had slipped by since our meeting with Mr. Brigg and he had explained the generous offer made by Jan de Haas. I remember our astonishment as we came out of Mr. Brigg's office, struggling to absorb the implications of the news.

'Now I think I understand,' Rose had said as we emerged into the sunlight. Seeing my puzzled expression, she explained: 'You remember when they invited us to dine with them?' I nodded. 'Maryke talked with me while you were busy with Jan. She asked so many questions – what were our plans? How would we start our own business? Jan was determined to help, but it would have meant going to live in Bruges. Then Maryke said, "I think I know a way" – well this is it. This is her way of thanking you Tom,' Rose rationalised. 'So what next? What will you do?'

St. Paul on his way to Damascus could not have had a greater moment of inspiration:

'I shall make Martin an offer for his business – buy him out. His health is poor, and he needs rest. This way, he and Alice will be able to live comfortably, while I shall be independent.'

And so life became resolved for us all, perversely thanks to Jasper Griswold.

'You know, without that awful business with Jasper, we would not be where we are now,' Rose observed. 'We might never have met Jan and Maryke.'

***

The August sun held its power, even at the end of the day, and I enjoyed the sensation of its warmth on my face as I closed the workshop door and set off for home. My eyes lit up with pleasure as I saw my young wife walking over the green towards me. I looked at her lovingly as she approached, her slight limp invisible beneath the dark green gown that swished over the short grass and emphasized the wonderful natural poise that she managed so effortlessly. I watched, and in those brief moments, loved her as much as on the day when we had first met. The sway of her hips and the glimpse of auburn hair swept carefully under her white bonnet made me catch my breath.

'Rose! This is a nice surprise. What are you doing here?' my curiosity overwhelming my subtlety; for some reason today Rose had put on a gown and walked to meet me.

'You have no manners Thomas Gifford! Can't a woman come to meet her husband without being interrogated?' she asked in feigned annoyance. She was smiling broadly so I knew it could not be bad news.

'But you have dressed up. Why are you so smart? Are you going somewhere?' I was not helping myself at all, but I was completely taken by surprise.

She gave a loud sigh of exasperation and pointed to a bench on the edge of the green. 'Sit down; can you not see that I need to speak to you?'

We sat in the September sunshine, and I waited. She turned to me and smiled: 'I wanted to look my best for you because I have news.' She paused, grinning impishly and withholding for a tantalising moment longer. 'I am with child, Tom. At last I am with child!'

There was silence as she looked at me and waited. I knew I should say something – had to say something, but I sat and looked at her stupidly as I fumbled for the right words.

'... well, are you pleased?' she asked.

'Are you sure? Can there be a mistake?'

'Quite sure, and there is no mistake,' she replied, smiling. 'I have missed my courses.'

'How many times?' The questions tumbled out of me as my mind raced to take in her words.

'Twice now, so there is no doubt.'

'So that would make it...' I started counting on my fingers.

'March next year,' she interrupted.

I paused, still astonished by the unexpected news. 'Then when your time comes, you will need this,' and I produced the sunstone from around my neck, where it had lain hidden and almost forgotten.

She took it from my outstretched hand. 'What is it?'

'Godwin's mother gave it to me. She used it as a talisman during birthing. It will keep you safe in childbed.'

'When my time comes, I want my mother to keep me safe – but I shall be glad of your sunstone too!' She smiled, and leaning across, kissed me.

'A son!' I exclaimed. 'I shall have a son!' I flung my arms round her, tingling with delight.

***

'Tomorrow you must go to the minster, Rose,' Alice announced as we sat after supper was finished. 'It is time to pay the smoke farthing.'

'Oh, Saint Peter's Pence Day,' added Martin. 'It's that time of year again, is it?'

I looked at him curiously. 'It's a tax that we have to pay each year for the privilege of having a fire,' he explained. 'They call it the smoke farthing, I suppose, because it is a hearth tax. They set up a kiosk at the minster on the feast of St. Peter ad Vincula and people go to pay their bill for the coming year.'

'I will go tomorrow morning,' Rose decided.

'If you wait till later, I will come with you. Keep you safe.' I felt that I had almost become a parent already and could not risk any mishap to her in the crowded city. I saw Alice turn to Rose and give a knowing smile.

It was early evening, and the bell was ringing for Vespers as we left home and set out on the short journey to the minster. It was September, the day had been dreary and a chill mist hung over the city, clinging to the rooftops and lacing the cobwebs on the thatch with droplets of moisture. It would be dark early tonight, and the prospect of a fire and a hot supper made us walk quickly. As we passed through the churchyard, the path led amongst the gravestones and past the great outer wall where statues were set in high niches; the sightless eyes of saints looked down upon the sinners below in their last resting place. I noticed that behind one of the great tombstones, someone had left a bundle of rags, no doubt as an act of charity for the poor.

The kiosk was a small tent with an ornamental fringe round the canopy. It looked as if it belonged in a fairground rather than a churchyard. It stirred a memory of the day I had been to Ravengill Fair with Godwin, and he had won his bout at the wrestling booth. I smiled irreverently to myself; they are wrestling money out of poor people's pockets I supposed. We entered the tent, and I declared myself to the clerk at the desk. I noticed his thin hands were blue with cold as he looked up our household in his ledger. I handed over the coin, a tick in the column and it was done, and we set off for home.

'It moved!' Rose was pointing to the bundle of rags we had passed, piled loosely against a blackened headstone. 'There is somebody lying there.'

Before I could reply, she had crossed the grass and was bending over a prone figure. Lying slumped in the meagre shelter of the stone, was the bedraggled shape of a woman, with a shawl pulled across her face.

'We must help the poor creature, Tom.'

Reluctantly, I joined her and stood looking down at the pitiful figure, while Rose spoke to her and tried to rouse her.

'She may have the plague, Rose. For God's sake leave her.'

'I will not!' she answered hotly, 'and neither will you. It is our Christian duty to help her!'

'Then at least pull the shawl back so we can see she is not a leper.'

Rose leaned forward and gently removed the shawl to reveal a face that was grey, lined with fatigue and streaked with grime.

'Ursula!' I exclaimed.

***

We made up a bed by the fire and between them Alice and Rose bathed Ursula and dressed her in a clean nightshirt. She was barely conscious and occasionally muttered wildly in her delirium.

'She had a bundle that she clung to. I had to force it from her.' Rose pointed to a ragged cloth bundle lying beside Ursula's feverish body. I knew beyond doubt what it contained.

'Look inside,' I instructed.

Rose opened the cloth, and withdrew the Book of Hours: even as she lay close to death, Ursula had clung to her precious book, as if her life depended on it.

Rose looked up at me, her face a mixture of surprise and disbelief. 'Who *is* she to have a book like this?' she whispered.

'Her real identity has always been a mystery. She was my father's woman after my mother died; she tried to have me killed; she drove me out of my home. That's who she is as far as I'm concerned.'

'But just look at her Tom. No matter what she has done, we could not have left her to die alone.'

'I feel nothing for her plight, but if I must help her, it is only out of duty.'

Rose frowned as she considered for a moment. 'She has clung on to this book as though it is as precious as life itself. I have a feeling that it may hold the answer to many questions.'

I remembered once taking a huge risk and asking Martha to see if she could decipher it.

'Don't forget, I have seen inside this book long ago. It is just a prayerbook with some curious inscriptions inside the cover. We would need someone with the knowledge to understand their meaning.'

'Then I know just the person who can get to the bottom this,' Rose concluded. 'I shall take it to Mr. Brigg and ask him if he can make anything of it.'

***

'Have you any idea who this woman really is?' Mr. Brigg's face was worried. 'For a start, she is not Ursula Gurnard, although that is the name she has called herself. I have traced some of her history through the court rolls at the assizes. It seems she has been before the magistrates here some time ago, when she was only sixteen. She gave her name then as Ursula Greenwood.'

'What about her book? Does that tell us anything?'

At this, his face became even more worried. 'If you take my advice, you will destroy the book, regardless of its value; deny that you have ever seen it, and forget all about this "Ursula" as if she had never existed.'

'Why?' we asked simultaneously. I could tell that the warning had frightened Rose but had also aroused her curiosity.

'Because she is dangerous; the book is dangerous, and its very existence is a threat to our lives. If I were to be caught with it, I could be arrested for treason.'

We stood, speechless; we had not expected this.

'I will refute all knowledge of this once you leave here, and I do not want you to ask me for details.'

'Please,' begged Rose, 'if we are to help her, you must tell us what you can.'

There was a long pause; it was clear that he was torn between his personal safety and providing the information we needed. 'Very well,' he said finally, 'but you must not speak of it beyond this room, and I am only telling you this because it may help you to understand the gravity of the situation. All our lives may depend on it.'

Mr. Brigg drew a deep breath, leaned forward and opened the book. He glanced furtively towards the door, then in a voice that was barely more than a whisper, he continued: 'Firstly, there is the name of a place written inside the cover.' He pointed: 'The Priory of Saint Agnes. I have made enquiries, and it is a nunnery only thirty miles north of here, at a place called Rosegill, run by the order of the Poor Clares.'

'Do you think she stole it?' I interrupted but was instantly shushed by Rose.

'I think that her mother has been wealthy and forced to abandon her child. She left this expensive book as a keepsake for the daughter she would never see again – but more than that, she left her a puzzle that would reveal her birthright. Look at the first page.' He turned to an inner fly leaf, where an illustration of a tree had been neatly hand drawn. 'See the tree? Each branch has a fruit with a name beneath it.

One fruit does not have a name, just a shape like an empty beaker – what letter does that look like to you?

I looked at the diagram, but shook my head; it meant nothing to me.

'Could it be the letter U?' Mr Brigg suggested quietly.

'For Ursula you mean?' Rose was beginning to grasp the importance of the message here. Her face was worried as she looked up at him. I could tell that she already felt that she knew more than was safe, but we were too committed to turn back now. 'What else do you see, Mr. Brigg?'

'If you study the trunk of the tree, you will see that letters have been cleverly disguised in the curls of the bark.' He traced with the tip of a knife and spelled out: R, I, C, H ...'

'Richard?' I offered.

'And the names of the fruits?' Rose could barely speak.

'Edward, George and Richard,' murmured Mr. Brigg. 'The sons of Richard, Duke of York - and if that were not enough, there is the prayer to St. Egina. Let me read it to you.' He cleared his throat and in a voice that trembled slightly read...

'Invocation to St Egina.
Yea, though my heart be rent, and deep in sorrow me escry,
Behold, with nurture how I rise, in whole and glorious harmony!'

We looked at each other, still none the wiser.

'Like you, I had never heard of Saint Egina, so I sent my clerk to the minster to make discreet enquiries. When he returned he was quite definite. There is no such saint. That made me most curious, and I looked more closely at the wording of the prayer: *"though my heart be rent"* so I spelled out the saint's name like this,' and he took a scrap of paper and scrawled "ST EGINA".

'I tore the paper up to make individual letters that I could play with... "*though my heart be rent*" you see? Torn up.'

Rose was enthralled. 'And what did you discover?'

"*How I rise in whole and glorious harmony*" he quoted. 'Harmony, by rearranging the letters.'

'This is a code isn't it? A coded message from mother to daughter!' Rose's quick mind had grasped what I could not understand.

He continued: 'I shuffled the letters and made the word "GENISTA". It is the Latin name for the broom plant - the emblem of the Plantagenets.' He paused, gathering himself for what he was about to say next.

'Ursula is a Plantagenet! She is a displaced member of the nobility; robbed of her birthright; destined to live her life in poverty and obscurity, never having known her origins. I would hazard a guess that her mother was a lady of noble birth, quite possibly a member of the royal household, perhaps even a lady in waiting and close to the throne. She has faithfully guarded the only link she has ever had to her mother – the book that sits in front of us, although she never knew its significance. Now do you understand the danger you are in? She is the bastard half-sister of Edward IV - the king, and we, the people of York saw their father's head put on a spike at Micklelith Bar after the Battle of Wakefield. How do you think the king would react if he found that his half-sister had been living in poverty like a common whore?' Mr. Brigg's voice had risen in volume in response to his anxiety. 'How would his wrath descend on the people who denied her a title, a great household and the wealth from the estates due to a Plantagenet half-princess of the blood royal?'

He paused, regaining his composure and lowering his voice. 'And let me put an alternative case to you. Supposing that Margaret of Anjou succeeds in restoring her husband Henry to the throne and discovers that there is another Plantagenet, albeit a half-sister, who could claim status and wealth. This woman does not have a reputation for noblesse and forgiveness. How would she react if she discovered that we had supported Ursula, offered her shelter and saved her life?'

He sat back to let the full implication of his disclosure sink in. My head was spinning, and I could barely believe what he had told us. I had assumed that this woman that my father had brought home was a tavern slut, yet now it began to make sense. Perhaps the nuns at Saint Agnes had inadvertently let slip some hint of her origin. Although she had shared our hearth, she always seemed aloof and had never been comfortable in the company of working people. Yet here was the woman who had betrayed me, and left Godwin and I with no choice but to answer the muster. I could even persuade myself that she was responsible for Godwin's death, because without her betrayal, we would have escaped and he would be alive now. Why would we even consider helping her? Once again, Rose was the voice of my conscience:

'She is dying you know, and when she is awake, she says the name "Rosegill" to me. Now I think I understand. She was trying to make her way back to where she came from. She wants to die in a state of grace among familiar surroundings and with the nuns who raised her ... end her life where it started I suppose,' Rose concluded.

‘Then, wicked though it may sound, you must hope she dies soon...’ Mr. Brigg said, crossing himself. He closed the book and handed it back to me.,, ‘and when she does, destroy this book. Until it is done, none of us is safe.’

***

The late summer sun beat down with shimmering heat as we left York on our way northwards. Our destination was within a day’s travel, and I had hired an enclosed carriage for our journey. Even beneath its canvas awning, the heat was stifling. We had arranged Ursula with cushions and a blanket to make her as comfortable as possible, and Rose sat beside her. I perched on the high box seat and steered the pair of horses to avoid the worst of the ruts as best I could. From my seat, I could hear Ursula’s occasional bouts of coughing and several times had to halt our progress until she was recovered.

The road was baked hard after the dry summer and while it assisted our horses, the bumps were unforgiving, and we could only make slow progress. The green canopy of the great Forest of Galtres had offered dappled shade, but now in the early afternoon, trees had given way to open, rugged countryside, and we sweltered. Even though she was wrapped in a blanket, Ursula had bouts of shivering, and Rose began to worry that we had overtaxed her strength. As afternoon became early evening, the air began to lose its fierce heat, to be replaced by a delicious coolness. We were now surrounded by purple heather, and the rich, heady scent of flowers mixed with the smoky fragrance of peat moorland pervaded our nostrils. Here the road had narrowed to a track with grass growing in the centre of the wheelways. Finally, we entered a sheltered valley with a broad stream running at its centre, where the rocky, steep sided hills on either side were covered in bright green bracken and birch trees.

It was the sound of a bell's rhythmic cadence that gave us our first indication of the presence of the priory. In this remote valley, its silvered tones echoed off the rocky slopes as Vespers was announced. Then, as we rounded a shoulder of the hillside, the Priory of St. Agnes came into view.

A collection of stone buildings lay ahead, securely surrounded by a high wall, above which rose the tower of the church. Outside the perimeter, a series of low thatched buildings provided accommodation for the few lay workers that were allowed to assist with the heavier duties. There were barns, stables and a granary, with a large fishpond, supplied by a cleverly diverted channel from the stream. A thin column of smoke rose from the kitchen building, hinting at the supper that had been served before the nuns had gone to their prayers. The bell's summons had ceased, and above the creak of the carriage wheels, the faintest hint of the antiphon's chanted invocation drifted intermittently to our ears in the evening air.

The outer gate to the priory was of stout oak and studded with nails; at head height was a small grill with a hinged flap behind the protective metalwork. It reminded me of the visor on a knight's helm, and when I knocked boldly on the door, I expected a male voice to challenge me. After a second, louder knock, my summons was answered by a young woman with a brown headdress, whose face appeared timidly at the grill.

'Yes? What is it that you want? We have closed our doors and no more alms will be given until tomorrow,' and the flap began to close again. Rose stepped forward and brushed me quietly aside.

'If you please, we do not seek alms; we have a woman here who says she was once a member of your community, but she is gravely ill and needs your help.'

The sight of Rose had clearly reassured her because the flap opened again. 'I am Justine, an oblate at St. Agnes. The sisters are attending Vespers, and I will need to speak to Reverend Mother: I cannot admit you without her permission. You must wait – the service will soon be over.' The flap closed and we looked at each other in resignation.

True to her word, Justine reappeared, and a second face looked out on us, wearing the wimple of a nun, as she surveyed us closely. Once satisfied, there was the sound of bolts being drawn, the door opened slightly and the nun stepped out, upon which, the door was closed behind her, and she spoke to Rose: 'I am Sister Isabella. Show me this person you have brought to us.'

Rose led the way to the cart, where a sudden bout of coughing revealed that Ursula was indeed unwell.

'How long has she been like this?' Sister Isabella leaned into the carriage and looked closely at Ursula's grey face.

'Nearly two weeks, but she has become much worse over the past day.'

'And she claims to have been a member of this community?'

'So she says,' Rose replied.

Pausing in thought for a moment, Sister Isabella came to a decision. 'Wait here,' and she hurried back through the outer door. After a short while, the door was pushed wide, and two nuns emerged carrying a litter. They carefully transferred Ursula, then carried her through the gate.

'You will wait here please. Reverend Mother wishes to speak to you.' Sister Isabella had a foreign accent although her English was perfect.

***

We were shown into an outer courtyard, surrounded by doors which could have led to stores or even workshops. Sister Isabella opened a door adjacent to the gatekeepers lodge and we were ushered into a square, whitewashed room which had the appearance of a chapel. A table stood at one end, upon which was a simple wooden crucifix.

'This is the room where the priest comes to say mass for our lay workers. Please be seated and Reverend Mother will see you.' This time, Sister Isabella stayed with us as we waited. When the door opened, the tiny figure of a nun wearing a plain brown habit and white wimple entered, taking small, mouse-like steps. The portion of her face that I could see was tanned a leathery brown and was deeply wrinkled. She gestured to us to be seated while she sat behind the table, and regarded us in a silence that unnerved me. It was her eyes that I noticed; they were like little brown beads, alert and never still.

'I am the Prioress of St. Agnes, Sister Louise.' We introduced ourselves. 'Now tell me about the woman you have brought to me.'

'She used to be my father's....'

Rose interrupted me before I could go any further. 'Reverend Mother, her name is Ursula Gurnard, although I do not think that is her real name. We found her close to death, trying to make her way to your priory. She says that she came from here long ago.'

‘She is indeed very ill,’ agreed the Prioress, ‘and unlikely to live long, but I do not recognise her – nobody can recall her.’

‘Then perhaps this might help,’ I said, producing the Book of Hours and passing it across the table. The Prioress picked it up curiously and looked inside; immediately her face changed.

‘Where did you get this,’ she asked sharply…‘Wait.’ She left the room and was gone for what seemed a long time. When she returned, she was not alone: a very elderly nun was helped to a seat by two female lay workers, where she lowered herself painfully with a sigh of acceptance.

‘This is Sister Marie – the most senior member of our community. She is our archivist and wishes to speak to you.’

Although her voice wavered slightly, Sister Marie’s mind was as clear as a crystal pool, and she regarded us critically, almost daring us to speak.

‘So, she has come home!’ Sister Marie’s voice sounded like the rustling of dry parchment.

***

‘Long ago, when I was a novice, an event took place here that none but I will remember.’ Marie was quietly spoken, and I strained to hear. ‘The Poor Clares are a strict order with rigorous rules on fasting and abstinence. We are dedicated to an austere life here - more so than most. I think that is what she found so difficult. Our founder sisters came from France and set up our mother house at Newcastle. Here at Rosegill we have established our small community, thanks to the generosity of a wealthy patron.’ She paused to regain her breath as though speaking was a considerable effort, lapsing into silence until the Prioress prompted her gently from her reverie:

'An event, sister?'

'Ah yes. There was an arrival here. A young woman with a baby only a few weeks old came to our gate, escorted by soldiers. She was expected because I was told to accompany our Reverend Mother to meet her - I was a young nun then and had only just taken my vows. She was a noble lady, dressed in fine clothes but so distressed, and I remember there were tears in my eyes, too, when she handed her baby to me. Then she was hurried away by her escort.'

'But who was she?' I asked impatiently. Rose gave me a look that silenced me in an instant.

'I was never allowed to know,' Sister Marie replied. 'I did hear that she was a lady at court, and had been sent home in disgrace because she was with child. She must have been the daughter of a nobleman to aspire to such high duties. The poor young woman was weeping and in a state of great sadness, but before she left, she gave our Reverend Mother a keepsake to be given to her daughter when the time was right – the Book of Hours that you have brought with you. I have not seen that book for over four decades, and yet here it is again.'

'What became of her as she grew older?' Rose quizzed gently. She could see that recalling events from so long ago was exhausting Sister Marie.

'Ursula was a wild, resentful child who needed correction and time for solitary repentance on many occasions. Although she was an oblate, she never accepted our values and rebelled against the stringency of our rules. Eventually, she ran away and although we tried to trace her, all we discovered was that she had met a man and left with him, and that is all I know. And now, with your leave Reverend Mother, I wish to rest.'

When Sister Marie had been escorted to her cell, only the Prioress, Rose and I remained in the tranquillity of the room, considering what we had just heard.

'I have had time to give thought to this troubling matter, and I am certain that your interpretation of the message in her book is correct – Ursula is indeed connected to the Plantagenet dynasty, but her true name and title can never be known for certain. She is close to death and once the Lord takes her, her secret will have no significance.'

'And what of her book? What of the secret that it holds?' I felt sure that the book must have a relevance under such circumstances.

Sister Louise, Prioress of Rosegill, looked away for a moment, then spoke with a quiet intensity: 'We live in troubled times. There are secrets here that must never be discussed beyond the walls of this room. The book will be sealed, and then sent to the mother house, where it will be locked away in our archive vault and be forgotten. You, too, must forget, but to help you, I ask you to kneel before me.'

We complied, looking up at this small nun who had assumed a stature of timeless authority.

'I bind you both with the seal of the confessional, that you may never speak of this matter again. We murmured our oath "My silence is bound before God," with reverence. 'Should you break the pledge that binds you now, your immortal souls will be held to account for it on the Day of Judgement.' She made the sign of the cross over our heads. 'May God bless you and keep you.'

As we were gestured to rise, Rose returned to her knees. 'Reverend mother, I am with child. Will you give me and my unborn baby your blessing?'

For the first time since we had met, I saw the Prioress smile. Her tanned face beamed, and her small brown eyes twinkled.

'You have shown Our Lord's charity towards a woman whom you could have left to die in anonymity. You have gone to considerable trouble to give her peace in her final hours. Of course you may have my blessing.'

She made the sign of the cross once more above Rose's head: 'May your birthing be easy, and your child be blessed with health and piety.'

***

Chapter 33

Three years later: Autumn 1468

Martin died two days before Michaelmas, shortly after our return from Rosegill Priory, and Alice seemed unable to live without him: 'It is as if the light has simply gone out of her,' Rose sighed, and when Alice, too, was taken in the spring of 1466 it had seemed inevitable. She had always been such a bundle of energy; even when she had nursed Martin through his illness she had stayed strong and resolute. Without him, she had lost her purpose; she had scarcely eaten, and slowly went from us like an autumn leaf drifting down a millstream. Alice had been so thrilled to greet our firstborn whom I named Alan; "Fathers name sons, mothers name daughters." I can still hear her, as if she were standing beside me, so proud and excited. "Martin and I prayed for this to happen for us, and it never did. It seems that our prayers may have been answered after all - just not how we expected. I'm going to be a grandmother – well, sort of." She lived to be a grandmother for only three short weeks.

Such changes to my family in the space of so short a time. I sent for Martha to join our household the following spring, after we had seen through the worst of the winter. I commissioned the masons at the minster to make a headstone for Godwin and I took Martha to visit Saxton Church, where she wept for her son, and laid primroses and cowslips on his grave.

Rose had looked forward to the Martinmas Fair for weeks, but she was great with our second child, and it was Martha who came with me, with instructions from Rose to buy ribbons. 'And see if you can find some bright cloth – if this one turns out to be a girl, she will need dresses,' she said, pointing to her ample girth. 'And see if you can get something for me,' she asked, turning to Martha. 'I would like to have a new gown for Yuletide - something warm.'

And so it was that Martha and I strolled among the stalls at the Martinmas Fair, taking in the sights and sounds of the busy streets. She had bought ribbons, some red and some green, and now she was concentrating on a stall that sold bolts of cloth. She had selected a fine grey worsted with a thin black stripe running through it. 'She will love that!' I said as I paid the stallholder.

Our attention was distracted by the sound of hooves, and we gave way for a small detachment of cavalry, clattering through the market on their way to the castle.

'By the Virgin's tears, it is Gifford the archer!' The officer at the head of the troop reined in his mount beside me.

'Roland Green!' I returned, astonished that he had remembered me.

'Garrison Commander Green!' he corrected with a grin. 'I am on a mercy mission for Sir Richard de Coverdale. His favourite horse, Midnight – you remember? The Percheron that he rode at Towton? He has gone down and rejects all attempts to get him on his feet. He has been lying in the paddock for two days now, and stubbornly refuses to get up – almost as if he is sulking. Sir Richard is beside himself with worry: he loves that horse dearly; they are old comrades. I have been seeking a horse doctor because if we don't get him up soon, he will die there.'

A thought began to form itself – a memory from the back of my mind was struggling to break free. 'Twitcher!' I exclaimed. 'I know who may help you – young lad who works in the stables at the Angel called Barnaby Glover. He has an amazing way with horses. Try him!'

Roland gave me a celebratory salute and led his troop off. I prayed that I had not given him false hope.

***

'Rosie, you will love to hear this!' I could not wait to bring her the news at the end of the day. She straightened uncomfortably, massaging her aching back, and awaited the cause of my good humour.

'Roland Green called at the minster yard in person. You remember I suggested that Twitcher might help him?'

'Barnaby!' she corrected sternly. 'He is called Barnaby. Well, go on.'

'He took my advice and let Barnaby have a look at the horse. Here's what he told me: he said, Barnaby took a long look at Midnight, then sent for bedding straw. He laid it out on three sides of the horse with a gap behind him. Then... you'll never guess... he set fire to the straw!

The horse was up on its feet in a flash, snorting in panic. Barnaby took his head and led him round the paddock, talking to him all the while. Now he's back in his stall and all is well. Oh, and we shall receive a barrel of wine from Sir Richard in thanks.'

'And what of young Barnaby? What thanks did he get?' Rose was always quick to champion her young friend.

'Ah well, Sir Richard was so impressed with his skills that he hired him on the spot! Taken him on as his personal groom – it is a huge advancement for the lad.'

Rose smiled with pleasure, then grimaced as her baby gave a painful kick. 'This one wants to be out. It won't be long now.'

Rose entered her confinement in November, with Martha and her mother, Mary Cooper in attendance. It was cold, and the first fall of snow came in the middle of the month, blanketing the city streets and silencing the horses' hooves. The moment I opened the door and stamped the snow from my boots, I could tell that the child was on its way. All was a scene of purposeful activity. Mary had prepared an infusion of herbs to ease the birth pangs, but Rose's cries were pitiful to hear. She lay in our chamber, surrounded by pillows and blankets while Amy, our maid was directed hither and thither first by Mary, then Martha, fetching one essential after another. I reached inside my shirt and taking the sunstone from around my neck, thrust it into Amy's hand. 'Give her this to hold. It will help.' I waited in an agony of apprehension until at six of the morning, just after the bell had rung for Prime on the sixteenth day of November, she gave birth to a girl on the feast day of St. Margaret.

***

As the month turned, December announced its arrival with the early fall of snow giving way to gales and driving rain. Rose and her baby were well, and after protesting at the fuss and pampering, she had been allowed to resume a nearly normal life. Now, with a fed and freshly clothed infant in her arms, Mary Cooper held her new granddaughter while we enjoyed the last hour before we retired to our beds.

'I have chosen her name,' Rose announced. 'Remember what Alice said? "mothers name daughters?" I have decided to call her Margaret. We could shorten it to Maggie perhaps?'

'That was your mother's pet name, Tom. She was called Magdalene, but everyone called her Maggie,' Martha explained.

Rose thought for a moment: 'Then we shall choose something different– Meg! I like the name Meg for short.'

'I think I like Margaret better than Meg. You shorten her name if you will, but I shall always call her Margaret. She was born on St. Margaret's day, not St. Meg's day. I like the name and it seems a shame to shorten it.' I knew that whatever I said, Rose would have her way, so Meg it would be.

The barrel of wine from Sir Richard had been delivered that morning, but we would keep it for our twelfth night celebrations. The wind had picked up outside and we sat in comfortable silence beside the fire as the rain pattered on the shutters. Rose saw that her mother was tiring so she gathered up Meg and laid the child in its cradle, where Amy sat rocking her with her foot as she concentrated on her stitching. Rose had held the sunstone tightly all through the hours of her labour, and now she hung it above the cradle, where it twisted on its cord, the firelight making it glow with colour.

‘That Ursula never was any good,’ Martha observed unexpectedly. I shot a glance at Rose but she studiously ignored me as if she had never heard. ‘She vanished straight after your father’s accident - probably taken up with some other man now.’

Silence resumed for a while, broken by the steady breathing of Grandmother Mary, who had fallen asleep.

‘Sir Hugh Thain was arrested you know,’ Martha continued.

That was an unwelcome name to hear again: ‘What had he done?’ I asked, although I felt that I knew the answer.

Martha looked pleased to have news that she could share: ‘He was arrested for sedition and assisting the king’s enemies. He was lucky that he was spared the death penalty. As it is, he has been…’ she struggled for a word, ‘… attainted!’ she announced. ‘He has been attainted. It means that he has been disgraced. All his lands are confiscated and he cannot bequeath anything to his heirs.’

‘That is a fitting punishment for someone who chose to support the enemies of our king,’ I commented. ‘He backed the wrong side.’

Little Meg lay contentedly, lulled by the gentle rocking of her cradle and the sound of our voices. Outside, the gale blustered, making the candles flare and gutter in the draft. An unusually strong gust shook the shutters, and Grandmother Mary gave a cry. She stared ahead, her eyes unseeing; not in our company – lost in a half-world between wakefulness and sleep. I got to my feet out of concern for her health, but Rose gestured me to be still.

‘The Sight is upon her,’ she whispered. ‘I have known her to be like this before.’

Mary took a deeply indrawn breath, followed by a shuddering sigh. In a faltering voice that was barely more than a whisper she spoke:

'This innocent bairn has a long road to travel... a fey child who carries our gift. She will mix with the greatest in the land... she will dine with kings, and queens will seek her counsel.'

Rose put a hand to her mouth, stifling a gasp, and stared at her mother in disbelief. In the silence that followed, Grandmother Mary sank back into her chair, and soon her steady breathing showed she was asleep. A log settled in the fire with a crackle of sparks, and Meg cooed contentedly in her cradle.

***

Afterword

Thank you for reading my book, the first in the saga of the Gifford family. These are ordinary people who lived in extraordinary times, when the country endured periods of turmoil as the houses of York and Lancaster clashed for supremacy and ultimately for the crown. Inevitably, the lives of the population were entangled in the ambition of their overlords; the duty to fight, and often to die, in service of their superiors was inescapable and yet the loyalty they gave was unquestioning.

The research for this book took over two years to complete and involved several visits to the bleak and windswept battlefield site at Towton. I must thank my long-suffering wife for her patience (and endurance!) on these expeditions. The site is unusual because it is still open farmland and virtually unchanged over the last five and a half centuries. It is hard to imagine today, the many thousands who were slaughtered on what is now a peaceful English landscape. For Tom

Gifford it was the start of a chain of events that would change his life. I have such respect for the people who lived through these times. They were tough, resourceful and above all, resilient in the face of extreme hardship.

I have made use of artistic licence to weave a story that, whilst based on the history of the time, features characters who might have populated this imaginary world. The mysterious Ursula has no basis in fact, yet she represents the measures taken by the gentry to disguise or dispose of their indiscretions.

Similarly, the company of archers to which Tom and Godwin were conscripted is entirely fictional, although it is a fair illustration of the way that men were mustered by their lords. Their forced march northwards saw them arrive just after the preliminary battle at Ferrybridge had been fought, and the Lancastrian troops had been driven off, only to be annihilated at Dintingdale, prior to the battle of Towton on the following day. There is no doubt that the loss of life at Towton was considerable, with some estimates reaching as high as twenty thousand. While this figure seems unlikely, what is certain is that the worst of the death toll occurred when order broke down within the Lancastrian ranks, and the battle turned into a rout. The topography of the battlefield contributed to the final tally as the fleeing soldiers became trapped by the flooded valley of Cock Beck, later known as the 'Bloody Meadow'. This is where Tom Gifford thought he had finally rid himself of Jasper Griswold.

Rose is an intelligent young woman, and her aspiration to be valued as an equal partner in marriage is unusual; women in this era, regardless of social status and rank, were regarded as the property of their husband, with all that that entails. We must wish her well in the full expectation that Tom appreciates her loyalty and the contribution she can bring to their life together. I hope she achieves her goal for her sake, and the sake of women everywhere.

About the author

CB Smailes is a writer who lives in the North York Moors National Park, where he has resided for over thirty years, amidst a moorland landscape that is the haunt of grouse and curlew. Chris studied history at Leicester University and has devoted his life to teaching, whilst continuing to write as time allowed. Martha's Gift is the first book in the Gifford Trilogy, set in and around the medieval city of York and the vast wilderness of the royal hunting ground , still known to this day as the Forest of Galtres. Amongst his other interests, Chris lists local history, archaeology, and a lifelong passion for beekeeping, which has brought him national awards and recognition.

You can find him on:
www.facebook.com/westfieldshoney/
cbs.author241@outlook.com

,

Acknowledgement

I would like to express my thanks to Betty Martinez (Connecticut, USA) for her stunning cover design. I would also like to thank my friend and former colleague, Jane for her invaluable role as co-editor and 'critical friend'.

If you have enjoyed this book, you may wish to know that the second in the series is already in preparation. Perhaps you might like to leave a review on Amazon?

Printed in Great Britain
by Amazon

49441034R00207